DON'T KILL THE MESSENGER

"Someone's coming," Candace reported, excitement threading through her voice. "But I can't see them, yet."

Roda followed them toward the door and Wang sniffed the air. "Do you smell something?"

Rieka nodded. "They're gassing the room." Knowing the effort would be all but futile, she willed Roda to hurry out the door. Seconds later, it closed behind them.

"They're here!" Candace gasped.

Rieka looked down the corridor to see a squad of six Ophs running around the corner, their weapons drawn. Pinned in the short hallway, she stepped forward beside Wang.

"Shoot, shoot!" Rieka ordered. She lifted her maitu and discharged it just as they received return fire.

Earth Herald

JAN CLARK

A ROC BOOK

ROC
Published by the Penguin Group
Penguin Putnam Inc., 375 Hudson Street,
New York, New York 10014, U.S.A.
Penguin Books Ltd, 27 Wrights Lane,
London W8 5TZ, England
Penguin Books Australia Ltd, Ringwood,
Victoria, Australia
Penguin Books Canada Ltd, 10 Alcorn Avenue,
Toronto, Ontario, Canada M4V 3B2
Penguin Books (N.Z.) Ltd, 182–190 Wairau Road,
Auckland 10, New Zealand

Penguin Books Ltd, Registered Offices:
Harmondsworth, Middlesex, England

First published by Roc, an imprint of Dutton NAL,
a member of Penguin Putnam Inc.

First Printing, July, 1998
10 9 8 7 6 5 4 3 2 1

Cover art by Donato

 REGISTERED TRADEMARK—MARCA REGISTRADA

Printed in the United States of America

BOOKS ARE AVAILABLE AT QUANTITY DISCOUNTS WHEN USED TO PROMOTE PRODUCTS OR SERVICES. FOR INFORMATION PLEASE WRITE TO PREMIUM MARKETING DIVISION, PENGUIN PUTNAM INC., 375 HUDSON STREET, NEW YORK, NEW YORK 10014.

The author would like to acknowledge the following individuals for their help in making this book possible. Your input and support are dearly appreciated.

In return, let me take this opportunity to remind us all that—*anything* is possible.

Many thanks to: Jim Allen, Bunnie Bessel, Jan Christensen, Alec Disharoon, Dr. Arthur Ehlmann of Texas Christian University, Chuck Gatlin, Laura Anne Gilman, Mr. Coke Kohli, Jonathan Shipley, and David Williams.

ONE

"I *hate* politics. Whatever made me think I wanted to do this?" Rieka Degahv muttered to herself. She rubbed the ache in her temples and frowned at the Commonwealth News Sheet she'd been studying on the screen.

The Bournese Herald had made a deal with her uncle to purchase 27 percent of all imported produce from Earth, beginning on Commonwealth date 135.00. In exchange for that business, Alexi had agreed to hire three Bournese excavation companies to do the prep work for the next subterranean Earth city, New SubNairobi.

It sounded simple enough. But Rieka knew there were subtleties in the agreement, even if she couldn't see them. And 27 percent was a huge amount. Some other planet, probably Aurie, would suffer the consequences of such a deal. And they were sure to resent it. But who would be criticized? The Bournese Herald, the Earth Herald, the commercial middlemen, or Humans in general?

"With my luck, this will turn out to be some kind of huge disaster—and *I'll* be blamed for it." She raked a hand through her dark hair and activated her datapad. "Notebook, remind me to get some numbers on the agro business between Aurie and Bourne."

She called up the next News Sheet page. Nothing of interest appeared, so she scrolled through the next few sheets.

A communiqué has just come in for you . . . from Yadra, Triscoe's mind-voice told her.

Rieka warily pulled her attention from the computer screen and tried to decipher what her husband had meant. That he hadn't used the intercom implied the news was personal.

From Alexi?

No. I'm bringing it down.

That isn't necessary, just transfer it to—. She felt it when he stopped listening, as if a barrier had been erected. "Men," she grumbled. "It doesn't even matter what species."

Rieka tapped the proper keys to save her place, then left the desk to walk the confines of their quarters. They'd been living on the *Providence* since she'd given up her command of the *Prodigy*. The arrangement had worked out, so far, since she'd needed a way to get from planet to planet, and Triscoe's current tour would not be over for several months. But after her inauguration as Earth Herald, all that would change.

Only a few more days, she told herself. It had become her mantra.

Waiting, her least favorite pastime, served to fuel her irritation at Triscoe's strange behavior. Since he'd refused to discuss who'd sent the message, her mind worked at the small mystery. Having come from Yadra gave the impression it had been sent by someone from the Fleet. Admiral Nason was her first choice, since she hadn't yet signed her acquittal papers. But there were others who might be inclined to send a communiqué.

The only other thing Rieka could deduce from their short conversation was that they'd come close enough to the Centauri world, Indra, to drop out of their quantum-slide and power down to quarter light speed. Another ten hours or so and they'd be visiting Triscoe's parents at their home near Bedron. The next morning she and Triscoe had an appointment at Sati Labs. And then she'd be interviewing Jeniper Tarrik, the last on her list of potential Earth adjutants.

The door slid open behind her and Captain Triscoe Marteen stepped inside the room, wearing a tentative smile. His light hair matched his pale skin, in direct contrast to the deep blue-and-rust tunic of his Fleet uniform.

"Let's have it," she said, holding her hand out for the message.

He gave her a steely look, and replied, "In a minute."

"This is beginning to sound very bad, Triscoe," Rieka

warned. She tilted her head up to maintain eye contact as she stepped closer. "Is it from Nason?"

"No. It's private."

"Private?" she repeated. "My cousin, Edell?"

Triscoe shook his head. "Your mother."

Dumbstruck, she stared at him before finding her tongue. "What?"

"It's from your mother." Cautiously, Triscoe dug into his trouser pocket and pulled out a small blue disk. He held it up for her to take. "After what happened at Paden's funeral, I didn't think you should see this alone."

Rieka's heart hammered in her chest as she recalled her mother's threat to prevent her from becoming Earth Herald.

"Look, Yadra's fifteen light-years from here, Triscoe," she began, hoping her bravado would hold. "I'll admit Candace has some pretty lengthy tentacles, but we've discussed this before. Her threats are just that. She can't do a thing now. The election's over."

"Then let's have her prove that to us, together." He flashed her a carefree smile, both dimples appearing on his cheeks.

Rieka appreciated and ignored the tactic. Mentally connected by their marriage bond, she could tell his grin was completely cosmetic. She studied the proffered disk for a moment, then snatched it from his fingers. "Fine." Two strides put her back at the computer console, and she slid the disk into the proper slot. Triscoe pulled up a second chair as the small screen activated. She eased into the desk chair and glanced at him once. Grim, she thought. Now he looks ready to kill. She could only hope her expression wasn't a twin to her husband's.

"Hello, Rieka," her mother began. Rieka immediately recognized the stern expression and frosty tone. Seated behind her immense white desk, Candace meant business. That she'd chosen her home office to produce this message provided several other subtle hints as to its content. The custom desk and furnishings, as well as her expensive suit and coiffure spoke of money. A lot of money. The recording had been made in private—so Rieka figured her mother wanted no one else to know about it for as long as possible.

"This message is for you alone," Candace said, confirming her only daughter's assumption. "The communiqué is encoded with some sort of scrambling program—so my engineers have informed me—and can only be played once. So you had better listen well."

Rieka rolled her eyes. Scrambled communications were the norm, but single-play recordings were illegal. "She's such a bitch."

Triscoe nodded but didn't comment. He kept his eyes on the small screen as if memorizing every image that flashed by.

"I have told you how I feel about what you did to Paden," Candace went on, her voice bitter. "Your brother's death will be on your hands for all eternity, and I can only hope the guilt you feel will cause you to suffer as he did—for the rest of your life."

Rieka sighed. "The woman needs medical help," she muttered.

"But I do not intend to dwell on the fact you have committed fratricide. Perhaps justice will be served, and the court will one day see to it you pay for your crime. I am sending this message to you for one purpose—to stop you from committing a second crime, more heinous than the first. A crime against Humanity itself."

"What is she up to?" Triscoe wondered aloud when Candace paused for effect.

Rieka sat straighter. "I'm sure we'll find out."

"I warned you not to attempt to become Earth Herald, and you ignored me. Rieka, Rieka, do you not see the pattern? Your father, the consummate Human sympathizer, left me—and died in that 'esteemed office' because you encouraged him in his dream to make the Earth viable again. It cannot happen. Do you understand? It mustn't be allowed."

"No, I don't understand," Rieka told the recording.

"You may think I have turned my back on your little crusade, but I know you well enough to realize you want the same thing your father did—all Humans living on Earth. You are wrong. That is the worst possible thing for the Commonwealth. You may have been elected, but you will fail as badly as your father, Rieka. The Earth cannot support civilization. Period. I want you to consider abdication."

"Can you believe this?" Rieka wondered aloud.

"She apparently does."

"You do not have to believe me," Candace went on as if she'd heard the comment. Her blue eyes suddenly turned steely. "I have many expert opinions to back me up—and they have not come cheaply. Roughly ten and a half billion Humans exist in the Commonwealth, the bulk of them here on Yadra. Less than two million currently reside on the Earth—all working feverishly to complete the subterranean cities begun by your father over twenty years ago. You expect ten billion people who have lived their entire lives on worlds such as Yadra, Aurie, and Indra—to return to Earth just because their ancestors once lived there? Thank heavens they will not, but if they did, can you imagine the social upset? The economic turmoil? An exodus to Earth will cause more damage to the Commonwealth than rescuing the four billion refugees did two hundred years ago.

"Think realistically, Rieka. Your charming ideal of our species returning to its homeworld won't work. It can't work. And I will do everything in my power to stop you—should you try to go forward with that plan."

"She's out of her mind," Rieka grumbled. "She can't possibly think I'd—"

"I will grant you the planet that spawned our species has been rejuvenated. I have reports here," Candace offered, gesturing toward a console on the desk, "that tell me the oceans are healthy again. The land arable. The air sweet and clean. That is wonderful news. A tremendous accomplishment. But you mustn't take it too far.

"Consider this, daughter—the Earth is new again. Fresh. Vital. Why not make every effort to keep it that way? Encourage only limited repopulation—with essential self-supporting industries on-site. But the bulk of the Earth should remain the paradise it has become. Turn it into a resort world—if you insist the rest of the Commonwealth should be inspired to visit there on a regular basis. Rethink the marketing and turn the Blue Planet Future into a performance advertisement for vacationing on Earth—not for going there to live.

"Rieka, my people have done all the research and compiled the data. If you would discard your pride and study my documentation, you would see where you are about to go terribly wrong. What you want for Humanity cannot be allowed to happen. It will not only bring ruin, again, to our species, it will serve to upset the very foundation of the Commonwealth's economic structure."

Candace stopped and took a breath before lifting her chin and staring directly into the video pickup. "You may have saved the Commonwealth from a Procyon invasion six months ago, but I can assure you they'll only stay away for as long as we continue to appear strong. Your concept as a Reaffirmed Earth will bring the Procyons back faster than any quantum-slide. Think about that, daughter."

The screen went blank.

Rieka let out a long sigh. "That was quite a tirade."

"She certainly likes to cover herself," Triscoe commented. "By sending you a self-destructing threat, you have no grounds for retaliation."

"But it wasn't really a threat," Rieka said, turning to face him. "She never actually said she'd do anything."

He frowned. "But she implied something. Just like she implied she'd make you pay for Paden's death."

"And that's starting to make sense now, too," Rieka said. "If he hadn't been killed, I would never have considered running for Herald. And as obnoxious as he was, Paden would have been elected over either Edell or Peter. I'm sure of it. Mother's clout, if not her money, would have bought him the position. Add to that the fact she had him completely under her control; he would have been the Earth Herald in name only. His death effectively stole that power from her. It's why she blames me."

"And in light of that, I don't understand why she's opted to ask for your cooperation. You'd think she'd be looking for a way to control you just as effectively as she did Paden."

"You're right." Rieka nodded. "I'd have to guess Candace hasn't found that angle, yet. But she's right about one thing. If Earth repopulates, the Commonwealth's economy is going to react. The agro business will experience a big shift. That's already starting to happen," she added, thinking of the News Sheet. "Other industries will probably follow. I just can't see how that would hurt the general economy."

Triscoe leaned back in his chair and crossed his arms over his broad chest. "Apparently, your mother can."

"So why should she be right?" Rieka argued. "For the last two centuries Humans have been trying to recover from the Collision. We're almost there now, and because she's comfortably rich on Yadra, she doesn't want that to happen for fear it'll upset her power base." She banged her fist on the desktop. "Well too bad, Candace. You're not getting your way this time."

"She may not get her way," Triscoe echoed ominously, "but I can guarantee she'll do whatever she thinks is necessary not to let you get your way, either."

At that, Rieka smiled slowly. "She's certainly welcome to try."

Triscoe Marteen felt that same sentiment aimed at him two days later. She was stubborn, his Human wife, and quite often that particular characteristic could be endearing. But she'd been saving the "baby" issue for their arrival at Indra, announcing it to his parents almost as soon as they'd arrived.

Now, as he sat watching his bridge crew begin the mid-tour inspection, Triscoe wondered how he could possibly convince Rieka to give up on the idea of motherhood. Twanabok, the *Providence*'s medical superintendent, had told him Indran-Human hybrids were impossible, but he knew Rieka would never accept defeat.

The console at his elbow beeped softly, bringing him back to the present. Aarkmin, his executive officer, turned toward him from the navigation console. "Your appointment, Captain?"

"Yes." Frowning slightly, Triscoe pushed himself out of his chair. "You have the bridge, Commander. Page me for any reason."

Her shadowy smile did not escape his notice. Aarkmin had retrieved him from other unpleasant meetings with a simple and not necessarily urgent page. "Of course, sir," she said. He wondered if she thought rescuing him from Rieka was funny.

Not bothering to acknowledge her awareness of his apprehension, Triscoe strode from the bridge. A few moments later, the InterMAT deposited him in the Indran city of Korval. A short walk from the station put him in front of the planet's foremost genetic-research facility, Sati Labs.

The beveled-glass facade sparkled in the afternoon sun, causing him to squint as he entered the foyer. A familiar dark-haired figure walked toward him, and Triscoe leaned to welcome her with a light touch on her jawline. "I didn't forget," he said softly.

"I didn't think you would," Rieka answered lightly. "I've already signed us in. It shouldn't be much longer. There's a place to sit over here."

He followed her, noticing she'd worn a skirt today as opposed to her usual jumpsuits. Rieka claimed she'd worn the Fleet uniform for so many years she'd never be comfortable in anything else. But he knew she liked variety. Most Humans did. And the skirt had a certain appeal that slacks did not.

"That color suits you," he said. She looked at him and smiled slightly but said nothing. Studying her, Triscoe noted her hair had returned to its original nut brown color, but her skin still looked paler than he remembered. Dr. Twanabok had sworn her normal pigment tones would return within a year. His ministrations had been the key in allowing her to appear Indran when Admiral Nason had ordered her to spy on the Procyons. Twanabok had also suggested removing her breasts, but Rieka had bound them instead. For that, Triscoe was grateful. The alien structures fascinated him, as did the Human concept of recreational sex.

After their marriage's shaky start, they'd grown more comfortable with each other. But now, Triscoe felt the distinct murmurings of unrest. Rieka had left the Fleet to pursue her father's wish that Earth be managed by a Herald who both loved the planet and her peoples. Now, on the brink of achieving that goal, Rieka had already grasped at another.

And this one would be far more difficult to attain.

"The doctor we'll be speaking to is Wilmstos," she told him, once they'd settled into a pair of padded lobby chairs. "He's their . . . sounding board, I suppose you'd call it. He gets to interview the potential patients, then makes recom-

mendations to the board." Enthusiasm sparkled in her
voice, and her hands gestured as she spoke.

"Rieka," he offered hesitantly, gauging his words by the
anxious amber he sensed in her subconscious. "I've been
talking to Vort—just hypothetically, and—"

She cut him off with an accusing look. Slowly, she asked,
"About us?"

"Not exactly," he explained. "Just about . . . possibilities."

She huffed. "It's on your face, Tris," she hissed quietly,
obviously not wanting to draw the receptionist's attention.
"You talked to Dr. Twanabok about our personal business,
didn't you?"

"I didn't," he insisted innocently, knowing she had been
asking certain questions herself. "I just inquired about the
possibilities of DNA recombination among any two Commonwealth species."

"And?"

"Degahv and Marteen?" an Aurian woman announced
from a nearby doorway. When they both turned to her, she
offered them a sunny smile while her bibbets flushed a light
pink. "Dr. Wilmstos will see you now."

Almost thankful for the interruption, Triscoe stood and
followed Rieka and the woman down a short corridor to
Wilmstos's office. The man was shorter than expected,
Triscoe realized, as they performed the formal Indran
greeting of touching palms. The top of his head looked to
be almost level with Rieka's. His hair had gone white,
though touches of tan were still visible in the braid that fell
from just behind his left ear to his shoulder. His face appeared smooth, smile genuine.

"Captain Degahv, Captain Marteen, a pleasure,"
Wilmstos said. "I'm Helegi Wilmstos. Please, sit down."
He gestured to a small arrangement of furniture near a
corner window.

"Thank you," Rieka said as she settled onto a chair.
"But please, call me Mrs. Degahv, or Rieka. I've given up
my Fleet commission."

"Of course. Although we will soon be calling you Herald," the doctor added with a smile.

Triscoe couldn't help but grin at the look on Rieka's
face. She still found it difficult to accept even such a subtle

compliment. How would she ever manage as a public figure? At least she didn't blush readily or have to worry about bibbets turning dark, he mused. Perhaps, it would just be a matter of getting used to that type of attention. For her sake, he hoped so. Rieka hated feeling self-conscious.

A moment of silence passed. Wilmstos said, "Before we begin, let me say one thing. Today's interview is simply the groundwork—nothing physical will happen. No samples or testing. You've filed your request with us, and it's my job to make sure we get all the pertinent information before sending your case on to the review board. It will be up to them to decide whether or not your situation is one that will be mutually satisfactory for Sati Labs. Are we clear on that?"

"Yes," Rieka said, while Triscoe nodded.

"Good." Wilmstos reached for a datapad on a nearby table and activated it. "Now, I have here you've been married for approximately eight months. You were both captains at that time—and Rieka had since left the Fleet."

"Correct," Triscoe said.

Without looking up, Wilmstos continued. "Captain Marteen is a native Centauri from the planet Indra. And Rieka is a native Yadran of Human descent."

"I prefer to think of myself as simply Human, if you don't mind," she told him sternly.

"But you and two prior generations were born and raised on Yadra, is that correct?"

"Yes, that's correct," she replied, her tone flat.

He tapped something into the small machine and continued. "Do the two of you share physical intimacy?"

Triscoe tried hard not to smile at the incredulous look that crossed Rieka's face. Before she could utter a sound, he said, "Frequently. That has never been a problem for us."

"Good, good," Wilmstos said, tapping more information into his computer. "Now, you are aware of the impossibility of any kind of natural fertilization, are you not?"

"Yes," Rieka answered, her eyes on the doctor's datapad. "That's why we're here. We both possess the ability to reproduce. We just want to do that with each other."

"And that's the tricky thing, Rieka," Wilmstos commented as he set aside the datapad. "What we've got here is a loving, married couple. They're compatible emotionally, mentally, physically . . . and they want to produce offspring. But the undeniable fact is—even though you may look very much alike—you are not the same species. Far from it." Wilmstos gestured with his hands. "And that is a huge obstacle."

"But is it possible?" Rieka asked.

Triscoe felt his chest constrict as he waited for Doctor Wilmstos to answer.

"Of course," he told them. He reached for the datapad again, tapped a few keys, and looked up. "Actually, just about anything is *possible* in the field of biology. *Probable* is another thing altogether."

"But you've combined closely related species before," Rieka urged. "And the results—well, the published ones anyway—have been tremendously successful."

Wilmstos nodded. "True. But there have been serious failures. And the parent species have always been indigenous. We're talking about something altogether different here."

Triscoe clamped his teeth together and nodded, relieved. He refused to argue with her in front of a stranger, but if the doctor told them trying to produce a child by artificial means even at the most basic level was ludicrous, he would not give up the opportunity to agree.

Rieka glanced at him, frowned, and turned her attention back to Wilmstos. "Are you trying to tell me that since something hasn't been tried previously—you're not willing? This is supposed to be Indra's most advanced lab."

"It is," Wilmstos told her. "But our reputation comes from the fact we are very careful about what we do. We and our clients must honor both moral and legal obligations to society."

Triscoe watched as Rieka puckered her lips in a displeased frown. "I'm simply trying to find a way to have a child with my husband," she argued. "I appreciate the necessity for being careful . . . you just aren't being very helpful."

"Are you saying we should give up?" Triscoe asked.

"No, Captain Marteen, I'm not. There are certainly things that can be done to aid in your having a baby. Quite simply the idea of trying to genetically recombine chromosomes from *alien* species is . . . not a good one. We could clone a child—even go so far as to alter the sex—give you a boy. But we would only be creating a genetic reproduction of you, Rieka. I cannot recommend trying to hybridize an Indran and Human. It is far too complex. Too dangerous."

"Why? You've just pointed out how alike we are—aren't there enough genetic similarities?" Rieka asked sarcastically.

Wilmstos remained unruffled, and Triscoe silently applauded him. "Of course there are. I would be a fool to deny the obvious. Every new discovery made in the last four decades gives credence to the theory of a common ancestor. Most of the advanced scientific minds now agree with that scenario. But after a few billion years of evolution, even the most hardy bacteria—and that is all our supposed forebears are guessed to have left behind—are going to be genetically incompatible."

Wilmstos leaned forward. "The three of us are sitting here sharing this atmosphere, but your lungs are absorbing oxygen and releasing carbon dioxide. Triscoe and I are taking in carbon dioxide and breaking it down at the cellular level."

She sighed. "I know that. I simply thought you could genetically engineer the desired traits. You make a decision on what you want—and then go with that."

"An essentially accurate assumption," agreed Wilmstos. "But every decision made must be followed through with utmost precision."

Triscoe felt himself frowning at the complexity of their request. If Sati Labs started working on the problem today, it might take years before they were ready to attempt anything involving a physical subject. "You're saying this is like designing an entirely new species."

He nodded. "Yes, Captain. But I would not recommend it in this case. There is no guarantee that the chemistry of the fetus would not adversely affect Rieka in some way. Or vice versa. The risks are simply too great."

Triscoe reached for Rieka's hand as the crestfallen look swept across her face. He sensed her disappointment and refused to discount it in the face of his own triumph. Not that he didn't want to be a father. He just didn't want her desire for a child to outweigh common sense.

"I'm sorry," Wilmstos offered finally. "I simply need you to understand the facts."

She stayed silent another long moment, kneading Triscoe's palm with her fingers. *What do you think?*

He's right. The risks are too great.

She sighed. "Look, Doctor, I've done an awful lot of things in my life, a great many of them risky. What's the worst that could happen?" Without waiting for an answer, she continued. "The chromosomes wouldn't combine—or if they did, the embryo would die quickly. And if you got past that, maybe it wouldn't survive being implanted—or my body chemistry. Anything. But you'll never know what can be accomplished unless you do try.

"This is the best facility Indra has to offer, but if you're unwilling to even attempt what we ask, we'll just go somewhere else. We'll keep going until we find someone who *will* try."

"I understand," Wilmstos said finally. "But you are not looking at the entire scenario. Implanting a viable embryo with incompatible chemistry could also kill you, Rieka. And if you somehow managed to bring the fetus to term, it is possible the infant would have an abnormal appearance . . . perhaps even freakish. Above everything else, I must make sure you understand that." He looked squarely at Rieka, then Triscoe.

Rieka nodded once. "It's understood."

Wilmstos tapped his datapad again and set it aside. "I think I've got all the information I require at this point. I'll take your request to our board of directors and contact you in a few days."

Triscoe nodded, and they said their good-byes. Walking back to the InterMAT station, he realized now more than ever that he could do little to dissuade her from this crusade. Rieka saw no point in avoiding something simply because it hadn't been done. His arguments for her safety would, as in the past, be conveniently ignored.

And with all the complications and stresses of being Herald added to the equation, Triscoe saw only disaster ahead. How would he ever manage to convince her that her concept of life was not necessarily the only acceptable one?

He would love a child cloned from her Human cells just as deeply as one that they might have had—had Rieka been Centauri.

This procedure could also produce an abomination instead of the cherubic baby she envisioned. And simply carrying a hybridized child might kill her, the doctor had said. She would fight him, of course, but under no circumstances would Triscoe allow Rieka to make such a sacrifice. Whether or not Sati Labs accepted their case, he needed to find a suitable argument in order to stop her.

Unfortunately, nothing came to mind.

TWO

"I'm simply saying if you *can* control something, you should make every effort to do it completely," Ker Marteen told her as he leaned back in his chair.

Rieka studied her father-in-law for a long moment, trying to judge whether or not he was serious. "Really, Ker, that is the most moronic thing you've ever said to me. We're talking about creating babies, not inanimate objects." She sighed and looked at Triscoe. He seemed relaxed in his father's presence, or at least less tense than she'd remembered from the last time they'd all met in this house. Of course they'd been newlyweds then, and Ker had been completely opposed to the idea his son had married a Human.

"It is not moronic," the older man insisted, flipping his long silver-blond braid over his shoulder. "If you'd just look at this sensibly, you'd see that."

Rieka glanced at the expensive artwork on the wall and shook her head. "I'll tell you what I see around here, Ker. You live in this private art gallery surrounding yourself with images created by mortals. Look at this place." She gestured to various pieces in the room. "It's a shrine. And a group of individuals created it. but it's not *natural*. It's affected. Created to your whims. And that's fine," she added with a shrug. "I would be pleased with the challenge of helping to design a house or a spaceship to my specifications. But I draw the line at designing a *person*."

Ker pounded a big fist on his knee. "You're not listening." He pointed a finger at her. "You made that decision when you went to Sati Labs. I'm simply saying as long as they have agreed to try to combine your DNA with

Triscoe's, you ought to find out if they can preselect some traits. Intelligence would be nice, for one. General health. Coloring. Temperament."

Rieka lifted a hand, wanting to stop him while it was still possible. "Please. Let's change the subject. The lab hasn't even agreed, yet. If they determine they can do the job, we'll take whatever we can get. I'm not going to manipulate nature any more than absolutely necessary."

"Why ever not?"

"Because it's dangerous." Rieka huffed again and looked out the window. "Triscoe and I are not about to risk any more than we have to in order to have a child. I'm determined in this, Ker." She turned and glared at him. "You aren't going to change my mind."

Ker looked at Triscoe. "You agree with her?"

"For the most part," he replied. "The thing you don't seem to want to understand, Father, is that this is our decision, not yours. Yes, I know—this would be your first grandchild. But you must allow the two of us to be parents. Rieka has made some incredibly hard decisions in the past few months. I think the least we can do is offer a little slack."

"Thank you," she said.

Ker grumbled but offered no comment.

"Well, I see we're all getting along famously, as usual," Setana quipped from the doorway. Rieka bit back a snide comment and watched as her mother-in-law offered them all a wry smile before seating herself near Ker.

Rieka sighed and gnawed at her lip. Would she ever learn self-control the way Setana had? Triscoe's mother, the Indran Herald, possessed the *quantivasta* gift—the ability to pick up on other people's thoughts and emotions. She used that gift to manage everything and everyone with gentle determination. Rieka's experience in the Fleet taught her how to issue orders. Persuasive tactics, she supposed, could be learned. She hoped.

For some reason, that thought made her think of her father. His untimely death had given her good reason to find her own subtle ways to help both the Commonwealth and Humanity.

And Stephen Degahv had also disagreed with Candace on the most basic principles. He truly believed Humanity belonged on Earth. That the people needed a common place to connect on a most basic level—not live scattered by chance rather than choice on eight of the Commonwealth's ten member worlds.

She hadn't been on Earth the day the transport ship crashed, but she'd always known the circumstances surrounding the accident were murky. Pilot error? Mechanical or electrical failure? Rieka could never be sure of that any more than she could say for certain Candace had had nothing to do with it.

And now, out of some warped sense of responsibility, she'd been elected Earth Herald, her campaign focusing on her role as Earth's champion. Her father would have loved it. While protecting the Commonwealth from the Procyons, she'd made a shocking discovery: The meteor collision that had nearly destroyed Earth had been a deliberate attack.

Humanity had been manipulated for the past two centuries, and it had to stop.

Jeniper Tarrik sat at the table in her small apartment in Bedron staring at the News Sheet on her IndraLink screen. She blinked once and realized she hadn't actually read any part of the article. Her breakfast, now a lump of soggy mush in her bowl, had lost its appeal. In a few hours, she'd have her interview with Herald-elect Degahv. Why couldn't Jonik have waited until tonight to contact her? After all, she hadn't heard from him in months. Now, on top of being nervous, she'd become preoccupied. She couldn't help wondering what trouble he'd gotten himself into, this time. And the price tag he would quote for her help.

As the third child, Jonik had grown up with many handicaps. Both Jeniper and Edrin, their older brother, had always tried to help him however they could. But sometimes Jeniper thought he'd gone beyond help. Ever the adventurer, Jonik would never conform.

In a way, though, she envied him. She'd worked as the Earth Herald's Attaché on Indra for four years. At first, the job had challenged her, but recently Jeniper found herself bored with the routine. If the new Earth Herald didn't hire her, she'd already decided to resign her post here and find something better.

Glancing at the time, Jeniper sighed into her now-inedible breakfast. "Thanks, Jonik. I get to go to the biggest interview of my life—on empty *ribah*—then meet with you. Can't imagine a better day."

Pushing away from the table, she disposed of the uneaten food and switched off the screen she hadn't even read. On the way toward the door, she checked herself in the mirror. Her hair looked fine, as did her outfit, but the dark mauve bibbets on her forehead wouldn't do.

Hoping she could grab fifteen minutes to get herself under control, Jeniper grumbled, "This can't possibly get any worse," and closed the door behind her.

"Dammit, this is impossible!" Rieka raked her fingers through her hair and heaved a tired sigh. "I've been invited to six civic dedications—all on Earth on the same day— and a state wedding between two people I've never met. There are one, two . . . five corporate meetings I've been asked to attend. I don't know what the companies expect, or even the topic of discussion. I don't negotiate contracts. At least I don't think I do." She looked at Setana for confirmation.

"Not necessarily, though I'm sure you will be asked to mediate from time to time. A Herald whose planet means to be productive knows who is doing business with whom. And Herald sanction of a business deal can be quite significant."

"Well, I'd better mark those as "should attend," she muttered.

"You also should have several appointments scheduled for protocol briefings and at least two fittings for your inaugural dress."

"Got that." She tapped another key and glanced back at her mother-in-law. Six more entries had come in during their short conversation. "I knew I'd be busy, but this is ridiculous."

Setana smiled gently. "A new Herald is bound to get a great deal of attention, Rieka," she advised. "It will all settle down in a few weeks, I'm sure. The most important thing to remember is you must never allow the public to see you distraught. A nervous Herald is an ineffectual one."

"I'll keep that in mind," Rieka said. "Actually, this isn't that much different than commanding a Fleet ship. It's just that I had over a hundred people crewing the *Venture*. More than three hundred on the *Prodigy*. Right now, it's a solo performance until I get my staff in place."

Setana smiled. "You are *pemila kaye*." She made a complex gesture with her fingers. "That's an Indran expression which seems to fit you rather well. You are trying to be ahead of where you are," she offered with a slight frown. "Is there a Human equivalent?"

She thought about that for a moment. "Putting the cart before the horse?"

Rieka watched as Setana considered the idiom. "Why yes. That is very similar. Rieka, have you ever considered how closely Human phrases are to those of the Boo? Everything is so visual. Indran and Peratan concepts are characteristically thought processes. Really, it is quite remarkable."

Rieka shrugged noncommittally. "And what does that have to do with my being . . . *pemila kaye*?"

Setana refocused on Rieka and smiled. "You already have a staff, you know. And an office on every planet."

"Well, yes, but they're Uncle Alexi's people. I didn't think it would be right to just walk in and . . ."

"I'm sure there are people at the Earth Embassy here on Indra who would be happy to assist you in any way—even though Alexi is still the legal Earth Herald."

"I suppose so. I'm interviewing Jeniper Tarrik this morning. My Herald's Adjutant is the most pressing decision to be made."

She'd already interviewed four people for the position. Unfortunately, none of them had both the self-motivation and willingness to work Rieka sought. She needed to find someone who wanted the same things for Earth she did, and soon.

"You will find someone suitable," Setana told her.

"I'm sure I will. It would be nice, though, if I could do that sooner, rather than later." Rieka hesitated a moment, then asked the questions she'd wanted to know for weeks. "Did you know I'd be elected?"

Setana looked up from her computer screen. "I wondered if you would ask." With a wistful smile, she answered, "Yes, I did. Yillon mentioned it some time ago. After you'd announced your candidacy."

"I see. And that's why you invited me here and cleared your calendar—so we'd be able to spend time together?"

"Since there is no point in trying to cover up that fact, yes. Precisely." Intelligent brown eyes studied Rieka for a long moment. "I always knew you were quite intuitive."

Rieka glanced at her mother-in-law and realized the woman expected her to explode.

"Are you angry?" Setana asked.

"A little," she answered honestly, knowing Setana's *quantivasta* gift would sense any deceit. "I realized you couldn't tell me what you knew—but it's still hard to accept. I suppose I would have gotten very *pemila kaye,* if I'd known ahead of time."

At that, Setana laughed lightly, and Rieka joined her.

"If it is any consolation, I doubt Yillon will be predicting any significant changes in your life in the near future."

"A comforting thought," Rieka jibed. She glanced out the window toward the trees in the distance and bluntly changed the subject. "You and Ker have built this sanctuary where you can come and find a little peace. I have nothing like it."

"You will someday, I'm sure."

"Is that a prediction?"

"No. Just an idea. A thought. We all need a place to retreat when things threaten to overwhelm us."

"I used to call that place home."

"And where was that?"

"My mother's estate on Yadra. It's a huge place in the hills outside of Kilpani called Olympus. I was just a child, though. I didn't know any better." The great stone edifice surrounded by outbuildings, fields, and rolling terrain skimmed across Rieka's mind. She hadn't thought of the estate in a long time. No. She had no home. Setana's gentle advice had proven far more valuable than her mother's constant criticism.

"You're thinking of Candace?"

"Are you reading my mind?"

"No." Setana smiled. "Just your face. You look as though you've swallowed something awful."

Rieka laughed.

Setana tilted her head slightly and Rieka felt her mother-

in-law's scrutiny like a tangible thing. "Was she that bad?"
Setana asked. "I've only met her once or twice."

"Bad doesn't begin to describe Candace Degahv," Rieka
began. Her voice turned cold. "She loved Paden because
he let her tell him what to do. And she resented me because my father stood up for my independence. Now that
Paden's dead, she's become even more unreasonable."

"How so?"

"At the funeral she took me aside and told me she'd
make me pay for Paden's death. She's convinced I killed
him."

A frown crossed Setana's brow. "But he was shot by a
Procyon. You tried to save him."

"I know that—and so does everyone else in the Com-
monwealth. But Candace will never believe such a story.
She called me a murderer and promised to see justice done.
The funeral was . . . quite a show."

Setana frowned thoughtfully at Rieka. "Do you have any
idea what she meant?"

"No. And until recently, I've ignored her. She threatens
people all the time. But she wanted Paden to be Herald.
And now I am. She sent a message to me on the *Providence*
threatening to stop me from trying to make Earth viable
again."

"Threatening to do . . . what?"

"She didn't say." But Rieka had recognized that look in
her mother's eye. She'd seen it before. At the funeral. And
the day she and her father had left for Earth.

Candace meant to have her way.

THREE

As she entered the small waiting area at the Earth Embassy, Rieka decided she wasn't particularly impressed with either its cramped size or the ecru decor. And aside from the furnishings, all of Centauri design, she was alone. Irritated by that fact, she strode past the vacant receptionist's desk and opened the door.

"Oh, you can't do that," a voice scolded her from behind.

Rieka turned and looked at the speaker, previously hidden by a profusion of greenery set in an alcove. The slight Centauri man in his middle years stood holding a watering can. Rieka wondered if she'd ever figure out why Alexi hadn't hired a completely Human staff.

"And you are . . . ?" Rieka demanded.

"I'm the receptionist here. Mr. Kelind Barq." He left the can near the plants he'd been tending, walked to the inner door, and closed it securely. He then turned and stood behind his desk like a sentry.

The man's posture reminded Rieka of a Fleet security officer, and she tried hard not to smile. She covered it by clearing her throat and offering, "Good morning, Mr. Barq."

"Good morning," the man returned. "But I have no appointment scheduled for this early in the day. Whom did you wish to see?"

Rieka watched as Mr. Barq plopped onto his chair and began tapping orders to his computer. In addition to the interview with Ms. Tarrik, she'd intended to check up on Alexi's recent business dealings and see what was required of her in order to pick up the reins efficiently. Ms. Tarrik, apparently, had not informed anyone of her impending visit, which Rieka found curious.

Mr. Barq finished with his console and looked up at her expectantly. "I'd like to see Jeniper Tarrik, if I may," she said politely.

"Have you business concerning Earth?"

"I would say so."

"A residential or commercial license?"

"No."

Barq frowned. "Construction permit of some kind?"

"No."

"Scientific research?"

Rieka shook her head.

"You look familiar," Barq told her. "Have we met before?"

"I sincerely doubt that, Mr. Barq."

"Well, I feel I should know you." Barq frowned and studied his computer screen. "I have an opening for tomorrow morning at eleven hundred hours."

"I don't want an appointment. And I know I'm a bit early. But I just need to see Jeniper Tarrik." Rieka clenched her jaw to keep from smiling. Their droll conversation was a lot like getting past Admiral Nason's secretary. A lot of double-talk and little progress. "I should be on the schedule," she repeated. "I'm sure Ms. Tarrik confirmed the appointment."

"Ms. Tarrik is the Planetary Attaché," Barq countered, shaking his head. "She's quite busy. One can't simply walk in and expect—"

The door behind him opened abruptly and a statuesque Aurian woman appeared. Jeniper Tarrik resembled her holofile exactly. She wore her hair pinned up off her neck in a trio of neat coils. Her pale blue eyes were both sharp and guileless, and, despite the row of bibbets adorning her hairline, the sprinkle of freckles across her fine-boned cheeks gave her a Human look. She glanced at Rieka then did a double take. "Captain Degahv?"

"Just Rieka—for now," she replied, offering her hand and catching a better glimpse of the woman's forehead, or what she could see of it beneath the carefully coifed red hair. The Aurie's hivelike bibbets had flushed from pink to rose but the welts had stayed relatively flat, indicating her emotional state had gone from nominal to somewhat stimulated.

"Jeniper Tarrik, Centauri's Attaché to Earth Herald Alexi Degahv." Jeniper shook hands firmly, and Rieka extended hers again, to Barq. The Centauri man had gasped but regained his composure quickly enough to accept and return the greeting.

"I am so sorry, Herald," Barq mumbled. "Please accept my apologies. I should have recognized you. I knew you looked familiar."

"Think nothing of it Mr. Barq," Rieka told him, slightly self-conscious of that title, since it wasn't yet completely hers. "I dressed this way on purpose." Not wanting to be recognized on the street, she'd made a special point of looking as ordinary as possible today. She'd worn an old jumpsuit, no jewelry, and didn't even carry her datapad.

Mr. Barq nodded hesitantly. "Please call me Barq. Everyone else does."

"It's a pleasure, Barq."

Alexi's attaché pulled herself straighter. "Please don't let us be disturbed, Barq. I imagine our guest will need my full attention while she's here."

"Of course, Ms. Tarrik."

With that, Jeniper gestured Rieka through the door. "Let me show you around, Rieka."

"First door here, conference room. Next on the left is my office. Next to that is the media room. Across here, the kitchen. Can I get you anything?" When Rieka shook her head no, Jeniper turned to the next doorway. "Here is where the rest of the staff works. Yime is on Perata at present. Mr. Giff is attending a corporate meeting between Fielmar Services and JoirWen Incorporated this morning. And Yoe is in the data center, on the fourth floor. That is where the rest of the secretarial staff works. A complement of seven there, total."

"So, with seven there plus two out of the office and one on Perata—and you and Mr. Barq, Alexi has a staff of twelve, here. Is that enough?"

"I believe so," Jeniper said. "Of course one of the junior staff is always stationed at the small office on Perata. They rotate that position on a monthly basis."

"Whatever works, I suppose."

"And the end office will be yours. It's got a wonderful view of Bedron."

Jeniper threw open the door, and they entered. The office had all the personality of a dormitory. Dark blue floor, pale blue walls, large desk with an equally large chair. Near the window, which did boast an impressive view of University Park and the city beyond, sat the usual grouping of chairs and low tables for informal conversation.

"Ugh," Rieka groaned. They would have to redecorate completely in order to achieve the comfortable, open feeling she wanted to create. Visitors here should feel as if they were on Earth, not Indra. "It's almost as bad as out front. Who decorated this place?"

"I have no idea, ma'am," the Aurian answered dryly. "It was this way when I came."

"It was a rhetorical question, Jeniper," Rieka murmured, still taking in the view. "I suppose Alexi doesn't spend much time on Indra."

"Only a few weeks out of the year."

Rieka turned. "And that must be because the office here manages quite well without him."

Jeniper looked away, and her bibbets colored slightly. "I wouldn't begin to guess the Herald's reasons for doing what he does, Cap—Rieka," she answered diplomatically.

Rieka nodded, pleased the woman had neither denied herself the compliment nor augmented it. Still, she hadn't forgotten that odd scene in the reception area. "And now that we're alone, would you mind explaining why your interview for the position of my adjutant is a secret?"

She watched Jeniper clench her fingers, then nod. "Of course. The answer is quite simple, really. The application is my business, not theirs. If I'm hired, I'll appoint one of the junior staff to take my place and leave it to him or her to fill the empty spot. If I'm not hired, routine here will go on as usual." She shrugged slightly. "Routine is important, Rieka. I do everything I can to maintain it."

Rieka found herself admiring the woman's honesty. "Mmm. Have you ever been to Earth, Jeniper?" She gestured to the chairs, and they sat.

"No, I've never been to Earth. Travel there is restricted until the Reaffirmation."

"I know that—but you're the Herald's attaché. I would

have thought Alexi might have sent you there for some reason." Jeniper shook her head. "We'll have to rectify that oversight. Can't have people working for me—and the Earth—who haven't even been there, can I?"

"I suppose not," Jeniper said. Her watery blue eyes sparkled in a way that reminded Rieka of her Aurian friend, Robert DeVark.

"How old are you?"

"Twenty-nine, ma'am."

"And why do you want to leave Indra? A bit bored here?"

"Excuse me?"

Rieka shrugged. "I was just thinking you're awfully young, and despite the importance of this embassy and your dedication to routine—you're probably not very challenged."

At that, Jeniper smiled slightly. "I don't mind routine. But I will admit looking forward to the Earth's Reaffirmation into the Commonwealth. I've been considering hiring more staff to compensate for the additional activity."

"Sounds like a good idea."

"I take it you've gone over my application."

"Yes." In fact, she'd gone over it several times. Scrutinized it. Jeniper Tarrik was qualified, dedicated, and willing to work for Earth. Rieka just needed to get over the idea of having a non-Human as her adjutant.

"And?"

"And I'd like to get to know you a bit before I decide," she admitted, intrigued that the interview had somehow pivoted. She hadn't expected to answer questions, just ask them. "I'd prefer to hire someone with a personality compatible to my own. One I can trust to make decisions in my absence."

"Very reasonable." Jeniper rose and went toward the Herald's huge desk console. "If you want to explore that aspect, then perhaps we should try working together. I could acquaint you with our data-processing system."

Rieka pushed herself up from the cushions and went to sit in Alexi's large chair. Jeniper Tarrik had to be the most intriguing person she'd met in some time. "Great. Then how about giving me a quick tutorial on this console. For the moment, I'd like to know exactly who works for me and what my uncle has been doing for Humans who live on Indra and Perata."

Five hours later, the intercom beeped. Barq's face appeared on the small screen. "You have an incoming call, Herald. Captain Triscoe Marteen from the *Providence*."

Rieka didn't bother to correct Barq. She would have to get used to it eventually. She glanced at Jeniper, then rolled her head to loosen the cramped muscles in her neck. "Put him through, Barq."

Triscoe's amused expression told her Barq had probably questioned his request to speak to her. "So what's with the formal call, Tris?" she asked. "I would have bet money you'd simply get my attention . . . the Indran way." He hadn't even nudged a sense of nearness into her thoughts.

"None of that for the new Earth Herald," he replied seriously, though Rieka could tell he was biting his tongue.

"Right," she told him, her voice oozing with sarcasm. "What do you want, then? Did I forget an appointment or something?"

"No, love. I just wondered if you'd forgotten to eat. I have. And since my inspection is now complete, I thought I'd invite you to lunch."

"Well isn't that sweet?" Rieka looked at Jeniper with a wry grin. The Aurian woman seemed uncomfortable at being privy to the personal byplay. Her bibbets flushed slightly even as Rieka watched. An idea clicked in her mind, and she asked, "On the *Providence*?"

"I suppose that could be arranged," Triscoe replied. *What's going on?*

There is someone I want you to meet. "Great, I'll be bringing a guest with me, if you don't mind."

Even on the small screen, she could see his eyes glimmer with curiosity. "Of course not. I'll meet you at InterMAT Station Four in—fifteen minutes?"

"We'll be there. Earth Embassy out." She flipped the toggle to "off" and turned to Jeniper. "What do you say we shut this down for a while and take a break. Ever been aboard a Fleet ship?"

When Jeniper didn't answer right away, Rieka wondered if she'd made other plans for lunch. Then her expression brightened. Apparently whatever Jeniper had expected to do had been overridden by an invitation to lunch with a Herald-to-be and a ship's captain. Rieka saw only the barest hint of rose in the spots on her forehead and commended her for being able to adapt quickly.

"Actually, I traveled quite a bit before I took this position."

Rieka shook her head. "Commercial passengers don't see half the interesting stuff. I think our relationship is about to become mutually educational."

It took a few minutes to shut down the terminal and put away the hard copies of the files Rieka had requested. Then they told Barq they'd be on the *Providence* until further notice and headed for the Embassy's InterMAT station.

Triscoe met them as soon as they stepped from the chamber. "Permission to come aboard, Captain?" Rieka asked.

"Granted."

She accepted the traditional Indran greeting of husband to wife, allowing his thumb to caress her lower jaw before turning her attention to her companion. "Jeniper, I'd like you to meet the *Providence*'s captain, Triscoe Marteen. Tris, this is Jeniper Tarrik. Confusing as it may seem, Humanity's Centauri Attaché is an Aurian."

"A pleasure, Captain," Jeniper said, smiling. She offered her palms in the Indran greeting.

"The pleasure is mine," he replied, touching his palms to hers. "Tarrik. The name is familiar." He gestured them to accompany him into the hallway. "Does your family do business with the Fleet?"

Jeniper nodded. "My brother Edrin owns a hydroponics company based on Aurie."

Rieka watched while he nodded thoughtfully. "Yes. I thought I recognized the name. And you resemble him, do you not? Though his hair is darker as I recall."

"It is."

Rieka remained quiet through lunch, watching both Triscoe and Jeniper. The woman had an easy rapport with just about everyone, Rieka observed. She was intelligent, inquisitive, adaptable, and highly motivated. She had all the qualities of the adjutant Rieka needed, save one: she wasn't Human.

While Rieka wrestled with that, Triscoe regaled Jeniper with the story of how Rieka and the Boos had saved the

Prodigy during the Procyon War. When they'd finished eating, he offered to take them on a short tour.

"That would be wonderful," Rieka said. "Jeniper was telling me earlier that she's traveled a great deal but never really seen how a Fleet ship functions. Engineering would be the perfect place to start."

"I have wondered, of course," Jeniper began.

"Then we'll endeavor to answer all your questions," Triscoe told her. "This way." They walked down the main corridor to the nearest Chute and were deposited on quadrant B, deck two before Jeniper finished asking if they ever had trouble with the gravity pod.

Rieka smiled wryly. The Pod, located a kilometer below the vessel's main curved hull and manned only by Boos, produced the gravitational field that allowed both the passengers and crew to move about normally. "Problems occur now and then," she said. "But Memta is one of the best engineering supers in the Fleet."

"The best," Triscoe corrected.

They followed him through the huge doors and entered an immense room that spanned all three floors of the umbrella-shaped vessel. The room brought back fond memories of her own engineering suites on the *Venture* and *Prodigy*. Men and women from five races worked together here on the main engineering deck. Far below in the gravity pod, only the Boo could withstand the immense stresses they generated with their almost magical equipment.

Rieka noted Jeniper's slight reaction as a huge Boo shuffled up to Triscoe and began to speak. "Captain has a problem?"

"Negative. Roddik. We slide to Varannah," Triscoe told him. "I have visitors who wish to see the curve of the dawn. Is Memta close?"

"In the Pod. I'll super here until his return."

Lieutenant Roddik, an immense blue creature with multi-faceted eyes and a translator box sutured to his chest, turned toward Rieka. "Captain Herald Degahv," he gurgled, "your visage is weightless."

She offered him a grateful smile. "I am honored you recall my visage, Roddik," she said. "And I am glad to see you aboard."

"Always shall I work under Memta," Roddik replied. He

Jan Clark

took a brief pull from his atmosphere compensator, and added, "His command is the square of the nth. All equality."

The odor of chlorine swept over her, but Rieka had trained herself to ignore it long ago. "That is good. I would introduce you to my friend, Jeniper Tarrik."

Rieka watched as Jeniper stood her ground while Roddik sidled closer. He was nearly half again her height and probably outweighed her ten times over. "Honored am I Jeniper Tarrik," he said, wiggling the fleshly folds over his gleaming black eyes. He double-blinked and added, "The *Providence* slides to Varannah on the dew, does it not?"

"Well, yes, I suppose it does," Jeniper replied. "Where exactly is Varannah, Lieutenant?"

"It is the place on the horizon which touches our *ckla*. Here we find symmetry."

"So it's really more like a feeling than an actual place."

"Yes."

"Well then, I suppose you are right."

The odor of chlorine grew heavy. While Rieka watched Jeniper wipe her eyes, Triscoe silently asked, *What's going on?* She knew his curiosity had been piqued even before lunch.

Have Roddik show her around, and I'll tell you, Rieka offered, tempting him with a quizzical grin.

A brief request from his captain was all it took to send Lieutenant Roddik shuffling off with Jeniper. She threw them one questioning look over her shoulder before frowning up at the Boo, probably trying to fathom what he'd said.

"What is going on?" Triscoe repeated aloud.

"As if you couldn't guess. She's my adjutant."

Triscoe looked down at her skeptically. "You didn't introduce her that way."

"Well, that's because I haven't exactly hired her, yet."

"Rieka!" he chided.

"What?" She looked at him innocently. "She knows what I'm doing—that this is part of her interview. I wanted to see how she dealt with an unpredictable situation. Roddik is about as unpredictable as they come—though Memta would have been more intimidating."

Triscoe turned, effectively blocking her view of the suite.

"I cannot believe this behavior is coming from you. Do you realize you are manipulating this woman? You, of all people." He put his hands on his hips. "A Human who swore never to be caught acting like any of those—"

Rieka poked him in the chest. "Don't you start with me, Centauri. And I'm testing, *not* manipulating. And Jeniper knows it."

She watched as a dimple puckered in his cheek. "You are quite beautiful when you're defensive, my wife," he said softly. "Your face gets pink and your eyes start to—no, now that is definitely not a defensive move." He smiled. "I am teasing, Rieka," he added, catching her raised fist in his hand.

Triscoe kneaded her fingers gently. She knew he still didn't understand the appropriate times for things, but he was working on it. "I knew that," she lied, pulling her fist from his hand. "And Jeniper will be a wonderful adjutant. Alexi's kept her holed up as his attaché here for four years. She's ready for a challenge."

"Then why are you waiting to tell her she's got the job? She meets all your criteria. I imagine you'll know soon enough if you've made the wrong choice."

Rieka glanced up into his face and decided not to comment on that. She'd simply have to have faith in her own judgment. She sighed and made an exasperated face, then waved her hand as if to dismiss him. "Go play captain and annoy someone else, Triscoe. Jeniper and I have work to do." She turned on her heel and went to collect her soon-to-be adjutant.

"I'm such a *bimoosh*," Jeniper muttered to herself as she studied one of Olm's early watercolors. After leaving the Herald's office, both stunned and thrilled by Mrs. Degahv's decision, she'd hurried to the museum, afraid she'd missed Jonik. Her baby brother was nowhere to be seen. Thinking of little else beyond the enormity of her new position, and the fact she'd been hired almost on the spot, Jeniper examined the painting a few minutes longer, then moved on to a wall wearing an abstract oil. If Jonik's reason for wanting to see her had anything to do with money, he'd arrive soon. She stood there, feeling a sudden connection with the wide, abstract bands of color, and tried to concentrate on what she'd need to do before she left Indra.

"Took you long enough to get here," a familiar voice said.

Jeniper turned and looked into her younger sibling's face, wondering how long he'd been studying her while she'd thought she'd been waiting for him. His appearance had changed enough for Jeniper to feel a jolt of maternal anxiety. He now wore his dark hair long and over his bibbets, effectively covering all but those near his eyes. Stubble covered his jaw line. He seemed thinner than the last time she'd seen him, and there were worry lines around his mouth. And his clothes, though clean, looked old and threadbare.

"I had business to attend to, Jonik," she explained with an air of superiority. "I have a good job. And responsibilities. I realize you aren't familiar with those sorts of things, but—"

"I didn't come here to be insulted," he grumbled, setting himself down on a bench in front of an immense Pollock. "Now this one I can relate to. One great big mess." He leaned back to get a better view. "That's me."

Jeniper glanced up at the paint-splattered canvas, then folded her skirt under her as she sat next to him. "What sort of trouble are you in now?"

"Who says I'm in trouble?"

"I hear from Mam and Pae once a week, Jonik. And Edrin sends a message every now and then. I hear about what you've been doing."

Jonik shrugged and said nothing.

"You haven't asked me for money in nearly a year. I suppose I'm due." Jeniper sighed. "How much do you need this time?" she asked resignedly.

"Just a loan, Jen," he said.

"And like all the other loans—I'll never see a credit of it again. How much?"

"Fifty-eight thousand."

Jeniper felt her jaw drop, and she snapped it closed. "You are out of your mind, Jonik. What have you done?" she whispered in disbelief. His silent reply irked her further. "I don't have that kind of money, and if I did—I certainly wouldn't throw it away on you. Go ask Edrin. He can put it in his books as a bad investment." She pushed herself up from the bench and headed for the museum entrance.

Jonik caught up to her on the street. "You don't understand, Sis," he told her. "This isn't just money I owe someone. It's more. She means business. If I don't pay up in less than a week's time, she'll . . . do something." His eyes grew wide and he pressed his lips together, a nervous habit he'd developed as a child.

"Grow up, Jonik."

"I'm serious."

Jeniper huffed and kept on walking. Jonik had tried this approach too many times. She no longer had a soft spot for his problems. He was a grown man now, able to look after himself. "I'm sorry you've made some bad decisions," she began. "But they've been your decisions to make. The entire family has gone out of its way to help you. This is too much." She shook her head at his incredulous expression. "Don't try to hold me accountable. I've got enough responsibilties to worry about for myself." Wasn't he tired of hearing this speech by now?

"But Jen, you don't understand," he babbled, dogging her as she crossed to the next block. "I can't go to Edrin. He's got worse problems than I do. And besides, he just gave me ten thousand six months ago."

She stopped and looked into Jonik's worried face. "Worse problems? What are you talking about?"

He jammed his hands in his pockets and wouldn't look at her. The stance reminded her of a little boy, though Jonik had just turned twenty-six. "Uh, nothing," he muttered. "Edrin expressly told me not to concern you about it. Just a temporary thing."

Jeniper could tell he was lying and wanted to shake him, but not here on a public street. Instead, she balled her fists, and, through a stiffened jaw, said, "Jonik, go to the police and tell them this woman has threatened you." He rolled his eyes. "Then go to Mam and Pae and tell them you're in trouble, again." He shook his head.

Jeniper almost caved in to his forlorn look. She was about to offer him what credit she could when she remembered Barq's advice. Living alone on Indra, Jeniper had welcomed the older man's friendship and counsel and

thought of him as a mentor of sorts. Barq had told her
Jonik would never learn to depend on himself unless he
was forced to face the consequences of his decisions alone.

Strengthening her own resolve, Jeniper set her jaw.
"Leave me alone, Jonik. I am *not* going to help you." At
that, he looked her directly in the eye. She lifted her chin
and added, "I don't know you anymore. You *aren't* my
brother." Maybe the threat of being disowned, even by her,
would wake him up.

It didn't. He shrugged. "You may get your wish," he said
cryptically. "But let me tell you something, Jen. This . . .
person craves satisfaction. Even if she finds me and . . .
does something . . . she'll still want her money. She knows
everything about me. About my family."

Jeniper felt her bibbets darken. He'd gone too far, now.
"You're not going to intimidate me. I'm through listening
to you whine. Do you understand that, Jonik?"

"I understand. Perfectly. You've sold out Aurie to work
with Humans in some *vikkat* job for an equally self-cen-
tered Herald. You only care about yourself."

Stunned by his outburst, Jeniper said nothing. She stood
on the sidewalk and watched him disappear into the crowd
of moving bodies. She had her own problems to think
about, she told herself. She had a new job and a new boss,
and she had to be ready to leave for Earth by tomorrow
afternoon. She should be concentrating on that.

But all she could think about was the color of Jonik's
one visible bibbet when he'd said the mysterious person
would "do something." He'd managed to school his expression enough to seem simply serious about the threat. But
he'd never been able to control his bibbets. When they
were kids, she could read him like a book. And just now
he'd gone maroon. He'd tried to hide it with his hair
brushed forward, but a breeze had come up, and she'd
caught a glimpse of one near the corner of his eye.

Maroon.

FOUR

Rieka massaged the banded muscles in her neck and wondered if she'd ever get rid of her headache. She thought she'd understood the eco-political system that drove the Commonwealth, but the documents in Alexi's files made her want to quit before she started.

"Okay," she said to herself, glad that Jeniper had run off on an errand. "In addition to their own planetary set-ups, each member world elects five senators, three judiciary ministers, and one Herald to coordinate Commonwealth interests." She sketched out a crude diagram with a stylus and sheet of paper, starting with three circles at the top of the page.

"Then, there's the Fleet." Rieka drew a line from each circle to a box below them marked "Fleet." "And the races on the member worlds." She wrote out the names of the eight sentient species and the member worlds they claimed as home. For the two planets that had been terraformed and had no indigenous species, Yadra and Medoura, she drew a line to the primary inhabitants there: Indrans, Aurians, and Humans.

Rieka gazed at her crude diagram. "So, the Senate writes the legislation, and the Judiciary enforces it—as long as it doesn't countermand local practices. The Heralds work as an intermediary between the citizens and the government. And all anyone really cares about is the amount of profit they can earn."

She sighed. It had seemed a lot simpler when she'd learned it in school.

A tone sounded from her console. "A message has just come in for you, Herald," Barq told her.

Glancing toward the screen, Rieka studied Barq's Centauri face, his eyes expressing a curious uncertainty. Curious herself, Rieka pushed aside her frustration with the mechanisms that ran the Commonwealth. "For me? Not for my uncle?"

"Yes," Barq replied. "It has your name on it, Herald."

"Thank you, Barq," Rieka said. She tapped the appropriate keys on the desk console to play the message. The Earth Herald's logo appeared, and she wondered for a moment if Barq had been mistaken. But then Alexi's round face sprang from the graphics and she knew she should have expected him to send a message.

"Rieka," he began, his welcoming smile somehow managing to look sincere despite showing all his teeth, "I hope you are well and beginning to find your way through the myriad of new responsibilities being Earth Herald–elect has brought. I am sure Setana has offered her assistance—which is why I did not ask you to come to Yadra before now."

She watched Alexi nod, a habit he'd developed that somehow managed to coerce people to agree with him, and Rieka found herself fascinated by the cloud of white hair on his head and how it contrasted with his steely beard and dark skin.

"So get to the point, Uncle," she muttered to herself, waiting for the message to continue.

"But circumstances here have changed, and I need you to come to Yadra right away," he went on, as if knowing she'd asked the question. "There is a matter of some urgency I must speak to you about, in person. If you have not already selected your staff, I suggest you do so before you leave—and use the time spent in transit to work out the details of how you wish to handle your office. In any event, I need you to come to Yadra as soon as possible."

"You're not going to tell me what it's about, are you, you old hustler?" she grumbled. She could simply fast-forward to the information she wanted, but Rieka dutifully let the message play, noting the day and time he wanted to see her.

"I am sure you wish to know the reason our meeting must occur as soon as possible," Alexi went on. His pudgy cheeks rounded even more when he smiled again. "I must brief you on several agreements I have pending with certain businesses and planets. There will not be ample time for this prior to your inauguration, since I am not scheduled to arrive until the day before the ceremony. I am sure you understand the necessity of coming to Yadra, first. Please notify me as soon as your ship makes orbit. I look forward to seeing you soon, Rieka.''

She watched while his image was replaced by the Earth Herald's logo. A moment later the screen went dark, and Rieka sighed. Had she really thought she could tolerate all the folderol that went along with the job?

Before she had a chance to consider the question, the console beeped, and she touched the intercom button. "Yes, Barq?"

"Incoming call from Captain Marteen," Barq replied.

"Thank you." She touched the button again and frowned at the anxious look on his face. "What's wrong, Tris? Barq didn't interrogate you again, did he? I thought I'd already made it clear to him before we left for lunch.''

"It wasn't Barq," he said, schooling his features to disguise whatever had been bothering him. "It's nothing. Nothing at all to worry about, love. I have good news, in fact.''

He'd said the words, but his tone reminded Rieka of a time months ago when Admiral Nason had sent her on a covert mission Triscoe had opposed. "It doesn't sound very good so far," she commented.

He mustered a sickly smile. "Dr. Wilmstos from Sati Labs spoke to me a moment ago."

She sat straighter. "What did he say?"

"The board reluctantly gave the go-ahead to the experimental combination of Centauri and Human genotypes."

Rieka exhaled a breath she didn't realized she'd held. "So soon? I thought they'd take several days to decide."

"Apparently not," he said tersely.

"And that's a bad thing?" When Triscoe looked away from the camera, she felt her heart begin to thump in her chest. The fact that he hadn't communicated this mentally told her he knew something and wanted to keep it to himself. A dozen ideas coursed through her mind while she watched him hesitate, none of them what she wanted to hear.

"Before you say anything," she began, lifting a hand to

indicate he shouldn't interrupt, "I want to know why you're so upset."

"I'm not upset."

She sighed. "Triscoe, do you take me for an idiot? We wouldn't be talking like this if you weren't upset." She leaned an elbow on the desk and perched her chin on her hand. "Tell me everything."

He took a deep breath and looked into the video pickup. "They have also accepted your request—to follow through the complete process and attempt to hybridize a child."

Rieka didn't need to be in mental contact to see that something was definitely bothering him. She decided she could probably get him to tell her if she could keep him talking long enough. "You just said that. Or am I not following the conversation?"

"I said they'd decided to do the experimental lab work—and attempt the pregnancy."

She'd watched carefully as he'd explained himself. He'd actually grimaced when he'd said the word "pregnancy."

"You don't want me to get pregnant, do you?" she asked softly, feeling the hairs rise on her forearms.

He sighed. "I would love for you to be pregnant, Rieka. Just . . . not this way. Not with your life at risk, and the child's. It seems so—"

"—engineered?" she finished.

He shook his head. "Futile."

She said nothing for a long moment. "I think we need to talk about this. But we'll need to do it in person. This sounds like a subject for Yillon's little white room."

"It does," he agreed, his sober tone almost frightening. "Perhaps we can sit with the *wruath* instead."

Rieka recalled the shimmery scarf he'd wrapped around her shoulders when they'd said their marriage vows aboard the *Providence*. It symbolically compelled them to be truthful with one another. "Perhaps," she agreed. "But it had better be soon. I just got a message from Alexi. He needs to have a meeting with me on Yadra in three days."

"I'm scheduled to depart for Tau Ceti tomorrow," he offered. "The *Providence* would be honored to transport you."

"Have you got room for my Planetary Adjutant?" she asked with a grin.

"And the Indran Herald."

"Sounds like a crowded ship."

"More so than you think. I've got two crews of steve-dores loading the cargo holds as we speak. We'll be 87 percent capacity by zero-eight-hundred tomorrow."

Rieka nodded. That kind of activity was nothing new. "Are we supposed to go to the lab before they close today?"

"That would seem best, since it is unclear as to when either of us will be back." He paused briefly. "Unless you'd rather wait for a while."

Rieka sat straighter in the chair. "No. Not at all. Nothing like the present, we Humans say. I'll just wrap up what I'm doing here and tell Jeniper we're going to Yadra instead of Earth. Then I'll get myself over to Sati Labs before seventeen-hundred."

"Good," he said softly. "I will see you later, then. Marteen out."

The screen went blank, and Rieka heaved a concerned sigh. Triscoe was always overprotective when it came to her safety, she told herself. Still, she had to admit this situation was different. No enemies. No weapons to discharge. She faced technological risks, chemical imbalances, untried techniques. But everything would turn out fine. Triscoe would forget all about his uncertainty when he held their baby in his arms. Of course he would, because this was a risk she had to take.

The Earth Herald needed an heir. That was all that mattered.

Rieka didn't know what to expect when she got to Sati Labs, but Wilmstos greeted her at the door and ushered her in with enthusiasm. He led her to a room that looked remarkably like the surgery suite on a Fleet ship.

"Doctor Saleem?" he asked, looking around the room.

An Indran female stepped out of a peripheral office. "Yes?" When she noticed them, she came forward, smiling. "Hello."

Rieka returned the smile. "Good afternoon, Dr. Saleem. I'm Rieka Degahv." She extended a hand, and the doctor gripped it without hesitation. "I can't tell you how much I appreciate your taking this case."

Nodding, Wilmstos interjected, "Dr. Saleem will supervise your procedure and prepare your sample. Captain Marteen is having his sample taken in the suite across the hall."

Rieka looked at him. "I didn't know he was here," she said, irritated he'd avoided her again.

"Arrived shortly before you did," Wilmstos told her. He nodded at the doctor. "I'll leave you to it, then."

With Wilmstos gone, Saleem grabbed up a datapad and gestured toward a bodypad. "If you would position yourself on the table, Mrs. Degahv, we can get started."

Rieka nodded amicably and complied, lying face up. "Don't I need to disrobe?" she asked, watching Saleem roll a large piece of equipment toward her.

"Not necessary for this," the doctor said. "The extraction needle is quite thin and the sterilization field is not encumbered by fabric."

"Great." Rieka watched her pivot the device and lower a section of it over her abdomen.

"Don't move, please," Saleem said. "You may breathe, but your legs and hips need to remain immobile."

"Okay." The lowered section clamped itself to the table, and Rieka didn't see how she could move even if she wanted to. Saleem checked the clamps, then moved around the unit to the control panel. She tapped her fingertips on its surface and explained what she was doing.

"I'm now using the sonic device to load in the exact location of your right ovary. Sterile field established. Extractor needle ready to deploy. Deploying needle. You may feel a slight—"

"—poke. Yes, I did," Rieka said tightly, trying not to complain.

Saleem ignored her. "Needle on target. Cell extraction under way."

"How much material are you taking?"

"The unit will secure one hundred viable eggs from each of your ovaries," Saleem replied.

"That sounds like a lot."

"Not really. The experiments planned for your case have a high failure projection rate simply because they have not been done before. Actually, it is arguable that two hundred cells are not enough."

"I suppose that sounds reasonable." A moment later the doctor announced the procedure had been completed, then repositioned it and extracted cells from Rieka's other ovary.

"You may feel a slight soreness for a few hours," Saleem told her as Rieka sat up.

She nodded. "When will you know anything?"

The doctor shook her head. "Unknown. Days. Possibly months. As I said, we're dealing with new territory here, Mrs. Degahv."

"I understand." She said good-bye and left the surgical suite. Down the hall, she saw Triscoe talking to Wilmstos.

"Everything went well?" Wilmstos asked as she approached them.

Rieka smiled. "I think so."

"As I was telling Captain Marteen, we'll get started first thing in the morning. I'll send reports to you every week. Hopefully, something will happen sooner rather than later."

"Hopefully," she agreed. "Thank you again, for everything."

As they left the lab, Rieka couldn't help feeling elated. Glancing up at Triscoe's serious expression, she knew in her heart he wouldn't regret what they'd done this afternoon once he held their baby.

Three days later, Rieka notified Alexi's office the *Providence* had achieved orbit. She turned to say something to Jeniper when the console on Triscoe's desk beeped with an incoming call.

"That was fast." She quirked an eyebrow while Jeniper grinned, and tapped the respond button. "Degahv."

The second eyebrow joined the first and she sat straighter. "Admiral Nason, this is a surprise."

The admiral's bibbets, clearly visible on his receding hairline, deepened from pink to rose. He smiled genuinely before speaking. "I hope I haven't interrupted anything important, Rieka," he said with a small nod. "I need to meet with you as soon as possible."

Rieka felt a wave of uneasiness pass through her at his tone. But she grinned at him, and crooned, "And it's so nice to see you, too, Admiral. You're looking well."

Nason's response was predictable. His bibbets flushed

slightly, and he looked suitably humbled. "I beg your pardon. Welcome to Yadra. I hope your trip was uneventful."

"Remarkably so," she confessed, since she hadn't had a chance to deal with Triscoe's fear for her safety.

"And congratulations."

"Thank you. I was a little worried there, for a while. But then I suppose all elected officials must endure elections." She paused, and when he didn't immediately jump in, offered, "Now that we've gotten through the social niceties, what can I do for you?"

"You learned that from Setana, no doubt."

"What?"

"Circumventing the problem at hand with social niceties, as she calls them."

Rieka watched as the admiral leaned back in his chair and crossed his arms over his chest. His smile seemed more relaxed now, and she noted that the beard he'd begun to grow when she'd seen him last had filled in. The red hair on his chin was infused with as much white as that of his head, giving him a peachy glow. "Yes, actually I did. I've noticed every Herald has a certain way of approaching a pending problem. The goatee becomes you, by the way," she told him.

"Thank you."

"And the problem is?" she prompted.

"Something I'd rather discuss in person."

She studied him for another moment before nodding and consulting her datapad. "I have a tight schedule, Admiral. I'm afraid I've only got from now until eleven-hundred open." She glanced at Jeniper, who nodded and mouthed the words: only one hour.

"That will do. I'll notify my secretary to send you in as soon as you arrive. Fleet Headquarters out."

The screen went blank, and Rieka let her jaw drop slightly in indignation. She huffed and glanced up at Jeniper. "What are you grinning about?"

"He's still giving you orders—and yet allows you to banter with him like an equal. I find that very entertaining."

"I'm sure you would—since the two of us do exactly the same thing." She pushed herself out of the chair. "I suppose I'd better change into something befitting my station if I'm to visit Fleet Headquarters. What do you think of that navy blue outfit with a white blouse?"

"That should be fine." Jeniper followed her into the sleeping room Rieka shared with Triscoe.

Rieka retrieved the outfit from the closet. "How much more work are we going to need to do on that speech?"

"It looks fairly smooth," Jeniper replied. "A bit more polishing should do it."

Rieka grunted her agreement and began to change. "And what about our schedule once we get to Earth?"

"Nothing is doubling up so badly that I won't be able to manage it. But I'm going to need at least two assistants to handle the itinerary. And we're going to have to hire local people right away to supervise the details for the social events. Entertainment. Tours. Catering. Lodging." Jeniper paused and her tone became more serious. "Oh, and remember to ask your uncle if his legal staff plans to switch over to you or stay with him once you're inaugurated. And his PR staff, too, if you think of it."

"Two of a hundred or so questions on my list," she quipped. "I doubt we'll get to them all today."

"Do try to remember the important things, at least," Jeniper countered. "That outfit does look very nice on you. The admiral will be impressed."

Rieka glanced at herself in the mirror and nodded with approval. The white collar curved upward around her neck much like her old uniform, but beyond that, there was no comparison. The silky, deep blue overvest and pants clung to her in all the right places and followed her every move. "The admiral," she murmured, though silently agreeing with Jeniper, "is rarely impressed by anything, even heroics."

Admiral Nason rose and came around his desk to greet her as she entered his sanctum. "Rieka, you're looking well. I am glad you could come on such short notice."

She grinned and shook the hand he offered, noting his silent appraisal. "It's a pleasure to see you again, Admiral. I think. You're looking fit."

He nodded and gestured for her to sit in the chair opposite his desk. He ambled back to his own seat and said, "Complete recovery. Both lungs are functioning at 96 percent—or so the doctors tell me. Of course I wouldn't be here at all if Captain Finot hadn't intervened."

Rieka's smile faded. "A noble sacrifice," she murmured. "We all miss him."

Nason's expression remained somber for a moment. "Indeed. But I believe he knew what he was doing. The risk he took in putting himself in the line of fire."

She cleared her throat. "Yes. Well . . . am I correct in assuming I'm here to sign my acquittance request?"

His pale blue eyes met hers, and she noted the stern set of his bearded jaw. "I'm afraid the admiralty was unable to grant you all the items you asked for."

Rieka accepted that with a slight nod. "How many were left out?" she asked, silently wondering if they'd altered her retirement or severance pay, or both, and by how much.

"Only one item, actually," Nason answered. "I have the hard copy here—for you to look over and sign—if you don't wish to appeal their decision."

Rieka frowned at him and pulled herself straighter in the chair. "Which particular point are we talking about?"

"Discharge."

"What?" she huffed, grabbing the proffered document. "They're going to make me stay in the Fleet for another year—until my contract expires? That's ludicrous. How can I possibly command a ship and act as Earth Herald at the same time? I thought we worked this out months ago."

"It's not exactly as complicated as I may have implied," he said softly, obviously trying to soothe the blow. "Look on page six."

Rieka read through the paragraph that had been marked in the margin. "It's just Article Nine that they want changed?"

"Yes."

She glanced at Nason and noted his bibbets were uncharacteristically dark. He was worried that she'd make a stink about this, but it really didn't matter all that much.

"I think you're worrying over a stonefoot," she said, using an Aurian phrase that meant the problem did not really exist. "The circumstances listed here in which I could be recalled to duty are simply not going to happen."

Nason had the decency to look relieved, but still held

himself with an aura of caution. "I'm glad you see it that way."

"Invasion," she read. "Medical Emergency. Epidemic. Insurrection. Mutiny. These things are hardly on the horizon for the Fleet, Admiral."

He nodded. "I thought so, too, but I've given up trying to predict the future," he told her sagely. "At any rate, I'm sure you understand the value of your command experience."

"Mmm." Rieka flipped through the pages, glancing at all the other articles in the acquittal contract. "It looks like everything else is in order. If you'll hand me a stylus, I'll be glad to sign this and be done with it."

"You're sure?"

"I'm sure. Is there something else I need to know?" she asked jauntily.

Nason placed his stylus on her side of the desk in such a way to make her hesitate to pick it up. "Perhaps."

She sighed and braced herself. "Then let's have it."

Nason leaned back in his chair again, and looked at her with a curious expression. "I am not sure, exactly, if anything is happening. But I have a sense of uneasiness."

"How so?" For Nason to make this statement, something had to be up.

He shrugged. "Nothing in particular. Huge shipments have been made recently. Mostly to and from Aurie. In some instances, valuable items have been lost. Oph stocks have been rising and falling hundreds of points in a very short time." Rieka nodded; she'd seen the stock reports, too. "Something seems to be shifting in the business world. The analysts all have ideas—but who can say what is really going on? My understanding is the business community is concerned about Earth's Reaffirmation—and how the Commonwealth economy will react. Still, I can't see that as the entire reason for this odd behavior."

Rieka took a moment to gather her thoughts before she spoke. "You know my opinion of the negative attitude the Commonwealth has toward Humans." She raised a hand to stop him from interjecting before she finished the thought. "And I'll admit there's a lot of speculation going on—about how the Reaffirmation will unbalance things," she said. "Even my mother has given me the end-of-the-world scenario. But let me assure you it is not my intent to disturb the economic status quo. I think everyone is blowing this out of proportion." She paused, and added, "I did everything in my power to keep this civilization out of Procyon hands. Why would I ever jeopardize it in any way?"

She felt a welcome wave of relief when Nason smiled and pushed the stylus closer to her side of the desk. "I'm glad to hear you say it, Herald. And I trust you to do what you say."

"Thank you, Admiral." She picked up the writing instrument and leafed to the contract's last page, then signed her name with her characteristic scrawl and handed the paper back. "I see you even managed to come up with a new rank—in the event of my return to the fold."

He tucked the contract into a drawer, and she watched in amazement as he actually grinned. "That was my recommendation," he admitted.

She grinned back at him and silently hoped no one in the Fleet would ever refer to her as Captain Herald Degahv.

She left the Fleet building a few moments later and stepped to the curb to hail a taxi. Momentarily blinded in the bright sunshine, Rieka squinted and caught herself as she collided with someone standing near a car. "Excuse me," she said.

"No problem," the man replied. Then, in the space of what seemed like a heartbeat, he opened the door and shoved her into the passenger compartment.

"What the hell?" She immediately turned and pressed at the door release, but nothing happened.

Out of the sun, she could see that the vehicle's interior was plush and the divider between the passenger compartment and the driver deeply tinted. She banged on it as a man, presumably the one who'd shoved her, took his place at the control.

"What is going on here?" she demanded.

By the time Rieka realized he couldn't hear her no matter how loud she yelled, the vehicle had left the curb. She searched frantically for an intercom switch and found one among several buttons under a uniquely disguised panel.

In as pleasant a voice as she could muster, she asked,

"Where are you taking me?" They glided silently past several Fleet office buildings before he answered.

"I've been asked not to say, madam."

"Stop this car immediately and let me out."

"This is not possible."

Rieka huffed. "You'd better do as I ask if you care about your standard of living for the next thirty years."

"I'm simply doing my job, madam," the chauffeur replied. "I was told, quite specifically, to fetch the Earth Herald."

FIVE

Rieka gave up banging on the window and watched as the scenery whizzed by. They'd left Rhonique some minutes ago. Once out of city traffic, the driver pushed their speed to the maximum, 150 kph.

Despite having been kidnapped, Rieka didn't feel threatened. Quite the opposite, in fact. Her curiosity was piqued. Knowing she could mentally contact Triscoe for help if she needed it, Rieka dismissed the abduction and concentrated on who the driver's boss might be. She couldn't decide whether it had been the cavalier way the man had spoken, or the interior elegance of the car, but somehow this "kidnapping" had the feeling of a command performance.

She knew for certain when they passed Kilpani township. It went by quickly, the few buildings little more than a multicolored blur. Then the road sign told her everything she needed to know. Olympic Drive was the next exit.

The driver turned off the main highway, and, a few minutes later, she could make out the tile roof over the tree line. Situated on a modest hill, her mother's manor house, Olympus, loomed like a reclining god. She watched, transfixed, as the edifice appeared for a brief moment only to be hidden again by the trees. She remembered the pony she'd had, and the huge closet, where she had often hidden to get away from the yelling. The clash of voices echoed across her mind, her father and mother in lengthy, bitter arguments over every detail of their lives.

A strange pain pulled her from her reverie. Looking down, Rieka realized her hands had balled into fists, the knuckles white. "You have no power over me now, Candace," she whispered, consciously relaxing her fingers. "You can't hurt me anymore."

They approached the hill quickly, and her captor did not deign to slow down until he pressed the control for the gates to open.

He continued to reduce their speed until they came to a stop before the three-story monument to Candace Degahv's business acumen. The driver opened her door, and she stepped out, glancing daggers at him before stepping between two of the four massive columns guarding the front entryway.

Rieka paused at the door, a grotesquely ornate thing made of wood, twisted metal, and beveled glass. Deciding she must be expected, she turned the knob and opened it. Stepping into the entry, Rieka was overcome by the fact that nothing, as far as she could see, had changed. The fragrance of fresh-cut flowers on the foyer table brought back even more childhood memories. Even a few pleasant ones.

"Hello," she called. "Mr. Dokins? Kenna? Mother?"

"Well, Miss Rieka, they said to expect you this afternoon, but I didn't believe it until this moment."

Rieka spun and looked at her mother's housekeeper, Kenna. The woman looked the same as she had nearly two decades ago. Her once blond hair now looked tinged with gray, but her dark eyes still spoke of an inner calm, and her smile still lit her entire face.

"Kenna." Rieka stepped forward and embraced the woman she'd known as a child. "You look wonderful. I would have recognized you anywhere."

Kenna's hug was fierce. "I'm so glad to see you," she said, stepping back to hold Rieka's hands. "And look at you. All grown-up. We followed the news last year, we did. The battle and all, and you're being a hero. And I voted for you last month, you know. You're so much like your father, Miss Rieka. I just know you'll be a great Herald."

"Thank you, Kenna." Letting go Kenna's hands, Rieka blinked back unexpected tears and turned to glance into the huge front room. "I see you never convinced Mother to change the flooring in there."

"Marble," the housekeeper grumbled. "Most idiotic flooring to choose for such a room. So cold. So hard. I daresay it's gotten a few nicks since you left. But she won't cover it, and she won't replace it."

"Probably only because my father suggested both those options."

Kenna nodded. "Probably. But I'm keeping you, prattling on so. Mrs. D. said you were to come to the office as soon as you arrived."

Rieka nodded. She stepped toward the lift and pressed her palm against the panel to call the car. "It was nice to see you again."

"The same here, Miss Rieka. Now don't let her bully you."

"I wouldn't think of it." She smiled to herself as the lift ascended. How long had it been since she'd answered to "Miss Rieka"?

The office door was closed. Not bothering to knock, she barged through.

Candace looked up from some papers on her desk.

Rieka noticed the ominous glare and ignored it, knowing Candace thrived on intimidation. She'd been a kid when she last lived here and had long outgrown empty threats. "Don't ever do that again, Mother," she warned. "Abduction is a felony."

"And you expect me to believe the new Earth Herald would actually grant me an audience through a mere request?" Candace shot back.

Rieka leaned over the desk slightly, enjoying the fact her mother had to look up to her, for once. "I promise you— do it again, and I'll file charges. You'll be running your precious empire from a prison cell."

Candace had enough sense to blanch at the threat. She took a deep breath, then indicated a cushioned chair near her desk. "Sit down, Rieka. Please."

Sure she'd made her point, Rieka pulled up the chair and sat. "I received your charming message almost a week ago. Has something changed since then?"

"Actually, no." Candace sat back in her chair and crossed her manicured fingers in her lap. "I had expected a response from you and did not receive one. So I thought it necessary to speak to you while you were here."

Rieka didn't bother to mention her presence on Yadra was not public knowledge. She'd long ago realized Candace had "retainers" in well-placed positions in both the Fleet and the Commonwealth's legislature.

"I don't respond to threats," Rieka answered with a shrug. "Just a little habit I picked up."

Candace frowned slightly before she schooled her face to the appearance of calm. "I have no idea what you're talking about. I didn't threaten you."

Rieka nodded. "Right. Not in so many words. But that big, 'Do what I say, or else,' was pretty obvious, Mother." Candace's face hardened into an expressionless mask and Rieka sighed. "You seem to think I'm planning to ship every last Human back to Earth. Tomorrow. I don't know where you got that insane idea—that is *not* on my agenda."

"But there are already a dozen underground cities on Earth ready for occupation," her mother countered. "You have prepared accommodations for almost ten million people. And more cities are under construction—or on the drawing board."

"So? Ten million people on a planet is nothing. Even ten million in a *city* is not that unusual."

"But by encouraging Humans to move to Earth, you're going to deplete the workforce on every other Commonwealth holding. And what do you intend to do with your ten million residents?"

"I don't intend to do anything with them." Rieka leaned forward and put her elbows on the edge of her mother's pristine white desk. Carefully, as though she were speaking to a child, she said, "A list of jobs has been compiled—everything from farming to engineering to bankers and teachers and plumbers. People will find out about these jobs and apply for them. If they get the job, they'll come to Earth to live and be a part of the community. What's so hard to follow?"

Candace sighed. "You're oversimplifying, trying to make me look like some kind of naysayer. I'm telling you to look at the numbers, the statistics, the projections."

"I understand that you're worried your little kingdom here might loose its firm foundation. But you're welcome to invest in the Earth, Mother. If the bottom line is so damned important to you, why can't you see this as a re-markable ground-floor opportunity? Projections tell me we're going to pay off our Commonwealth debt in only twenty-five years. Thirty-eight percent of that will be from the agro businesses. It's amazing."

"And it's going to ruin the economy of ten other worlds in the process."

"Oh, don't be ridiculous."

"You are the one who is being ridiculous."

Rieka leaned back and massaged her forehead with her fingertips. "Obviously we're not communicating. This endeavor will not happen overnight." She dropped her hand and stared purposefully into her mother's dark eyes. "It will take years. I agree if I were to suddenly InterMAT a million people off every planet it would cause problems. But we aren't talking mass exodus, here. We're talking about emigration. That takes time. And I promise you, it isn't going to be racially exclusive, either. Every race that can stand the atmosphere will find themselves welcome on Earth."

They glared at each other for a long moment. When Candace did not reply, Rieka considered an idea she hadn't thought much about, before. For a split second it seemed ludicrous, then she realized the argument might have some merit. "Or is this discussion about something else, entirely?" she asked, curiosity tinging her voice.

"I don't know what you mean."

"I think you do, Mother." Rieka sat straighter. "I think you've had a hidden agenda all along and the noise you've been making is simply to keep me from seeing the obvious."

"There is no other agenda," Candace replied innocently. "My concern is for the financial security of not only my business interests, but that of the entire Commonwealth. What you don't seem to comprehend—"

"—is the race issue," Rieka finished. "I hadn't thought of it before, but I can see where it might leave you and your business associates . . . a little nervous."

Candace furrowed her brow ever so slightly. "What do you mean?"

"Oh, it can't be that hard to follow, Mother, especially since you've already thought it through." Rieka took a breath and put her theory to words. "Triscoe once told me the other races in the Commonwealth were frightened of Humans because of our spirit. Our tenacity. Our ability to rise to a challenge. When free from the limitations we've endured for two centuries, Humans will exercise that incredible drive to succeed, to discover things, to become more than what we were. And that will only happen once we live on our own planet again. We'll be walking with the Earth under our feet. We won't be the orphaned aliens anymore. We will be *home.*"

"But Rieka—"

She raised a hand. "And we will thrive without that burden of prejudice. And when a Human thrives, he or she is unstoppable. Yillon predicted it—of me. He knew I could save the Commonwealth from the Procyons. And I did, much to everyone's surprise. A mere Human. Can you imagine millions of us out there—doing our best?"

For a moment, Candace looked stricken. Then, she seemed to pull herself back together, and said, "What you are not considering—"

Rieka laughed then, cutting off her mother's sentence. "Gods! You have imagined it. And that scares the hell out of you, doesn't it?"

"You just don't seem to realize the damage this can do," Candace finally blurted. "Humans, when we lived on Earth before the Collision, were horrible creatures. Why do you think we weren't contacted? Why did it take a devastating meteor strike before the Centauris insisted on providing aid?"

Candace pushed herself out of the chair and paced behind the desk. "Because Human weren't fit to be Commonwealth citizens. We were barbaric. We fought petty wars over religion and land. We abused every sense of ethics. Young people purposely poisoned their bodies while the adults did everything they could to poison the world. Pollution was incredible. The air, land, and water were unfit."

Candace stopped for a breath, and Rieka saw the intensity of her conviction. Without the thumb of alien ethics to hold them in their place, Candace believed Humans would rise up and destroy the Commonwealth as they had almost done to the Earth.

"You're right, Mother. One hundred percent. I admit it: the textbooks tell us Humanity was an abomination. But even then, it was worth saving. And we have changed in the last two centuries. Out mind-set is completely different.

Mine is the third generation to have been born in the Commonwealth—right next to Centauris and Auries and Ophs and . . . whoever. Our consciousness has been raised by simply existing in an interplanetary community. You actually shock me with your shortsightedness."

Candace waved a hand dismissing that thought. "You are so incredibly naive."

"I don't think so." Rieka walked around to her mother's side of the desk and perched on the corner. "I fought in the Procyon War, Mother. I had the opportunity to kill. And I killed from a distance because it was them or me. And during that war I also had the option to murder. But I didn't. Believe me, I had both motivation and opportunity. And even in hand-to-hand combat, I did not kill Commander K'resh-va. I left his fate in the hands of our judicial system."

Her mother's face went white for a moment. "You fought with that animal?"

Rieka ran her tongue along the inside of her lip, where the scar still remained. Smiling crookedly, she murmured, "I'm not sure who enjoyed it more."

"There. See. Exactly. You enjoyed it!" Candace aimed an accusatory finger. "This is precisely what I'm talking about, and you aren't listening."

Rieka stayed motionless, amazed that her mother felt so deeply about this. "Mother, he'd wanted to kill me for a long time. And when I found out he'd set me up in the first place and then kidnapped me," she paused, making sure Candace heard the comparison, "I wanted to kill him, too. More importantly though, I had the opportunity—but *didn't.*" Knowing it would be detrimental to her case, she purposely kept to herself the part about Triscoe's intervention in the fracas.

"I don't believe you," Candace said softly.

Rieka shook her head. "About what?"

"About your innocence. You wanted to control K'resh-va's fate more than you wanted him dead. So he was placed under arrest. It's as simple as that." Candace shook her head. "But we shouldn't be talking about war. We live in peace, now. And peacetime struggles can be far more vigorous."

"But no less important," Rieka noted.

"Correct." Candace glared at her once, then turned and walked to a window. "And lives are always at stake."

"What is that supposed to mean?"

Her back to her daughter, Candace said, "Paden would have understood."

Rieka pulled her fingers through her hair and sighed. "Let's not go into that, again. Under your influence, Paden refused to believe me. He took matters into his own hands and put his life and that of Ker Marteen in jeopardy. If he'd trusted me, he would be alive right now—as Herald-elect."

Candace turned toward her, and they locked eyes. Rieka's gaze remained steady. "Quit trying to lay the blame on my shoulders, Mother. I wasn't the one who pulled the trigger. And I wasn't the one who brainwashed him not to trust his own sister."

Candace's eyes widened as she absorbed the innuendo. "Are you blaming me?"

"Is there anyone else in the room?" Rieka left the desk and faced her mother's angry grimace. "He thought the way you wanted him to think, Mother. You taught him that his father had made a mockery of being Herald and his sister would never be anything more than a public servant. You told him he would be Earth Herald after Alexi. And he believed you. You held him in your grasp like a puppeteer does a marionette. And because you couldn't influence Dad or me, you hated us."

"Don't presume to speak for me, Rieka," Candace warned. A flush of pink spread over her cheekbones and chin.

Rieka could see her mother had been pushed far enough. She doubted anyone had been as candid with her since her last argument with Stephen. But if she did nothing else, Rieka meant to show her mother that the new Earth Herald was a considerable force.

"I don't need to. You've said and done enough on your own."

"Say what you mean."

"You need help, Mother. For all your wealth and power, as a Human you don't amount to much. You poisoned your son's mind. You disowned your daughter. And I'm beginning to believe you actually had a part in creating the accident that killed Dad."

Candace gasped, but Rieka went on as if her mouth had control of her mind instead of the other way around. "Now I have the power. And after your little stunt today, you can make sure the Earth Herald's security will increase tenfold. I'll not have you threatening me. Is that clear?"

"You don't actually believe—?"

"It doesn't matter what I believe. What *you* believe matters. And the *truth* matters. The minute I have any extra time, I'm going to investigate Stephen's shuttle accident. Thoroughly."

Rieka stormed from the room and headed for the lift, Candace behind her.

"You'll never prove anything with an investigation, Rieka," Candace shouted, her voice echoing through the entryway. "You're a fool if you try to go up against me. You'll never prove anything. And if you try—I'll see to it that you'll never succeed. At anything!"

The lift door opened, but Rieka turned at her mother's last comment. Did she know about Sati Labs? "I told you I don't like being threatened, Mother," Rieka told her calmly. "But since you've screamed you across the house, and I'm sure every servant has heard you, I'll tell you this." She aimed a finger at her mother's angry face. "If anything at all happens to me, the first person the authorities are going to investigate is *you.*"

Rieka took a deep breath and let her tone take on a lighter lilt. "Good-bye, Candace. Unless you want some bad press, the car had better be waiting for me by the time I get to the front door."

"I simply can't understand why she's so obstinate, Robet," Triscoe said as they ambled down a corridor in the Fleet Administration Building. He considered it a fortunate coincidence their schedules had brought them to Yadra today. Robet DeVark had a unique way of looking at things, especially when it came to Rieka.

"Rieka's always had a mind of her own," the Aurian captain offered sagely. "She managed fairly well when she was in the Fleet because she respects authority. But now . . . ." He shrugged lightly. "Now she's got the clout."

Triscoe shook his head helplessly. They both returned a lieutenant's salute as they left the building, then went into the plaza between the Fleet's two huge office buildings. There were low walls around the plantings and statues, offering places to sit, but he didn't want to discuss his personal business in public.

He slowed his pace and glanced at his red-haired Aurian friend. Robet wasn't one to offer the practical answer to any problem, though he usually did bring a hidden side to light. "Rieka hasn't changed since the election, Robet. That will be obvious to you once you see her. But she simply won't back down on this business about having a child."

"It might be better if you understood why she feels so strongly," Robet offered. He gestured to a path through a small park.

Triscoe turned with him down the shaded lane and shoved his hands into his trouser pockets. "I understand why she feels the way she does," he said finally, "though I'm not sure she's completely conscious of the motive, herself. The problem is—the Earth Herald has been a position held by her family for two centuries. She means to have an heir."

Robet shrugged. "I'm certain there are other Degahvas in the Commonwealth. She doesn't have to produce another one to keep it in the family."

"Of course. But a child raised to think a certain way about Earth would make a far better Herald than one who might be indifferent."

"That's . . . probably true," Robet conceded. "I can't understand why you're not fighting her on this, Tris. You've already given that lab your tissue samples."

"I suppose I could have been conveniently too busy to do that," he admitted. "But it would only prolong the inevitable—and Rieka would have been furious."

They approached a bench that faced a small glade. Robet sat and Triscoe joined him, wondering whose side the Aurian was on. Then he realized Robet couldn't choose sides. He had a longtime friendship with both of them.

"It really isn't that I'm so adamant about the pregnancy—I just don't want her risking her life over something so—unnecessary. And the child might suffer terribly, too."

Robet nodded. "I can't disagree with you, Tris. If there were some way gestation could take place outside her body, you wouldn't have a problem, I suppose."

"That would solve the physical risk for her," Triscoe conceded, "but not the emotional one." He leaned forward and propped his elbows on his knees. "She's picturing a perfect infant with her hair and my eyes. But in truth, they still don't know what kind of . . . thing, would come from our combined cells."

"What are you saying?"

"Robet, our species have been living side by side for nearly two hundred standard years. We've become accustomed to the physical differences between us. But we evolved on different worlds. To attempt to ignore that is simply foolhardy." Triscoe stared at the ground between his feet and watched a bug crawl up a blade of grass, silently cursing himself for being the biggest fool of all. How could he have let so much time pass without explaining to Rieka their mental link's one negative aspect?

"You mean you think the doctors wouldn't let you know if something went wrong?" Robet asked softly. "Or can you trust them that much?"

Triscoe sighed. "I trust them to do their jobs. They are the best in the Commonwealth. And we're paying them an exorbitant amount to do this research. But the thing that has begun to really worry me is—will they even know if something is wrong? In attempting to combine two alien races, they'll be creating something totally new." He raked his fingers through his hair and looked into Robet's pale blue eyes. "I don't know what to think, or feel. But I know this is wrong, Robet. Beyond my fear for Rieka's safety, I know she's wrong."

Robet stayed quiet for a long moment. His bibbets remained a steady rosy pink. "And you haven't discussed this with her?"

"I've tried. She doesn't think I'm being reasonable. She knows I'm worried for her safety and dismisses it as anxiety."

"Can't she tell, though—in your mind? That this whole thing really disturbs you?"

"Through the Singlemind? No. I don't want to worry her with this. Until now, I've been counting on Sati Labs to fail. That would be the simplest thing, wouldn't it?"

"I suppose so," Robet agreed. "But it's also conceivable that Rieka's a lot stronger than you know. Gods, Tris, remember what she went through with her arrest and the Procyons? And I might remind you she didn't have a particularly pleasant childhood either. It's entirely possible you're jumping to some wrong conclusions, yourself. You two need to talk."

Triscoe didn't think so. "My mother has advised me to wait, so I haven't made myself available for such a conversation. Rieka will simply rant that I'm being unreasonably overprotective. She'll refuse to listen, I'll become frustrated—and that won't get us any closer to solving the problem."

"You've worked this all out ahead of time, haven't you?" Robet asked, then chuckled to himself.

"How can you possibly find anything funny about this?"

"It's just," Robet began with a smile still in his voice, "ridiculous. You both know each other so well, you think you can predict what will happen. But dammit, Triscoe, if Rieka is anything at all—she's completely *un*predictable."

Triscoe thought about that for a moment before he answered. "You may be right. But you haven't talked to her since Dr. Wilmstos interviewed us. It's become . . . a given. She expects to have a baby. A perfect, healthy hybridized child."

Robet shrugged. "I guess she's confident she can overcome any obstacle—even those beyond her control."

"I don't think I will ever understand how Humans believe they can change the immutable."

Robet laughed and slapped Triscoe on the shoulder. "Sorry, friend. But I'll have to disagree with you on that one. It isn't Humans that think they can change everything, it's *women*."

SIX

Unlike the greeting she'd gotten on Indra, Alexi's receptionist on Yadra welcomed Rieka as soon as she came through the door. She was ushered immediately into a private waiting area complete with comfortable furniture and a refreshment buffet. While she helped herself to some fruit juice, the woman told Rieka that Herald Degahv would be with her shortly.

"A ruse," she murmured after the door closed. She'd been among the elite long enough to realize waiting was merely a psychological tool, appointment or no.

From what she'd seen of the outer office, Alexi ran this embassy with a bigger budget than he did on Indra. Budgeting, she thought, another thing on my list.

She opened her datapad and tapped some notes from her meeting with Nason. He'd told her once the board of admirals had signed the contract he would forward a copy to her, or else bring it himself when he attended the Reaffirmation ceremony on Earth. She added in the terms of reinstatement so she wouldn't forget to tell Jeniper or Triscoe about them. It would be a good conversation starter, anyway, she mused. She and Triscoe had had too few of them, recently.

The door opened, and Alexi bustled in with outstretched arms and a smile that bordered on sinister. "Rieka! Oh, my little Rieka. Just look at you." He beamed when she stepped forward and into his padded embrace.

Rieka endured a squeeze, a back rub, and finally several pats before he released her. "How are you? You look great," she told him.

He rocked his head from side to side. "I am fine now.

Last year was bad, you know. With the liver problem and such. And it is good that I'm retiring—and leaving the family business to you. The doctors claim that the stress of the office has not done me any good."

"I wish you wouldn't call it that."

"What?"

"The family business."

He raised his eyebrows and chuckled. "And what else is it? Earth's Herald has been a Degahv since the Collision. It was written into our constitutional agreement that only a Degahv represent the Earth to the Commonwealth—unless and until another agreement is reached. I see no reason to change what has stood for two hundred years."

She gave in to his argument and raised both hands to signal surrender. "And please accept my apology for being late. I had a—an experience—with Candace."

Alexi sobered. "Oh. I see," he murmured, his bushy brows furling over his eyes. "Nothing too horrible, I hope?"

"I'll handle her, Alexi. Now, what is so important that it can't wait for a few weeks?"

"Come. Bring your drink." He turned so quickly Rieka thought he'd lost his balance. But he hurried out the door without so much as a glance over his shoulder. She followed him into his richly paneled office. He gestured for her to sit on the sofa, then lowered himself into a cushioned armchair and heaved a sigh.

"I must lose some weight, the doctors tell me," he explained, breathing more heavily than she thought healthy. She couldn't tell if he really felt ill or was simply acting. While he'd always been rotund, Rieka decided that he did look heavier than the last time she'd seen him, only a few months ago. There was a ruddy flush to his skin, making his black eyes sparkle and his hair look even whiter than it was.

"I hope you intend to do what they say," she warned him. "There aren't many of us left, and I'd just as soon you stick around with the living as long as possible."

"Fond of your father's brother, are you?" he asked with a laugh. "I haven't seen you come visiting much in the last few years."

"We've gone over this before, Alexi. The Fleet doesn't

give captains a great deal of time off. And your schedule has been as busy as mine. I didn't even get to see you at the *Prodigy*'s dedication."

"I hadn't meant to be tardy," he apologized. "But it was a fortunate happenstance, yes? Joel Ciccone's housing contract with Aurie was under dispute. I missed the attack and arrived on the *Varannah* shortly before the Fleet left for Medoura."

"And I suppose I'm lucky you did," she said candidly. "I can't imagine how Triscoe must have felt with both parents on the Little One during the skirmish. If you'd been there, too, I never would have been able to concentrate."

"How flattering." An aide knocked on the door and entered discreetly, bringing a tray of crackers and cheeses. "Thank you, Deborah," he told her. She nodded and left.

Rieka quirked a brow at the healthy selection. Alexi had always preferred to serve high-calorie treats to his guests as an excuse to eat them, himself. "Now that we've caught up on the recent past, would you mind getting to the point? You told me you'd be available for at least three months after the inauguration—as my advisor, I believe you put it."

Alexi drew his bushy brows together and pursed his lips but didn't say anything. Rieka decided that wasn't a good sign. "You're not. Well that's great, Alexi. Tell me, did you decide this—before or after you gave me your assurances?"

He put up his hands defensively. "The circumstances now are regretfully different than when I promised to help you ease into the job. Immediately following my next trip to Earth, I am going to Perata. The doctors there are quite the experts. They've said if I don't deal with my liver problem as soon as possible—I won't have any problems at all."

It took a second for Rieka to realize he was making light of an apparently serious illness. Her heart skipped a beat. "It's that serious?"

"I am afraid so."

Rieka sighed and dipped her head. Her uncle had always been there, distant perhaps, but ever-present. The thought of his mortality hit her like a maitu stun. She rubbed her right temple for a moment before raking her hand through her hair. "When did you plan on telling me?"

"I . . . just did."

He looked at ease with the problem and the decisions

he'd made, so Rieka went along with him. Her father's death had been sudden, unexpected. Alexi's apparently would be slow. She wasn't sure she preferred one way over the other. In any case, she would make a point of visiting Perata as often as possible.

Looking him in the eye, Rieka said, "I want you to promise me you'll keep me up-to-date on your . . . condition."

Serious for once, he answered, "Of course."

She nodded. "Then let's get started on this tutorial. It looks like I'm going to need it." She reached for her datapad, and turned it on.

When he smiled at her, his entire face lit up, and the rest of his body relaxed as if he'd been waiting for her to reject his offer or argue his decision. "Good. Good." He leaned forward and picked up a small chunk of cheese. "Food for thought, eh?"

"Yeah." Having missed lunch, she reached for a cracker and devoured it.

"First," he began, gesturing emphatically with his hands, "the position itself. As you know, by definition, the Earth Herald is Earth's diplomatic ambassador to the Commonwealth. Since Peter and the time of the Collision, however, none of us has actually done that—simply because Earth has had no population to speak of. So, it has been subdivided, if you will, into representing the Earth—and representing Humanity on all the other words. A difficult task.

"But we have managed fairly well," he added.

She nodded, hoping he'd get to the point. "As Herald, you are empowered by the people to act in their best interest with regard to the Commonwealth. You have no power between individual—that is to say—personal contractual agreements and the like. Such conflicts are for the courts to decide. But if there is a difficulty in conceiving an agreement or living up to one involving a government body, your involvement is mandatory if requested by either side.

"The Heralds meet annually, of course, to decide on a budget and equally mundane things. And perhaps to negotiate certain problems on a less formal level.

"But basically you are an ambassador. Humanity's foremost public-relations tool. Your position gives you great flexibility, for you can choose to mediate a dispute yourself, or go to the Judiciary—and they are compelled by the

Commonwealth Constitution to address any issue brought forward by a Herald. But generally you will be participating in goodwill activities. You will attend functions. Be a public figure. A model Human. This is the best thing you can do for Earth. Keep it in a positive light with everything running smoothly. Or the appearance of running smoothly. Does this sound remotely familiar?"

She finished another cracker and swallowed. "Of course. I lived with my dad for years. And recently with Herald Marteen. But you said so yourself—Earth's situation is unique. I may have to push the rules from time to time. Be outspoken."

"One of your many talents," he said trepidatiously.

Rieka chuckled. "Now, something a little more pressing is the budget. This year it was six million credits. Since we pay a flat rate for travel and embassy real estate, I don't see how I can possibly spend that much. Salaries and business expenditures, as far as I can tell, come to a little over four million."

"Yes, but you are forgetting the incredible amount of entertaining you will do. Lunches, dinners, parties. My dear niece, it all adds up."

She cleared her throat, and told him, "I intend to work, too."

"Of course you do. And you will. But politics is not physical labor. It is a business of strategy, strength of character, and patience." He smiled knowingly. "You will develop patience soon enough, I'm sure."

"Very funny. I suppose that's why everything takes so long to get approved, or budgeted, or completed."

He frowned. "You must understand that we are required to look at any decision from all angles. From every point of view. If information is lacking, we must have studies done and wait for the data to come in. This does take time, yes. But it is necessary. We need to make the best decision possible, especially if the Council of Ten is convened. As a body, the Planetary Heralds are equal in power to the Senate and Judiciary. We have even overturned their decisions on occasion. You must learn to work with them—to your advantage."

"Are you discouraging me on purpose?" she inquired with a sideways grin.

"You will be a wonderful Herald," he came back, his eyes wide. "I don't doubt that for a moment."

"Because I'm the antithesis of what you just described? Demanding. Straightforward. Impatient."

"No. Because you remind me of your father." He paused, then beamed at her. "He was a great Herald, Rieka. And you are very much like him."

Several things came to mind, but all she said was, "I hope so."

He leaned toward her and rested his forearms on his knees. "Now, I must tell you about the meetings I've been having with RadiMo."

She set up a new file on her datapad, typed in the Bournese Herald's name, and looked at him. "I hope you don't mind if I take notes on this, too."

"Not at all. The Bournese are interested in mining certain ores and gemstones. There are several spots on Earth they are interested in. RadiMo has been gathering information for three Bourne companies: Kimcon, BeliCo, and MiliCorp. They all intend to bid for the contract. You should plan to speak on Bourne's behalf to the Senate in the event we require legislation on the matter. It is in Earth's best interest to encourage trade with all Commonwealth planets."

Rieka shrugged. "Doesn't that go without saying? This doesn't sound terribly complicated, Alexi. I should be able to handle a mineral-rights contract."

"Good. Now, as a gesture of good faith, RadiMo is also lending his services to us. In addition to gathering information for his own planet, he has been overseeing the plans for three more subterranean cities."

"And they are?"

"New SubMoscow, SubBeijing, and SubBrasilia."

"Got them," she said, tapping at the datapad.

"You should assist RadiMo in whatever way you can, Rieka," he told her. The tone of his voice urged her to comply. "He represents the first of the member worlds not only to take an interest in capitalizing on Earth's many resources—but to offer his help as we try to repopulate."

"I hear you, Alexi," Rieka said. "And I know negotiation with the Bournese is very difficult. Almost as bad as trying to talk to a Boo. I respect what you've done so far, and I'll do my best to see that RadiMo is happy. I'll even ask Setana if she can give me any tips."

"Good. Good," he said, beaming. "She has a wealth of information in that regard. It was she, in fact, who told me of the Bourne's interest in rubies. That conversation sparked this entire relationship."

Rieka shut down her datapad and smiled at her uncle. "I'm sure she was happy to help. Is there anything else?"

"Yes. Do not trust RadiMo completely."

Rieka looked into Alexi's face. He was serious. "Say that again."

Alexi gestured vaguely with a hand. "The Bournese are very . . . literal. And also secretive. Perhaps it comes from living underground, I don't know." He shrugged. "Anyway, they have a certain talent when speaking the standard language through their translator computers that—for want of a better term—lies through omission."

"So you have to pay attention to what they don't say in addition to what they do?"

"Precisely."

Rieka returned her attention to the datapad. "Thanks, Alexi. This is exactly the type of information I need. Now, not to change the subject, but I will," she began, reactivating her datapad. "I've got a few questions. The first one is about that other deal with the Bournese—involving produce."

They went on for nearly an hour more, Rieka asking her questions and Alexi answering them. Finally, seeing he'd begun to tire, she nodded. "I think that's it, for now."

"I wish I could do more," Alexi told her, a sad note in his voice. He sat straighter and studied her. "You have selected your adjutant?"

Rieka nodded. "Her name is Jeniper Tarrik. I believe you know her."

"The Aurian who runs the office on Indra?"

She smiled. "She ran the office. We promoted her replacement just before we left."

"Are you sure you want a non-Human?"

"Yes," Rieka told him irritably. "I've met a lot of people in the last six months. She's the best person for the job—which means she actually *listens* to what I say. And unless she gives me cause to fire her, she's my adjutant—as of next week."

Alexi nodded. "That's fine, I'm sure. She never had any problems handling Indra."

Rieka winked. "Don't worry. I'm a decent judge of character. And Setana likes her, too."

"I'm sure she'll be fine," he repeated, then glanced at the wall behind her and made a strange face. "I hadn't meant to keep you so long. I will see you before you leave for Earth, yes? For dinner tonight. At my residence. And bring Triscoe and Jeniper."

"Another party for your expense account?"

Alexi laughed, a full rolling chuckle. "Perhaps."

Triscoe sat at his desk in his quarters, reading through Aarkmin's daily report without much real interest. Robet's words kept coming back to him, and he couldn't help but wonder at his friend's newfound wisdom. Robet DeVark's reputation for seeing little beyond the obvious was slowly being replaced with a mature, objective outlook. Perhaps his mother was correct when she predicted Robet would be settling down soon.

But Triscoe knew explaining the real reason for his concern would not be easy. Rieka's reaction to the one last aspect of the Singlemind he hadn't yet explained would be explosive. Not wanting to upset or distract her during the election process, he'd let the days slip by. Now he realized he might never find a proper time.

Unable to concentrate on the report, Triscoe shut down the computer just as Rieka came through the door. Immediately, he noticed her gray eyes had turned to steel. She nodded at him, her jaw set. "We have to talk."

He rose and cautiously moved toward her. A brief touch with her mind gave him a sense of anger and frustration. "All right," he said softly, gesturing toward a chair. When she sat, he gently asked, "Did you see Nason this morning?"

"Yes."

"And he gave you the acquittal papers?"

"I signed an edited version." She gestured vaguely with her hands. "No problem. I'll get a hard copy once the board of admirals okays it."

Her terse response gave him a distinctly uneasy feeling. "And you had an appointment with Alexi," he coaxed, hoping to discover the force behind her reined ire.

"Yes."

"How did that go?"

"Fine. He's seriously ill. We talked. I took notes." She tossed her datapad onto the table beside her.

He wanted to question her about that revelation, but sensed her uncle wasn't the problem. "And after that?" he coaxed.

"After that, I came back to the *Providence*. It's what happened after Nason and before Alexi that was, shall we say, disquieting."

"Rieka," he began, waiting until she looked at him to finish his question, "what happened before you met with Alexi?"

She sighed. "It isn't like it sounds—but . . . I was kidnapped."

Before he could respond to that outrageous statement, she raised a hand, her expression hard. He hadn't seen such determination since he'd stopped her from killing K'reshva.

"This time, it was relatively harmless. My mother sent her driver to 'fetch' me. But that doesn't alter the facts. I need security, Tris. I need a bodyguard."

Though he agreed with her, Triscoe knew she chafed at anyone assuming even the slightest responsibility when it came to her safety. "Are you sure that's what you want?"

"I'm sure," she replied, her voice a grating monotone. "A bodyguard is going to look conspicuous, but Candace isn't going to give up, and I don't believe she's completely rational."

Triscoe frowned. "What are you saying?" he asked softly, almost afraid of the answer.

"I'm saying this abduction was just a way to prove her point. And if I don't do what she wants—which I won't— I think she'll do something really stupid." She sighed and shook her head. "Maybe even try to have me killed."

SEVEN

Rieka knew Triscoe had been furious with her for not contacting him immediately when she'd been abducted. But two days had gone by and each silent moment now fueled her own anger. He's busied himself with ships' business day and night during their trip from Tau Ceti to Sol. He'd used every possible excuse not to be alone with her and had had almost no contact with her mind.

Which was why Rieka became curious when he entered their quarters and sat down as if to stay awhile.

She looked up from the console to acknowledge his presence, then turned some of her concentration back to the projected attendance at the Reaffirmation ceremony, pitiful though it was.

"Rieka, I need to talk to you," he began, echoing her own words from two days ago.

As she punched a key to suspend the data, a sense of apprehension tingled down her spine. "I thought you might," she said, wondering what topic had taken precedence on his agenda.

He smiled crookedly, a dimple appearing on his right cheek. "I would like you to interview several people. I'm going to hold you to your word that you will accept protection—even if I'm not the one providing it."

She shook her head, confused. "How could you have lined up job applicants in such a short time? We've been in transit for over thirty hours."

"I made inquiries before we left Yadra," he told her. Rieka thought the permanent frown he'd worn since she'd told him about the visit with her mother showed signs of cracking. "As soon as we came out of phase, I received notice that two individuals would be waiting at Earth to apply for the position of your personal bodyguard. There is another, here on the *Providence,* who wishes the job as well. A member of my crew."

She shook her head. "I can't do that. Mixing politics and Fleet personnel is strictly taboo. You know that."

"This one is willing to give up his career."

"From what rank?"

The frown became slightly more apparent. "Lieutenant."

"Who?"

"Martinez in Security."

She shook her head. "No. That's crazy." She paused a moment to think. Perhaps Martinez had a reason to want to leave the Fleet. She'd have to wait and see. "Look, the best I can do is interview them all and be fair. Let's hope your crewman isn't the most qualified."

"I am relieved to hear it—to a certain extent." She watched the frown ease slightly as he relaxed a bit against the cushions.

"I admire that kind of conviction, Tris. I just won't be party to destroying a budding career. A lieutenant, for heaven's sake." She took a breath and considered the possibility of hiring a bodyguard before she left the *Providence.* That notion felt good.

She watched Triscoe rub his hands on his thighs, a sure sign of stress. "So why are you still worried? I'll have a guard soon. Jeniper has plans to line up an entire security team once we're in Earth orbit. Everything will be fine."

"Yes. Everything will be fine."

"Except . . ." she prompted.

"Except us." His brown eyes were hard when they met hers, and Rieka realized more than just her steadfast independence bothered him.

"I told you before—I didn't feel threatened," she explained, knowing the excuse was lame. "Well, not in so many words. Being kidnapped isn't like being invited to a party. But it's happened to me before, and this time I didn't feel my life was in danger. If I had, I would have notified you right away."

Frustrated, Rieka stood and walked back to the desk. They'd gone over this before, and she still felt her judgment had been sound. Rehashing old worries did no one any good. She picked up her datapad and began to set up three files for the applicants so she could keep them straight.

"I appreciate your thoughtfulness," he said, and she sensed he wasn't being facetious. "But we have not reconciled several personal issues."

Rieka put down the datapad as he came toward her. He grabbed up her hands and held them both tightly as if fearful she would escape. "You are married to a Centauri, Rieka. A Centauri with the *quantivasta* gift. Problems cannot be ignored."

"I didn't think I was ignoring anything," she said softly, feeling an overwhelming sensation course through her at his touch. "I've set some things aside recently, so I could focus on more important . . . issues."

"I think it is more than 'things' you've set aside."

"I get it," she said, hoping her bravado held while she felt a wave of something strong and insistent work its way through her. "You mean I've ignored *you*. Well, since we left Yadra, it seems to me that *you're* the one who's been too busy to talk—or do anything else for that matter."

"I have been preoccupied with finding a way to tell you how I feel. I admit that."

She heaved a little sigh. "Okay. I take it you've come to a decision."

"Precisely. You've always been intuitive, Rieka," he murmured.

The compliment didn't boost her confidence. She felt him tug her, and she followed willingly as he moved back to the sofa.

"Sit."

She did. "I don't under—"

"Shh. Close your eyes."

It was almost a relief not to have to look at him. He'd placed her at the sofa's end, her back braced against the arm as she faced him. She felt it when he joined her, his weight shifting the cushions. He held her there, his hands gripping hers, working themselves up toward her wrists.

"Open your thoughts to me, love."

Why didn't you just say you wanted to Singlemind? she asked silently. *I would have understood.*

I don't think so. His next thoughts weren't clear enough

for her to understand in words, but he seemed both motivated and reluctant to continue.

Rieka relaxed and felt him ease into her mind. He
seemed more chaotic than she remembered. Knowing he
wouldn't believe her unless he experienced it for himself,
she purposely recalled her visit with her mother, including
how she got there.

She felt him accept it, and welcomed a small reprieve
when he finally agreed she hadn't really been in danger.
But then she felt something unexpected happen.

He receded into his mind. It left an unpleasant void between them, and she didn't know what to do.

Triscoe must have understood her confusion, because she
heard him whisper. "Come to me, Rieka."

"I don't know how."

"Let go of yourself. Fill in the empty space and come
to me."

Eyes still closed, she tried. But letting go of herself didn't
seem possible. She sensed her mind inching away and then
snapping back as if some kind of self-preservation instinct
refused to let go.

"It's not working," she whispered. "I'm trying but—"

"—don't try," he told her. "Just float. I will lead."

Floating, she guessed, would be a kind of nothingness
she could manage. Carefully, purposely, she made herself
hover not far from that instinct that kept her centered,
aware and able to withdraw into herself in a heartbeat.

"You're doing fine," he coached. "Now I'm going to
reach out to show you the path."

Not quite sure what path he meant, Rieka waited. She
felt him come back toward her, the emptiness recede, and
a kind of necessity encroach on her consciousness. She
needed to go to him. Somehow, he'd given her a compul-
sion to enter his mind. Unable to recall her motivation, she
inched forward.

"Yes. That's it."

Rieka continued, albeit slowly. Her consciousness eased
across the emptiness until it touched him. She felt the orga-
nization of his thoughts, so alien from hers. A palette of
colors and patterns and textures. The depth of his
emotions.

She felt tears sting her eyes when she touched the sensation of gold that seemed to be fused with everything around her. Instantly, Rieka realized this was his love. It overwhelmed her, caressed her, held her in its gentle embrace. It had no boundaries, though she could sense places where it had been tempered with logic. She began to comprehend the vital differences between them. Centauri love was more complete than she'd ever imagined.

Come here, his voice silently told her mind.

She eased away from that deeply emotional part of him and toward more rational thought, and wondered if he felt the same things when he came to her mind. If he became so involved with her being that he forgot how to be himself.

Where? she asked, suddenly realizing the vastness before her.

Here. A bluish area grew brighter. Feeling overwhelmed and exhilarated, she moved toward that light.

As she reached it, Rieka felt the blue and him together, as if she'd touched his very essence. Then, surprisingly, she also sensed herself. Or a reflection of herself. She didn't know which. But there seemed to be a double being within him—as if Triscoe, by himself, was not complete.

Correct, he told her. *You are always here with me. It is the Centauri way.*

Is this a recollection of me?

No.

Then, that means . . . what?

Both of us exist here within me. If you die, part of me will die, as well. It is possible I would not survive alone.

Rieka felt her body, somewhere out there far away, shudder. During the war with the Procyons, her life had been almost constantly in danger. Now she understood that his fear for her safety wasn't as irrational as she'd thought. It had to do as much with self-preservation and instinct as it did common sense. She'd taken so many chances since they'd exchanged their vows all those months ago. And he'd stood by, allowing her to risk both their lives for the greater good. How could he stand it? Why hadn't he told her sooner?

Then another thought struck her. *But not every mate dies. I've met widows and widowers.*

Few Centauris have the gift, he reminded her.

Rieka felt like kicking herself for not realizing that sooner. *Then why tell me now?*

She felt him hesitate as the answer came to her. He'd kept this knowledge apart from their conversation because he'd waited for her to come to the conclusion herself.

The child. Their child. Just as she held his fate in her hands, she held that child's fate, too. If something were to happen during the pregnancy, all three of them would suffer.

She absorbed the impact of that realization and felt herself recede from him. She slid through his love, again, and was surrounded with overwhelming devotion before easing back into the void. When she left him, Rieka felt her body shiver. She gasped for air, suddenly aware she'd forgotten to breathe.

"Rieka." Triscoe's hands cupped her face, and she felt his thumbs slide along her cheeks. "Rieka, don't cry. Open your eyes, love."

She blinked at him once before sliding her arms around his neck and pressing her cheek into his shoulder. She felt his arms come around her and marveled at their strength in the face of such fragility.

Promising herself to determine the necessity of everything she did from now on, Rieka allowed herself to sob quietly against him, feeling a tremor run through him almost every time she made a noise.

"I didn't do it to frighten you," he whispered finally. "I did not know any other way to make you understand."

"It isn't as though you haven't tried," she admitted, sniffing and pulling back to look at him. His brown eyes were no different than before, but now she saw so many new things in them.

"And now I must ask you a difficult question." He paused, then asked, "Why do you wish to have a child?"

Sure she hadn't heard him correctly, Rieka made a face. "I want a family. You know that."

Triscoe nodded. "So do I. But *why* do you want one?"

She shook her head, confused. "Why does anyone?"

He offered a soft smile. "For many reason, I would guess. But you said nothing about children until after Paden died and you decided to run for Earth Herald."

She thought about that, then said, "I suppose that's an accurate observation."

"So then, why? Do you seek to replace that sense of belonging you haven't felt since your father died? Or, are you looking for an heir?"

The questions stopped her. Insulted, Rieka started to make a snide comment, then realized he was right. She turned away and tried to think.

Gently, his mind voice whispered, *I don't know, either.*

"I've been selfish, haven't I?" she asked finally, glancing up into his concerned face. "And you're right, Tris. I want an heir. And I want a child to fill an empty space." She shook her head. "But those reasons don't outweigh the risks I've been willing to take with—with our lives."

The look of relief on his face conjured feelings of both guilt and happiness. She felt a sense of pale blue serenity as he asked, "So what shall we do now?"

"Wait," she answered instantly. "It seems like the only thing we can do until a lot of questions are sorted out. I think the biggest one, for me, is understanding how my father died." His death and what caused it had been bothering her for days. Had that and Alexi's health problems brought on a sense of her own mortality? Rieka didn't know, but dwelling on it probably wouldn't help. "We should tell Wilmstos to put everything on hold until we're both emotionally ready to start a family. Maybe when your commission is over and you're not touring anymore."

She smiled faintly, and sniffed. "And we don't *have* to try to combine our genes. Ker's idea may have been a good one, after all. We could simply tell Wilmstos we want a Human child that *looks* Centauri."

Triscoe nodded and the sense of pale blue faded into a deep midnight. "I'm due back at Indra in a few days," he said. "I think it best one of us should speak to him in person."

Her smile faded. "How can you stand being married to me? It must be awful."

He shook his head. "It's wonderful." She watched him quirk his mouth. "You are the most vital, spirited, inspirational person I have ever met. You are my *wife*. In my mind that makes me the more fortunate one."

Rieka didn't realize she'd moved until she felt the warm

softness of his lips against hers. She kissed him gently at first, then as the moments passed the tenderness and respect evolved into passion.

Triscoe responded in kind. By the time she'd worked his tunic loose, she felt cool air across her shoulders and his hands on her breasts.

He was murmuring something into the skin at the base of her neck when she heard a noise in the corridor. "Tris, the door."

"Mmm. No one would enter my cabin."

"But Jeniper . . ."

He sat back. "Lock it."

Rieka got up, activated the lock, and turned back slowly, knowing his attention would be on her breasts. Indran females didn't have them, and Triscoe's fascination with them bordered on obsessive. When she returned to the sofa, both his dimples were shamelessly displayed. "What?" she asked innocently, her hands on her hips.

"I am simply enjoying the view."

Flaunting herself inches from his face, Rieka tried not to smile. "Which is precisely why you asked *me* get up to lock the door," she murmured.

He leaned forward but didn't touch her. Still, she could feel his breath on her skin when he said, "You did it, anyway."

She could only see his crown of blond hair as she looked down at him. When his lips finally made contact, Rieka gripped his shoulders. "Gods, Triscoe, you are a quick study."

I accept the compliment, he told her gallantly.

Her voice sounded raspy, even to her. "Then you should remember that after the last time, I swore I would never again make love on this sofa."

I haven't forgotten.

Taking her hand, he led her to the bedroom and set her gently on the mattress. She reached for him, but he stepped away and slowly began to remove his shoes.

Rieka groaned and stood up. He set his shoes by the bed, then turned and pushed her back on the mattress. She reached her arms around him, but he pushed her away. Taking a step back, he slowly began to undo his waistband.

"Triscoe—"

"Patience."

"You are such a tease," she complained.

His answering chuckle sent a shiver down her spine. "I learned it from you."

Jeniper rang for admittance at Captain Marteen's door and wondered what the day would be like. She and Rieka had finished the inaugural speech and were working on the Reaffirmation details, but things were not going well.

Problems seemed abundant in Damascus, and Rieka wouldn't rest until they were resolved. Two caterers had canceled. Florists had informed them the arrangements that had been ordered weeks ago were unavailable. The stadium crew had yet to complete the infield stage. Jeniper found herself nothing short of amazed. At each piece of incoming bad news, Rieka would come up with at least three alternative plans. The woman's energy in her approach to unexpected obstacles could be staggering.

Captain Marteen appeared as the door slid open. "Good morning, Jeniper," he said. "Are you ready for your first close up look at Earth? It will only be another hour or so."

"Good morning," she replied, as he stepped back and she entered. "Is it so much different than the DGI image?"

Seated on the sofa, Rieka looked up from her datapad, an intense look on her face. "Is ice different from water?"

Jeniper felt the captain's eyes on her, as if waiting for her to fall into some kind of rhetorical trap. "Yes. No. It—it depends upon how you look at it."

"Well—there you go," Rieka said.

"And here I go," the captain told them. "I'll notify you once we're nearing orbit."

Jeniper nodded and smiled at him as he left. "Your husband is . . ."

"What?"

She shrugged. "I was going to say an enigma. But then I've never known a Fleet captain personally, before. Maybe his behavior is normal, and I am simply seeing more than there is."

Jeniper thought she saw Rieka flush a bit before she answered. "You see exactly what he wants you to see. No more, no less," she replied sagely. "But basically, you're right. And I've known plenty of Fleet captains. Triscoe is . . . arcane."

Not quite sure how to respond to what she decided must be a Human term, Jeniper changed the subject. "Working on the Reaffirmation speech?"

Rieka shook her head. "I'm going over the questions to ask my potential bodyguards. Triscoe and I were just discussing whether or not to ask if they'd ever killed anyone."

Jeniper felt herself frown as she sat on one of the chairs. "Is that something you want to know? Would it make a difference?"

She knew she'd been set up when her boss grinned. "It isn't the answer that really matters, Jen," Rieka told her. "It's how the person responds to the question. If they did, are they proud of it? Or were there extenuating circumstances that warranted the act? Lots of possibilities, there— not just a yes or no."

Jeniper nodded. The thought of murder, either in self-defense or not, made her think of Jonik's predicament. Surely he was just stretching the truth in order to gain her sympathy when he'd spoken of that threat. He'd already used nearly every other ploy to persuade her to give him a loan. She'd been expecting the life-or-death gimmick for some time. Still, the thought of his bibbets when he'd walked away gave her plenty to think about.

"Are you okay?"

Jeniper gave herself a little shake as Rieka's question penetrated her reverie. "Oh, of course. I, uh . . . suppose the question is reasonable," she offered, going back to the original topic. "After all, the person is supposed to be able to defend you against any adversary."

"I thought so," Rieka agreed. "Except Triscoe wanted me to change the question to: *would* you kill someone? There's a lot more happening in the subconscious when you ask something like that."

"Perhaps you should include both questions," Jeniper suggested.

"Maybe, but the interviews have to be conducted in just under ninety minutes. Once we make orbit, neither of us is going to have a lot of time to do anything. I've got to eliminate every question I can."

Jeniper found herself making a small noise in agreement.

Once they reached a stable Earth orbit the word "busy"
would be an understatement.

Rieka sat mesmerized by the blue planet on the DGI in
Triscoe's quarters. She hadn't been to Earth in almost a
year, and couldn't help wondering how she'd be received.

The door opened. "Permission to enter?" Jeniper asked
from the corridor, though it sounded more like a statement.

Rieka shifted her attention from the three-dimensional
vista. "We seem to be getting awfully formal all of a sudden," she jibed. "It isn't as if you weren't here an hour
ago. Come in."

"This planet is your seat of power, Herald," Jeniper reminded her, stepping forward and following Rieka's silent
gesture to sit. "You must command respect here, of all
places. If you do not . . ."

"I'll be looked on as a fool," Rieka finished. Jeniper's
silence made her smile. Little did her companion know
she'd played the fool often enough in the past. "When you
agree with me, say so, Jeniper. I've asked for your candid
opinion at all times, and I expect it."

"Of course."

Rieka sighed. It would take months for this woman to
feel comfortable enough to be a friend. She glanced back
at the DGI. Triscoe had brought them to a high, stable
orbit, and she could just make out the curve of North Af-
rica as they approached it from the southwest.

"Do you know much Earth history?" she asked.

"What they teach in school," Jeniper replied, looking up
at the planet's image.

"That's a bunch of sh—" Rieka caught herself before
she embarrassed Jeniper again. "Excuse me, I'll rephrase
that. The textbooks don't explain the half of it. And quite
probably only a handful of people will ever know what
really happened."

Jeniper leaned forward. "You're saying the Commonwealth teaches a lie?"

Rieka smiled. "Not in so many words. The lie is purely
by omission. We discovered the true facts during the trouble with the Procyons six months ago. That knowledge convinced me to run for Herald."

When Jeniper said nothing, Rieka glanced at her again. The Aurian woman sat staring at the DGI with a look of wonder. "Would you like to hear the story?"

"Yes."

Relieved that it hadn't been, "Yes, ma'am," Rieka turned her attention to the screen as well. "About two hundred years ago, the Commonwealth united the civilizations on seven planets. Earth had been considered, it being so close to the Centauri system, but the people there weren't ready for nonterrestrial contact.

"Around that time, the civilization residing in the Procyon system decided they needed to move on—and the Commonwealth stood in their way. Instead of trying an overt attack, they figured their best bet would be to weaken the Commonwealth first, then pick off whatever planets they wanted. They decided to use this scenario on the only local planet with no defense."

"Earth," Jeniper supplied.

"Exactly. They found an asteroid, hollowed out one end and fit it with an ion propulsion drive. Then, they sent it on its way and sat back to watch what happened."

Jeniper turned, wide-eyed. "You mean the meteor wasn't a natural cosmic occurrence?"

"The astronomers of the time called it an anomaly," Rieka told her. "That much, at least, is in the history books. No one could explain where it came from or how it maneuvered itself to hit the Earth as it did. It was noticed months before the impact—and watched carefully. Everyone thought it would be a near miss. But just three weeks before the collision, it mysteriously changed course. Everyone figured it had been influenced by some other, equally anomalous phenomenon.

"Astronomers scrambled to figure new data trajectories. The people were warned not to panic, but nothing could be done. By that point, Humanity had banded together and started working on a plan to try to destroy it, but even if they had some way of detonating an explosion to push it off course, I'm sure the Procyons would have found a way to turn it around."

Rieka leaned forward and gestured at the DGI image. "The exact point of contact couldn't be calculated, but they worked out the correct latitude. Thirty-three degrees north.

A latitude that would affect over two-thirds of the global population.

"So the four-and-a-half-kilometer-wide rock came hurtling out of the sky at something like thirty kilometers a second. The entry angle of seventy-six degrees was way too high for anyone to hope the atmosphere might slow it down."

Rieka paused and looked at Jeniper, then stood and stepped close enough to the DGI to point to the impact site. "It hit here, about five kilometers south of an island called Cyprus in the Mediterranean Sea. The island was destroyed instantly, as were about twenty-five million people along the coast on the mainland."

"How?" Jeniper stammered. "I mean, instantly?"

"The kinetic energy was changed by the impact to heat energy. The people were incinerated, Jeniper. They estimated the temps to be upwards of a million degrees Celsius. The firestorm swept an area over seven hundred kilometers in diameter. That part of the Mediterranean coast was pretty dry. The whole thing went up in flames in a matter of minutes.

"Of course the rest of the Mediterranean suffered as well. Tsunamis—oceanic waves hundreds of meters high destroyed nearly every island and coastal town. More millions killed without a chance to save themselves."

Jeniper's bibbets got darker, but she said nothing, so Rieka went on.

"And the jolt from the impact set off hundreds of earthquakes worldwide. There's a particularly unstable area called the Pacific Rim where the continental plates move against each other. Those plates shifted. The result—more tsunamis. Underwater volcanoes erupted. No major port city made it through that time without suffering tremendous damage.

"And then there was the ash—from the fires, volcanoes, and the Collision itself. It bubbled up into the upper atmosphere and got picked up by the jet streams—prevailing movements in the air—and eventually spread out to cover the globe. Components of the ash were nitric and sulfuric acid. So when things cooled down—and they did by a good twenty degrees—the rain that fell was acidic. It wreaked havoc with pH in both fresh and salt water."

"Nothing was spared. Not plants, animals, people, water . . . even the rocks eroded under that kind of torture. In the first three months, before relief came, a billion people died. A sixth of the population. And with their deaths came disease . . ."

"I can't imagine living through anything so horrible," Jeniper whispered.

"My great-great-grandfather did. He was an astronomer—the Human who discovered the Centauri relief ship. When Delik Silva became the first Centauri to visit Earth, Peter Degahv was the man he chose to speak to. And because of his ability to stand tall in the face of adversity, old Peter took the post of Earth Herald."

"It's quite a story," Jeniper said.

Rieka smiled. "Yes, it is. And now it's come full circle. Earth has been resurrected like a phoenix from the ashes, and a Degahv is still her representative. I just hope I can manage half as well as he did."

"I am sure you'll do very well, Herald," Jeniper told her firmly. Rieka could tell she truly believed that.

Glancing back at the digital image, though, Rieka felt her jaw tense. How could one person consolidate the needs of an entire race? And then execute that agenda without disrupting the rest of the Commonwealth? "I wish I had your confidence."

"I can't understand why you don't. There are two centuries of Heralds in your family. Surely that must bring you some sense of assurance."

"But none has ever done what I have to do," Rieka said, turning away from the DGI to look directly at Jeniper. "I'll be the first Earth Herald to try to make the Commonwealth respect us for what we did. What we've done. And what we intend to do."

EIGHT

Adjutant Gundah preened the fur on her arms as she sat at the conference room table listening to the Herald's staff's weekly reports. Periodically, she glanced at the Ophs around her, but her mind calculated its own agenda. There would be many things to do before the next two weeks were out.

Cimpa, the Oph Herald, nodded at Beresh and told him to see to an agreement between the Boin clan and the Daskar. He pronounced his decisions on two short-term business deals and told his office secretary, Gabah, he wanted the arrangements for his trip to Earth on his desk by eighteen-hundred. Then he dismissed them.

Gundah pushed herself up from the table, her hollow ear jewelry clinking pleasantly, and headed toward her office. As Cimpa's adjutant, she intended to accompany him there though he had not yet included her in his party. She had always managed to profit from her position in his shadow. It would be a simple thing to do it again.

Her desk console blinked with incoming mail, so she sat and perused the files, finding a few things vaguely interesting. Once certain nothing needed her immediate attention, Gundah accessed the Commonwealth NewsNet and flipped through the various News Sheets. She took notes here and there, where business interests were concerned. TechLine stocks were unchanged. Aurie Quadrant 3 produce apparently had a good season. Three companies were reporting record profits this year.

Gundah smiled. She held a great deal of stock in two of them.

She sifted through a mass of useless information and was

about to switch off when her incoming mail icon reappeared. Curious, she opened the directory and recognized the file source as one of her people on Indra.

Her black lips pursed as her pads touched the appropriate keys. Then, as she skimmed the page, Gundah felt her ears prick up and immediately eased them back down lest someone come in the office and wonder what she was reading.

Casually, she jacked in her datapad and transferred the message onto it. Then she deleted the file from her console. She needed to read the entire missive slowly, probably several times. Then, she would decide the best action to take, although she already had the basics in mind.

An aide named Kaffah stepped into her office, the distinct odor of *ciffa* wafting in with her. "Herald wants you. Now," she said, her eyes wide.

Gundah snorted slightly and switched off her datapad. Kaffah had not yet been Advanced and knew only the academics of sex. She stood in awe of her superiors who engaged in the activity on an almost-daily basis.

"I am on my way," she told the girl, then pushed away from her desk and walked to the door. "How long to your Advancement?"

"Four more months," Kaffah said, managing to look both proud and embarrassed.

Gundah offered her a consoling growl, then said, "Always remember the males among us rut. It is a thing they do. And though it is the female's place to bear young, it is also our duty to control them in their need. Their release. You will learn how to accomplish this only with practice."

"Of course," Kaffah replied, her ears flattening to her head.

Delighted she'd completely mortified the precocious girl, Gundah strode past her and toward Cimpa's private office. Unable to bear pups of her own, she'd been servicing the Herald since she'd become his adjutant eighteen years ago.

It was a mutually beneficial practice. Long after his mate's death, Cimpa remained a remarkably functional Herald—due, Gundah thought, to her sexual services. A male in his position simply couldn't ignore his urge to rut by pounding *ciffa* every seventy-two days. And ignoring the obvious would eventually have worn on his sanity.

She opened the office door to discover an empty room. She detected the faint odor of *ciffa* and followed it to Cimpa's private bath. There, she found him leaning heavily against the sink, his eyes glazed. A huge block of *ciffa,* a refined tree sap, stood beside him, its top worn with many claw gouges. His paws were covered with the pungent white dust.

"Cimpa, *bigotch do vou kriktan,*" she chided, indicating the mess with a paw. He bared his teeth at her, but she ignored that and threw the bolt on the door.

"*Vash. Vash,*" he growled. "*Gundah, vash.*"

When he stood straight, she saw that his *cile* had already protruded alarmingly and the three *pictiles* were well extended, ready to engage.

"*Korik noi grunda mah,*" she scolded, ambling to the half wall near the cylindrical commode and leaning on it with her arms. After taking a deep breath, she arched her back.

Cimpa leapt on her almost immediately, engaging himself and clawing at her fur. She let go the wall and grabbed at his paws. He knew better than to damage her coat. He growled, but Gundah growled louder. Now fully engaged, she felt his paws relax against hers and she released them.

"*Tondon da na,* Cimpa," she told him softly.

He growled, but this time with satisfaction. Now, as his breathing became both labored and rhythmic, she felt him stroke her back, nails held in check. She could barely feel them through her fur.

His paws made their way down her sides and reached around to knead her chest. She watched as they clenched again and tugged her wheat-colored coat. She tilted back her head and growled her displeasure. Again, he eased off.

Gundah held her position dutifully, knowing Cimpa would return to himself in a few moments. How many times had they done this, she wondered. A thousand? More? Sometimes it seemed like forever. Sometimes it felt completely new.

Another moment passed and she heard him snort, then a few seconds later she felt the *pictiles* release her as he disengaged. By the time she turned around he had restored himself completely.

He smoothed his coat and looked at her. "Again, you have my thanks, Gundah."

"I am always at your disposal. You know that," she told him. She had known his time would nearly coincide with the Earth's Reaffirmation and had wondered if he would gamble on leaving her on Oph. Obviously that was out of the question. Now, all that remained was for him to say the words.

He heaved a great sigh and flipped his left ear. "Then it is apparent that you will accompany me on my trip to Earth." He looked at her carefully, and she could almost detect a fondness for her in the way his left ear tipped forward. But perhaps it had more to do with his physical state as opposed to his emotional one.

"Of course. It is a good idea," she said. "It would be most unpleasant to have you pounding *ciffa* every hour and swollen beyond belief."

"Most unpleasant," he agreed.

"I have wondered," she began, her curiosity overcoming any hesitancy, "why do you not simply find a new mate?"

"This arrangements suits," Cimpa said, pulling himself up and expanding his chest. "A wife would wish pups. I have them. You wish only to continue as my adjutant. You perform your job to Oph—and to me, admirably. And you are sufficiently compensated."

Gundah nodded. He'd answered her question, and although the term "sufficiently" was subjective, she both understood and agreed with it. "Perhaps you would find a female who did not wish pups."

"Perhaps. But I am not looking for one." Cimpa pulled himself straighter. "I will notify you if I need you." He twitched his nose, growled softly, and left.

After making sure her coat was properly groomed, Gundah casually made her way back to her office. She reseated herself at her desk with a thoughtful sigh and reached for her datapad.

Candace's people had unearthed some news about Rieka, on Indra. Gundah hoped the report was not a repeat of anything she already knew.

It wasn't. Gundah could tell that much as soon as the name Sati Labs came up. Her breath caught when her agent reported both Rieka Degahv and Captain Marteen having visited the place twice. What were they doing there, she wondered. Sati's reputation, not to mention their fee, was beyond any other genetic-engineering lab in the Commonwealth. They were cutting edge, but staunchly ethical. Gundah couldn't imagine what Candace's daughter and her husband would be doing in such a place.

Then, a thought struck her. Outrageous as it seemed, it might be possible. They could be attempting to have a child of their combined species. Certainly Centauri and Human genomes wouldn't combine on their own. Other thoughts began to tumble in her mind.

Degahv. Sati Labs. Genetic material.

Perfect.

She touched a toggle on her console, and her secretary's voice responded almost immediately. "Zeliah, I will be accompanying Cimpa to Earth's ceremony," she began. "Inform Gabah and tell him to make the arrangements. I wish to be notified once they are finalized."

"Of course, Gundah."

"And I want you to conduct a Search. Bill it to my private expense account. Flag it urgent and express."

"Understood. Who am I searching for?"

"An Aurian. Male. Last known residence was here on Oph, but I believe he may have traveled to Indra recently."

"And the name?" Zeliah asked.

"Tarrik, I need you to find a man named Jonik Tarrik."

Having already interviewed the other two applicants, Rieka asked the third candidate the last question on her list. She and Hong Wang-Chi had been chatting in her quarters for almost thirty minutes, and the interview had gone well, she thought, until now. He looked suddenly tense and began to fidget in the chair.

"Yeah," he answered quietly. "I did kill someone once. An accident—but he's dead, anyway. And that's what counts."

She nodded her head in agreement and noted his reply on her datapad. Seeing the cautious look in his eye, Rieka said, "Well, we've gone this far, I might as well ask the circumstances."

Hong shifted in the chair. He was a big Human, close to Triscoe's height, but had to weigh half again as much.

Though he didn't look bulky, his musculature could not be ignored. The chair looked about three sizes too small.

"It was a martial-arts competition. I'd been to a lot of them, even before I started working for Norik Security. Never even hurt anybody at a competition—well, not anything more than a bruise or two. It wasn't even a top round," he explained, leaning forward and looking her in the eye. "An Aurie, his name was Freni Cabel, got assigned to me. We were at it for about twenty-five seconds—I was doing well. I threw him. That's it. I threw him. Just like I'd done a thousand times before. But for some reason he twisted in the air. I don't think I did anything to make him do that. The force of the fall, even on the mat, broke his neck. They put him on life support and started nanotherapy right away." He shrugged and said no more.

Rieka looked down at Hong's resumé. His last competition had been three years ago. "Was that at the Sepin High Trials at Pikoom?" she asked.

He nodded. "The last time I ever competed."

"But it was an accident."

Mr. Hong nodded. "Like I said though, dead is dead." After a tight sigh, he seemed to let go of the incident. The pitch of his voice rose slightly when he said, "I was on assignment on Medoura when you stopped that meteor the Procyons tried to hit us with."

Dumbfounded, Rieka nodded but made no reply. She'd seen the chaos that day on Medoura. But it would have been far worse had the Fleet not destroyed the rock she considered a twin to what had nearly annihilated the Earth two centuries ago.

"And then there's . . ." Hong began quietly, then shook his head.

"What?"

He frowned as if what he wanted to say simply wouldn't come out. "I've hurt a few people, too, Herald," he managed finally. His dark almond-shaped eyes held hers while he spoke. "I'm big for a Human. Sometimes I don't know my own strength."

"Can you explain what you mean?" she asked softly. Obviously, he felt remorse for every act that had caused someone else to suffer. Though commendable, she didn't need a bodyguard so concerned for others that he'd put her in danger.

"Back on Medoura. During the confusion when they thought they'd be hit . . . the people went crazy. That's the best way to describe it. I was on a ground-level tram in Eskitou and the driver just—well she went crazy. She just took off down the street with her load of passengers. There must have been twenty of us aboard. We watched her cause three accidents before I decided I had to do something."

He leaned toward her but looked at his hands while recounting the incident. Rieka sat enthralled. Neither the Oph nor the Indran lieutenant had seemed anywhere near as responsible.

"Her box was isolated, of course," he went on, "so I had to break through that. I got this scar, here, from busting through the plexi with a guy's walking stick." He showed her the back of his left hand where a fine line ran from his thumb to his little finger. "When I finally got the door open—she was completely gone. I mean, she wasn't in the real world, you know?"

Rieka nodded. "I think so."

"Medourans are sensitive people," he explained. "They take everything personally. When I yelled at her to stop, she accelerated. Anyway, I couldn't pull her out of her chair—so I hit her. Hard. Knocked her out. I stopped the tram then, and let the rest of the passengers out."

"Sounds like you saved everyone."

"Maybe, but I broke the woman's jaw. That's what the medics told me when they finally got there."

Rieka considered that last statement and decided Mr. Hong didn't count himself a hero as much as he did a bully. Yet no brainless tough guy would stand watch over his victim until paramedics arrived. She let a long moment of silence go by before she asked, "So why have you decided you want the position of my bodyguard?"

Hong sat up straighter and looked at her as if the answer were obvious. "The Fleet saved us that day, Herald. All the people on Medoura. We would have died if that meteor had struck. And *you* were the one who figured out what was happening."

"Who told you it was me?" Rieka asked, confused. Only

a handful of Fleet officers knew she'd been the one to deduce the Procyons' tactics.

"I know somebody who knows somebody," he replied cryptically.

"It isn't common knowledge, then?"

"No."

Relieved by that tidbit of information, she asked, "And you think you can protect me?"

He pulled himself straight, all but dwarfing the chair. "Yes, ma'am."

Realizing she'd made her decision during his story about the tram, Rieka took a moment to collect her thoughts. Hong Wang-Chi was twenty-eight years old. He'd worked for Norik Security for eight years. Before that, an excellent education on Yadra had taught him electronics, computer science, and psychology. He hadn't experienced life in the Fleet, but he did know the difference between doing something and having to do something.

"I'm used to giving orders. Do you think you can handle that?"

He offered her a cocky smile. "Not if it goes against my better judgment. If I thought you were taking too big a risk, I'd give *you* the orders."

They locked stares until Rieka laughed. "Then I suppose I should say, welcome aboard, Mr. Hong. I am using your name correctly, am I not?" she asked. "Your given name is Wang-Chi, family name Hong."

"Right."

She offered her hand, and he shook it firmly. "I'll call you Wang-Chi if you'll call me Rieka."

"Thank you, Rieka. And just Wang will do. I appreciate your confidence. And I promise I won't let you down."

Jeniper stood near the entry to the InterMAT chamber watching Captain Marteen say good-bye to his wife. She had noticed their odd behavior before, and still couldn't quite figure out what passed between the two of them. It almost seemed as though they could communicate without speaking. The Centauri *quantivasta* gift was rare, she knew. But even if Captain Marteen had it, Rieka was Human. Thought interaction didn't seem likely.

"We'll be fine in Canberra," Rieka told him. "Wang's

checked everything out with the Embassy security people and the hotel. Stop worrying."

The captain looked skeptical. Jeniper tried to hide her smile by shifting her briefcase from one hand to the other. They had a mountain of confirmations to go through for both the inauguration and Reaffirmation ceremonies. And she needed to reschedule two press conferences and organize a dinner at the Herald's hotel.

Rieka huffed and frowned at her husband. "Quit that or I'll take back what I said before about inviting your parents to stay with us before the Reaffirmation."

"I didn't *say* anything," he replied, a distinctly innocent tone in his voice. Jeniper saw a dimple appear in his left cheek. She watched Rieka's face contort into another incredulous frown.

"As if that meant something," Rieka muttered. The captain moved to stroke her chin, but his wife would have none of that. She reached to cup the back of his head and pull him down for a kiss. Self-conscious, Jeniper studied her shoes.

"See you when you get back from Mars Colony," Rieka said softly.

Jeniper could tell the captain still wasn't comfortable with leaving her, but he nodded. Wondering if she would ever find someone with whom she could be so comfortable, Jeniper scolded herself for being jealous. There was no room for that in either her job or the friendship that had taken root with her new boss.

And she needed that friendship now, she realized, in the light of Jonik's latest message. She'd received it a few hours after they'd reached Earth. Since then, thoughts of her brother were never far away. He said he'd see her soon. How could he do that? And why? What was worse, he hadn't mentioned anything about the loan he'd begged for on Indra.

Rieka turned to her, an inscrutable smile on her face. "Are we ready, then?"

"I think so," she replied.

Jeniper watched Rieka slip her datapad into a small briefcase on the console as Captain Marteen entered their destination. They stepped into the chamber. The captain looked at them both and nodded. "Two days," he said.

Jeniper smiled and meant to say good-bye, but before she could speak, she found herself looking at a wall that read: Welcome to Canberra. Knowing her new job meant a great deal of traveling, she hoped she'd get used to InterMAT transport sooner rather than later.

"Well, I expected someone would be here," Rieka murmured, openly annoyed. She heaved a disgruntled sigh and shook her head. Jeniper followed her out of the chamber and Rieka strode past the InterMAT technician and toward the outer door. It opened before she reached it.

Wang's smile apparently disarmed his boss's ire. "Transport okay?" he asked.

"A lovely way to spend nine hundred nanoseconds, Wang," she told him. "Where is everyone?"

"Downstairs. The more secure the Earth Herald's image, the better. Trust me."

"I agree," Jeniper said, smiling at him. She turned toward Rieka. "Once we're in the conference room, I'll have the Australian Administrator announce you."

Jeniper watched Rieka nod and wondered what she must be feeling. This would be her first public appearance as Herald-elect. Squeezing her briefcase a bit tighter in her hand, Jeniper followed Wang and Rieka down a short flight of stairs. She stepped around them and spoke quietly with a dark-skinned man she recognized from prior communications aboard the *Providence,* Wesley Stafford, the Australian Administrator. About a dozen journalists of nearly every race sat before them, and an untold number of holo-cameras were set up along the back wall.

After assuring Jeniper all was in order, Mr. Stafford moved to the podium and introduced Rieka, then eased aside while she came forward to greet the news people. "Good morning," she told them. "I can't tell you how glad I am to be back on Earth. Words simply aren't enough. I hope that one day soon you will all experience this feeling—of coming to a place where you are welcome simply because you are Human—and not in spite of it." She shot the journalists a wry smile. "And if you aren't Human, you're welcome anyway."

When she paused, an Aurian in the front row asked, "Were you concerned the electorate would not choose you,

Mrs. Degahv? I understand you have not completely sev-
ered your ties from the Fleet."

Rieka frowned slightly at that. "Mr.—?"

"Silkam," he supplied.

"Mr. Silkam, since I did not consult the Indran Oracle
on the matter, I was *not* sure I'd be elected," she told him,
her voice edged by a touch of humor. "And the Fleet and
I still entertain an amicable disassociation. More than that
I am not at liberty to say. But I can tell you my agenda
doesn't include commanding a starship anytime soon."

"Is it true you'll be launching a billion-credit campaign
to lure Humans back to Earth?" an Oph asked.

Jeniper smiled to herself as Rieka responded with an
openhanded gesture before speaking. They'd gone over this
type of inquiry yesterday morning. She had thought her
boss felt nervous then, but now Rieka seemed as confident
as if she'd been Herald for a decade. Jeniper could only
guess at the manner with which she'd commanded a Fleet
ship. It must have been something to see.

A few questions later, Wang nudged her, and whispered,
"We need to go."

Jeniper glanced at the wall chrono and nodded. Nearly
thirty minutes had passed. She hated taking Rieka from an
obviously positive interview, but it couldn't be helped. She
moved to stand a short distance from the podium and, before the next question could be asked, said, "Thank you
very much, ladies and gentlemen. I'm afraid that's all we
have time for today. Herald-elect Degahv has an extremely
tight schedule."

Jeniper had to gesture in order to get Rieka to leave the
podium. Stafford followed her out of the pressroom.

Wang ushered them back into the hallway and smiled
down at Jeniper. "That went well, don't you think?"

Jeniper found herself nodding, then looked at Rieka.
"You did great. The reporters all seemed pleased with
your answers."

Rieka's response was a terse laugh. "We'll see—once the
NewsNet is updated," she said. Then she looked up at
Wang. "Where to next?"

"I've arranged a tour of the city, Mrs. Degahv," Mr.
Stafford offered. "Canberra was saved from a lot of damage simply because of its position in the southern hemi-

sphere. Many of our above-ground buildings are not only maintained, but occupied as well."

Jeniper saw Rieka nod and glance at Wang. "It's all been approved," he told her. "My people will flank the touring van. I'll ride with you."

"Sounds like fun," she quipped, her tone disclaiming the words. For a moment, Jeniper wondered if she didn't want to go. Then Rieka suddenly smiled, and said, "I haven't seen Canberra in years, Mr. Stafford. And I would appreciate a tour. It's probably the most beautiful city this planet's got left."

"I'd think Sydney would like to argue with you on that, ma'am," Stafford replied. "Or possibly Winnipeg."

"I think the Herald simply means the overall effect," Jeniper supplied. "I know that from orbit the river and parks give it an esthetic appeal something like Rhonique."

"Aye, they do, Miss Tarrik," he said, smiling. "And I'm sure you'll find it that much more appealing from the ground."

Wang ushered them outside and into a waiting vehicle. Jeniper was impressed by the elevated seats and panoramic view. While the convoy assembled, she took note of the way Rieka beamed.

"Isn't it beautiful, Jen? Look at how clear the sky is. We're going to do whatever it takes to keep it that way."

"We can do with a bit of rain now and then," Stafford told her, his tone light.

"I didn't mean clouds. I meant pollution."

He smiled and glanced around. "It looks as though we're ready. Now, when we get down to the end of Brisbane and turn onto State Circle, I want you to look out to the left past Capitol Hill and see the new sculptures on the far side of the Parliament House—which is, of course, where you'll be inaugurated tomorrow."

"Herald RadiMo, this is an unexpected pleasure," Rieka said later that afternoon, bowing her head to the Bournese Herald. Wang had accompanied the Herald's *skiff* into the sitting room of her hotel suite. He stood discreetly to the side, she noticed, watching the small creature as it poked its head and shoulders from the center area of the coffin-sized floating device used for both transportation and comfort whenever the Bournese left their homeworld.

"RadiMo gives greetings to Herald-elect Degahv and wishes to inquire as to the health of Herald Degahv," the synthesized voice announced.

"The Herald Alexi is well," she replied. "And he is honored that you remember him in your greeting to his niece." This time she bowed formally, tipping her body forward from the waist. She'd dealt with few Bournese as a Fleet captain, but a short tutorial with a protocol program had hopefully honed her diplomatic skills.

"Enter my domain, Herald RadiMo," she told the small, dark being. "You are welcome and no harm will come to you."

She watched as a hole formed in the top of the *skiff*'s forward area. RadiMo's brown, fist-sized head disappeared from the center area and reappeared at the new hole, followed by narrow shoulders and forelegs. He began to tap rapidly on the miniature console before him, and the voice translated almost immediately. "You are gracious. I am comfortable."

The *skiff* edged farther into the room and settled lightly on the floor. RadiMo disappeared down the hole and emerged again a moment later from another opening.

Rieka watched while he sniffed the air. Noting the arch of what she could see of his back, she realized she'd never actually seen an entire Bourne. Computer images, yes, but never a whole living being outside a *skiff*. They were tubular, warm-blooded creatures that looked something like an otter, she decided, but with very little fur. In fact, the only hair she could see on his deep brown body was a fluff emanating from each ear and a sort of goatee below his pointy chin. RadiMo had huge eyes, dark enough brown to be considered black, but the things that most fascinated Rieka were his hands.

Bournes had eight-fingered hands, not paws. Four fingers stood out straight and two struck out the back, similar to that of birds. This opposition of digits gave them an amazing ability to grasp things. The last pair of fingers stretched over the top of the forward-facing ones. Thus, they could manipulate objects while clinging to cave walls, stalagmites, or whatever happened to offer a fingerhold. When it came to the messages emanating from their consoles, a Bourne could type faster than the machine could speak.

When the small being finished sniffing, Rieka asked, "And how are you, Herald RadiMo? How is your mate, RagiMo?"

"This creature is well," the voice replied, its sweet, child-like tone close to what Rieka figured a Bourne might actually sound like, though she'd long ago stopped trying to anthropomorphize things. "And RagiMo finds health in the birthing ring with others preparing for the event. She would ask your health."

"I am well, thank you," Rieka replied. "And I would congratulate you on your kits."

"Their arrival is not for many days, yet, though they may arrive before I return home."

Rieka nodded and sat in the chair closest to RadiMo's present position. "Alexi tells me you have been helping us plan three new cities."

"This is true."

"I understand your wish to survey the areas for the purpose of mining gemstones. It is my pleasure to assist in negotiating the contract with the Bourne."

"Rubies are cold fire."

Rieka offered a slight smile and glanced at Wang, still standing just inside the door. She had no clue what RadiMo had meant. "I'm sure. Are you interested in any others?"

"Sapphires have the warmth of water," he said.

"Yes." She waited a moment for him to speak again, then said, "You have been here on Earth many days, Radi-Mo. How much longer do you think you'll stay? When will the work be finished?"

"This is a question," the voice said. "RadiMo seeks great opportunities. Departure will wait until after the Reaffirmation."

At least another two weeks, Rieka guessed. "Earth has always been a place which offers opportunities. I hope you find what you are looking for. May I ask to have your report on the excavations of the New Subcities—Moscow, Beijing, and Brasilia?"

"You may ask."

Not sure he'd agreed with her request, but not wanting

to insult him, either, Rieka smiled softly. Offending him by pressing the point wouldn't do her any good.

She meant to ask about his plans for actually mining the gems, but RadiMo, apparently, felt the meeting had concluded. After a few parting words, he scurried back down into the *skiff*'s bowels and came up facing the door. A few adjustments of his console and he'd negotiated his way back out. Silently Rieka recalled Alexi's warning. What RadiMo had chosen *not* to say was just as important as what he had.

Wang closed the door and turned to her. "Funny little guy," he offered, "but I guess I liked him."

Rieka shook her head, laughing. "How diplomatic of you, Hong Wang-Chi," she said, trying not to sound too disapproving since her own response to RadiMo was almost identical. "I'm so glad you waited until he left to share your opinion."

NINE

Jeniper stood near the window, feeling distinctly on edge. Late this afternoon, the *Prospectus* had arrived with Herald Degahv aboard, and she had been invited to dine with Captains Marteen and DeVark, Rieka and Alexi.

But socializing with powerful people didn't bother her half as much as the latest message she'd received from Jonik. He had actually followed her to Earth. He expected her to meet him in an old mining village northeast of Canberra. Bywong, he'd called it. Before the Collision, it had been a tourists' point of interest, if one was interested in panned-out gold mines. She couldn't imagine the state it might be in after two centuries of neglect.

Questions bounced around in her mind. Why had he come? How had he paid for his ticket? What purpose did it serve to keep pestering her? She'd already told him he'd get no money.

Jeniper turned as Rieka entered the suite with her three male companions. "Jen, there you are. Why weren't you at the reception this afternoon?"

Jeniper smiled and stepped closer. "I got there a little late—another problem with the TechLine supplier at Damascus—but I did attend," she replied. "I must have spoken to half the people there. You just weren't one of them."

"I've been working you like a dog, I know," Rieka said, her expression concerned. Jeniper wondered how one worked a dog, but didn't think it prudent to ask. "But once we settle in New SubDenver, you'll be able to hire a decent staff. Then you'll only have me to deal with."

Jeniper saw a smirk appear on Rieka's face and nodded at the implication. "You're not a bad boss."

Rieka chuckled. "Compared to whom?"

She intended no response to that question, and apparently Rieka wasn't looking for one. Instead, the Human woman turned and gestured toward an Aurian in a Fleet uniform standing near Captain Marteen. A silver stripe ran down his arm, indicating the rank of captain as well. "Robet, if you're not too immersed over there, there's someone I'd like you to meet."

The man excused himself from his discussion, turned, and walked toward them. Jeniper felt a *ribah* flip deep in her chest as she looked at him. Red hair, ice-pale eyes, and the most attractive row of bibbets she'd ever seen. And apparently either he didn't care about his image, or didn't choose to flaunt it. He smiled easily at them as he approached.

Rieka extended her hand, and he took it. "Jeniper, I'd like you to meet an old friend, Captain Robet DeVark. Robet, this is my Planetary Adjutant, Jeniper Tarrik."

"A pleasure, Miss Tarrik," the captain said. He extended his right hand in the typical Earth welcome. Impressed, she took it, and he gripped her hand firmly. "A Human custom, I know," he told her. "But when on any Commonwealth planet, one should assume the local etiquette. Don't you think?"

Jeniper smiled as he let her hand go, and the warmth of his palm lingered. "I think, Captain, that your primary purpose in this particular handshake is in deference to Mrs. Degahv."

She noticed his bibbets darken to mauve and felt her own darken in turn. Rieka, apparently oblivious, laughed and clapped him on the shoulder. "I told you she was sharp, Robet."

"Sharp as a *tack,* was the term," he said, looking both entertained and embarrassed.

"Mmm," Rieka replied, quirking an eyebrow. "I suppose I might have said something like that." Jeniper watched as Rieka turned back to her. "Don't mind Robet's mouth, he often regrets what he says."

"I should think a Fleet captain would be in control at all

times," Jeniper found herself saying, glancing again at the captain's bibbets. They'd faded to pink.

"All times," he agreed, smiling. "Please call me Robet."

"Well, I'll leave you two to get better acquainted," Rieka told them. "And I expect you to discuss things other than your association with me." She looked pointedly at Robet. "Dinner should be ready in a minute. You can go in and sit down, if you like. I'll collect Triscoe and Alexi."

Though she'd originally expected to feel somewhat self-conscious at dinner, Jeniper found it the opposite. Robet DeVark regaled her with stories about Rieka and Triscoe, many of which were of great interest to Alexi as well. Her former boss looked tired, Jeniper decided, and noticed Rieka inquiring as to his comfort several times. She wondered if his health had anything to do with his retirement, but knew better than to ask such a personal question at the table.

Jonik's call still buzzing in the back of her thoughts, Jeniper reluctantly declined Robet's invitation to visit the *Prospectus* after dinner. Taking in his disappointed expression, she looked him in the eye.

"I have an appointment, Robet. But I would love to see your ship, another time."

"Sure. Can I walk you out to the taxis, then?"

"There's really no need—"

"It isn't a bother, Jeniper," he insisted. "And I thought I'd walk a bit after that meal." He tapped his stomach. "The *ribah* aren't what they used to be. My third's been giving me trouble for months. Usually a walk settles it."

She nodded and allowed him to accompany her down to ground level, and then outside. Jeniper decided she liked him rather more than she thought wise. He was charming, witty, and handsome. She particularly liked his bibbet pattern. And the way he smiled. And the way he looked at her.

When a taxi rolled up and its door slid open, Jeniper turned. "It's been very nice meeting you, Robet," she told him, noting the way his pale blue eyes swept over her face. "I hope I'll get to see you again sometime."

"The pleasure's been mine," he replied. "And you can count on it."

She smiled and stepped into the vehicle. "Bywong village, please," she told the computer. It responded with an affirmative tone when she slipped her bank card into the slot, and Jeniper breathed a small sigh of relief. Jonik hadn't said if this place could be reached by city services. She looked up and waved as the door closed and felt a jolt of delight run through her when Robet winked and waved back.

Thoughts of Captain DeVark stayed with her until she reached the dilapidated remains of Bywong. Ordering the vehicle to wait until she returned, Jeniper got out and looked around. Though lit by three tall lamps in the parking area, every structure was dark inside. All looked as if they had suffered too many years of neglect to stand even a moment more. With the car humming pleasantly behind her, Jeniper spotted a modern-looking module-type building. Glancing around once more, she headed toward it.

The door opened when she turned the handle. "Hello? Jonik?" And waiting a few seconds and receiving no reply, she stepped over the threshold and peered about in the darkness. Littered with construction materials and tools, the structure looked to be a covered work area—for whom, she had no idea. Perhaps, with the expected rush of visitors to Earth, the Australian Administrator's office had decided to renovate the village into a modern tourist attraction.

A draft came through the open door, and Jeniper shivered. Right now it held no attraction at all.

"Jonik, are you here? Answer me, you two-toned *bimoosh*."

Name calling had always unnerved him, but it did not have any effect, that night. Wondering if she had misunderstood him and had come to the wrong place, or perhaps arrived on the wrong evening, Jeniper carefully moved toward what looked like a computer workstation.

As she came around the desk, she noticed a blinking light. The station was functional. Another step and she realized the console's screen had been set to "suspend," not "off." The small oval cursor shone steadily in the lower left corner.

Not knowing what else to do, Jeniper touched a key. She sucked in a small breath when the screen sprang to life, though that was exactly what she'd expected it to do.

Jonik's face appeared, and for once, he did not even wear

his counterfeit smile. "Jeniper," he began, "I wasn't able to get here tonight. I hope you understand."

Not knowing whether or not she understood, or even wanted to, Jeniper impatiently muttered, "Get on with it."

"I need to warn you—she's coming to Earth. You're not safe, Jen. I don't think you believed me before, so please, believe me, now. She's not giving me any slack, and I'm sure she's able to make good on her threats. She's got people on her payroll everywhere. Please be very, very careful. Wherever you go—whatever you do, take a weapon with you. I'll try to find a way to meet with you as soon as I can. Until then, take care of yourself."

When the screen went blank, momentarily blinding her in the darkness, Jeniper felt all three of her *ribah* flip, one after the other. She had to force herself to let go the console and walk back to the door. Trembling with both cold and fear, Jeniper hurried back to the taxi. As the vehicle turned and headed toward Canberra, she could only hope Jonik was safe and that he'd try to contact her again.

Standing in front of Parliament House on Canberra's Capitol Hill, Rieka took a deep breath and stepped to Alexi's side. She raised her right hand and rested her left on the book he'd placed on the podium.

"I, Rieka Amelia Pirez Degahv, do solemnly swear to uphold the rights of Humans, once native citizens of Earth, a member world in the Commonwealth of Planets; to further the interests of the Human planet, Earth, and to promote peace and goodwill among all Commonwealth residents.

"As Earth Herald, I will make myself an advocate for Humanity. I promise to promote my people in every possible instance, both on and off the homeworld. And I promise to make myself as accessible as possible—so that any Commonwealth citizen, Human or not, might use my office to secure assistance, in whatever form, from the local or planetary authorities."

She lowered her right hand and looked out on the thousands that had gathered on the lawn. Her uncle slipped the huge, sealed volume from beneath his left hand and set it on a small shelf inside the podium. Then, he said, "As Earth Herald, I, Alexi Mikhail Bordeux Degahv, do hereby transfer all powers of my position to my niece, Rieka Amelia Pirez Degahv, who has sworn to uphold this office in the name of Earth and Humanity."

He then gripped her by the shoulders and kissed both her cheeks. When he hugged her, she squeezed him back and felt the crowd's approving applause roll over them.

"Congratulations," he said, offering her his hand. She shook it and turned to Triscoe who nodded. He caressed her cheek, then leaned and kissed it.

I am very proud, he told her, the thought infused faintly with a golden hue.

Alexi had turned back to the assembly and lifted the huge book sealed in cryofilm from the lectern. "As tradition dictates, I turn over the possession of this, the Commonwealth Constitution, including all amendments, to the current Earth Herald—Rieka Degahv."

Another wave of applause swelled as Rieka accepted the book, now over two centuries old. She cradled it carefully in her arms and stepped closer to the microphone.

"Fellow Humans, brothers and sisters of the Commonwealth, tradition dictates that I give a speech now, promising great challenges ahead and providing assurances of the bounty that is sure to come from our united efforts. That speech I will not give today."

A low rumbling emanated from the audience, and Rieka squeezed the book tighter. "For the last two centuries we have struggled with the greatest challenge a planet and its citizens can face. We were orphans, existing in the shadows of those on whose planet we lived. Now, we seek the rewards of a habitable homeworld where peace and prosperity are available to all. Fourteen days from today we will rededicate Earth. I urge you to join me then and celebrate all that Humanity has to offer."

She waited while the applause swelled, then faded before she continued. "This planet owes the Commonwealth a great deal. I have challenged myself to make sure that debt is repaid within my lifetime. But while we attend to our finances and the bottom line, let us not forget the reason any of us are here at all." She paused for effect and looked out on the people.

"The Human spirit, my friends, is dauntless. Since before recorded history, it has conquered disease, despair, and devastation on an order so great as to be almost incomprehensible. Let us look forward from this day to a brighter future. One where we can celebrate who we are and what we have become.

"I invite you all to visit the Site and to attend the Reaffirmation in Damascus. Until then, be well."

The crowd applauded again, and Rieka couldn't tell whether it was for the content or the short duration of her speech. She smiled and waved for several minutes. When it became almost embarrassing to accept their acclaim, she nodded and waved one last time, then turned and stepped down off the dias.

Wang was there, along with a half dozen guards. They surrounded her as she made her way inside Parliament House, followed by Triscoe. Alexi, and Jeniper. The only downside of the day, Rieka thought, was that Setana and Ker hadn't been able to be there.

"That was excellent. Excellent," Alexi told her, as they strolled to the InterMAT terminal. "The people love you, my dear."

"That remains to be seen, Uncle," she told him. "I can hardly declare success after five minutes in office." She heard a soft chuckle in her mind and glanced at Triscoe. He seemed to be trying desperately not to smile, but a dimple showed, nonetheless.

"But the people consider you a hero," Alexi insisted. "They know already you are a Degahv who will fight for them. And they respect this."

"Respect is good," she admitted, casting a glance at her now official Planetary Adjutant, who had looked grim all morning. "I suppose veneration will come in time."

Jeniper nodded. "Possibly," she agreed.

"It was a joke, Jen," Rieka told her.

"Of course."

Sensing something wasn't right, Rieka leaned toward Jeniper, and said softly, "We've got three hours before the party tonight. I'll want to talk to you before then."

"Of course," she repeated.

Tightening her grip on the book she'd inherited, Rieka sighed and entered the InterMAT chamber with Triscoe. Something had happened to Jeniper after dinner last night. She knew it as well as she knew the Earth orbited the Sun.

And just as immutably, she could tell Jeniper didn't want her to know what was wrong.

An hour later, Rieka sat at a writing table near a window in her hotel suite. Wang lounged on a nearby sofa, talking quietly to one of his men on his private comlink. The datapad she'd been using waited patiently while she looked out at Canberra, imagining how things must have been two centuries before.

The door chime sounded, bringing her back to the present.

"Come," she said, her voice drowned out by Wang's baritone as he spoke the same word. When Jeniper came in the door, Rieka added, "We've got to stop doing that, Wang." He nodded agreeably but said nothing.

To Rieka's surprise, Jeniper stayed near the entry. "Herald," Jeniper began, "I have some people with me who would like to meet you."

"Really?" Rieka couldn't imagine what Jeniper meant. "I'm sure I don't have anything scheduled before the party."

"You'll want to see them," Jeniper told her. To Wang she added, "They've already been cleared by your staff." Jeniper opened the door wider and stepped back to accommodate five young people.

"This is the Blue Planet Future's Performance Committee," Jeniper announced. "Herald Degahv, I am proud to introduce you to Dale, Samantha, Po, Maria, and Kathy."

Rieka looked into the most hopeful faces she'd ever seen. "I'm so glad you came," she said, smiling as she shook each of their hands in turn. "Come in and sit down."

Leading the way to the living area, Rieka gestured for the young people to make themselves comfortable. She offered refreshments, but they declined. Rieka pulled a chair away from the dining table and sat. "So, tell me a little about yourselves," she said.

"I'm Po," the littlest one began, his dark almond-shaped eyes barely visible below straight, black bangs. "I'm eight. My parents are electronics. They're in New SubAtlanta. Kathy wants to marry Hans."

"I do not!" an older girl snapped. "And your parents are electricians, not electronics. I'm Kathy, Herald. I'm thirteen, and I sing alto. My parents are wheat growers here in Australia. And I do not want to marry Hans. I just like him, that's all."

Rieka nodded sagely. "I understand completely how others mistake things about us, Kathy," she said. "And I'm glad you took the time out of your busy schedule to come and visit me." She looked at the three other young people. "And, Dale, isn't it?" she asked the redheaded boy. "What do you do?"

"I'm a dancer. And I get to be assistant stage manager sometimes."

"That sounds challenging."

"Yes, ma'am."

"And your name is Maria?" Rieka asked of the pretty, dark-haired girl sitting next to Po.

"Yes, ma'am. Maria Fortua. I sing soprano. I'm fourteen, and I don't have a dad anymore, but my mother works in the Seven Seas pavilion at World Zoo. Her name is Dr. Angela Fortua."

Rieka nodded, and softly said, "I'm sure you're very proud of her—just as she's proud of you. I don't have a dad either, and I know that can be tough, sometimes." Maria studied her hands and shrugged. "What do you like best about being in the Blue Planet Future?"

Maria thought about that for a moment, then said, "Coming home. I don't mind performing and traveling to the other planets. But I like Earth the best."

Grinning, Rieka said, "Me too." She turned to the last member of the group. "And you are Samantha?"

"Yes, ma'am. Samantha Mackay. I sing soprano and dance. I'm seventeen and my family lives just outside of Winnipeg—so when I'm not traveling with the BPF, I live at home."

Rieka nodded, studying the blue-eyed blond. "Jeniper called you the Performance Committee. What is that?"

Samantha shrugged. "We get to help design the shows. And then we critique the performances during final rehearsals. The show changes every six months. That's how long any one of us can be on the committee."

"So you rotate the privilege. That sounds fair." She looked at the youngest boy. "Po, you're the littlest. What do you think about all this?"

"The committee is boring," he replied seriously. "Even more boring than lessons. But it makes you learn how to be fair—'cause if you're mad at someone, you have the power—and then they have the power when it's their turn. You know?"

"I think so," Rieka told him.

Jeniper stepped closer, and said, "I promised Mrs. Gambo to have you back in an hour. Sorry to cut short the visit, but we need to get moving or you'll be late."

Rieka stood as the young people rose and followed Jeniper to the door. "It was very nice to meet all of you. I'm looking forward to your performance tonight."

They followed Jeniper into the hall, then Maria stopped and turned. "Good-bye, Mrs. Degahv." It looked as though she meant to say more, but she only shrugged.

"If you want, you can write to me on the comnet," Rieka said. "Jeniper has the address."

Maria's expression brightened. "Really?"

"Knowing how she'd struggled at that age without her father, Rieka nodded. "Really."

Have I told you you look quite delectable in that dress? The words, wrapped in a warm, rosy color, came to her mind above the noise of the milling crowd.

Triscoe, standing some distance away, looked up from his conversation with Administrator Stafford. Rieka made a face at him when his eyes dropped to her low neckline, then resumed her conversation with Wint Zevak, a Vekyan hydroponics supplier. She couldn't fault him for inquiring as to Earth's possible needs, though she wished he'd be a little less dogmatic.

"Well actually, Zevak—and you probably already know this—we do a great deal of agro production on the surface," she told him, hoping she used the right words so as to avoid any misunderstanding. Some Vekyans could be painfully literal. "But there are certain products, most notably those staples in the Vekyan and Aurian diets, that can't be produced without artificial cultivation—here on Earth, that is. I can't see why we wouldn't set up a few test labs in a couple of subcities."

"This would be acceptable," Zevak said. He uncurled his

tongue and carefully speared the piece of fruit floating in his drink.

"I'll have to speak to the architects and overall designers, of course," she went on, "to make sure it's feasible to plan such a facility into the structure. And I'm afraid I just don't have time for that in my schedule for at least three weeks. But I can tell you it wouldn't hurt to invest a little thought in this. Set up a meeting with my adjutant," Rieka advised, wondering if Zevak would have better luck pinning Jeniper down. Probably not.

"Thank you for the information, Herald," Zevak told her. "I will have my designers draw up some preliminary plans." He bowed slightly, dipping his great head toward her, then stepped back and disappeared into the crowd. She noticed Alexi, seated for once, in a lively discussion with Dzan, the Boolian Herald, who stood towering over him. Wondering at that odd pair, she scanned the crowd until she spied Jeniper at the buffet table.

Irritated that Jeniper had managed to avoid her after her visit with the children, Rieka slowly made her way through the mass of bodies. When she finally got close enough, she touched the Aurian woman on the arm. "I need to speak to you."

Jeniper turned, a worried look crossing her brow before she brightened. Rieka thought her half smile looked strained, but said nothing more.

"I'm just getting a bite to eat," Jeniper told her. "Can I get you something?"

"No. Thank you. All I want is to talk to you."

"Certainly." Jeniper scooped up a half dozen *kimbie* and set them on her plate. The large Aurian sea seeds, soaked in brine until they burst, rolled about, and Rieka wondered if any would fall off the plate before they reached the table. Jeniper collected her fluted glass and turned. "Which way?"

Rieka was about to suggest they head for her table when an uproar sounded across the room. At least two voices raised above the noise from the milling crowd, which now hushed considerably.

"You didn't plan this, did you?" Rieka jibed. She signaled Jeniper to follow and looked around to find Wang and several of his people hurrying toward the disturbance.

The crowd parted before her as they stormed toward the angry voices. An Oph female and a Human man continued to argue despite the fact they were causing a scene.

"What is going on here?" she demanded as her bodyguard stepped up to her shoulder. She glanced at Wang, her look telling him she'd handle this, and hoped he had the sense to behave.

The man turned from his opponent and had the decency to look embarrassed when he recognized her. "I am Luis Mendoza, Herald," he said with a curt bow. "I beg your forgiveness for creating this disturbance."

Jeniper tried to interject something, but Rieka raised her hand, and said, "We'll see about that, Mr. Mendoza. What is the problem?"

"I am a farmer. North American continent. And this Oph is Grulah. She is from Aurie's Quadrant Two."

"A farmer as well, I suppose."

"Of course," Grulah told her. She looked down her nose at Rieka before glaring up at Wang.

Taking in the silent affront, Rieka could understand how Mendoza had gotten into an argument with this Oph. She looked back at him. "And what seems to be the problem?" she repeated.

"Grulah has challenged that her beef is of better quality than that which I, or anyone else, produces on Earth. Herald Degahv—cattle evolved on Earth! How can they not be—"

"—yes, I understand." She glanced again at Wang, who responded by rolling his eyes. Though this threat to honor could escalate, he obviously didn't think it likely. The most important thing she could do, she realized, was not offend anyone. "Perhaps we could discuss this later. My adjutant here, Miss Tarrik, can schedule an appointment."

"There is nothing to discuss, Herald Degahv," Grulah spit. "Aurie has been the premiere producer of all agricultural products for centuries. Our animals are the best to be found anywhere. To imply that beef from Earth could possibly be superior—is ludicrous."

"There, you see!" Mendoza shouted.

"Yes, I do see," Rieka told him quietly. She allowed a look of disgust to mar her expression in the hope that these two would realize they had chosen the wrong time and place for such a debate. "I see a great deal, Mr. Mendoza. And so do all my guests."

Mendoza suddenly looked contrite. "I beg your pardon, ma'am."

"You may beg my pardon—and that of everyone else here, but the problem isn't solved, is it?" She looked back at Grulah and noticed Triscoe standing not too far away. "While I applaud your loyalty to your profession, I remind you that this venue is no place for such rivalry."

"I understand," Mendoza said softly.

"Now Grulah, I'm sure you do realize the creatures to which you refer, did, as Mr. Mendoza has pointed out, evolve on Earth. I will grant that in two hundred years both Oph and Aurian animal-husbandry techniques may have improved the original stock. But that remains to be seen." She turned to Mendoza. "I suggest that you postpone this debate and let the consumer decide who has the better product."

"Of course," Mendoza echoed, his dark eyes flashing the challenge.

Grulah took a deep breath and held it for what seemed like an interminable amount of time. Finally, she exhaled, "I shall look forward to proving my point," she said. "If you will excuse me." She bowed slightly, then headed for the door. A security man followed at a discreet distance.

"My sincerest apologies, Herald," Mendoza offered, inclining his head toward her. A relieved sigh deflated him for a moment before he puffed out his chest again, this time with pride. "I too, will look forward to—seeing her proved wrong!"

Rieka studied him for a moment. "Mr. Hong's men will accompany you to the exit. Good evening, Mr. Mendoza."

"Good evening, ma'am," he said respectfully. "It was a pleasure to meet you—despite the circumstances." A huge blond woman took his arm and turned him toward the door.

"Wasn't that fun?" Triscoe asked her as he stepped closer.

"Can't remember when I had a better time," she replied dryly.

"It looks as though we're secure for now, Boss," Wang told her. She could tell when he frowned and put his finger to his ear that he was using his own security net. "Uh-huh. Okay. Thanks." Wang looked back at her. "The Blue Planet Future is ready. Could I get you to return to your table?"

Flanked by Wang, Jeniper, and Triscoe, Rieka returned to her chair. They seated themselves, and she leaned toward Jeniper. "Later, I mean it."

Triscoe nudged her as the youth band struck up their first song. *What is wrong?*

Something's going on with Jeniper. I haven't been able to talk to her.

Something bad?

I don't know.

They listened to the next song, a duet performed by Samantha and a talented young man. Rieka was glad Alexi had endorsed the group. The Blue Planet Future, made up of youth who had been born on Earth while their parents readied it for repopulation, had become ambassadors in their own right.

When the duet ended, Wang moved closer and touched her arm. "There seems to be a problem with RadiMo," he said.

"What now?" she mumbled, and excused herself from the table. Po and a group of the younger children lined themselves up and started to sing.

"What's the problem?" she asked the Centauri attendant stationed near the Bournese Herald's *skiff*.

Wang caught up with her as the man replied, "I don't know, ma'am. Herald RadiMo went down a hole, squealed terribly, and switched on his red light."

"Do you have a remote control for the *skiff*?" Wang asked. The attendant nodded. "Then let's take it out into the hall before this song is finished."

She watched him guide the floating platform out a pair of double doors, while at the same time listening to the Future's singers and a muffled but distinct Bournese wail.

Once out in the hall's quiet, Rieka leaned close to the *skiff*. "Herald RadiMo, it is Herald Degahv. Are you ill?"

She heard a series of snorts and clicks but could make nothing out. Softly Wang said, "The translator boards are all inside the unit."

Rieka nodded. "RadiMo, I do not speak Bournese. You must translate for me to understand the difficulty."

Slowly, a portal opened and he crept toward her. She backed away from the hole and stood at a discreet distance. "The noise," the synthetic voice finally said.

"Is it quiet enough here, or would you rather depart?"

"Departure is preferred."

Rieka nodded and offered him a soft smile. "Your comfort and happiness are my concern. Do not trouble yourself to stay."

His fingers moved quickly over the board. "RadiMo thanks Herald Degahv for her graciousness."

"Anytime. I hope you enjoyed the party before the music started."

"It proved . . . interesting. Good evening." He slunk back down the hole, and the attendant accompanied the *skiff* down the hall.

Rieka heaved a sigh and looked up at Wang. "Aliens." She chuckled, shaking her head. "I'll never figure them out."

TEN

Triscoe watched Rieka walk across the suite's bedroom, marveling at how a mere garment could capture his attention. "Where did you get that dress?"

"You're awfully interested in my wardrobe, recently," she commented. Then, after glancing his way, answered, "Rhonique. There's a little shop not far from the Fleet Administration Building. On Senate Boulevard."

"Perhaps you should open an account there," he told her. There must have been something in his voice that caused her to chuckle. "What?"

"Triscoe, dear heart, I love you, but I don't ever think you're going to understand the Human concept of romance."

Indignant, he stood straighter. "And what gives you that idea?"

"Obviously, this dress—or rather *me* in it, is something you find attractive."

"Almost to the point of distraction, if you must know." He watched her breasts push against the fabric when she heaved a sigh and wondered whether or not she'd worn anything under the shimmery, deep blue material.

"It's the neckline," she told him. "Anyway, the point is—if you find me sexy in this thing," she lifted the skirt a bit and let it fall, "and want to open an account at the store where I bought it—that's fine."

He frowned. Rieka had completely lost him, again. "Didn't I just say that?"

"No. You said *I* should open an account there."

Confused, he sat and nudged off his shoes. "Why . . . shouldn't you?"

"Because *you* should."

Triscoe dropped his chin into his hand to think. Finally, he gave up. Again. "I fail to understand why I would wish to open an account in a women's dress shop. I have no intention of wearing a dress—or is that *your* idea of romance?" he finished warily, hoping humor might actually enable them to communicate.

He watched her fidget and make a strange, disgruntled noise. "No. Don't be ridiculous."

Triscoe felt as if he were in his first conversation with a Boo. Nothing followed or made any sense at all. "I think *you're* being ridiculous. How would I know what style to choose? What size?"

"You like this one, don't you?"

"Unquestionably, but I don't see why you would want more of the same." He found himself shaking his head, again.

Rieka sat down across from him and leaned forward, her elbows on her knees. Her eyes twinkled, silently challenging him to grasp an obviously Human concept. "You pick out presents for me—to please you. I'll buy things for you that please me. Get it?"

He took a moment to think it through. "This sounds like a paradox. I should buy things for me to give to you. And this is romantic?"

"No. Yes." She made a face. "Well, not the way you put it."

He liked her confused scowl. At least it made him feel as if they'd found an equal, if not precarious, footing. "Perhaps," he suggested, "we should just both go around without any clothes and the problem will be solved."

"Very funny."

He sighed. "Really, I am not that dense. I believe I understand the concept, now, although I am skeptical."

"I'll take what I can get."

Triscoe was smiling softly at her, his eyes consuming everything about her from the jeweled comb in her hair to her satin slippers, when his TC clicked. He switched it on. "Marteen."

"Saw you leave the party a little early," Robet's voice reverberated in his head. "Wanted to say good-bye before I left for Dani."

"That was thoughtful, Robet." He watched Rieka put her hand to her mouth.

"Tell him I'm sorry I didn't get to say good-bye," she whispered.

"Rieka says good-bye, Robet. And she'll try to find a way to spend some time with you when you return for the Reaffirmation."

"Ugh! I can't," she huffed. "My schedule is—" He waved at her to be quiet.

"Tell her I understand."

"He understands, love."

Rieka rolled her eyes and went to the bar for a beverage.

"Anyway," Robet's voice continued, "I missed Jeniper, too. I really like her, Tris. She's a fascinating woman."

"Yes, I suppose she is," he agreed uneasily.

"I know you're leaving tonight, too, but I thought you might pass on a message. I had intended to speak to her before I left."

"And what's the message?"

"See you in two weeks."

"That's it?"

"Yes. I didn't want to seem to pushy. I don't think she'd appreciate that."

"That's rather thoughtful of you," Triscoe told him dryly. "I'll ask Rieka to give her the message. Anything else?"

"No. I suppose I'll see you in two weeks, too."

"Undoubtedly. Marteen, out."

Robet switched off his end of the communication, and Triscoe leaned back into the sofa's cushions. "Robet asks you to tell Jeniper he'll see her in two weeks—and he's sorry for not telling her good-bye."

"I'll be happy to. I think it's very sweet," Rieka said.

"You know I don't approve of your pairing them up."

"Yes." Her gray-blue eyes flashed at him, and she lifted her chin. "I could tell you weren't overjoyed when I sat them together at dinner last night, but for heaven's sake, Triscoe, it's been months. Robet's a big boy. He's bounced back from that . . . that leap of stupidity. Jeniper is a nice, safe girl. And she's Aurian. They'll get along just fine, given a chance."

"A chance is all he needs. You know his reputation."

"Stop. That isn't nice. Robet is capable of a meaningful relationship. He's friends with us, after all."

Triscoe closed his eyes and rolled his head on his shoulders to ease the tightness in his neck. "I don't feel particularly 'nice' at the moment," he told her. "You've berated me over this 'romance' concept—again. I can't seem to fathom why I should buy clothes for you to wear—or vice versa. You've gone against my better judgment in pairing Robet and Jeniper. And now, I have to leave you when I would much rather—"

He heard her soft footfall and drew a deep breath when she put her finger on his lips. She then traded her lips for her finger and slid into his lap. "Me too," she said finally, her voice uncharacteristically deep. "Let's make a truce for now," she told him, nibbling her way along his chin toward his ear. "When you leave, we still may not agree, but at least we'll both be . . . satisfied."

Triscoe slipped his fingers beneath the skirt's long slit. "Deal."

Rieka tried to shove her way around Wang as he blocked the cockpit door. "I said let me pass, Wang-Chi."

"And I said you are not going to pilot this craft."

She huffed and put her hands on her hips. "I've already cleared it with the pilot. And you've had your people go over the ship. We're all going to be as safe as if we were home in bed. Now, *let me pass.*"

"You said you'd take orders from me," he persisted.

"You're forgetting about the part where my life might be in danger. It isn't, here. For heaven's sake, we're only taking this tiny shuttle on a puddle jump." Rieka waved a hand in his face to help make her point.

"You are not cleared to pilot this ship, Herald."

Rieka set her jaw. "Actually, I am. I have a current Commonwealth pilot's license for everything from a shuttle like this—to the *Prodigy.* And for your information, Mr. Hong Wang-Chi," she added, using his complete name the way a parent would to an obnoxious child, "in addition to being Earth Herald and your boss, I am *still* a Fleet captain."

Knowing it would take him a second to digest that interesting tidbit, Rieka rushed past him. Lieutenant Verde looked over her shoulder and saluted.

"Welcome aboard the *Kimbell,* Herald," she said. "She's small, but she's a good little ship."

"Why thank you, Lieutenant," Rieka said, throwing a glance at Wang as she returned the salute and assumed the captain's chair. Verde had already moved to the copilot's seat. "I haven't flown one of these in a couple of years. Please don't allow my position in the Fleet or the Council of Ten to intimidate you. If I forget to do something—I expect you to tell me."

Verde looked skeptical. "I doubt that, ma'am. You've been piloting ships for years."

Rieka's laugh sounded more like a sigh. "I'll take that as a compliment."

Wang hovered in the cockpit door and Verde glanced at him. "Is there something I can do for you, sir?" she asked.

"No," he grumbled, glaring at Rieka.

"Really, Wang," she offered, doing the preflight check, "you're safe with me. I promise I won't crash the *Kimbell.*"

"You'd better not. Half your staff is along. And we've got another four passengers, too."

Rieka happily tapped the console and studied the systems reports. She hadn't realized how much she missed spaceflight, and no amount of Wang's grumbling would dent her enjoyment of it. "Which reminds me," she told him over her shoulder, "send Jeniper up here as soon as we level off in the exosphere." She glanced at Verde. "About ten minutes from now."

Rieka watched Wang's reluctant return to the cabin, then waited, her fingers poised over the controls, until Verde announced, "We're cleared." A moment later the *Kimbell* shot down the short runway and angled up through the clouds.

When they hit the first elevation mark, twenty kilometers, Verde said, "You're doing great, Captain. Maybe you should've let that big guy stay in here and watch."

"Mr. Hong?" Rieka chuckled. "I admit he sometimes takes the job a bit too seriously—but then again, that's one of the reasons I hired him."

They continued on in companionable silence, broken only by Lieutenant Verde's one-sided communications with EarthCom Asia. Once the shuttle leveled off in the exosphere, the door opened to reveal Jeniper. "Come on in,

Jen," Rieka said, waving her into the cramped space. "I'd like you to meet your flight crew, Lieutenant Allana Verde and Captain Herald Rieka Degahv."

"No wonder Wang's having a fit back there," Jeniper told her, smiling. "You shouldn't be flying this ship."

"I'm the most experienced person aboard."

"Maybe so, but really . . . it's . . . it's not right. You're the Earth Herald now. You need to consider that."

"I did. For about four seconds." Rieka checked her readouts and nodded to herself. "Verde, I wonder if I could speak to Jeniper alone—if you don't mind. It'll only take a minute or two."

Verde touched a few controls. "Certainly. We're just now coming over the Indian Ocean. I'll be back in about fifteen minutes." She eased out of her chair and, with the help of her magnetic shoes, changed positions with Jeniper.

When the door closed with a soft click, Rieka noted the dusky pink of Jeniper's bibbets, and said gently, "Is everything okay? You seem a little tense."

Jeniper fidgeted and stared at the instruments on her control panel. "A little. The job is new to me. I want everything to be just right."

Rieka nodded and checked their altitude. "I can empathize with that. If you get overwhelmed, say something, Jen. There's no use suffering in silence."

"Yes. Of course."

Sensing that Jeniper had just improvised a generic excuse for her behavior, Rieka decided being subtle might get her closer to the truth. "How'd it go with Robet the other night?"

"Who?"

"Captain DeVark."

"Oh. Well, the captain is quite charming—as I'm sure you know. We chatted about a variety of topics. He is easy to talk to."

"That he is," Rieka agreed. "I noticed you and he left together after dinner," she coaxed, hoping Jeniper would offer an opinion of him.

"Really?" Jeniper asked, sounding more confused than wary. Her bibbets darkened a shade or two. "Oh. Oh, yes."

Now they were getting somewhere. "Look, I don't mean to pry into your private life Jen. That isn't what this conversation is about. But ever since that evening when we all had dinner together . . . you have to admit you've been acting strangely. If Robet said or did anything improper, I'd be glad to speak to him about it."

"Oh." Jeniper's expression shifted from confused to pensive. The bibbets lightened a notch. "Well, I wouldn't go so far as to call it . . . improper."

"He's pushy, I know. And he loves women. I apologize for anything he might have done to offend you." Encouraged by Jeniper's sympathetic expression, Rieka continued. "It was my idea to seat you together, Jen. The whole thing is entirely my fault."

"No, don't blame yourself, Rieka," Jeniper told her, relief obvious in her tone. "It was nothing. Really."

"You sure?"

"Yes. Absolutely." Rieka watched as Jeniper's bibbets faded to a very pale pink.

"Mmm. Well, in that case, I suppose I should relay his message. He apologized for not saying good-bye before he left—he looks forward to seeing you at the Reaffirmation ceremony."

"He told you that?"

Rieka nodded. "Actually, he told Triscoe. I don't have a TC anymore." She paused, trying to gauge Jeniper's mood. "So, it's okay, then?"

Jeniper turned, and Rieka saw the hopeful look in her pale blue eyes. "Yes. Yes, of course. Everything's fine."

Rieka gladly let Verde pilot the *Kimbell* as it made the descent over the Arabian Peninsula. Jeniper had returned to the passenger cabin, and Rieka had no desire to explain the landscape to anyone. She simply wanted to enjoy the view.

"Can we swing out over the Mediterranean before we land?" she asked.

"Sure, Herald," Verde replied.

Smiling softly at the appellation, Rieka leaned closer to the window. The water shone like a thin silver ribbon on the horizon. It widened as they approached, its deep blue mirroring the nearly cloudless sky.

"Crossing the thirtieth parallel now, Herald," Verde told

her. "The ruins of Cairo are about five hundred kilometers due west."

Rieka nodded and rested her chin in her hand, eyes scanning the horizon. Almost eight years had passed since she'd been here, and even in that short time things had changed. The desert seemed dotted with more agro-oases than she'd remembered. And she was almost sure the Char had reached the thirtieth parallel. When they neared the coast, Rieka realized she could see no burned sections amid the various croplands below. Her heart surged with a mixture of pride and relief.

As they shot out over the sea, Rieka noticed that their altitude had dropped considerably. "What's the alt?"

"Six kilometers."

She nodded absently, gazing at the deep blue Mediterranean below them. "I've seen enough water this morning. Swing back east over the mainland at the thirty-third parallel and drop to two kilometers."

"As we speak, Cap—Herald," Verde replied.

Rieka turned away slightly to hide her grin and felt the lieutenant's attention shift from the control panel to her, then back. A silent apology for almost calling her captain, she wondered—or hesitation at traveling over the actual impact site? A lot of people didn't like to look at the scar. For her, it was a reminder of just how long they'd suffered and how far they'd come.

Collision Gulf loomed before them on the horizon. "Slow forward speed to 250 kph." As Verde complied, the panorama before them shifted slightly and grew slowly.

This is how she'd always imagined it, Rieka realized. Riding the meteor's path. Sometimes she could even conjure it in her mind's eye—falling from the sky, plunging into the Mediterranean Sea, and ramming the coastline hard enough to change it forever.

Their speed, though slow, was too fast at this elevation for more than a quick look. Rieka saw waves breaking against the limestone cliffs, a waterfall, then scrub-covered mountains. The *Kimbell* swept over them, and Verde turned the ship south toward the long flat valley once farmed by Humans calling themselves Syrians.

They skirted the blast zone's edge and made their approach to Damascus. Now restored as a tourist base and historical point of interest, Rieka was sure this new, above-ground city would soon become Earth's focal point. She figured anyone visiting the planet, even businessmen and women, would eventually wind up here. Curious about Humanity's past, the Collision, and what had happened in its aftermath, they'd find all their answers, however incomplete, in Damascus's On-Site Museum.

It was the perfect place to hold the Reaffirmation.

After they set down in a shuttle parking facility, Rieka, Jeniper, and Wang walked across a short open space to the Chute that would take them to the terminal and waiting ground transport. Rieka breathed in the heat, the dry tang in the air, and a quality of freshness that invigorated her. "Wonderful, isn't it?"

"Amazing," Wang said before stepping forward and speaking to the person waiting at the Chute door.

"Amazing?" Jeniper asked.

Rieka purposefully said nothing. She waited while Wang finished with the attendant and ushered them into the Chute.

"Amazing how, Wang?" Jeniper repeated when they were under way.

"This place was completely devastated, Jen," he told her, waving his hands to indicate everything outside the Chute. "Gone. A century ago most everything around here was still black. The Char, they called it. Any place within five hundred kilometers of the Site. Burned. Even the ground itself. The restoration is amazing."

Jeniper nodded, apparently comprehending the project's immensity. She turned to Rieka. "And your father and uncle are responsible for the transformation."

Rieka found herself smiling wryly. "Not exactly." The Chute door opened and Wang stepped out. He looked around and signaled someone waiting a few paces away. The two men spoke, and he turned.

"This way, Herald." The ground transport waiting for them looked identical to the one they'd used in Canberra. When they'd settled in their seats, Rieka reached for her datapad and noticed Jeniper doing the same. Wang sat up front with the driver, watchful but relaxed.

The ride into Damascus took only a few minutes. Rieka managed to catch up on her notes and check the calendar before shutting down the datapad to look at the incredible city built to honor the many civilizations of man.

Nowhere else in the Commonwealth would Humans find such a firm foundation of their peoples' past. She saw a building that looked remarkably like the Parthenon, a mosque, a pyramid, and a three-story brick building among modern structures both short and tall. She saw tents of various types, all constructed of something far sturdier than the original woven or hide materials they resembled. There were thatched roofs, totem poles, and great, granite walls wearing parapets like jagged crowns adorning their corner towers.

They passed a huge domed structure, and, even from several blocks away, Rieka could identify it as the On-Site Museum. "We'll need to go there, Jen," Rieka told her, pointing toward its hulking blue form. "Make sure you schedule it sometime before we leave for the Senate meetings on Yadra."

Jeniper nodded and made a note on her small computer. "Did you want to do that before or after the World Zoo?"

"Doesn't matter. But I'm sure Wang'll probably want the entire facility closed to the public when we go—so try to find a time that won't be too invasive to their schedules."

Wang turned at the sound of his name. "It's nice to know I'm appreciated—or at least considered competent."

Rieka smiled. "Oh, you're appreciated, Wang-Chi—even if only for your scintillating conversation."

She watched him absorb her subtle barb, then laugh in that good-natured way she'd come to expect. Since their first meeting, Rieka had sensed that Hong Wang-Chi much preferred criticism to praise. Consequently, they got along quite well when she wrapped one in the other. It was like talking in code.

Watching him turn back toward the driver, Rieka couldn't recall meeting anyone else with hair so black it reflected a blue tint.

"That must be Olympic Stadium," Jeniper said.

Rieka looked left through the trees and glimpsed the immense structure. "The place seats ninety thousand people. How many tickets are left?"

Jeniper shook her head. "Earth NewsNet reported the Reaffirmation's ticket sales at 56 percent this morning."

Rieka sighed. It was almost as if a conspiracy brewed, intent on making the ceremony a circus. Low ticket sales, balky caterers, entertainers backing out. She couldn't imagine her new career starting off on a worse note.

"Shit!" Wang snapped. For a moment, Rieka thought he'd simply been reacting to their conversation. But when he left his seat and reached for something under his jacket, his eyes trained on the stadium, she realized his comment had nothing to do with them.

He pulled the maitu into view, and Jeniper gasped. "Everyone stay here," he ordered. For once, Rieka simply nodded and let him do his job.

Candace Degahv turned at her stateroom door and looked at her personal secretary, Barbara Smith. The Human woman sat at the console studying a News Sheet. Apparently sensing her employer's attention, Smith looked up. "Mrs. D?"

"Schedule my dinner for eight this evening," Candace told her. "I'll be dining with Captain Gimbish. I'll let you know the location later."

Smith nodded, nonplussed. "Of course."

Purposefully, she left the suite and went directly to the captain's quarters. He opened the door with a surprised flip of his ears. "Mrs. Degahv, welcome aboard. I had not realized you would be making this trip." He bowed formally, from the waist.

"An oversight of your registrar, no doubt," Candace said easily.

"Come in please. Make yourself comfortable. Can I offer a refreshment?"

Candace strode into the room and seated herself in a cushioned chair. "No. Thank you, Captain." She studied the Oph's now-familiar coat pattern. Generally cream-colored, Gimbish had darker paws and ears and a mask across his eyes.

Gimbish sat on a nearby chair. "Is there something I can do for you, Mrs. Degahv?" he asked.

Candace smiled for his benefit. "Actually, there is. I'm going to be sending several large shipments to Earth in the next few weeks. And I was wondering if you would be amenable to . . . taking my word as to the contents."

The captain's ears pricked up. "This sounds like an interesting prospect. Can I have some assurances from you that this mysterious cargo is not hazardous?"

"Oh, it's completely benign, Captain. Tools and equipment—things like that. And I plan to compensate you, as usual, for your cooperation." She waited patiently while the Oph considered the proposition.

"The usual fee?" he asked.

"Yes. And I'll throw in a bonus if you can give me any information as to any plans TechLine might have for Earth. You do have access to someone on the executive board, do you not?"

Gimbish seemed to hesitate, apparently unsure of how much she knew and what he could safely tell her. "I have some, limited connection," he admitted. "I am unsure of when I will next have contact."

Candace nodded. "I understand completely, Captain. Of course, compensation will not be forthcoming unless I receive the information. But the cargo business will be handled as usual."

He growled lightly. "Of course."

She glanced around the room and noticed a ceremonial blade mounted to the wall. It was for some part of the Oph Kori-death ritual, but she had no idea of the thing's name or function. Still, it struck a cord Candace had been grasping at since she'd first boarded the *Garner*.

"Was there anything else, Mrs. Degahv?"

"No. Thank you for your time, Captain," Candace said, eyeing him as she stood. "But I would be honored if you dined with me and my staff before this trip is over."

He seemed to consider the invitation, then nodded. "It would be my pleasure," he said, his black lips thinning slightly.

"Good. Tonight at eight in the VIP dining room."

Gimbish hesitated only a moment. "I will look forward to it."

They made their way to the door and Candace turned to study his dark eyes. "You seem to have many more Ophs in your crew than I remember," she remarked lightly.

He glanced away before responding. "Yes. We've had an influx of new personnel during this tour."

"I'm sure I'd love to hear all about it . . . at dinner,"

she said. "Thank you again, Captain." Her face an impenetrable mask, Candace allowed a smile. Sure Gimbish had business with entrepreneurs other than herself, she decided dinner would be the perfect means to find out what was going on, and perhaps find a way to capitalize on it.

ELEVEN

When Triscoe walked through the now-familiar doors at Sati Labs, he was surprised to see Wilmstos waiting for him behind the reception desk.

"Captain Marteen," the man said, a trace of excitement in his voice. He came around the desk and extended his hands, palms up. "I have marvelous news for you, Captain," Wilmstos told him, eyes gleaming excitedly. "Come. Let me show you."

Triscoe followed, but with a good deal less enthusiasm than the doctor. He had convinced himself it would be easy to tell Wilmstos simply to hold the DNA samples until more research could be done or some other way to have a baby could be explored. But the man acted as impatient as a child in an amusement park, and Triscoe sensed telling him to postpone their request would come as a great disappointment.

Instead of going to his office, the doctor led him into the main laboratory building, where they entered a lab observation deck.

"I've brought you here so we can actually see the work in progress," Wilmstos began. "Of course, I could get you clearance to enter the lab proper, but we would have to be sterilized and wear biotech suits. And, frankly, I didn't want to waste the time."

Triscoe nodded as he glanced around the floor below. "I appreciate the forethought, Doctor," he said. "But I'm not sure why you've brought me here."

"I wanted you to witness the people and the place that has created a modern-day miracle," Wilmstos explained. "One which you and your wife instigated."

This was sounding worse than he'd imagined. "It's only been a week since your board accepted our proposal and tissue samples," Triscoe said, a hint of uneasiness in his voice.

"Yes. Yes, I know. And who could have predicted such incredible success?"

Triscoe studied Wilmstos's exuberant face and glanced back over the lab, the technicians busily working and paying them no mind. "I think, Doctor, that we should adjourn to your office."

Wilmstos frowned slightly, then smiled. "Of course, Captain. We need to sit and discuss what will happen next. Timetables. Additional questions you might have. When the Herald will be able to schedule a trip to Indra. And I've taken the liberty of ordering a bottle of *kiova* and some *darvin* to celebrate the occasion."

Triscoe frowned slightly, nodded again, and followed the doctor back to the Chute. Now that the lab both had their DNA and had managed to do something remarkable with it, he needed to find a diplomatic way to explain their new goals without minimizing the achievement, whatever that was. After all, he and Rieka had made the request in good faith. No one should be blamed if plans had changed.

A few moments later, they found their way to Wilmstos's now-familiar office. Seating himself at the doctor's request, Triscoe watched the man collect two small glasses and a short round bottle from a shelf. He pulled the stopper and poured about fifty milliliters of thick white liquid into each glass, enough for a couple of swallows.

Keeping his hands on his thighs, Triscoe waited for Wilmstos to sit, then asked, "What, precisely, has happened?"

"I must tell you first, Captain, that as soon as you approached us, I had a team running virtual simulations and working on techniques that might be useful in our quest. We worked through several dozen possibilities, most of which were unsuccessful, before your samples were even taken. Nine did show promise."

He studied Triscoe for a moment, apparently wondering why his client lacked enthusiasm at the news. Then, with a little shrug, Wilmstos continued his story. "Yesterday afternoon while some preliminary testing was being conducted with sections of the genomes you and the Herald provided—a most astonishing thing occurred. We got natural cohesion. It's unheard of between alien species, Captain. But it happened. The lab notified me immediately as soon as they got a positive turn. I went down and looked at the films, myself. Several pair of chromosomes had correctly aligned themselves. Not all of them, I should add, but enough to show promise. The tech-pro assured me the event happened without our intervention."

Triscoe eased back in the chair and felt light-headed, as if all the CO_2 in the room had been removed. "What are you saying, Wilmstos?" he asked, hoping he didn't sound as alarmed as he felt. "That I could impregnate Rieka myself?" he asked incredulously.

"Of course not. Well, I don't think so, anyway. Not exactly—but this is remarkable. Hundreds of additional processes are still to come. But our job has been made infinitely easier by this affinity between the two species' genetic material. No one's ever tried anything like it before." He stopped and took a breath. "We've gone through that already." He waved his hand, dismissing that old news. "But this is . . ." He shook his head, unable to find the proper words.

"Incredible?" Triscoe offered.

"Beyond that."

Sighing quietly, Triscoe felt the war within him bubble back to the surface. He'd come to tell Wilmstos to delay the attempt, but now nature had accelerated the plans without warning. He did want to have a child. Maybe this remarkable cohesion foretold the possibility of that. But he didn't want Rieka to endanger herself—and that was still a sobering factor.

"Wilmstos, I came here today to make a request on behalf of both Rieka and myself," he began, calling upon all his diplomatic talent.

"Yes?"

"Yes." He looked into the doctor's brown eyes for a moment, then at the glasses of *kiova*. "Yes. The thing of it is, you see, she couldn't possibly have realized the time involved in her duties as Herald until she'd actually become Herald. Which she hadn't when we first approached you.

I . . . other factors have become apparent, recently, forcing us to change our plans."

Wilmstos's smile faded. "I understand. Can you tell me exactly how the plans have changed?"

"We need to . . . postpone the pregnancy," Triscoe told him softly. "I don't know how long—"

"You're halting the process?"

"No," Triscoe said firmly. "We *do* wish to have a child. But Rieka frequently jumps into things without all the facts. The situation now, precludes us having a baby until things have . . . calmed down."

"I'm afraid I don't understand, Captain," Wilmstos said, a wary look on his face. "This interview—indeed—every conversation we have is completely confidential. If there is some unique reason you must postpone the pregnancy, I would like to know."

Triscoe had debated telling him both everything and nothing. Now as he sat here looking the doctor in the eye, he realized Wilmstos had taken a big career risk in supporting their original request. If only for that, he deserved the truth.

"There are two reasons, Doctor. Both quite serious and both, as I assumed you've deduced—have very little to do with Herald's duties."

"I'm listening," Wilmstos said. He picked up his glass and swallowed the *kiova* in one gulp.

Pausing a moment to gather his thoughts, Triscoe finally said, "I have the Gift. When we were married, Rieka was unable to communicate with me mentally without my performing a Singlemind. During the Procyon War, she received a severe blow to the head. When she regained consciousness we found the link had bridged our minds. And it has grown stronger in the last few months."

The doctor's eyes grew round. "You are a Gifted Pair," he whispered reverently.

"I wouldn't go quite that far," Triscoe said. "But there is a significant risk to all three of us if we aren't absolutely sure the fetus will be chemically compatible with Rieka's Human body."

Wilmstos took several deep breaths. "I can see why you are concerned, Captain. This is most serious. It certainly supersedes anything I might say to the contrary. And, since the chromosomes are so compatible, we can shift our attention from whether or not they will attain mitosis to exactly what might grow from that single cell. That, of course, is your biggest risk. And I assure you we planned to investigate thoroughly any possible complications before even suggesting implantation. The extra time—" he made a small gesture with his hands, silently telling Triscoe of his relief, "—will allow a more unhurried approach."

"I am pleased that you're able to accommodate our request without very much difficulty."

Wilmstos smiled, and Triscoe felt thankful the man had understood the situation's complexities without having them explained. "Of course, Captain," he said. "We always intended to move cautiously, of course, but now there will be absolute certainty the cells will be compatible or, I assure you, there will be no mention of implantation."

"Thank you, Doctor."

They sat in companionable silence for a moment, then Wilmostos asked, "And what was the other reason to delay?"

Triscoe shrugged slightly and exhaled through his nose. "There is no delicate way to say this, I'm afraid. It is quite possible someone means to do Rieka harm."

"But who? Who in their right mind . . . would . . . would consider such a thing?" Wilmstos stammered, obviously aghast at the notion. "She's a Fleet hero. Humanity elected her as their united voice. Surely she hasn't made an enemy in the last few days."

"The situation began almost two decades ago, as I understand it," Triscoe began. "Suffice it to say there is at least one individual who—"

The floor suddenly shook. Triscoe's chair shifted. He held on to it and watched Wilmstos lurch forward. An incredible sound assaulted their ears.

"Take cover!" Triscoe yelled, barely able to hear himself over the noise. An explosion? Earthquake? Somewhere in Korval, he decided, though the notion seemed ridiculous.

He dropped to the floor and tipped his chair forward, creating a small but serviceable shelter. Another concussion shook the building. A second tremor or rubble falling from above? He had no idea. Sections of ceiling slammed into the floor around him. Shelves tipped and crashed. Triscoe heard Wilmstos whimper once and hoped the man was unhurt. The air became so thick with dust Triscoe found it difficult to breathe. He pulled his tunic up over his mouth and nose, hoping the cloth would filter enough to keep him breathing until they could escape the building.

Finally, after what seemed like minutes but probably amounted to seconds, the noise abated. He could still hear things occasionally crashing, but the building itself seemed to have stabilized, at least for the moment.

"Wilmstos, are you all right?" Triscoe began what became a complicated process of extracting himself from the chair and the debris that had fallen around him. When he finally looked around, he was astonished at the amount of dust in the air, and the mess. The ceiling had caved in, leaving barely enough room for him to crawl around.

"Wilmstos?" he said again, picking his way through the rubble to the desk's farside. "Doctor, can you hear me?"

A small sigh sounded from somewhere in the vicinity of where he expected the doctor to be. Triscoe carefully picked up chunks of ceiling, books, a smashed picture frame. When he'd cleared enough away to see some of the floor, he heard another sound and saw the doctor's hand protruding from under a fallen shelf.

After checking first to see whether or not moving the shelf would cause an avalanche of debris, Triscoe levered it up as far as he could and braced it against a small table. Wilmstos lay facedown, his right arm twisted at an unnatural angle. He moaned slightly.

Triscoe knew ground assistance was out of the question. Rescue crews would never enter a collapsing building. He clicked on his TC and pulled his tunic back into place. "Marteen to *Providence*."

"Aarkmin here, Captain," his EO replied. "I was about to contact you. There has been an explosion in the vicinity of your signal. Are you all right?"

"An explosion? Not an earthquake?"

"Definitely an explosion. Are you injured?"

"I am fine, Aarkmin," he replied, confusion washing over him. The dust clogged his throat and he coughed. "However, my companion requires medical attention. Have us InterMATted directly to the Medical section."

"As we speak."

In another moment, Triscoe was looking at Vort Twana-bok, his medical superintendent. The Vekyan glanced at him and waved at an assistant. A mask attached to a small compressed air cylinder was slipped over his face. Another was placed on Wilmstos.

"I'm fine, Vort," Triscoe assured him through the mask. He pulled it off and took a deep breath. "Swallowed some dust, that's all." He pointed to the unconscious man on the floor.

"See to him, Vort," Triscoe ordered. "His name is Dr. Wilmstos. Helegi Wilmstos, I think. He's employed at Sati Labs."

"I'll report as soon as I know something," Twanabok told him.

Triscoe nodded and left the Medical suite in search of some answers. When he got to the bridge, Aarkmin vacated the command chair. "Captain on the bridge."

"Report," he spit, confusion and anger swirling in his mind like tangible things.

"Sir, there isn't much to say. Shortly after you In-terMATted to the surface, Sati Labs was destroyed."

"Only the lab? Nothing else?"

"Nothing else, Captain," she said.

Wang ordered the driver to stop before turning toward Rieka. "Stay here," he said. She nodded, catching a glimpse of the maitu he'd pulled from its holder. She frowned when he began walking across the pavement, holding the small but lethal weapon in full view.

He stopped about ten meters away and gestured the gate attendant to come down from her tower. Once she stood on the ground with him, Rieka smiled at Wang's obvious height advantage. The woman responded to his questions, waving her hands at her tower, the roadway, and the stadium behind her.

"What the hell is going on?" Rieka grumbled.

They watched him speak to the woman for another moment, then turn and stride back to the transport. "Sorry," he said with an apologetic shrug, then instructed the driver where to park. "Security isn't what I wanted. The stadium manager is waiting in the main lobby to show you around.

Before we take his tour, I'll need about fifteen minutes with him. Privately."

Rieka found herself smiling at the determined look on Wang's face. She schooled the expression to a faint curve in her lips, and said, "Whatever you think is necessary, Mr. Hong. This is your specialty. But I'd rather not wait in the transport, if you don't mind."

"That can be arranged." He turned as they parked and the driver opened the door.

"Oh, and Wang—"

"Yes, Herald?"

She smiled. "I don't mind the inconvenience."

They had just finished touring the stadium and were walking toward the third-level VIP lobby when Jeniper looked up from her datapad, confusion and concern clearly written on her face. Rieka felt her heart speed up when Jeniper's bibbets actually darkened.

"What's happened, Jen?"

She watched Jeniper work her jaw for a second, then she managed to say, "Herald RadiMo is . . . missing."

"What do you mean missing?" Rieka snapped, snatching Jeniper's proffered datapad and looking at the missive. His aide, CariMo, clearly stated the Herald had been expected in New SubAtlanta. When he did not arrive at the scheduled time, a search was conducted. Neither he nor his *skiff* could be found anywhere on the Australian or North American continents. Searches on the other five continents were still under way.

"Well, this is just great," Rieka mumbled. She handed back the datapad and tried to think where he might have gone. "Dammit. As if things weren't already a mess. I suppose I should be prepared for stuff like this."

"I don't see how," Jeniper advised. "You aren't responsible for the Bournese Herald. In fact, he has been on Earth at his request."

"True. But that doesn't really make any difference, Jen," Rieka told her. She signaled Wang that she was going back to the transport, then turned and led her people to the ground level, where the vehicle waited.

When they'd all taken their seats and the transport had turned down the long, landscaped driveway, Wang asked,

"Where are we going?" His look told her he took Rad-iMo's disappearance quite seriously.

"Well, they've already scoured New SubAtlanta," she replied. "We'd probably do well to start in New SubDenver."

"I was wondering when we'd get a look at the central office," Jeniper quipped.

"Then you don't have long to wait. We'll be there in a few minutes."

Jeniper frowned. "I don't understand. It'll take at least an hour and a half—if a shuttle is ready to go—which I wouldn't expect since this is an unscheduled trip."

Rieka smiled and glanced at Wang. She activated her own datapad and tapped at the pads. Seconds later, she looked back at Jeniper. "The *Capitol* is now in orbit. And though under normal circumstances we'd shuttle in our destination, I'd say this situation requires my immediate attention. I'm proclaiming a diplomatic emergency. We're InterMATting to SubDenver. In fact, as long as there's a ship within range, we're InterMATting everywhere until RadiMo is found."

Wang's frown had appeared and seemed glued to his face. "But—"

"No 'buts' from you on this, Wang," Rieka told him. "We've got an emergency. I'm responsible for both Earth and its image. The day after I officially become Herald, a visiting Herald disappears without a trace. Does this sound like coincidence? Not to me." She paused for a breath and looked at Jeniper. "Am I sounding paranoid to you?"

"I don't know. This could all be quite innocent," Jeniper told them, glancing at Wang. "On the other hand, it could be very serious. At the moment, there's no way to tell."

Rieka leaned her elbow on her seat's armrest and dropped her chin into her hand. RadiMo's disappearance had obviously been planned carefully. Only someone who knew both why he'd been on Earth and his daily agenda could pull off the Herald's kidnapping. How many people had access to that kind of information? Not many, she figured. But for one of them, abducting a Herald wouldn't be terribly difficult. After all, she'd already done it at least once.

Now, she only had to deduce Candace's intent. To intimidate? Or was there a larger scheme? Thinking back to her conversation with RadiMo, she couldn't tell if he'd been behaving with characteristic shyness—or had been deliberately obtuse. With the Bournese, it was anyone's guess.

"Wang-Chi," she said, and he immediately jerked to attention.

"Yes."

"You're with me from now on. Every minute. Is that understood?"

He nodded, a look of conviction in his eye. "Of course."

"And I expect you to hire someone you trust to do all the itinerary work—what you've been doing yourself, so far. He or she will coordinate between you, Jeniper, and wherever I happen to be planning to go, if possible."

"Right." He gave her a slight nod. "I . . . I think I know someone who can do that."

"Good. Now, I can't predict where I'll be going after New SubDenver, but I can give you a few places that you need to secure."

He pulled his own datapad from his pocket while Rieka consulted hers.

"Is there something I should know?" Jeniper asked warily, her bibbets flushing a delicate pink.

"Not yet, Jen. Let's not all worry about things that may simply be phantoms." Jeniper said nothing, but Rieka noticed her bibbets darken slightly. "Okay, Wang. Odds are I'll be in SubDenver, SubAtlanta, Winnipeg, and possibly Jerusalem—sometime within the next twenty-four hours. I'll be InterMATting whenever possible, so there won't be any forewarning on the receiving end, if you understand my meaning."

"Unfortunately," he grumbled, and began tapping commands into his datapad.

"If we go anywhere else, it'll be equally unpredictable. Only the InterMAT chief on the *Capitol*, or whatever ship we use, will be privy to that knowledge. Does that ease your palpitations even a little?" she asked, smiling wryly.

He didn't return the expression. "Not exactly. Can I ask why we're doing this?"

"You can ask whatever you want. And this time I'll even try to reply. Someone wants to control my Heraldship—wants me to keep Earth isolated rather than opening it up to the Commonwealth for repopulation and trade. If I'm guessing correctly, she's decided to go a different route. Now, she intends to tarnish my image, raise questions about my abilities, stir up old lies about my loyalty. All this she can do without ever threatening me. A clever plan, I have to admit. And somehow, I have to figure a way to throw it back in her face."

"Who would do this to us—I mean to you?" Jeniper asked, a tremor in her voice evidence of her concern. "I mean, who could possibly have that kind of power?"

"Plenty of people, Jen," Wang volunteered without looking up from his computer. "Especially those with interplanetary businesses."

"But you have someone specific in mind, don't you, Rieka?" Jeniper persisted.

Rieka nodded, thankful again for Wang's expertise in things beyond his ability to protect her physically. "Right now, I'm betting it's Candace Degahv. But knowing her, that will be difficult to prove."

"Your mother!" Jeniper gasped.

"A lovely woman," Rieka quipped. "If you're lucky, you'll never have to be in the same room with her."

"Have the records come in from Atlanta, yet?" Rieka asked, looking across her desk and Wang's head to catch Jeniper's glance. They'd been in New SubDenver for three hours, and reports were coming in slowly. The local community directors in Winnipeg, New SubBrasilia, and Canberra had all sent identical communiqués. RadiMo was not anywhere to be found.

"No," Jeniper answered. "Mr. Moore's secretary said there was a problem in one of the school facilities, and he went to see to it, personally. She assured me he'd send word as soon as he had any information."

Wang shifted in his chair and looked at her. "You seem safe enough, here. Do you think you can survive without me for about an hour?"

"I suppose so."

"Don't you want to know why?"

"I know why, Wang-Chi," Rieka said. "You've been studying those résumés for, what—two hours, now? You've made the decision on whom to employ to replace you as security chief—so you can do what you were hired to do."

He made a face at her. "Do you read minds, too?"

"Only one," she replied trying to keep a straight face. "Thankfully, not yours."

He grumbled, and Jeniper cleared her throat. Rieka waved him off. "Go, Wang. I have the maitu you gave me here, in the desk. I know how to use it. Jeniper and I will be okay for an hour or two."

He stood but didn't leave. When Rieka looked up to see a strange expression on his face, she offered him a one-sided smile. "Yes, Wang," she admitted, glancing once at Jeniper, "I can kill if I have to." When shock did not register on his face, she continued, echoing the same things he'd told her during his interview.

"It was during the war. And given a choice, I would have found another way. But when it's a them-or-me situation, there is no choice."

He watched her for a moment, then apparently made his decision. "I'll be back in an hour. If you need me, my datapad page will be on."

She waved him off, again. "Good luck."

When the door had closed, Jeniper moved to sit in the chair Wang had vacated. "You really . . . killed someone?" she asked gently.

"That comes as a surprise, Jen?" she asked, allowing only a trace of sarcasm. "Aren't we Humans expected to be barbaric—capable of every imaginable atrocity?"

When Jeniper looked at her as if she'd lost her mind, Rieka shook her head. "Sorry, just repeating something my mother once said."

"I still can't understand how she could hate you—her own daughter."

"It's a long story."

Jeniper's datapad beeped, and she moved to the desk console to receive the incoming message. Rieka didn't pay much attention to her until the printer spit a hard copy on the desk.

"What's this?"

"Just came in from EarthCom. It's the report you asked for on your father's shuttle crash."

Rieka nodded and grabbed up the sheets of paper. Glancing through them, she nodded to herself. "Nothing much new here. The shuttle had been inspected by the pilot and ground crew prior to liftoff."

"That's routine," Jeniper commented.

"True. But I wonder if this is?" She pulled the last page from the others and studied a column of names.

"What?"

"The ground crew that serviced the ship was made up of Ophs." She looked up into Jeniper's confused frown. "That seems a little odd, don't you think?"

"I have no idea," she confessed. "Is it?"

"Twelve individuals of the same species on the same shift sounds more than a little strange, to me." She raked her fingers through her hair and tried to think. "Okay. The next step is to verify how those Ophs were assigned. Eighteen years ago we were still using Fleet equipment. If there aren't records here on Earth, Admiral Nason should have them on Yadra."

Nodding her agreement, Jeniper tapped some notes into her datapad. "I'll find out about the Earth records, first. If they're inconclusive, I'll request Fleet records."

The plan sounded reasonable, but Rieka's sense of apprehension resurfaced. "Ask for both, now. We may find they don't match."

Jeniper's bibbets paled slightly, but she said, "Of course."

Her console beeped, and Rieka saw that the report from Atlanta had arrived. "Director Moore looks to be a good record keeper," she said, sifting down the index of residential, travel, and communication files. "From just looking at this I can tell our next stop will be Atlanta."

"I've been told you get a breathtaking view of the Atlantic from several above-ground sites," Jeniper said.

"Really?" Rieka said. "I can't remember. Last time I was there it was at night. And cold, too. Did you know the city used to be about three hundred kilometers from the coast?" Jeniper shook her head "no." "At any rate, by the time we're done in Atlanta, I'll be ready to head back to Damascus." She tapped in an access code to NorthAm Comm to find out if any Fleet ships were in orbit. Much to Rieka's displeasure, the *Capitol*'s captain, Durana, hadn't seen RadiMo's disappearance for a few hours as an emergency, but fortunately, she'd been willing to accept Rieka's need to InterMAT. "Oh, good."

"Good—what?" Jeniper asked.

"The *Currency* is due to attain orbit in about ninety minutes. I'm sure Bilik would love to help."

TWELVE

Captain Gimbish of the C.F.S. *Garner* sat alone in his room and thought about his cargo, his cousin, and what she planned to do.

He had always respected Gundah. She was older than he, held an enviable position in the Oph Herald's entourage, and enjoyed rough intercourse more than any other female he knew. She had wooed him to support her with tales of her unhappy adolescence and he had sympathized. Empathized. Sworn to help her right the wrongs.

But in the last few months, her suggestions had become requests and, finally, orders. Knowing she kept him cave-blind for his own good, Gimbish hadn't questioned what she did or why. Lately, though, he'd begun to realize Gundah's behavior was far from predictable. While on the one paw he credited that to her genius, on the other, he couldn't help but wonder if she required mental therapy of some kind.

Thus far, the cargo she'd transported on the *Garner* had been innocuous. Things in mismarked boxes. Shipments of goods they both knew were either damaged or defective. But now, she'd suddenly swayed political. And try as he might, Gimbish could not get past the feeling of blatantly breaking his Command Oath.

With a muffled growl, he slid a communication chip into his console and typed in her Ophiuchus address along with the encoding instructions to prevent the document from being read more than once. When the camera flashed its record prompt, Gimbish took a breath and began.

"Gundah. Greetings. As requested, I am notifying you that I have done as you asked. But I have grave concerns for this strategy. I see no point in risking everything in order to bait your quarry. I realize you have not told me the entire plan, but this does not sit well."

Both knowing and fearing her ire, Gimbish was glad many light-years separated them. He took a breath and continued. "RadiMo has told me this 'excursion' off Earth is unexpected. He seems upset that you have changed the original plan. I have done everything in my power to keep him happy—but who can tell such a thing with a Bourne?" He let his black lips pull tightly against his teeth, then twitched his nose.

"In any case, I will continue to hold him isolated from the crew and, as per the plan, deliver this last shipment before our next meeting. His carton will be addressed to you and will be waiting for your arrival at Mars Colony.

"I anticipate our next *grussha*. Gimbish."

He switched off the recorder and collected the communiqué chip. Staring down at the piece of plastic in his paw, Gimbish recalled how Gundah had helped their extended family financially. How she'd taught him the basics of investing and how he'd come to possess a small fortune from that knowledge. He closed his eyes and remembered how her fur rose when he panted in her ear just so, and how she growled at the back of her throat when he sniffed her.

Of late her eccentricities had diversified, but he still trusted her judgment. She had requested his help, and he looked on it as a repayment for all she had done. Her promise of wealth, power, and a harem on Oph only fueled his dedication to her. She was the cleverest person he'd ever met. How could he doubt her success?

Still, that small warning sounded at the back of his thoughts. Why hadn't she told RadiMo she wanted to see him before the Earth ceremony? And why did she keep her plans so secret? Had she become irrational, or were her tactics so incredibly complex they defied logic?

Gimbish realized he simply had to have faith in his cousin. She'd supported him and expected support in return. Knowing this was his last opportunity to back out of the plan and save his reputation, he took a breath, pushed out of his chair, and headed for the communications room.

*   *   *

The usual soft popping sound accompanied Setana Marteen as she transported from the *Currency* to New Sub-Denver. Rieka stood a short distance away, a huge, dark Human behind her. Their expressions bespoke both concern and curiosity.

"Setana," Rieka said, stepping forward and offering her hand. "Welcome to Earth. I'm glad you're here—but I was expecting to see Captain Bilik."

"He'll be along later," Setana assured her, gripping her daughter-in-law's hand. She let go and offered a firm embrace.

Rieka returned the hug, then stepped back. "Something bad has happened, hasn't it?" she asked softly.

Setana nodded, unsurprised by Rieka's intuition. "We must talk. Privately."

"Of course." Rieka turned and gestured toward the man behind her. "This is Hong Wang-Chi, my personal bodyguard. Circumstances demanded I step up security. Wang is never more than a room away."

Setana felt herself stiffen slightly. Rieka couldn't possibly have known what had happened on Indra. Her increased security had to be the result of something here, on Earth. For Rieka to take such measures, the problem had to be quite serious. "A pleasure to meet you Mr. Hong," she said pleasantly, offering her right hand. "I am Setana Marteen, the Indran Herald."

"I'm honored, Madam Herald," he replied. He shook her hand and stepped back, indicating he would follow them. Setana felt uneasiness in him as well and began to wonder at the scope of their combined problems.

"Let's go, then," Rieka offered. On the way to the guest suite, she explained that Wang had had a team go through it and several others in the Embassy's housing wing. She currently knew of four Heralds and a dozen offworld administrators who would attend the Reaffirmation.

"But I'm hoping a lot more will show up," she finished with a wry grin. "We can quarter them in other cities, but not with the level of security Wang has established here."

Mr. Hong stepped up to the lock and opened the keypad. He tapped in some numbers and eased back. "Now if I could have your left palmprint, Herald Marteen," he said.

"Of course." She placed her palm on the faceplate, and he tapped in another code.

"Thank you. We're set now. This door will only open for the three of us. If you need anyone else to access your quarters, let me know, and I'll add their print."

"Perhaps my husband and my adjutant. But neither of them is with me at this time," she told them.

When the door slid open, Rieka led the way into the suite. Mr. Hong positioned himself just inside the threshold.

"How bad?" Rieka asked, motioning Setana to sit on a sofa.

She settled on a cushion, deciding straightforward answers would be the easiest for her daughter-in-law to digest. "Bad enough. Would you sit, too, dear?"

Watching her carefully, Rieka eased onto a chair. "It isn't Triscoe, or I would know," she said softly.

"That is true," Setana agreed. "Even without the Gift, you would know if his life force had . . . departed. But this does have something to do with him—and you."

She watched Rieka frown, take a small breath, then gently ask, "What, Setana?"

"I was on Perata at the time—still involved with the problem that kept me from your inauguration," she began. "Triscoe had just come from Earth. He had a meeting with Dr. Wilmstos at Sati Labs."

"Yes. I know. He went to tell them there was no rush for a pregnancy. We had decided to . . . let things settle down a bit before attacking that problem."

"Yes," Setana said. "So Triscoe mentioned. But while he was meeting with Dr. Wilmstos, there was an accident."

"Accident? What kind of accident?" Rieka glanced once at her bodyguard. "The News Sheet this morning said something about an explosion in Korval. Is that what you're talking about? Are you sure he's okay?"

"Yes. Everything is fine. He is unharmed," Setana assured her, relieved when the sense of bright red alarm she received from Rieka eased off into a warm, orange concern. "Actually, that isn't quite correct. His message to me on Perata included a brief report not publicized on the News Sheets. I'm sorry to tell you—Sati Labs is . . . destroyed."

She felt Rieka recoil, but plunged ahead, knowing she needed to disclose every bit of information. "It was determined that someone used an antimatter device to consume the top twelve floors of laboratories. The entire building is unusable. Triscoe is fortunate he was on the ground floor when the explosion occurred."

She watched Rieka's reaction to the news. Her eyes widened, and her jaw dropped before she could snap it shut. She looked again at Mr. Hong. The man had gone motionless enough to remind Setana of one of Yadra's Living Statues. The sense of red flared again.

She watched Rieka stumble for something to say. "Sati Labs is destroyed? Did Triscoe say anything about—our samples?"

Setana tried to impress a sense of calmness in her words. "Yes. Triscoe wanted me to tell you Dr. Wilmstos said the samples achieved a partial natural cohesion, and he'd been encouraged by that compatibility."

Rieka nodded uncertainly. "And now all that work is . . . gone."

"Yes."

She took a deep breath. "Good. That's good, I think."

Surprised by that reaction, Setana sat straighter. "You've changed your mind about having a child?"

"No! Just readjusted my priorities. We'll find a way, eventually." She gave Setana a brief smile. "When Triscoe explained—showed me how the Singlemind really works—I realized how presumptuous I'd been. We decided to wait until a better time. Maybe even change the strategy." She shrugged, and Setana decided not to question her further.

"Considering the circumstances, you made a wise decision, dear."

Rieka appeared to be studying her hands, so Setana gave her a moment to reflect on what she'd been told. Glancing at Mr. Hong, she got a sense of uneasiness. His eyes skimmed from Rieka to her, then back to Rieka again.

"What's happened here?" Setana asked hesitantly. "You haven't been threatened since you've been sworn in, have you?"

"No. Nothing like that. RadiMo is missing." Rieka paused, but before Setana could comment, added, "I'm guessing you know about Candace abducting me."

"Triscoe mentioned it," she answered. "I can't say I'm surprised. Your mother has always been able to get what she wants—one way or another. But what do you mean, RadiMo is missing?"

"The day after my inauguration, we went to Damascus to tour Olympic Stadium and visit the Site." Rieka stood and paced behind her chair. "While we were there, we got a report that RadiMo had not shown up in New SubAtlanta as scheduled. We've been looking for him for two days. He's . . . gone."

"Or hiding," Setana suggested. "The Bournese are known to require several days of solitude when they become overtaxed."

"No." Rieka shook her head. "He's not aground. CariMo would know. And she has no idea where RadiMo is."

Setana sat back and wove her fingers together on her lap. "This does warrant serious consideration, Rieka," she said. "You don't even know whether or not he's still on Earth?"

"No. Not for sure, anyway. The *Capitol* was in orbit when he disappeared. And the interplanetary shuttle to the Moon and Mars has come and gone since then, too. He wasn't listed on any manifest."

Silently, Setana wondered how many challenges her daughter-in-law could take on at once. "Tell me how I can help you," she said. "I am expected on Yadra in three days, but my attaché there can take my place. This situation is infinitely more important."

Rieka seemed to deflate. She eased back into the chair, and the expression on her face reflected both relief and astonishment. "You'd do that?"

"Of course, dear. Not only are you Earth Herald, you are my family. I regretted having to miss your inauguration, but had I known you needed me, I would have come sooner."

Setana sensed Rieka's relief, yet could tell she held a great amount of thought and emotion in check. Dreading the addition of another enigma to their conversation, she knew it would be indecorous not to speak. "There is one other thing," she said softly.

Rieka stiffened. "What?"

"One of the reasons I was on Perata last week was to speak to the Oracle." She watched Rieka frown slightly. "During my audience, he asked that I relay a message to you. He said to beware for the children. Success or annihilation rides with them."

When Rieka lifted her brows, Setana understood her unasked question. "I am sorry. He did not explain further."

Rieka then let out a long sigh and sank back into the chair. "Whose children, Setana? Triscoe's and mine? Did he mean the samples destroyed in the lab? That prediction's both premature and late," she said sarcastically.

Setana didn't blame her for being pessimistic. "I don't think so," she replied evenly. "He seemed to mean the term in a broader sense. As in children belonging to more than one person."

"And his message was meant specifically for me?"

"Yes."

She shrugged. "Well, I haven't a clue what he's getting at—but I don't suppose I should be surprised. The man's an enigma."

Setana relaxed a bit at Rieka's light tone. "That he is," she agreed.

"But if he meant that for me, specifically, then we've got to assume he's referring to Earth—since it doesn't look like I'll be having children of my own anytime soon. Earth's children—meaning Humanity? Or children living on Earth?"

"I really couldn't say."

"Well, that isn't the most pressing problem on our agenda." She frowned. "What we really need to do is concentrate on finding RadiMo."

"Page me if anything comes up," Rieka said, looking into Jeniper's blue eyes. "We can be back in a few minutes."

"Of course," the Aurian woman replied, her bibbets remaining faintly pink.

"Captain Bilik on the *Currency* is standing by," Wang told her, touching a finger to the left side of his jaw where his new toy perched, an external TC clipped around his ear and activated by touch. Integrated with the Fleet's frequencies, the little device had enough power to reach a vessel in orbit.

"I'm ready," she said, picking up a small scanner. With the TC, they no longer needed to use an InterMAT chamber to lock the signal. Silently envious of her bodyguard's latest gadget, she stepped to Wang's side, and added, "Request transport for two individuals to RadiMo's apartment in New SubAtlanta."

Wang repeated the request and a heartbeat later they stood in what seemed to be a black void. Nothing appeared out of the blackness and the cool air held a distinctly stale odor. Obviously everything had been shut down for a long time.

She felt Wang tense and heard him draw his weapon. "Lights," she commanded. The apartment's environmental system immediately kicked on, revealing a typical biped habitation. Wang looked around warily but holstered the maitu.

"When Director Moore received my request to search this apartment, he said once it had been checked out by his people everything had been shut down, Wang-Chi," she said jauntily. "Judging by the stale air and coating by dust on everything, it doesn't look like anyone other than the search crew has been in here in some time."

"It stinks."

Rieka grinned. "Put your gloves on, hold your nose, and have a look around. I'll try checking some surfaces with the scanner." She busied herself with the small device, identifying individuals who'd left their cells on the computer console and the kitchen table.

While she worked, Rieka wondered why RadiMo had chosen this apartment rather than a VIP suite or one that more closely resembled a Bourne environment. This one held all the typical Human trappings: individual rooms containing chairs, tables, closets, beds. With his *skiff*, he really didn't need anything else. Maybe the conveniences were for his associates.

Wang caught up with her in RadiMo's sleeping room. "Kitchen is clean. Nothing in the cool units. The pantry's almost empty. None of the other bedrooms has anything either. Closets are clean. Find anything in here?"

"Nothing but this," Rieka replied, gesturing toward what appeared to be a platform bed. "It looks like a portable den of some kind."

"It is," Wang replied, stepping up for a closer look. "I've been reading up on the Bournese. They can use their *skiffs* for days at a time—but long-term visits away from the home den wear on them. These things," he added, squatting down for a better look, "provide all the comforts. Plus they have quadruple the space."

Rieka shook her head at the complexities spacefaring travelers dealt with and perched on the habitat's edge. About two meters across, the thing really did dwarf a *skiff*. A control panel of some kind hung on the wall. "What do you think this is for?"

Wang stood and examined it. "Let's find out." He touched an indicator and half a dozen holes opened on the platform.

"Interesting." Rieka tried looking down a hole, but couldn't see anything. "Does that thing control internal illumination?"

"Coming on now," he said.

The faint light didn't improve her vision. Frustrated, Rieka wished she could climb down a hole, but despite the spongy texture, the outlet wasn't even wide enough for her head.

Wang joined her on the mattress, peered down another hole and stuck his arm in up to the elbow. "Can't feel anything. Until I did some research, I didn't think they ever left their *skiffs*," he admitted, sitting up and bouncing lightly on the rubbery surface.

"Neither did I."

Wang stood and rubbed his hip. "I don't know what the Bournese call comfortable, but this thing's definitely got some hard spots."

Not quite sure why, Rieka studied the slight indentation he'd made. There wasn't any holes near it, so she chose one a short distance away and slid her arm down it as far as it would go. Her fingers felt nothing more than the tunnel's smooth sides, about twenty centimeters across.

Curious, Rieka activated the scanner and aimed it at the place Wang had sat.

"Is there something down there?" he asked.

"Maybe. Have you got a knife?"

He stepped closer, digging into a trouser pocket. "It isn't very big."

"Doesn't need to be. What I want is only fifteen centimeters down." She took the pocketknife and activated the laser. One swipe opened the bed's outer surface. "Remind me to tell Jeniper this comes out of my expense account," she muttered.

The second cut went deeper. Rieka deactivated the knife and handed it back to Wang. She shoved her hand down into the slit she'd made and pushed her fingers through the foam until she touched a solid object. She traced the surface to an edge and pulled it up.

"A datapad," Wang whispered, amazed. "Stowed in his bed. Looks like the Bournese Herald had a few things he didn't want anyone to know about."

"Could be," Rieka agreed, holding the compact machine and silently kicking herself for not personally searching the apartment two days ago. "But they're very private creatures—beyond simple shyness. Even checking the file directories can be construed as invasive."

"If he's in trouble, and we don't check for some kind of clue in this"—Wang pointed at the datapad—"we could be considered negligent."

"Tough decision."

"Not really."

"You'd just switch this thing on and find out whatever you could?"

He nodded. "Damn right I would. Lives are at stake."

"Maybe." Carrying both RadiMo's datapad and her scanner, Rieka went back to the computer console in the other room. She set both devices down, then reached for the datapad and activated it.

The machine turned on but refused her access without the proper user ID. She could still hear Wang moving around in the sleeping room. "How do I hack my way past this datapad's access lock?" she called.

"You don't," he answered, coming toward her. "Let me. If this isn't too customized, I should have you in in a couple of minutes."

Rieka stood up and gestured for him to take the seat. "Then by all means, Wang-Chi, work your magic."

An hour later, Rieka leaned over his shoulder. "You're going to wear the battery down."

"I'm almost in," he said, waving her away.

Returning to the chair she'd been sitting in, Rieka realized she'd heard him say that at least four times already. "Uh-huh. Maybe you should define 'almost.'"

He looked up and took a deep breath. "What do you want to know?"

She bounced up from the chair and slid the datapad from beneath his fingers. "None of your business, Wang. This is RadiMo's private stuff. You don't have authorization to—"

"—hack my way through the access code?"

"I asked you to do that," she snapped. When he glared at her with his face an imperturbable mask, she relented. "Okay. Look through the filenames and see if anything seems significant."

Together, they studied the entries and decided to open three directories. One involved notes he'd made during his stay on Earth, one had to do with Yadra, and the other looked to be a catalog of his offworld communications.

They checked the Yadra notes first, expecting to find some reference to her mother. When there wasn't one, they searched RadiMo's documentation on Earth. Most were dry reports on mineral deposits, geology, and the like. His communications had generally been to Bourne, but there were four messages sent to Ophiuchus 70, the star around which the planet Oph orbited.

"That's a bit odd, don't you think?" Wang asked.

Puzzled, Rieka rolled back to the directories and found a file for Oph. Unfortunately, the file had been recorded in Bournese, a language she didn't understand. A glance at Wang told her he didn't, either. She went back to the communications files and called up the messages sent to Oph. They were addressed to Herald Cimpa's office. Frowning, Rieka looked over other recent communiqués, but those were personal, to RagiMo on Bourne.

She sighed loud enough for Wang to comment. "Wha-dya think?"

"RadiMo's sent four and received two communications from Herald Cimpa's office in the last month. Most everything else looks personal. He doesn't usually have a lot of contact with other Heralds—as far as this log goes."

"So let's look in the files written to Cimpa. I'll bet he recorded them in the standard language. That would be a start."

Rieka made a face, but touched the proper spots on the datapad's surface. The most recent message switched on.

RadiMo's small face took up most of the screen, making his location impossible to guess.

"Adjutant Gundah," he began. The electronic translation sounded strange, almost contrived, but at least they understood it. "Greetings to Oph. This creature is most confused as to your request, but shall do his best to gain entry to the answers you seek. Business does well, here. It is not an unpleasant place. Not abundantly populated. Most work hard, readying for the Reaffirmation. I will bring the information with me the next time I travel to your planet. The travel is expected for two days after the Earth ceremony. I rejoice that our business will soon be concluded. RadiMo."

Rieka sat back and looked at Wang once the system shut down. "What's he up to with Cimpa?"

"No way to tell. Those little Bournese are too clever for their own good, if you ask me."

"I didn't. But I happen to agree with you." Rieka glanced back to the file and checked the date. "He sent this seven days ago. Could be Cimpa wanted his report earlier than RadiMo intended to give it."

"Could be," Wang conceded. "What could the two of them possibly have in common?"

"I have no idea. But Cimpa could have sent someone here to collect RadiMo. And even though there isn't a transport record for him on any Fleet ship, I'm willing to bet we'll find RadiMo on Oph."

Gundah reclined on her well-appointed bed and snarled at the video screen suspended from the ceiling. Jonik Tarrik's insipid Aurian face stared back at her like a frightened *kreget*.

Nibbling a chunk of raw beef, she said, "I don't care if she thinks you work for her. You work for *me*." She spoke in tones imperious enough to cow an Oph, though she had no idea of the effect on the furless being.

He turned his head, and she saw a bibbet grow dark. "Yes, I know. But—"

"There is nothing to add, Tarrik. You were sent for the item. Did you get it?" She watched as his eyes roved but wouldn't focus on his video pickup.

Finally, he mumbled, "I got it."

"Good. I expect you to bring it to Earth as soon as possible and wait for me to contact you, there. The Courier's ticket you've been issued will only pay for transit to Earth. Don't try to run out on me, Tarrik. I have many . . . acquaintances in the Fleet."

He nodded but refused to look into the camera. "I'll bring it."

She smiled and smacked her black lips as she dangled another bloody tidbit over her tongue. Savoring the flesh, Gundah gave in to the sense of accomplishment. Her plans were coming together nicely. Tarrik's part in them would soon be over, and she found herself anticipating his demise. The demise of everyone who stood in her way, in fact. She found the possibility of actually outliving the Human race uniquely entertaining.

Her amused smile wrinkled her nose and bared her upper teeth. "Perform well, Tarrik, and I may consider your debt paid," she said.

"But that was the deal," he whined. "You said this was the last thing I'd have to do."

"So I did," Gundah agreed, almost impressed that he'd stood up for himself. "Then all you need concern yourself with is getting to Earth. I want you there at least two days before the Reaffirmation—with the item."

"I understand."

"I'm so glad," Gundah drawled. She reached and deactivated the comm unit. She never ceased to amaze herself. She hadn't dared to dream she'd achieve her goal so quickly, so easily. Stumbling upon an Aurian who would do anything to pay off his debts, she'd seized the opportunity fate had handed her.

What Stephen Degahv had started almost thirty years ago, she would finish. They would call her Gundah the Redeemer, she thought, purring with anticipation. Her actions would restore the Ophs to their former economic dominance and bring an end to the puny whelps called Humans.

Gundah reached for her goblet of *sallanni* and held it high. "To me," she announced to the furniture. "Gundah the Redeemer."

THIRTEEN

"I would really feel better if you stayed on Earth," Rieka grumbled at Jeniper when the escort had left them alone in the *New Venture*'s guest suite. Aware of the potential danger involved in retrieving RadiMo, she couldn't shake the fact she considered Jeniper a civilian. Conversely, her own self-image was still that of a Fleet captain. Rieka wondered how long she'd be a Herald before she actually felt like one.

Jeniper sat on the sofa, leaned back, and stretched her legs out in front of her. "I've already told you—the staff will handle all the minor details. The new caterer is coming from Yadra and won't arrive for three days. The touring itineraries for Damascus, the Site, and World Zoo are mapped out, and my assistants can handle any little problems that come up."

"I'm sure they will," Rieka replied absently. She sighed and ambled restlessly around the room. Waiting was her least favorite pastime and the four day round-trip to Oph yawned before her like an eternity. Not discounting the necessity of retrieving RadiMo, she wanted this trip to be over before it began.

Glancing around, Rieka had to admit, this ship did look better than the *Venture* the Fleet had lost to the Procyons. The suite had three sleeping rooms with attached baths, a meeting area, and this socializing area, complete with comm console.

"With everyone doing their respective jobs on Earth, I doubt you'll be missed for a few days," Jeniper went on. "Herald Marteen is quite able to, how did she put it? 'See to things.' And in light of what we've found out so far about the events surrounding your father's death—going to Oph ties in with that, too."

Rieka nodded as she tried to walk off her sense of frustration. Jeniper's preliminary report on the evidence was woefully incomplete. Totally circumstantial. They needed to dig a lot deeper before they could begin to prove the accident had been staged.

She glanced at Jeniper. "I agree with you about the odd coincidence that the 'repairs' the shuttle required were both evaluated and performed by only Oph tech-pros," she said. "But I remind you we're looking for incriminating evidence against my mother, not someone on Oph."

"You've got to start somewhere."

"True. But it doesn't have to be now. I should never have listened to Setana," she grumbled. "Nothing is as it should be."

"Well, that's a comforting thought," quipped a voice from the doorway.

"Midrin!" Rieka hurried forward as the Indran woman entered and hugged her tightly. "Or should I salute and address you as Captain?"

"Midrin will be fine," she said, grinning. "You look as though the role of Herald fits you well."

"Looks are deceiving," she replied cryptically. "But a command of your own seems to suit you."

"Most of the time," Midrin replied with a smile.

"Did many of the crew get reassigned to you—or did they stay on the *Prodigy*?"

"A few," she replied. "Gorah is my Security chief. She's pregnant with her first pup."

"I'll have to make a point of saying hello," Rieka said, smiling. "I can just see the hair on her shoulders stand straight up when you tell her a Herald has asked to see her. Don't tell her it's me."

"Impossible, I'm afraid. Gorah knew the exact moment you came aboard. It was she who suggested this suite. And, you'll find she's changed a bit since her mating. Much more confident."

"Well, good for her." Rieka turned and tugged her old friend farther into the room. "Midrin, I want you to meet Jeniper Tarrik, my adjutant. Jeniper," she began, turning to see the Aurian had risen and come forward, a thoughtful expression on her face as she studied them.

"Captain," Jeniper offered, her hands stretched forward in the Indran custom. "You honor us by this visit."

Midrin returned the greeting. "The honor is mine, Ms. Tarrik."

"Everything looks wonderful," Rieka told her former executive officer. "Is the *New Venture* very different from the old one?"

"Not really. Once we're under way I'll give you a tour. You can decide for yourself."

"I'd like that."

"I know this trip was arranged on short notice," Midrin added, looking Rieka in the eye. "It sounds as if there's a problem."

Rieka recognized the question in her voice. "There is. Actually, several."

A door behind them slid open, and Rieka turned as Wang came out of his bedroom. "Everything is clean," he said, his comment directed toward her as he looked at Midrin.

Rieka nodded and gestured him to come forward. "Hong Wang-Chi, I'd like you to meet the captain of this ship, Midrin Tohab."

"A pleasure, Captain." He offered a hand, and Midrin shook it.

"Captain Tohab was my executive officer aboard the *Venture* and *Prodigy*," Rieka added. "The best EO in the Fleet. That's why Admiral Nason gave her this command."

Midrin sighed. Rieka clapped her on the shoulder. "And she *still* doesn't take compliments well."

"As if *you* ever did," Midrin shot back.

When Rieka laughed, Wang announced, "I'm Rieka's bodyguard," and brought the conversation to a standstill.

After a few silent seconds, Midrin looked up at him, and asked, "Is there a security problem I should be aware of?"

"Not aboard the *New Venture*, Captain," he replied. "But I'm not about to take any chances."

"I should think not, Mr. Chi."

"Actually, it's Mr. Hong," Rieka corrected.

"Mr. Hong," Midrin said with a nod. "Shall we sit?" She

gestured toward the sofas. "I'd like to know exactly what is going on and how the *New Venture* may be affected."

When they'd all taken their places, Rieka explained about RadiMo's disappearance and the problems Candace had created. Jeniper jumped in and added background information involving the curious circumstances of Stephen Degahv's death.

When the room was finally quiet, Midrin sighed and looked at Rieka. "I wish I could do more than provide you with transport to Oph, but my scheduled stop is actually the third planet in the system, Grita, and I won't even be able to stay with you long enough to—"

"Don't worry about us, Midrin. I'm sure we'll be fine. This is a surprise visit, and with just the three of us, we don't pose any kind of threat to whoever has got RadiMo. I'm sure we can see Cimpa, get some answers, and go from there. We'll leave as soon as we can."

"The advantage of unpredictability has been useful in the past," Midrin said, nodding. "But you're a Herald now, Rieka. Is it really wise to do this? I'm sure Captain Marteen would advise against it."

Rieka smiled ruefully. "Well, he'd have to take that up with his mother," she said, suddenly feeling a bit more confident about her travel plans. "Setana suggested this trip."

"Really? Well, then I suppose I shouldn't feel quite so . . . apprehensive about the idea."

Wang nodded and said, "And both the *Providence* and *Prospectus* are scheduled for deliveries at Oph soon after we arrive. The plan is for Captain DeVark to pick us up and get us back to Earth in plenty of time for the Reaffirmation ceremony."

Rieka watched Midrin glance from Wang to Jeniper to her. "Knowing this lady, Mr. Hong, plans tend to go awry. You may well need plenty of what you Humans call luck."

Jeniper watched Rieka come out of Herald Cimpa's office and walk down the corridor to the waiting area. Having known Rieka for several weeks now, Jeniper realized she could read her boss's expression even from a distance. She looked to be both disappointed and angry.

With a glance at Wang, Jeniper said, "Be back in a minute." She stood and hurried toward Rieka. When she got close enough for a private conversation, Jeniper asked, "What did Cimpa say?"

Rieka shook her head. "Nothing," she grumbled softly. "He doesn't know anything. And I mean that, literally. His office reeks of *ciffa*. It's a wonder he knows his name and what day it is."

"It can't be that bad."

"You're probably right, but he's never liked Humans, and I'm sure part of it was an act to make me go away." She sighed. "I'm not leaving here without some answers."

Jeniper recognized the frustration in Rieka's tone. "Maybe his adjutant knows something," she offered. "RadiMo did mention her name. The Herald may actually be as incapacitated as you say. If that's true, she probably runs the office during his rutting time."

"I sure hope somebody does."

"Let me talk to her," Jeniper told her. "Her name is Gundah. She's been the adjutant for nearly two decades. She's bound to know if RadiMo has had any contact with Cimpa."

She waited patiently as Rieka's face went through a variety of expressions while she weighed the decision. Finally, Rieka sighed and nodded. "Give it a try, Jen. It really burns me we came all this way for nothing. I was so sure that entry in RadiMo's diary meant he'd come here."

"He might have, and Cimpa doesn't know it. Almost anything is possible." She glanced at the clock on the receptionist's desk. "Gundah can see me in fifteen minutes—I already checked with her secretary. You and Wang go back to the Earth Embassy, and I'll meet you there when I'm done."

She watched Rieka take a deep breath and then smile with one side of her mouth. "You know, being a Herald is a lot like commanding a ship," she said. "Do it." Then she collected Wang and left Jeniper in the waiting area, still wondering what she'd meant.

The wait to see Gundah went by quickly. Jeniper busied herself with her datapad, trying to find a correlation between the Oph company, OSSI, and Candace Degahv. She figured if Candace had had a hand in Stephen Degahv's death, she would have been in contact with the company that built and maintained the shuttle in which he died. Who else would have the expertise to stage such a crash and make it look like an accident?

"Gundah will see you now, Miss Tarrik," the receptionist announced. "Third door to the left."

Jeniper shut down her datapad and walked toward the indicated door. She knocked once and entered before Gundah could reply. "Good morning, Adjutant Gundah," she offered, "I am Jeniper Tarrik, adjutant to Herald Degahv."

The Oph behind the large desk had a dark gold coat. The jewelry fused to her left ear was quite ornate, though Jeniper immediately noticed she wore no stones indicative of having had pups.

"Welcome," Gundah told her, rising and coming around the desk. She executed the straight-backed Oph bow of greeting and the traditional body sniff. Jeniper returned the bow only. "It is a pleasure to meet you, Adjutant Tarrik," Gundah continued smoothly. "Sit, please. May I offer a refreshment?"

Jeniper sat in the proffered chair and accepted a cup of *colan.* "Thank you."

She watched Gundah sip her drink and smile with black lips. "One is curious, Ms. Tarrik. With Earth so close to its time of Reaffirmation, why are you here, on Oph?"

Having anticipated this question, Jeniper replied cautiously. "It is a matter of some urgency. And discretion," she said, watching to see Gundah's reaction.

The Oph was unreadable. "I see."

"Herald Degahv just met with Herald Cimpa. The conversation left many questions unanswered. I thought you and I might have a more productive talk."

Gundah nodded and put down her cup. "On what topic?"

"Herald RadiMo."

Jeniper watched Gundah go very still for a moment, then flip her ears, apparently confused. "What about him?"

Hoping her strategy would work, Jeniper said, "Having spent the last several months on Earth, he is now missing."

"Really? And what has that to do with anything here on Oph?"

"He left documents on Earth indicating recent business transactions with Oph natives," Jeniper said, keeping her bibbets as pale as she could. "It was natural to assume he may have come here. Would you happen to know if he's made a recent visit?"

Gundah leaned back in her chair, and Jeniper could see something going through her mind. Unfortunately, she had no idea what. "Of course this office isn't privy to every individual itinerary," Gundah began, "but we are aware of all visiting dignitaries. To my knowledge, RadiMo has not been to Oph in the last several months. In fact, I believe he's spent the entire time on Earth."

"Yes," Jeniper replied patiently. "We know that."

"One moment." Gundah activated her console and tapped at the keys for a moment. "Yes. He visited here with his mate, RagiMo, just after the Procyon War, five months ago."

"That was an 'official' visit, I'm sure," Jeniper told her. "I'm wondering if there is a possibility he has come to Oph in another capacity. Perhaps under an assumed name."

"If that is so, this office would not necessarily be aware of it," Gundah replied. She pulled her black lips into a thin, tight smile.

Jeniper nodded. "Yes. But you have access to certain data. And a Bourne—any Bourne—coming to Oph would have specific physical requirements. . . ."

Gundah looked at her screen a moment, then glanced at Jeniper. "Naturally. They require a *skiff* when they travel."

Jeniper waited patiently while Gundah requested more information from her computer. A moment later, the Oph nodded and made a soft groaning sound. "It seems, Ms. Tarrik, that a Bourne may have come into the system several days ago. From Earth. Yona, our smaller moon, records the arrival of a crate having the dimensions of a *skiff*: point seven-five meters by one meter by two meters."

"Is there a colony on Yona?"

Gundah gestured with a paw. "A mining colony. The director there is a Lomii." She smiled. "Named Klikt."

Jeniper sat a bit straighter. Now they were getting somewhere. "Are there travel restrictions to Yona? Would I need any kind of clearance to see Klikt?"

"None," Gundah replied. Jeniper noticed a small light on the desktop begin to flash. Gundah glanced at it and slid her chair back from her desk. "You must excuse me,

Ms. Tarrik, the Herald requires my presence immediately. If I can be of any further assistance, please let me know."

Jeniper stood and, as Gundah left her office, said, "Thank you for your cooperation. I will."

"Well, then, I guess the decision's up to you, Wang," Rieka said. Uncomfortable in Oph's strong gravity, she leaned back into her chair's cushions and looked at him over the massive desk. Despite feeling as if she weighed almost twice what she did, Rieka had been delightfully surprised by the Human contingent here at the Earth Embassy. The office looked good and appeared to be running efficiently.

She glanced at Jeniper, seated in a nearby chair. Her news about the mining outpost had brought an unwelcome feeling of uneasiness, but Rieka decided to let Wang handle all the safety issues.

"You're sure this Lomii won't talk to you? Maybe you could try again," he asked.

"I doubt it would be worth the effort," she told him. "Lomii are very . . . uh . . . visual, Wang. Even with a two-way screen, it's not the same. And it would be very bad manners to use my position as Herald to examine the suspected *skiff* without a short audience. I may need Lomiian support in the future. Offending them isn't a good idea."

Jeniper looked at Wang. "I'll go and talk to him."

Wang shook his head. "We shouldn't split up."

"Then what do we do?" Rieka asked.

"We shuttle out to Yona, talk to Klikt, and check this . . . object, ourselves."

"You're sure?" Rieka asked, surprised he'd give in so easily.

Wang sat forward and looked her in the eye. "You're at risk wherever you are, Boss," he began. "As long as I can secure the shuttle and get a layout of the mine, we should be fine. This little excursion is so completely unpredictable, I don't see how it could be a trap."

"Okay." Rieka nodded at him. Glancing at Jeniper, she said, "You two make the arrangements for this trip. I'll work on my Lomiian sign language and book our passage back to Earth." She'd already called up the Fleet schedules and found that even though the *Providence* would arrive in another three hours, it would be going on to Aurie. The *Prospectus* would arrive at Oph tomorrow but could take them directly back to Earth.

Thanks to Wang's efficiency, they set down at Yona just two hours later. The shuttle's small DGI gave them an exterior image. The mine consisted of a series of seven domes connected by transport tunnels. The domes served as both air locks for the mine shafts and some other purpose, such as housing, administrative offices, storage facilities, and the like. The shuttle pilot docked inside one of them. Rieka looked out a portal and saw only one other shuttle.

After Wang inspected the terminal and found it empty, she disembarked and waited while Jeniper opened a comlink to the mining director.

Once video had been established, Rieka made a series of introductory gestures at the screen. Klikt responded in kind and bowed, which for a Lomii meant floating up a bit, then coming back to camera level. After a flurry of complex hand signals, most of which she didn't understand, Klikt's image disappeared from the screen and a map appeared. Wang stepped closer as a pair of indicators began to blink.

"We're here," he said, pointing. "And this must be where Klikt is. We'll just grab a personal transport and ride on out to him. It'll be a whole lot easier than trying to negotiate walking in this moon's weak gravity."

"It is about half what we're used to," Rieka agreed. "But definitely better than Oph." She noticed Jeniper try to walk toward one of three transports parked in the terminal. She leaned awkwardly before managing to right herself, then tipped again.

When they'd selected a transport and strapped into the seats, Rieka activated the locator system and programmed their destination. "It looks like he's near the mouth of shaft three," she said. "We'll have to go through two pressure domes before we get there."

Wang hit the accelerator. "Then let's get this over with."

During the ride, Rieka sensed Wang's increasing unease. He didn't like this situation any better than she did, but neither of them could find a reasonable excuse to leave. Protocol demanded she see Klikt before they inspected the *skiff.*

Finally, the last air lock appeared and they made their

way through it. Klikt, folded delicately into his own transport, met them near the shaft's sealed entry. Wang stopped their vehicle a short distance away and Rieka stepped off. She waited while Klikt extracted himself and balanced lightly on his six elongated toes. He began a long, formal sign-greeting accompanied by the high-pitched squeals the Lomiians called language.

Rieka replied as best she could, knowing Klikt could interpret her five-fingered hand motions. She wondered, though, if he pitied her for the handicap of having only ten digits. When she began to ask him if he knew where RadiMo was, Rieka realized she didn't know how to sign individuals names, so she used "Bournese Herald."

Klikt's pale blue, bony hands replied, "No."

Frowning, she asked about the recent shipment that included the *skiff*-sized box.

Klikt's sixteen fingers blurred with their immediate reply. Rieka raised her hands, palms forward, and he slowed to a point where she could catch the general intent. When he finally let his long, elegant digits relax, Rieka was sure she'd misinterpreted him.

"What'd he say?" Wang asked.

"I . . . I think he said a *skiff* did arrive last week. He hadn't requested one and sent it on a shuttle to Oph. As far as he knew, it was empty."

"So we're back to square one?" he asked.

"Possibly. But if someone wanted to hide a Bourne, a mine would be just the place, don't you think?"

"I've already thought of that," Wang replied. He draped his wrist over the steering wheel and scanned the dome. Rieka silently wondered what else he might be thinking.

Jeniper leaned forward from the transport's backseat. "Could a Fleet ship locate RadiMo if he were here?"

"Not specifically, Jen," Rieka said. "But it can detect the number of life-forms in a place. And once we know how many individuals are here on Yona, it's just a matter of mathematics."

"If RadiMo's alive."

Rieka shot Wang a disapproving look. "We assume that he is, Wang-Chi. There's a reason he's missing."

Klikt began to sign again, and Rieka snapped her attention back to his fluttering fingers. "Apparently, that wasn't the first *skiff* to be sent here. Klikt's returned two others in the last four months. Odd, don't you think?"

"I'd call it suspicious," he said. "Not to mention the fact that the Herald's office told us the *skiff* was here. We've come for nothing."

"The object was *skiff*-sized," Jeniper corrected. "They didn't know for sure."

When Klikt signed he knew no more about *skiffs,* Rieka thanked him for his time and wished him high profits. He signaled her a similar response, then folded himself into his transport and exited through the air-lock corridor to shaft number four.

Rieka flopped into the seat next to Wang. He turned the transport around to head back to the shuttle port.

When they stopped to wait for the air lock to open, Jeniper asked, "Are you going to request a ship to check for life signs?"

"Absolutely, Jen. The *Providence* should be here soon. Even the threat of an official protest from an Oph senator wouldn't stop Triscoe. It's always much simpler to apologize for doing something than waiting to get permission to do it."

"I don't think I've ever thought of things quite like that," she admitted.

"You're too caught up with protocol," Wang said. "People who get things done don't bother with—"

He didn't get to finish, Rieka thought perversely, as she slammed into him. The jolt that had pitched her in his direction sent Jeniper off the cart. With Yona's low gravity, the Aurian woman went sailing in an arc over their heads while Wang struggled to control the vehicle.

"What the—?" She gripped the handholds as the little transport skidded for a brief moment, then plowed into the wall. Wang had already slammed on the brakes, but the momentum bucked them back off the wall and they bounced sideways, tipping precariously.

"Get out!" he yelled, shoving at her.

Rieka let go and pushed off the seat. She floated up briefly, then hit the ceiling and fell back to the floor. She lay there, dazed, trying to decide what had happened, what she needed to do. The sound of a lethal crash snapped her attention back to the present and she pushed off the floor.

"Wang!" She saw that the transport had finally come to a stop about twenty meters down the corridor. It lay on its side. Wang was gone. She guessed, hoped, he was somewhere under it, maybe stuck between it and the wall.

A soft moan behind her made Rieka turn. Jeniper had ended up on the floor, a long streak of blood behind her, evidence of how far she'd slid once the minimal gravity had pulled her down from the tube's ceiling.

Struggling to her feet, Rieka stumbled forward. "Jeniper? Can you hear me?"

No reply. Rieka gnawed at her lip and watched for any movement. A labored breath. Good. "Okay. I'm here, Jen. You're going to be fine." Rieka ran her hands along Jeniper's arms and legs, looking for any injuries. She found nothing, then realized a puddle of blood was forming under Jeniper's neck. Following the dark, sticky path upward, she discovered a gash in her scalp.

"You'll be okay, Jen," Rieka whispered, yanking off her overtunic and ripping out the lining. "You're going to have a nasty headache, though."

Once she'd tied the bandage around Jeniper's head, Rieka covered her with the remains of her tunic and turned toward their mangled vehicle. Unused to the low gravity, she stumbled more than walked. The distance seemed to have grown in the last few minutes, but she finally managed to arrive, thankful the transport had slid no farther.

"Wang, where are you? Can you hear me? Are you okay?"

She found him, unconscious, pinned between the steering column and the wall. Rieka wedged herself against the backseat, pushed her feet against the wall, and shoved as hard as she could. The vehicle shifted slightly. "Guess low gravity is good for something," she told herself, then took a deep breath and shoved again. Two more tries gave her enough room to slide Wang from his seat. When she'd got him stretched out on the floor, Rieka reached for his communicator. But it wasn't in his ear. She looked around the floor and couldn't find it. Once she'd made sure he was stable, she'd have to go looking for a comm board.

He had a big knot on his forehead and a few scrapes but didn't seem to be suffering from any other damage. Rieka patted his arm. "You'll be okay, Wang-Chi," she assured him. "I'm going to get help."

She rose slowly, fighting unwelcome dizziness. Her own head ached mightily from having contacted the tube wall, and she had to blink several times before the floor looked level. She thought she remembered seeing a comm board near the shafts. One couldn't be too far beyond the next air lock.

Rieka took a few steps forward, swayed, and steadied herself against the wall. "Can't be far," she told herself. "Get going." She picked up one foot and put it down in front of the other. It slid helplessly out in front of her. Scrambling, she caught herself with her hands and realized she couldn't breathe. Her vision blurred and she rolled onto her side. When she forced her eyes open again, she realized the overhead seam in the tube's skin had breached. Just a crack, but the pressure difference was enough to pump all the oxygen out into space.

"Damn," she murmured, before the blackness enveloped her completely.

FOURTEEN

As the *Providence* approached Oph, Triscoe felt a growing sense of unease. Nothing seemed out of the ordinary, and yet the closer they came to achieving orbit, the stronger his anxiety became. Something was *wrong*. It took him a moment to realize the feeling had nothing to do with his perception of his ship or the crew. It had to do with Rieka, though that seemed absurd, here at Oph.

His heart lurched as the connection solidified. Rieka was here. And in danger. No. More than that, she'd been hurt. Closing his eyes, Triscoe concentrated on their subconscious connection. He reached out. Where was she? What had happened?

Once he identified a general direction, Triscoe glanced at his helmsman before calling up a tactical display of the Oph system. "Lisk," he announced, "we're detouring to Yona. Get us there immediately."

"As we speak, Captain," Lisk replied, no hint of curiosity in his tone. "Our ETA at Yona is three minutes."

"What has happened?" Aarkmin asked.

Triscoe gestured for her to be patient as he thumped a toggle on his console. "Zonne, security," the voice answered.

"Lieutenant, I require a team in InterMAT Station One immediately," he said.

"Yes, Captain. They're on their way."

"Rieka is in trouble," he told Aarkmin softly. "You are in command until I return."

The look she gave him spoke of both astonishment and concern. "Understood."

On the way to the Chute, Triscoe activated his TC. "Marteen to Kyliss."

"Station One. Chief Kyliss here, sir."

"Scan Yona, Chief. I'm sure the Earth Herald is there. If she is, another Human is with her. I'm not sure of anyone else."

"Scanning, sir."

He switched off his TC once he reached the InterMAT suite. Zonne's team had arrived and were awaiting orders. Kyliss looked up from his screen.

"I've got signals for about two dozen sentients on Yona, Captain," he began. "Most of them are cool—probably Lomii. But there are three stationary readings in a corridor near the shuttle dock that are much warmer. And—"

"—and what, Kyliss?" Triscoe demanded, waving the four security people into the chamber.

"There's a hull breach, Captain. That whole section is losing pressure. I don't know if there's time—"

"Out!" Triscoe shouted at the security team. While they scrambled to exit the chamber, he turned back to Kyliss. "Get those three up here. Now."

"As we speak, sir." Kyliss, ever efficient, had already been locking onto the heat signals. Seconds later three bodies appeared in the chamber, followed by a soft popping sound.

"Send for Twanabok immediately," Triscoe said, shoving past a wide Vekyan ensign as he made his way to the chamber. Rieka lay on the floor next to Hong Wang-Chi and Jeniper Tarrik. How had they gotten to an Oph moon? And why? She looked terribly pale but he saw her chest rise and allowed his anxiety to relax a notch.

Rieka?

He knelt and touched her face. Cool. The skin looked as pale as he'd ever seen it. His eyes swept over the others. Jeniper's head had been crudely bandaged, the cloth soaked through with blood. Wang's forehead had a huge swollen area over his right eye.

Twanabok arrived with a medical team and three mobile bodypads. Triscoe lifted Rieka and placed her on one while the doctor issued orders to his assistants. Once the bodypads activated, Twanabok studied the readings and muttered a few unintelligible sounds.

"How are they?" Triscoe asked, managing to keep his voice calm.

Twanabok gestured for his people to take the patients to the medical suite. He followed them, Triscoe at his shoulder. "None is critical," Twanabok said quietly. "The Herald will be fine in an hour. The male is the most serious. Concussion. Dislocation of the right shoulder. Fractured humerus. Possible kidney damage—I'll require additional scans since the bodypads are only designed to determine injuries for triage. The Aurie woman has a scalp wound and possible concussion."

"And Rieka?"

"She needs oxygen therapy. The others do, too." They crowded into a Chute and Twanabok ordered it to the Medical suite.

"And that's all?"

"Yes."

"There is no sign of . . ."

"Of what?"

"Mistreatment."

"If you're asking whether these injuries were the result of an attack—I'd say no." Twanabok glanced at him as the Chute door opened, then addressed one of his assistants. "Take the male to the surgical suite. The women go to the ward for treatment."

Triscoe waited until the Chute was empty before heaving a sigh of relief. He'd feel better once Rieka had regained consciousness, but Vort's lack of concern for her provided an ironic sense of comfort. She'd be fine. He followed the small parade of stretchers and crew through the wide entry doors but remained in the outer office.

He clicked on his TC. "Marteen to Memta."

"Clear as the morn, Captain," his engineering superintendent replied.

"Something odd has happened on Yona. I want to know what caused a breach in the conduit wall. And I need to know why three people were seriously hurt."

"An equation requiring multiple answers. Three engineers will I send to factor the variables," Memta's gurgling voice replied. "Will they require security?"

"Whether required or not, have Zonne send a team with them," Triscoe answered.

"Understood, Captain. I shall report to you as the first light touches Varannah."

"Good. Marteen out." He reactivated his TC and asked for Aarkmin. "Any communication from Yona?"

"None yet, Captain," she replied. "There's a small mining colony on the moon. The director there is a Lomii named Klikt. I've tried to reach him, but the comm system is automated, and apparently Klikt isn't currently accessible."

"Keep trying. I want to speak to this Lomii as soon as possible.

Rieka sensed Triscoe's anxiety before she realized she wasn't cold or struggling for breath. She blinked her eyes open and found herself clamping them shut again against painfully bright lights.

Triscoe, where are you? Where am I?

Here, love. I am here. You are fine.

She felt his hand on her cheek. He kissed her, and she smiled and opened her eyes again. "The lights are bright," she whispered.

He reached to adjust the control. "Better?"

"Yes." When Rieka saw the look on his face, she almost wished she were still temporarily blind. Finding her must have terrified him.

"You're on the *Providence* under Vort Twanabok's care."

"Where are Wang and Jeniper?" she asked. Her throat was painfully dry. She tried to swallow, but her tongue stuck to the roof of her mouth.

"Here, too. Wang is in surgery at the moment. Jeniper is in the bed to your left."

"Water?" she asked. Triscoe filled a cup, and she pushed herself up against the pillow before he handed it to her. She took a few sips, then gulped the rest. She felt him squeeze her hand as she looked at Jeniper. A bandage covered the top part of her head. Her eyes were closed, and her bibbets looked pasty white.

"She'll be fine," Triscoe assured her. "Vort says she's had a slight concussion in addition to the scalp wound."

Rieka took a deep breath and let it out. "And what about Wang-Chi?"

"A bit more serious," he said. Rieka sensed Triscoe's concern but couldn't be sure of its depth. "Vort is setting his arm and repairing an internal organ, I think. I'm sure he'll give us a full report once the procedures are completed."

Rieka nodded and watched Triscoe's brown eyes as he kept his own questions to himself. Finally, she smiled softly and squeezed his fingers. "By the time Setana got to Earth, we were dealing with our own little crisis."

"Tell me."

"You sure you don't want to tell me about Sati Labs, first?"

"I will tell you. Everything," he promised. "After you explain why you were on Yona."

Rieka nodded and sat up higher on her pillow. "By the time Setana got to Earth, we'd been looking for RadiMo for about forty hours. He's gone, Tris. Disappeared."

He frowned at the news. "Could he be aground?"

She shook her head. "No. His attaché, CariMo, wouldn't have reported him missing if he'd just gone into seclusion."

"I suppose."

"Wang and I found RadiMo's personal diary. There were some clues in it pointing to Oph. Your mother offered to look after things on Earth while Jeniper, Wang, and I talked to Cimpa. He didn't know anything, but his adjutant, Gundah, discovered that an object with a *skiff*'s dimensions had recently been delivered to Yona. We took a shuttle there and talked to Klikt, the mining director. Nothing." She shrugged, still confused about the accident. "Then . . . when we were leaving . . . something happened with the ground transport."

"Deliberate?" Triscoe whispered.

"I don't think so." She frowned at his cynical expression. "I don't know. It all happened too fast for it to be a setup, don't you think? There's no way Candace could have planned it. No one except Setana and Midrin knew we were coming."

Triscoe stood straight and crossed his arms over his chest. Rieka recognized the determination on his face. He watched her for a moment, then flicked his eyes toward Jeniper. "Memta has a crew investigating the—accident," he told her. "We'll know more once he reports."

"I suppose." Rieka sat, absorbed in her thoughts, picking up vague sensations of what Triscoe was thinking. She sighed again, loudly. "So tell me about the lab. The news release didn't say much. Was anybody hurt?"

She watched him purse his lips slightly for a moment, a habit she recognized as a stall for time. "Forty-two people were killed instantly when the antimatter shell decayed. Another fifty-seven were injured—Dr. Wilmstos included."

Rieka felt her heart leap. Setana had said nothing about the huge loss of life, probably to keep her from worrying overmuch. The News Sheets had only reported an explosion, claiming an unknown number of dead and injured. "Seriously?"

"Yes."

"No. I mean—was he seriously injured?"

Triscoe shook his head. "No. I was with him at the time. We were in his office. I wasn't hurt at all, but a section of ceiling fell on Wilmstos. Vort patched him up and sent him to the Korval Care Center for continued medical supervision. But the laboratory was destroyed. They had made amazing progress in their study of—combining our gametes. Wilmstos was very encouraged with the testing."

Rieka said nothing for a moment. "Then it's probably best that we . . . decided to wait." She sighed. "I'm sure there's an ongoing investigation by the local authorities as to the cause, but do they have any suspects? Should we be thinking Candace had a hand in that, too? Or am I just getting paranoid?"

"In your case, paranoia is preferred," Triscoe said.

"Very funny." While she watched, he tightened his jaw and glanced at Jeniper. "Is there something wrong?"

He shrugged, shook his head, and refocused his attention on Rieka. "They haven't found any evidence to point at a suspect yet—as far as I know. Since a Fleet captain was present, Admiral Nason has managed to gain access to unpublicized information. He has not mentioned anything to me."

"Yet," Rieka added.

"Yet," he agreed.

"I wish I knew if any of this is related to Candace," she grumbled. Her head ached, though it was probably nothing compared to what Jeniper would suffer when she finally woke. "Or maybe it's all coincidental."

"Be careful," Jeniper whispered.

Rieka turned immediately, causing her head to feel as if it had been split in two, but saw the Aurian woman was still asleep. Triscoe walked around the bed and stood near Jeniper's feet.

"Careful. She's a threat. She means it," Jeniper said softly.

"She's still unconscious," Triscoe whispered.

"Seeyouinbywong."

"What language is that?" Rieka asked.

Triscoe frowned. "I didn't recognize it."

"She means it," Jeniper repeated. Then she took a breath and settled into a deeper sleep.

"I wonder what that was all about," Rieka said softly, still eyeing her unconscious companion. "I wonder who 'she' is. Candace, maybe?"

"I don't know. Your anxiety may have rubbed off on her."

Rieka shot him an accusing look. "Well, thanks a lot."

Twanabok entered the ward and examined the readouts on Rieka's bodypad. "Nothing to keep you here, Herald," he told her. "I'll sign you out. But report back if you experience dizziness, nausea, pain—the usual."

"Thank you, Vort, I will. How is Mr. Hong?"

"Stable," the Vekyan replied, negotiating his wide body past Triscoe so he could examine the console at the end of Jeniper's bodypad. "The fracture is hairline and internal damage was not significant. He should be functional in a few days."

Rieka nodded and swung her legs over the side of her bed. "And Ms. Tarrik?"

"Suffering from a severe blow to the head." Twanabok clicked his claws together and stepped closer to examine his patient's bandage. "Lost some blood. Aurian and Human head wounds tend to bleed quite a bit. She will be fine."

"Thank you, Doctor," Rieka offered, smiling at his big green face. "You always seem to be patching me up. I'm grateful."

"This is my job." He shrugged, heaving his chest out and

in, then shifted his attention from Jeniper to Rieka. "We all serve the Commonwealth to the best of our abilities. Now go . . . and be diplomatic elsewhere. My patient needs rest."

Rieka couldn't resist a little chuckle. "You're a treasure, Twanabok." She pushed herself off the pad and stood on the floor. When the room didn't spin as she'd expected, she nodded at Triscoe, and they left the ward.

In the corridor, Rieka stopped. "Have you recovered our equipment? Jeniper and I had datapads. Wang had a mobile TC, a maitu, and probably some things I didn't know about."

"I'll find out," Triscoe told her as he gestured toward the open Chute door. "Let's get you cleaned up, first."

Some minutes later, as she zipped up her fresh jumpsuit, Rieka heard the distinct gurgle of a Boo voice. She shoved her feet into a pair of soft boots and stepped into the living area of Triscoe's quarters to discover Memta taking up what seemed like half the room.

The engineer swiveled his head toward her and double-blinked. "Captain Herald Degahv. A pleasure to see you on the morn," he said.

Rieka smiled and closed the distance between them. "Your visage is like a glimpse at Varannah, Commander," she said. "How do you function?"

"In balance," Memta replied, though he waved his starfish hand at her. "To a point. This I am equating to your husband captain."

"Then don't let me interrupt you."

She saw Triscoe pick something up from the low table in front of the sofa. "Your datapad," he said, handing it to her. "Memta's crew found Jeniper's and Wang's equipment, too."

"Were you able to determine what caused the accident?" she asked, looking up into the Boo's huge, multifaceted black eyes.

"The transport's tires are an inflatable type. Not magnetic," Memta replied, then inhaled a breath of chlorine from his compensator. "The right rear tire was defective as Schlimb's sails. Scanning shows a weak spot in the wall like Baro in the line at Horrahn. Three on the transport exceeded the pressure parameters. It blew."

Rieka nodded, relieved the explanation seemed innocent. "And what caused the ceiling to open?"

Memta made another gesture with his hand and wriggled a bit of flesh over his left eye. "This tire released pressure as an eruption of stored energy. A section of the material shot up like the waves into Trenno. It was enough to open the ceiling. The internal pressure in the conduit widened the fissure as Toroon displaced the air of Guye."

Rieka glanced at Triscoe. His face was unreadable and he even felt calm through their link. "So you're saying this . . . was an accident?" she asked. "It would have happened . . . eventually?"

Memta blinked at her again. "You perceive this like the dawn at Varannah, Captain Herald," he said.

"Thank you for the report, Commander," Triscoe said. "The information is vital to the equation."

"I am pleased to provide such important factors." Memta saluted them, turned, and left.

Rieka clutched her datapad and sat down. She looked up at Triscoe and sensed a color. A disconcerted reddish brown. Was he unconvinced by Memta's report? "What are you thinking?" she asked.

"I'm thinking I want you three back on Earth as soon as possible. RadiMo will turn up eventually—with or without your assistance."

Rieka felt her jaw drop at his tone, but snapped it up and used her own captain's voice on him. "You're being overprotective again, Triscoe," she warned. "Memta said this was just an accident. RadiMo disappeared while on Earth. I'm responsible for his safety."

She saw him clench his jaw and turn slightly away before he looked directly at her, and said, "I am also thinking that the easiest way to have you murdered—and avoid being suspect—is for someone to make it *look* like an accident."

That brought her up short. He'd just described her theory of her father's death. She took a deep breath and raked her fingers through her hair. "Okay, Tris. We'll transfer to the *Prospectus* as soon as it arrives—and return to Earth. Maybe RadiMo will have turned up by then."

As the *Providence* slid into orbit around Aurie, Triscoe heaved a small sigh of relief. He'd transferred Rieka, Jeniper, and Wang to Robert DeVark's protection before he'd left the Oph system. If the *Prospectus* had not yet arrived at Earth, it would shortly. He hoped they would stay in one piece until he arrived there himself, at the end of the week.

His helmsman, Lisk, announced their orbit was stable. A moment later V'don reported incoming communications. "Tell them we'll begin standard cargo transfer immediately," Triscoe advised V'don. "Commander Aarkmin, you may begin."

"Understood, Captain."

Triscoe listened to the interplay between the bridge and cargo hold while he scanned through their transfer schedule. They had roughly eighteen kilotons in their hold to send to the surface and were expecting to receive about half that amount. Glancing through the list of vendors, his eye settled on one. Tarrik Enterprises.

He accessed that file and found they were receiving nothing and sending out only one point six metric tons of cargo, all bound for Oph. Having just come from there, Triscoe wondered why Tarrik didn't wait for a ship that would run a direct route to his product's destination. Then he realized once the merchandise had been loaded on a Fleet ship, Tarrik could claim delivery.

His interest having been piqued when he'd met Jeniper, Triscoe had found Tarrik Enterprises' stock had been dropping steadily for six months. Unable to fathom why, since other agro suppliers had not suffered similar losses, he wondered if Tarrik himself had problems. Remembering Jeniper's cryptic words in the medical suite, Triscoe decided a few moments alone with her brother might be prudent.

While Aarkmin continued to coordinate their cargo transfer, Triscoe leaned toward his communications officer. "V'don, see if you can reach an individual named Edrin Tarrik. He runs Tarrik Enterprises. If you cannot speak to him directly, tell his secretary I require a meeting in person—as soon as possible."

Robet strode purposefully down the *Prospectus*'s main corridor and hesitated only a moment before he rang for admittance. Hoping he wasn't giving Jeniper the wrong impression, he schooled his bibbets to a soft pink and took a breath. The idea of seeing her privately had excited his libido more than he thought it would.

The door slid open, and Jeniper stood there, her pale eyes visible below the bandage. "Captain DeVark," she said. "This is a pleasant surprise."

"I hope I'm not intruding," he offered, the words sounding contrived, even to him.

"No. Please, come in. I was just doing some research."

She backed away, giving him room to enter. He stepped across the threshold and eased into a chair as she gestured for him to sit. "How are you feeling?"

Jeniper touched the bandage and sat in the chair next to him. "I'm fine. I don't really need this anymore."

Robet nodded and groped for something else to say. "I hope the room is satisfactory. If you don't like it, there are others. Rieka's fear the Reaffirmation won't be well attended seems frighteningly accurate."

"The room is fine . . . Captain." She reached to switch off her datapad. Robet had already glanced at the screen. She'd been "researching" a company called Tarrik Enterprises.

"Robet," he corrected. "All my friends call me Robet."

He watched her fiddle with the datapad before she said, "Well, yes. But we're on your ship now. It wouldn't really be proper—"

"—you're absolutely right," he conceded gallantly, "in certain circumstances."

"And this isn't one of them?"

"No." He heaved a sigh, thankful to be past that hurdle. "I . . . enjoyed having dinner with you after Rieka's inauguration."

"Thank you," she said smiling. "It was too bad I had to run off so early."

Robet found himself smiling simply because she did. "You should have stuck around. When I came back from my walk, Rieka got Alexi on the dance floor."

"That must have been a sight," she replied, her slender fingers reaching to pat the hair around her bandage. "I mean, they're both vivacious, but Rieka is thin compared to her uncle. Still, I think Alexi has lost some weight recently. I understand he's had some health problems." She stopped and smiled strangely.

Through the elastic gauze, Robet saw her bibbets darken slightly before she said, "I'm rambling, aren't I? I don't usually do that." He noticed her hands couldn't seem to find a place to light. "Really. Robet," she persisted, "I can't tell you—"

"—Jeniper, stop." Robet reached and caught her right hand. He held it loosely, allowing her the choice to pull away. She didn't. She did exactly what he asked. She stopped. Talking. Moving. Breathing.

"What's wrong?" he whispered softly, holding her hand a bit tighter. "You can trust me, Jeniper. If there's anything I can do to help you—just name it." He liked this woman, and although comforting her hadn't been on his mind when he'd been in the corridor, Robet realized she needed him as a friend right now more than anything else.

She shook her head. "It's nothing."

"I don't think so," he insisted gently.

Jeniper closed her eyes and seemed to pull into herself, even though she let him hold her hand. "Please," she whispered.

For a brief moment, Robet felt as though his world had tilted. Did she want him to please help her—or please leave her alone? This woman *needed* help, and he wanted to give it, but he had no clue what to do. Never having faced such roiling emotions, he let his bibbets darken and held her hand tighter. "Jen? Are you in pain? Is it your head?"

Her eyes snapped open and she looked at him. "No."

"Well then . . . tell me," he coaxed. "Whatever it is— is tearing you up. Don't do this to yourself." To me, he added silently.

"I'm . . . frightened," she said slowly. She pressed her lips together and looked away as though trying to decide what to tell him.

"Frightened of—what? Of me?"

She shook her head and for a moment, Robet thought she wouldn't answer. Then she sighed. "Everything's such a mess, and it's all my fault." She pulled her hand from his and brushed her fingers against bibbets that had thickened and darkened considerably. "Just look at this. I'm falling apart. I can't even control . . . myself." She dropped her face into her hands and gulped her breath.

"No. No, don't cry. Please," Robet pleaded. Dark bibbets he could handle, but not tears. He pushed out of his chair and moved to sit on the arm of hers. He slid his hand across her back. She was so tense it felt as if he were caressing a statue.

"Talk to me. I can't help if you don't tell me what's wrong. What's happened?"

She gulped great breaths of air, and not knowing what else to do, he rubbed her back. "Why would you want to . . . help me?" she asked finally, wiping her eyes with the backs of her hands.

Robet turned and sat on the table's edge so he could face her. He didn't touch her, but leaned as close as he dared. "I like you, Jen." He shrugged and looked into her pale eyes. "Honestly, I'm attracted to you. Very attracted. But if you're in some kind of trouble, I think you need a friend right now more than you need a—relationship."

She blinked at him, then sniffed. "My brothers are in trouble."

Robet shook his head. "What kind of trouble?"

"I . . . don't know. I don't know anything!" Jeniper stood and walked to the bathroom. A moment later, she came out with a wet cloth and pressed it to her eyes and bibbets. "My younger brother, Jonik . . . He's always in debt. Always trying to get ahead with crazy schemes or by working for people who—who flagrantly disregard the law. He's borrowed thousands and thousands of credits from me. The last time he asked, I told him no. But he was worried. He said someone had threatened him—and maybe they'd come after me."

"Did you believe him?"

"No. Yes." She waved her hands aimlessly. "I don't know." She sighed. "He always says things like that when he needs money. But this time his bibbets got really dark. I wasn't sure if he was truly scared or had learned how to make them do that."

"And when was this?"

"A few weeks ago. On Indra."

Jeniper sat down in her chair again and looked at Robet with such a painful expression he wanted to go find this guy and teach him a few lessons, himself. He brushed aside the sudden anger he felt toward her callous brother, and asked, "Have you spoken to him since then?"

"No. But he's sent messages to Earth. I was supposed to meet him . . . but he couldn't come. He left a video note for me. Another warning." She sighed. "And now, this!" She gestured to the bandage on her head.

Confused, Robet returned to his chair and leaned toward her. "But what happened at Yona wasn't anyone's fault. The transport had a defective tire."

"Yes. Of course it did," she agreed. "And there was no security problem at the stadium in Damascus and RadiMo isn't missing and the lab in Rhonique didn't blow up." She glared at him, daring him to disagree.

"Jeniper, those are all unrelated incidents. Two of them don't even have anything to do with you."

"They do—indirectly," she countered. "I'm the Earth Herald's adjutant. Whoever is trying to hurt me may be—"

"—or maybe not. It's possible this isn't directed at you at all," Robet told her using his best don't-argue-with-me captain's voice. "Rieka's got plenty of her own troubles. You may just be caught up in that. Do you know who is threatening your brother?"

She sighed and shook her head.

"I'm guessing you haven't spoken to Rieka about this."

"No. You said yourself—she has enough to worry about."

His mind churning, Robet nodded. "That's . . . what I said." Concern for both women made him forget his bibbets. He looked away from her long enough to get them back under control. Then, reaching for her hand again, he said, "I don't know what's going on, but I'm going to find out. While you're aboard the *Prospectus,* I promise you'll be safe. Once we get to Earth, we'll figure something out. Everything will be fine."

"I'm not so sure. My other brother, Edrin, is experiencing huge financial problems. It's like some kind of conspiracy. He can't make anything happen the way it used to."

"You can't be sure the two are related."

"I can't be sure they're not."

Robet sighed. Talking to Jeniper was like talking to Rieka, neither woman could be convinced their assumptions might be wrong. "Why don't you send Edrin a communiqué? Ask how he's doing. Tell him about the younger

brother and that you've seen the market reports—and offer
your support. See what he says."

"Just like that?"

"The direct way is usually best," he said.

He watched her consider the idea and make a decision.
"I'll do it. I've got to do something. I need answers. And
Edrin may be in danger, too, and not even know it."

FIFTEEN

"Captain Marteen, it's a pleasure to meet you. I'm Edrin Tarrik." The Aurian standing in the middle of the room looked at least a decade older than his sister, but the similarity of their features made it obvious they were siblings.

"Mr. Tarrik," Triscoe replied. They exchanged the formal Aurian greeting, a bow from the waist.

Tarrik gestured for him to sit and took his place behind a large desk. "I beg your pardon . . . Captain . . . but I don't believe my schedule—"

"It was short notice, Mr. Tarrik," Triscoe apologized.

Tarrik nodded, then glanced at the screen on his desk console. "If you will excuse me for one moment, Captain Marteen." He tapped furiously at his keyboard for a moment, studied his screen, then began tapping again. Finally, he took a deep breath and leaned back in his chair. "What is it you wish to discuss?"

Triscoe glimpsed the bibbets on the left side of Tarrik's forehead. They seemed dark, and he wondered if it had to do with the information Tarrik had just received, or perhaps his own unanticipated presence. Treading carefully, Triscoe slowly said, "There . . . is a . . . problem."

"Yes. That seems to be my *hoshan* of late." Tarrik banged the desk with a fist. "It's quite obvious, don't you think? Though I hadn't expected they'd send a Fleet captain to complain to me. The potassium conduits were defective when we got them from Oph," he explained, pointing a finger at Triscoe. "And as far as we've been able to tell, the oxygen and nitrogen mix synthesizers were also not up to standard."

"I see."

"And that doesn't even begin to explain the mismarked shipping cartons or why we're suddenly unable to get our suppliers to fill our orders."

"Suddenly?" Triscoe frowned at that fact but let Tarrik continue.

The Aurie waved absently. "Our parts have been back-ordered, in some cases for months. It's infuriating."

"I can well imagine."

"In each instance we are obligated to notify the customer. If the problem is defective equipment, we offer to replace the faulty hardware at no cost," Tarrik explained. "I have hired eight additional inspectors to guarantee such problems won't happen again."

"I am pleased to know the situation is under control," Triscoe began, "and that you are taking measures against future occurrences. I am sure this series of incidents has not been profitable."

"Quite frankly, Captain, it has been a nightmare."

Triscoe nodded and watched Tarrik's face. He couldn't sense much from the man, but hoped to pick up whether or not he was lying. "That is more along the topic I wished to discuss with you," he said. "From the published accounts I have studied, you never experienced such problems before."

"Never," Tarrik agreed. "Everything started after the Procyon War. The past six months have been chaos, Captain Marteen. Complaints. Recalls. Our profits are off. Stockholders are furious—as I'm sure you're aware." He braced both elbows on the desktop and leaned over them. "We're doing everything we can, but it will take years to recoup."

"Undoubtedly." Triscoe decided the man would continue to lament his problems if not nudged in another direction. "Do you have any enemies, Mr. Tarrik?"

"Excuse me?"

"Enemies, sir," Triscoe repeated. "I'm looking for a source. Are there people in the Commonwealth who would profit greatly from your ruin?"

Triscoe watched as Tarrik's face went through an array of expressions. "I . . . don't know. Certainly there is tough competition in the hydroponics industry. That is a good thing, of course. It keeps the standards up and prices steady. I sincerely doubt a competitor would want to see us fold."

"Then . . . someone else? Some person or group that would profit if Tarrik Enterprises didn't exist?"

Tarrik looked truly confused. "I don't think I can answer that question, much less believe our current difficulties are a deliberate attack. The idea is completely absurd."

Triscoe nodded. He hadn't picked up anything but surprise. The reports he'd read about Tarrik's integrity must have been true. He could only hope Edrin Tarrik was as conscientious in his personal life as he was in his professional one.

"Actually, Mr. Tarrik, my purpose for this meeting was not to discuss Fleet business, and I apologize for allowing you to think so." He paused briefly and added, "I needed to ask you a few questions about your sister."

"Jeniper?"

"Yes." Triscoe eased himself back against the chair. "Jeniper. She has informed you of her new job, has she not?"

"Yes. Several weeks ago. She's the Earth Herald's adjutant." Tarrik nodded and looked Triscoe in the eye. "Forgive me for being so dense, Captain. I see the connection now. She works for your wife. A big step for her—but I'm sure she can handle it." Tarrik took a deep breath and made a vague gesture with his hand. His bibbets lightened, and the tension seemed to drain out of him. He got up from behind the desk and gestured for Triscoe to follow him through a door.

"I apologize for that frustrated tirade, Captain Marteen," Tarrik said once they'd entered a comfortable-looking room. "I assumed you'd come about our current difficulties at T.E. Quite honestly, I've been expecting the Fleet to renegotiate our cargo contracts." He sighed, and Triscoe watched his bibbets fade to pale pink. "I'm a much better host in a social setting. Can I offer you some refreshment?"

"Fruit-water would be fine," Triscoe replied, and waited while Tarrik ordered beverages at a small console. They sat across from one another on thickly padded chairs. A small servebot rolled up a moment later, carrying two glass tumblers and a tray of snacks.

"Earth chocolate," Tarrik explained, picking up a small hunk of dark brown candy. "I admit I am addicted."

Triscoe smiled. He took a sip of his water and selected a piece of dried fruit. "Are you and Jeniper very close?"

"We are siblings," Tarrik replied after savoring the chocolate. "We keep in touch with one another, but we both have out own lives. I haven't seen her in almost a year, actually. Why do you ask?"

"Jeniper was involved in an . . . accident. Four days ago. On an Oph moon called Yona."

Tarrik leaned closer, his bibbets darkening slightly. "What kind of accident? Was she hurt?"

Triscoe shook his head. "She suffered a minor concussion and a small scalp wound. She was in the company of my wife and her bodyguard. None was seriously injured."

"Well, that's a relief—that none of them were hurt." Tarrik leaned back and Triscoe watched as his bibbets again paled to a neutral tone.

"Yes. But the reason I'm here has to do with the accident. I'm sure you understand my wife's safety is paramount—and that of her staff."

"Absolutely."

"Your sister, while still unconscious, said a most curious thing. And in light of your current business difficulties, I am wondering if there may be a connection."

"What did she say?" Tarrik sat straighter, and Triscoe picked up a distinct sense of anxiety from him.

"She said—while unconscious: 'Be careful. She's a threat. She means it.' Then she said something else in a language I did not understand." He paused for a moment, then said, "Does this . . . have any meaning for you?"

Tarrik set his glass down and tapped his fingers on the arm of his chair. Triscoe could tell he was trying to decide how much to reveal of whatever it was he knew. Softly, he said, "My concern is solely for the safety of my wife and her staff. I have no other agenda."

Nodding, Tarrik replied, "Of course, Captain. I appreciate your bringing this to my attention. And, unfortunately, I have few facts to give you. But I must ask—are you certain this incident involving Herald Degahv was an accident?"

"My engineers found no evidence to prove otherwise."

"But you are skeptical."

"Yes."

Tarrik nodded. "I would be, too. Let me explain, Captain. My sister and I have a younger brother. His name is Jonik. His birth was unanticipated, and though Auries do not give up their children to adoption as other races do, I sometimes think he would have been better reared in another household. My parents had planned and saved only enough for my sister and me to be well educated. Jonik understood at a young age that he would be earning his own way. By the time he finished his primary education, however, I had begun to turn a profit with Tarrik Enterprises. I offered to subsidize his education—but he refused.

"Jonik has worked in a variety of trades, the latest of which has been as a courier. I don't know for whom he works—or even if he's presently employed. He also likes to take risks. He gambles. Speculates occasionally. I have loaned him credit several times. And I know Jeniper has, too."

"How much are we talking about?"

"Tens of thousands of credits. I don't know the exact amount at this moment." Tarrik shrugged. "I have a record of it in my personal papers."

"Has he asked for money recently?"

"About a month ago. He wanted almost sixty thousand. My finances had already been bad for some time. I told him no."

"Do you think he went to Jeniper?"

"Possibly. She's given him money in the past."

"Would she have given him that much?"

"No."

Triscoe sat straighter. "You say that with certainty?"

Tarrik nodded. "I do. That's nearly a year's salary to her. Jeniper doesn't approve of Jonik's lifestyle. She wouldn't have done it."

"So do you think he might have threatened her?"

Tarrik shook his head. "No. Jonik would not threaten anyone." When Triscoe frowned at him, he smiled sadly. "You must understand. Jonik is easily influenced, but harmless. He could be holding a maitu to your head—and you wouldn't feel threatened."

Triscoe tried not to frown. "I'll have to trust you on that. But if not Jonik, then who?"

"I wish I knew, Captain. I'd also like to know where Jonik is."

"Is he missing?"

"Not as far as I know," Tarrik replied. "I simply don't know his whereabouts. He doesn't contact the family very often. Usually only for a loan. But our father's health is failing. I'd like to be able to find Jonik and ask him to spend some time at home."

"Does Jeniper know?"

"I think so. I believe Mam sent the message to Earth last week."

One look at Robet's face made Rieka glad she didn't have bibbets. "Come in, Robet," she told him airily from just inside the doorway of her suite. "Wang, Jeniper . . . would you excuse us?"

Wang hesitated. Rieka chafed at that. "I'm sure Captain DeVark isn't going to harm me, Wang-Chi." She flashed him a false smile. "And he's smart enough to know it would be stupid to try."

Wang gave her a halfhearted shrug and nodded. "I'll wait in my room."

When they were alone, Rieka relaxed. Slightly. "What's gone wrong now?"

"How do you know anything's wrong?"

"Because your bibbets are very pale, Robet," she told him gently. "You always overcompensate when you're trying not to show anxiety. And," she added, gesturing for him to sit on the sofa, "because we're inside Neptune's orbit, which means you've slowed forward speed enough to receive messages."

He frowned at her, his blue eyes cloudy with concern. "You know me too well."

"I know the routine," she corrected, seating herself beside him. "So what's happened?"

"An incoming communiqué, from Nason . . ."

"What about it?"

"He suggested I play it for you once I got to Earth. Of course he couldn't know you'd be on the *Prospectus* when I received it. I don't know whether to wait or—"

"Oh, for heaven's sake, give me the damn thing," Rieka snapped, holding out her hand. Robet fished in his trouser pocket and placed the small plastic square in her palm. He perched on the desk as she inserted it into the slot in her console.

The Fleet logo appeared for several seconds before Nason's face sprang three-dimensionally from the graphics. Rieka noticed the steely expression and the fact that his bibbets, like Robet's, were noticeably pale.

"Captain DeVark, you should be receiving this communiqué as you power down from your slide to Earth. The orders I am about to give you supersede your current tour schedule. I am issuing Contingency Order Three. Upon arrival at Earth, you are to remain there until you receive additional orders from me. Do not, for any reason, leave orbit."

Rieka flipped a toggle to suspend the replay. She looked up into Robet's odd frown. "What's going on? I haven't heard anything about a breach of security."

"Me either, until now," Robet told her. "Switch it back on."

She did. Nason sighed, looked somewhere off camera for a moment, then redirected his attention forward. "Contingency Order Three is being initiated for the following planets: Earth, Oph, and Yadra. And for the Fleet base at Dani. Persons en route to other planets who are *Prospectus* passengers may remain aboard at no charge—or may billet themselves on Earth at Fleet expense.

"The 'official' reason for remaining on Earth is a faulty valve in the exotic matter conduit. Your engineer is receiving a similar communiqué with a more technically complete explanation of the problem."

"Jeez," Rieka complained, "get to the point."

"I also want Rieka Degahv to be privy to the problem as it will quite probably affect her directly. Rieka, as you know, is still on the Fleet roster. It is possible we will have need of her services."

"See," Robet said, nudging her arm with his elbow.

She nudged him back but said nothing. A frisson of energy went through her. Excitement? Anxiety? She wasn't sure. But whatever was happening had to be serious enough

for Nason to pull ships off their tours. She wondered if
he'd actually recall her.

"Encoded communications between persons in the Fleet
and on Earth, Oph, and Yadra have been brought to my
attention by Admiral Veridok in Internal Affairs. The mis-
sives defy decoding. Once played, the audio and video are
rendered unintelligible. This type of programming is virtu-
ally foolproof. Copies are equally impossible to
comprehend.

"We do not know what is being relayed, nor to whom.
I am issuing the contingency order to provide additional
security for the planets involved. Other Fleet ships will arrive and depart without having been issued the order. Since
this action is covert, your excuse for staying on Earth is
the breakdown in your engine system. I may upgrade to
Contingency Order Two if and when the parties are
identified."

"I can't believe this," Rieka whispered.

"Travelers wishing to transfer to outgoing ships may do
so. No one is to be detained. I need you to double-check
all manifests for the last four weeks. Look for any inconsis-
tencies—among both cargo and passengers. Even if you
find nothing, forward all records to me. Brief only your
command-level personnel on this matter. Do not increase
ship's security. Do nothing out of the ordinary unless you
receive additional orders from me.

"Good luck, Robet. Let's hope this matter will resolve
itself as soon as possible."

The screen went blank, but Rieka stared at it for several
seconds before switching it off. "Damn, Robet," she said
softly. "I don't like this. Do you think it has something to
do with the Reaffirmation?" When he said nothing, Rieka
felt the hair raise on her forearms. Plans had been crum-
bling ever since she took office. Her mother's reach was
far, but Rieka hadn't anticipated anything like this. It resembled a coup.

She looked up at Robet. His jaw was clenched shut and
his eyes were almost closed. He seemed worried. "Do you
know something?"

He swiveled his jaw from side to side. "Not about this,"
he answered. "I'm concerned about Jeniper."

"Jeniper?" Rieka pushed herself up and away from the

console and went back to the sofa to sit. "I don't understand. She's fine now."

He sighed and followed her. She watched him fidget for a moment and swivel his jaw again. "She's so vulnerable right now, that's all," he said finally.

"Jeniper?" she repeated, incredulous. "I'm the one who's being threatened. I'm the one who's lost RadiMo. I'm the one who's plans for Earth's future are in jeopardy. And you think *Jeniper* is vulnerable?"

He had the decency to look contrite. "When you put it that way . . ." He gestured aimlessly with his hands. "It's just that—you're experienced. Gods, Rieka. You've commanded Fleet ships. You took on the Procyons. You're a Herald! Jeniper's just a nice girl from Aurie who works for you."

Rieka took a moment to absorb both what he had and hadn't said. She sighed and raked her fingers through her hair. "I see your point. But in that case, I need to ask—are the two of you . . . seeing each other? Are you worried about her because you care—or because anyone associating herself with me is probably taking a big health risk?"

Robet hesitated before he answered, but looked her in the eye when he did. "Both. Well, no. Actually we aren't physically involved, yet. That will happen . . . eventually. I hope." He sighed and looked at the floor.

"I'm proud of you, Robet," Rieka offered, hoping to ease him out of his apparent discomfort. "After that last horrible relationship you tried to jump into . . . I'm glad to see you getting some confidence back."

"I realized, then, what a fool I'd made of myself. I don't intend to do that again."

"You won't. Jeniper is a wonderful person. I'm sure once she gets to know you she'll see that you're a wonderful person, too."

"Yeah," he said sheepishly. "But now there are more important things to worry about than my social life. Do you have any idea what Nason's found out about those illegal transmissions and why he'd order CO-3?"

"Not exactly," Rieka answered, though her mind had already processed that information, and she'd agreed with the admiral's assumptions. "But I do know that my mother has people working for her who are willing to risk going to prison by programming messages to play only once. I actually received such a message from her. And Candace's base of operations is on Yadra. Since her goal is to stop me, we can assume she's communicating with someone on Earth."

"Then what about Oph? And the Fleet personnel?"

"I'm not sure. It may have something to do with Radi-Mo's disappearance. Or, it may have nothing at all to do with it. We don't have enough information. And though I'm usually willing to speculate on a lot of things, I'd rather not this time."

She looked at Robet and frowned. "As far as I know, my father and I are the only people who have ever successfully crossed Candace. If RadiMo is involved with her, he doesn't stand a chance."

Robet sat straighter. "You don't think she'd . . . murder him?"

Rieka thought back to her own speculation surrounding Stephen's death. They were still digging up evidence, but things were pointing toward something more sinister than a malfunction. Exterior coolant systems had backups and fail-safes. His shuttle should not have incinerated in the atmosphere.

"I suppose you could say with Candace, anything's possible."

SIXTEEN

Rieka couldn't quite suppress a smile for the motley group that followed her out of the InterMAT station at the Embassy in New SubDenver. Jeniper still wore the bandage on her head, Wang's arm would be in the sling for at least another day, and Robet looked as though he hadn't slept in several nights.

"I'm going to my office," she told Wang. "You don't have to come if you've got other things to do. I'm just planning on catching up with—"

"I'm not one hundred percent," he insisted, "but I can still do my job."

Rieka opened her mouth to berate him for his tone, then switched gears before she spoke. "Of course you can, Wang. If I didn't think so, you wouldn't be here." She offered him a wry smile and accepted the small nod she got in return. He still blamed himself for the accident at Yona. She figured she'd wait until his body mended before making any judgments as to his attitude.

Robet, having watched the interplay, took Jeniper gently by the elbow, and said, "We'll come along, too. I know Jeniper has some catching up to do, and I'd like to take a look at Earth security."

"The embassy is a clearinghouse for everything you might need," Rieka said. "Wang can take you through whatever security checkpoints we've got set up—and you can decide what you want to do with the *Prospectus*—security-wise." She watched him nod, and led the way to her office.

When the outer door opened, Rieka recognized Elena, Setana's adjutant, seated behind Jeniper's console. "Welcome back, Herald Degahv," the Indran said, a smile brightening her beautiful, pale face. "Herald Marteen is in your office. We have been rather busy in your absence."

"I can't imagine why," Rieka quipped. With the Reaffirmation now just days away, *busy* was a gross understatement.

Elena frowned, then nodded. "Oh, a joke. Yes. Well, I can certainly understand the value of humor in such a complex situation."

"I'm sure you can." She gestured for Wang to take Robet to the security office, then prodded them with, "Jen and I will be in my office. You can find us there when you're through." She watched Robet nod at Jeniper and follow Wang down the hall.

"I think I'll stay here and have Elena brief me on what she's been doing," Jeniper said.

"That's fine, Jen," Rieka replied. "I'll let you know if I need you." She turned and strode into her office, where she was greeted by Setana.

"I heard about what happened on Yona. How are you feeling?" Setana asked. "How are Jeniper and Mr. Hong?"

"We're all okay. Nothing sinister happened as far as Memta could determine. And there isn't any evidence to suggest otherwise. But that doesn't mean I accept his conclusion. *Something* isn't right." She sighed. "The most disappointing thing is that we still have no idea what's happened to RadiMo."

"It is very disconcerting," Setana agreed. "I do hope he turns up safe before the Reaffirmation."

"I wouldn't hold my breath." Rieka said. When Setana frowned, she realized she'd used another Earth idiom. "It means . . . we'll have to be patient."

Setana relaxed and nodded. "I shall not hold my breath, either."

Rieka covered her smile with her hand. "Right. Why don't you brief me on what you've done in my absence—and then you can go and . . . do what you'd rather be doing."

Setana adjusted her scarf and looked pointedly at Rieka. "I have been perfectly content as your temporary replacement. And I'll remind you I volunteered to help."

"Sorry. I didn't mean—"

"—I know exactly what you meant," Setana scolded. "Do not apologize for someone else's presumed hardship. It places you in a less favorable position." Rieka nodded. "Now then," Setana went on, "Elena has been coordinating the housing problems—there have only been a few—and I have overseen the social events. Everything is ready for the party tomorrow night in Versailles, and nothing untoward has happened in your absence—unless you consider your mother's arrival in that category."

"Candace is here?"

"She arrived yesterday."

Rieka sat back and digested that news. On the one hand, with Candace here to stir up trouble, there might not be a moment's peace. But on the other hand, it would be a lot easier to catch her trying to undermine their plans for Earth.

"Okay," she said, offering Setana a quirky smile. "If she's here, let's put her under the microscope. I'll have Wang order surveillance for her and whatever staff she's got. She might even provide Admiral Nason with some much-needed evidence."

"What is his connection to her?" Setana asked, confusion apparent in her eyes.

"Nothing is confirmed yet. I'll let Robet tell you about that, himself."

"Captain DeVark?"

"The one and only. But let's not digress. Who else is here?"

Setana smiled. "Herald Dets of Aurie arrived yesterday, as did Herald Honutik. We have been notified that six senators will accompany Herald Loome from Yadra. They will arrive the day before the ceremony. Dzan, the Boolian Herald is expected, but we don't know when. Several business leaders are here, as are some Fleet administrators. They're arriving slowly, but Earth is the place to be for the next week."

"Don't you just love the limelight?" Rieka asked, pushing out of the chair to return to her desk.

"Sarcasm? I thought you liked attention."

"In moderation," she explained. "From certain people. Sometimes I'm convinced I must have been insane when I decided to run for Herald."

"But it is your destiny."

Rieka shrugged. Destiny or not, she had the job, for life.

Slightly raised voices coming from the outer office made her frown. "What now?" Rieka went to the door and opened it to find Wang holding a maitu on her mother. Jeniper and Elena stood behind the receptionist's desk, and Robet blocked the outer door. "What the hell is going on out here?"

Everyone began talking at once, though the noise level rapidly elevated to shouting. Rieka rolled her eyes and grimaced at the cacophony, then yelled for quiet. Everyone responded immediately, with the exception of Candace.

"I cannot believe I would be treated with such—"

"Shut up, Mother. Just shut—up. Can you do that?"

The order apparently shocked her into submission. Candace clamped her jaw closed and sighed loudly through her nose.

Rieka glared at her for a moment. "Now . . ." She studied the crowd. "Elena first."

Setana's adjutant offered an odd gesture with her hands. "This woman insisted on seeing you immediately. I explained you were in conference, but she became . . . agitated."

"I have never been—"

"Shut up, Mother. You'll have your chance," Rieka barked. She turned back to the others. "So she started fussing at you, and I'll bet Wang came tearing down the hall with his maitu drawn." He'd already holstered the weapon, but she nodded her thanks.

"Well, yes," Elena said softly. "It all happened very quickly."

"I'm sure it did." She glanced at the faces around her. People looked angry, frustrated, and uncertain. "I think we'd better have a little chat. Mother. Wang." She gestured toward her office. "We're not to be disturbed," she said, addressing Jeniper.

"Of course." After a glance at Robet, Jeniper closed the door behind them.

Silence reigned for a moment, then Rieka shook her head. "Okay, we might as well get this ironed out right now. Conference room." She gestured toward a paneled door.

Wang went to it first, opened it, and switched on the lights. "It's clear," he announced.

Setana caught Rieka's eye as she waved her mother through. "Consider using the DGI, dear," she advised softly. "Perhaps a pastoral mural. Maybe running water. Something soothing."

Rieka nodded and went to the console to program the setting. Before she took her place at the oval table's narrow end, the room's DGI window revealed a forest lit with dappled sunlight. Speakers hidden in the ceiling played sounds to accompany the image of a running brook. The tension in the room dropped several notches.

Now, even though they were eight stories below ground level in the middle of a large city, it both looked and felt as though they could escape everything by simply leaving the room. At the moment, she realized she wished she could do just that.

"Okay. Let's start with introductions. Mother, allow me to introduce you to the Indran Herald, Setana Marteen. And this gentleman"—Rieka gently touched his arm—"is Mr. Hong Wang-Chi, my personal bodyguard." To Setana and Wang, she said, "This is the CEO of PirezCorp of Yadra, my mother, Candace Degahv."

A brief moment of silence passed, then they echoed various words of welcome. Candace, looking pleased with herself, "I didn't realize, Mr. Hong, that a Herald required a bodyguard."

"Under the circumstances, it is a prudent precaution," he replied.

"Under what circumstances?"

"Considering the fact that the last two Earth Heralds have suffered unexpected health problems."

"Such as?" Candace asked.

"Such as . . . let's drop this subject," Rieka interjected, throwing a warning glance at Wang. They'd get nothing out of Candace if they implied her involvement in Stephen's death. And as far as Alexi's liver was concerned, Rieka understood that to be a problem that had developed without Human intervention, though at this point she knew anything was possible.

"Mr. Hong has already saved my life and, fortunately, is on the mend. End of story."

"I don't think I like the sound of that," Candace said.

Rieka ignored the comment. "Your barging in unannounced this afternoon has been rather fortuitous, Candace. I need to ask you some questions. And Herald Marteen can tell us whether you're lying or not."

Candace gasped. "Well, I never—"

"—oh yes, you do. More than you think," Rieka said, recalling how sincere Candace always made herself sound. "But that's beside the point. You didn't want me to be Herald, and now that I am, you're determined to obstruct every effort I make on this planet's behalf, aren't you?"

"I'm sure I have no idea what you are talking about."

"And I'm sure you don't mean that," Setana said.

Candace huffed.

Rieka hid her smile behind her hand, then leaned slightly toward her mother. "You see, you're not going to get away with your scheme—whatever it is. Not everyone is on your payroll. I told you before—my plans for this planet do not include upsetting the Commonwealth's financial balance. Your fortune is safe. Can't you be happy with that? Tell all your people you've changed your mind and leave Earth alone. If you don't, I swear I'll see you prosecuted to the fullest extent of the law."

"I don't have to stand for this!" Candace announced, pushing out of her chair. "You are my daughter. My flesh and blood. I could not be here for your inauguration, but I came for the Reaffirmation—as a Human, as your mother. And look at what I find when I arrive. The Herald does not have time for an audience with me. I waited an entire day!" she hissed. "What kind of treatment is that—for anyone? How dare you sit there and accuse me of—of nothing—when you, yourself are far from blameless, Rieka.

"You carry on about responsibility—that you'll be responsible for Earth and the Commonwealth. But that's laughable. You don't know the meaning of the word. I have never seen or met a worse hostess. And your manners are deplorable. How dare you threaten me. It is unfathomable how you could have been elected, much less make a success of your position as Herald."

She stopped for a moment, her eyes daring Rieka to take the bait. Knowing better, Rieka simply sighed and said nothing.

"And your plans for Earth will fail without my help, certainly," Candace went on. "To expect to house people in these underground cities where everything is contained and accounted for as if you were aboard a spaceship . . . for heaven's sake, it's completely uncivilized. It's like living in a cave. Earth has spent billions with borrowed credit to create these civic abominations—and will never be able to pay it back."

It took incredible effort, but Rieka managed to keep her face relaxed and her mouth shut. She knew better than to try arguing with Candace in front of people. It would only serve to make her look less in control. She suddenly realized all that tongue biting she'd done as a Fleet captain did actually serve a purpose.

Candace continued ranting for several minutes more. Finally, when she paused for a breath, Rieka calmly said, "Thank you for that lovely tirade, Mother. Now, you will please leave us to get some work done. And if you ever barge into my office unannounced again . . . I'll let Mr. Hong shoot you." She looked at the man seated at her left. "Wang-Chi."

He stood and escorted Candace out. At the doorway, she stopped and turned. "You can't be rid of me this easily. And let me assure you, daughter, that even if you don't see how wrong you are, others do."

Ignoring a rumble from her empty stomach, Rieka poured a glass of fruit-water for Setana and joined her on the sofa. The apartment she'd selected was both roomy and well appointed. They sat quietly gazing at the large DGI Rieka had programmed to play a prairie sunset.

"That is quite lovely," Setana said. "Do Earth sunsets actually look like that?"

"In some places," Rieka told her. She heaved a great sigh and leaned her head back against the cushion. "I need more hours in the day."

"Triscoe will be here soon, dear," Setana soothed. "Things will be better."

"I'm sure I don't know what you mean—but I'm also sure I don't want you to explain it to me." She heard a door close and turned her head to see Wang come through the entertainment area. "Why aren't you wearing your sling?"

"Don't need it anymore." He poured himself a drink in the kitchen and joined them. "Nice sunset."

"We were just discussing it," Setana said.

"The DGI in my room is out of alignment," Wang complained. "Everything is blurry. Makes me dizzy to look at it."

"I can probably fix it," Rieka said, sitting up. "Shouldn't take more than a couple of minutes."

"Don't worry about it," Wang said warily.

"Who's worrying? I'm qualified to work on that type of equipment. I was a tech-pro only a few months ago." She pushed off the couch and glanced down at Setana's wry smile. "What?"

"The tech-pro that single-handedly *undid* the *Prodigy's* circuitry, I believe," she said.

Rieka lifted her chin. "I did what I was *ordered* to do, Madam Herald. Wang, I promise if I can't straighten out the problem, I'll admit it."

The big man shrugged and led the way. "Couldn't be much worse, anyway."

"Your confidence is inspiring, Wang-Chi. Be back in a minute, Setana."

They went through the entertainment area and down a short hallway to Wang's suite. His desk and several shelves were cluttered with various computer parts and other sundry hardware. The DGI was off, so Rieka went to his small console and switched it on. Sure enough, the picture looked so blurry she couldn't make it out.

Rieka picked up a pair of dirty socks from the chair and handed them to Wang. "Didn't realize you needed a housekeeper," she said.

"I manage."

Rieka laughed and sat. "Let's see what kind of damage I can do." Thoroughly enjoying herself, she accessed the programming files and called up those pertaining to the DGI. "Here you go, Wang-Chi. Your depth perception is way off. Who set this thing up, a Lomii?" She tapped a few more keys and reset the screen. When the DGI menu came up, she found a North Atlantic shoreline and entered it. "How's that?"

She saw the look of astonishment on his face, then a bit of awe added to it as he turned to her. "You really did it," he said.

She rolled her eyes. "Why are people constantly surprised when I do something completely mundane? It isn't that hard to reprogram a DGI. I'm sure you could have done it, yourself."

He shook his head. "I don't mess with that kind of software. It's Fleet derivative. Now, you want to talk anything else, or hardware—cameras, microphones, private TCs, any security equipment—"

"Rieka!"

Rieka heard Setana's strident calls and was out the door in a heartbeat with Wang on her heels. They ran into the sitting room and stopped short. Setana and Robet were staring at one another. Both looked concerned, almost fearful.

"What? What's happened now?" Rieka barked.

Robet turned to her. "It's Jeniper. I went to her apartment—we were going to a bar upstairs before dinner with you—and she wasn't there."

Rieka told herself to be calm, then looked into Robet's blue eyes and ignored his darkening bibbets. "What do you mean, she wasn't there?"

"I mean she's gone. When she didn't answer the door, I checked your offices and the bar we were going to. Then, I had SubDenver security come and open the apartment. She wasn't inside. Her datapad was on the kitchen table, Rieka. She's gone."

"Okay," she said gesturing for him to stay calm even as a frisson of worry went through her. "Now, Jeniper is pretty methodical. I'm sure she'd tell me if she planned to be late for dinner—which she isn't, yet. Let me just check my incoming messages."

Stepping past Setana, Rieka snatched up her datapad and accessed her comm file. "Here. She sent a message sixty-eight minutes ago. She asks me not to wait dinner. She's got an errand to run and she'll see me later."

Sure Robet wouldn't take her word for it, she handed the datapad to him. "Jeniper's fine." As long as the errand she's running has nothing to do with Candace, she amended silently.

SEVENTEEN

Jeniper took a deep breath and pulled her coat collar up against her neck. She couldn't believe she'd come back to Bywong just because Jonik had asked her to.

The old and new structures looked less frightening in the late-morning sunlight. There were two private vehicles parked near the small office she'd been in before. She stood next to the taxi that had brought her from Canberra and wondered what to do.

"This is so stupid," she told herself. The icy wind licked at her, and a line of strangely dark clouds loomed, blocking out all but the nearest peaks. A small voice in her head urged her to go back to New SubDenver. Now.

An Oph came out of the building. He glanced at her, walked to a vehicle, and got in. She heard a click as the flywheel engaged the electrical systems and watched as it maneuvered around the other car and her taxi. It pulled up alongside her and the window opened.

"He's in there," the Oph said. Then he took off down the narrow winding road that led back to civilization.

The wind picked up and Jeniper shivered. Glancing at the snow line, she realized it wasn't much higher than where she presently stood. The clouds looked closer now. She wondered how long it would be before it snowed.

Taking the Oph's advice, she walked cautiously toward the door. "Stupid, stupid," she muttered, knowing how foolish this gamble was. But she couldn't go on risking Rieka's life because of Jonik's disreputable actions. Somehow, she had to help him out of his current problem. Settle the overdue account. Whatever.

She knocked, but no one answered. Gripping the icy handle, Jeniper pulled the door open and stepped in out of the wind. She blew on her fingers to thaw them while she looked around the room. The blinds were drawn, but even in the gloom she could see there wasn't anyone at the console.

"Jeniper."

She swiveled her head. She had no idea where he'd been hiding, but he stood only a couple of meters away, now. She stared at him, taking in his gaunt features and dark hair that had grown too long since she'd seen him last. Apparently, he'd suffered more than she in that time.

"Gods, Jonik. You scared me. Are you all right?" She stepped closer to him and lifted her arms to offer a hug. He accepted it, and she got a better idea of how much weight he'd lost.

"You're too thin," she chided. "Mam would tell you to eat—that you look like a skeleton."

"I get enough," he said.

"And before we say anything else to each other, I need you to know that Mam sent me a message. Pae isn't well. Mam thinks . . . She thinks we should come home and see him soon. I'll probably go after the Reaffirmation. You should, too."

"He doesn't want to see me."

"He does. I'm sure of it. Mam and Pae always ask if I know how you are, where you are, what you're doing . . ." When he shook his head, Jeniper felt her patience waning. "Jonik, I want you to listen to me. Whatever it is you've gotten yourself into, I can help you. I work for the Earth Herald. I can—"

"—I know who you work for."

Jeniper shook her head. "I'm not the Indran attaché anymore," she said, not knowing how much news he'd heard. "I'm Rieka Degahv's adjutant to Earth."

"I know that!" He shoved her arms away and took a step back, putting the desk chair between them.

Jeniper made herself stay put. If she scared him and he ran, she'd never be able to keep up. She lifted one hand, gesturing for him to stay calm. "I came here because I got your message and want to help you."

"You refused to, before," he spit, the heat of his anger

and frustration darkening his bibbets. "Now things are different. You can't help me the way you think."

She didn't like his ominous tone. "How are things different?"

"She's already tried to kill me. Even after I helped her. I did what she asked, and she didn't care." He hugged himself and turned away.

Jeniper watched him in the room's faint light. She listened to his ragged breath and knew no matter how frustrated and afraid she'd felt, Jonik's terror had to be a hundred times greater. She raked her fingers through her hair, mindful of the healing wound, and tried to think of something meaningful to say.

"You're still my brother," she reminded him softly. "And even if you are a *bimoosh*, I love you anyway." She took a small step toward him. "Jonik, I didn't believe you, before. I do, now. I understand the kind of trouble you're in and—"

"No you don't, Jen. You don't understand anything." He looked at her and she could see the anguish on his face. The skin was so pale, and his bibbets stood out in stark contrast. She started to reply, but he went on. "You think you understand. But this whole stupid mess is my doing. Mine and hers. She'd kill anyone to get what she wants. You can't ask for your Herald's help—or anybody else."

"Rieka Degahv's a good person, Jonik. And she knows what it's like to be wrongfully accused. She's got a lot of power, too—and a lot of powerful friends. She can help you."

"I've already wrecked her life, Jeniper, and she doesn't even know it. I won't consider asking for her help."

"So the accident . . . It did have something to do with you." She had worried over that for days. Speculating whether or not it had been planned had almost driven her crazy.

"It was no accident."

Jonik's sober words doused her uncertainty but fueled her fear. Jeniper sighed and leaned on the desk. "I wondered about that, even after Captain Marteen had his engineer examine the wrecked transport. But of course, that had nothing to do with the hull breach."

He turned to face her, frowning. "What are you talking about?"

"About the accident. On Yona. How I got this." She pointed to the scab on her head. His bewildered expression told her this was news to him. "What are *you* talking about?"

She watched his eyes bulge for a moment, then a mask settled over his features. "I want to give you something, Jen."

"What are you talking about?" she repeated. "Don't change the subject." He shook his head. "Jonik, I'm prepared to help you, but I need some information. Just a fact or two. Anything." He didn't answer and she rapped her knuckles against the desktop. "Damn it, Jonik. You've got to trust me."

"I do. Come with me. I need to give you something."

Not knowing what else to do, Jeniper followed him out the door and toward a gaping hole in the mountainside. "I'm not going in there," she said.

"It's just the old mine," he explained, nodding for her to follow. "The developers have modernized everything. It's a tourist ride now. They finished laying the last of the tracks a couple of days ago. There's nothing to worry about." He walked into the cave's mouth and seemed to be swallowed up in the darkness.

"Jonik!"

"It's okay, Jen," his voice called out. "There's a blackout curtain right at the edge. Just come on through."

The blackout curtain turned out to be three curtains hanging about a meter apart. They'd been stretched and mounted to the cave's roof and floor. She pushed her way through slits in the heavy material, almost choking from the sense of claustrophobia.

"There you are," Jonik said, as she stepped into a well-lit room. "This place'll be open in another few weeks. But we can take a complimentary ride."

She watched him walk confidently to a console behind a large boulder, or more correctly, a console that had been constructed to look like a boulder. A string of dim lights came on down the tunnel, and a trio of connected ore cars with molded seats rolled into the room.

"Get in," he told her. Jeniper nodded and climbed into

the last car. Jonik stood a moment more at the controls, then stepped into the second car. "I turned off the audio," he said. "This'll only take a few minutes."

They rolled down the tunnel and Jeniper could tell it had been reinforced by modern technology and then decorated to appear old. What looked like antique wooden struts framed the underground passage every few meters, both small overhead lights and flickering lamps hung strategically on the uneven walls, lighting the mine shaft. The air smelled dusty, but dry. She imagined that would change once the snow melted in the spring.

He stood as they turned a corner and stretched his hand up high enough to reach the beams as they passed under them. He touched each one, and she realized he was counting them.

"Nine." He put his foot up on the car's seat. "Ten." He stood on the seat. "Eleven." He reached up and pulled something down from a recess behind the beam. Jeniper turned to look where the knapsack had come from, but she could only see shadows.

Jonik reseated himself. She watched him handle the dark cloth bag carefully. He set it on his lap and opened it. A burnished silver-colored cylinder appeared in his hand. It looked to be about the size of a large mug.

"What is that?" she asked.

"Insurance," he answered cryptically.

"For what Jonik? I don't understand. Why won't you tell me anything?"

"The less you know, the better, Jen." He slipped the cylinder back into the bag and leaned across the short space between the still-rolling cars. "Keep this for me. Keep it safe. Don't let anyone know you've got it."

Frowning, Jeniper accepted the proffered sack. "But why?"

"Our lives depend on it."

Robet could never remember being so worried about anyone. He couldn't get Jeniper off his mind. He'd watched her strong independence wilt until she blamed herself for every little mishap. He'd wanted to help her, and she wouldn't let him. Now, she'd mysteriously vanished. Even if the errand she'd supposedly been on had taken more time than expected, she should have checked in sometime during the night.

The secretary announced him, and he walked into Rieka's office. Setana Marteen stood before Rieka's desk, tapping notes on a datapad. "Is that all?" the Herald inquired.

"It's everything from her office's appointment book. You sure you want to do this?" Rieka asked.

"Endless Heavens, dear," Setana quipped. "Who better?" She turned and smiled. "Hello, Captain DeVark. How are you?"

"Good morning, Herald Marteen, Rieka," he replied, nodding to them in turn. "I've been better, to tell you the truth."

Rieka stood and looked him in the eye. "Wang's running a check on all modes of travel to and from this city. I asked him to wait until zero-eight-hundred just in case Jeniper came home late and didn't receive my message." She glanced at a nearby clock. "It's been almost twenty minutes. There should be something, soon."

Robet nodded. He sensed his bibbets coloring and concentrated on keeping them under control. He tried to think of something intelligent to say, but nothing sprang to mind.

Herald Marteen smiled at him gently before turning to Rieka. "I'll just get started on this, dear. If you need me, buzz my office."

"Thank you, Setana," Rieka said.

Robet nodded as the Herald glided by. When she'd left the room, Rieka looked at him sternly. "Robet, sit down before you fall down."

"I'm fine," he said, but he went to her office sofa and sat.

Rieka pounced before he'd even settled against the cushions. "You're not fine, my friend," she chided, sitting next to him. "You look awful. I've never seen you like this."

"I've never been like this," he admitted. "I mean, I was worried about you when you'd been arrested for treason—but it didn't feel like this. It didn't make me empty inside. All I do is think about Jeniper. I wonder if she ran away or was taken away. And if she ran—if it was because of me."

"It wasn't you." Rieka said it with such conviction, Robet took it as fact. "We'll know more once Wang finishes his search. And we'll get her back. And RadiMo, too."

Robet shook his head. "You don't know that."

"Maybe not, but I think Yillon probably would. And the most recent message he's sent to me is about children. Jeniper is not a child."

"No," he said, trying to remember the last time he'd felt this powerless. "Jeniper definitely isn't a child."

The door slid open and Mr. Hong strode into the office. "You're not going to believe this," the big man said. "Apparently, for some unknown reason, Jeniper went to the spaceport at seventeen-hundred hours yesterday. She purchased passage to Canberra, Australia, on an express shuttle. It arrived there at nineteen-thirty hours, our time. About noon in Canberra." He sighed. "I lost the trail after that. She didn't buy anything or register at any hotels there."

"Was she alone?"

Hong shrugged. "Hard to tell, but I think so. No other tickets were purchased within three minutes of hers. It's usually pretty obvious if people are traveling together. The ticket purchase is recorded almost simultaneously."

"Then why Canberra?" Rieka asked. "I don't get it. What errand could she have had there?"

"I don't know," Hong told her. "There could be a hundred reasons. But I don't think she stayed in Canberra—otherwise, she'd have made a purchase. Food. A hotel reservation. Something."

An idea began to coalesce in Robet's mind. "I think I can find her," he said.

"Australia's a big continent, Captain," Hong said.

"I know. But there's something . . ." He looked at Rieka. "Trust me on this. I think I can find her. It'll be faster if I go alone." He pushed himself to his feet.

Rieka rose and flashed him a skeptical frown. "All right, Robet. You know the rules about InterMATting into potential danger as well as I do."

He stepped closer and put his hand on her shoulder. "I'll be fine."

"Of course you will," she replied, her quirky smile proof of her confidence in his decision. "Just find Jeniper and bring her back safe."

He eased his hand down her arm and gave her fingers a squeeze. When she squeezed back, Robet released her and bowed. "Thank you, Madam Herald."

She chuckled and echoed his tone. "Get going, Captain DeVark."

"See you in a couple of hours." Robet left the office, then switched on his TC to contact the *Prospectus*. A few moments later, he stood on the bridge issuing orders.

"Dimish, I need you to get me some information," he said to the lieutenant at the communications console. "Start with EarthCom Australia and work your way down to someone in Canberra that can identify every taxi service."

"As we speak, Captain," the Indran woman said.

Robet turned to his helmsman. "We're altering orbit, Mr. Viktar. Bring us geosynchronous over Canberra."

"Yes sir." Viktar paused only a moment to check with his computer before adding, "It'll be about twenty-five minutes, Captain."

"Very good. Dimish, if you reach someone before we get back, page me. Strummik," he said softly, gesturing toward his executive officer, "let's have a chat."

"Indeed," the Vekyan said. She eased out of her chair and eyed him curiously before following him off the bridge and to a conference room. "You intend to do something beyond regulations, again, I take it."

"Not exactly," he replied, walking off his anxiety. "The Herald's adjutant is missing. I think I can find her. I'm going to try."

"But sir, I was under the impression that Herald's security office—"

"—I think I can find her, Strummik. That's all you have to know."

"Perhaps," she said.

Robet stopped pacing and looked at her. Strummik stared back, her pink eyes unblinking. He'd been reckless in the past, he knew, and she'd covered for him. He didn't intend a repeat performance, today. Fortunately, his TC clicked on before he had a chance to say anything more. "DeVark."

"Captain," Dimish's voice began, "I've reached the public-transit manager in Canberra. Her name is Emily Vasquez."

"Put her through to the conference-room console," Robet replied, guessing she'd be more responsive if she could see him. Strummik reached across the table and activated the system. He sat down before the console and motioned for her to stay out of camera range.

A dark-haired and dark-skinned Human appeared, her attention focused on something beyond his screen. "Emily Vasquez?" Robet began. "I'm Captain DeVark of the *Prospectus.*"

She looked into his screen. "Yes, Captain. I understand you require some information."

"A bit. Is it possible for me to find out where a taxi has taken a fare?"

"Possible . . . yes. You need to tell me which taxi service it was and the approximate date. The patron's name would be helpful, too. Or, an account number."

Robet frowned. "I don't know which service. The vehicle was white with red lettering."

Vasquez shook her head. "They're *all* white with red lettering in Canberra, Captain. It's a standard. How about the account number? That would be the simplest way—though the date would reduce the number of records I'd have to search."

"Commonwealth date 204:279," he answered. "I'm sure of that. I can have the Earth Herald's office forward the account information, if necessary. The name we're looking for is Jeniper Tarrik."

"I'll start with that," she said. "But the number would speed things along. Is there a reason—?"

"Yes, there is. But this is a secure matter, ma'am. I simply require your cooperation and the information from your records."

"I'll do what I can, Captain."

It took only fifteen minutes for Vasquez's computers to receive Rieka's reply to his request for Jeniper's account number and to correlate it with that day's records for the five taxi companies servicing Canberra. He spent the entire time poring over a detailed city map, trying to remember the name she'd given as her destination.

"Captain," Vasquez's image said, finally. "Miss Tarrik took a Green Hills taxi to Bywong. An odd destination. But our records show she made the round-trip."

Robet nodded. That name sounded familiar. "Why is that an odd destination?"

"Bywong is quite a distance northeast of Canberra," she

replied. "And there's nothing much there at the moment. An old gold-mining town is being refurbished as a tourist center. It isn't expected to open for a month or two, last I heard."

Robet nodded, absorbing the woman's skeptical tone. "Can you tell me if another fare has gone there in the last day?"

"One moment." He watched her check the information on her console. "Sorry, Captain. No one has taken any taxi from Canberra to Bywong in that period of time. Although there is a discrepancy . . ."

"What?"

"Corin Cabs is reporting a missing vehicle."

"I'll check that out. Thank you."

"Captain DeVark," she said, stopping him before he could cut the transmission.

"Yes?"

"All our cabs are Bitterlys."

He frowned. Having no idea what a Bitterly was, he asked, "Is this significant?"

"The vehicle uses energy supplied by a flywheel. Depending upon how long ago it was charged, it may not even register on your"—she waved her hand to indicate she had no idea of the correct term—"sensory equipment. And I'm afraid orbital imagery won't be available. It's been snowing in the mountains for several hours."

"Thank you, ma'am. I'll bear that in mind." Not that it mattered much, anyway, he added silently. He intended to do an on-site survey of the place. "*Prospectus,* out."

Jeniper shivered, furious with herself for getting into this situation. She huddled into the mining car's seat and sighed. The last few hours had been unbelievable.

When Jonik left, he'd warned her to wait at least half an hour before heading back to Canberra. He'd thought someone was following him, and he didn't want them following her, too. By the time thirty minutes had expired, snow was falling so hard she couldn't see past the cave's overhang. She saw no point in trying to find the office building, much less the car. The blowing snow would have her disoriented in less than a minute, and she couldn't possibly stand more

than a few minutes in the frigid air with the thin coat
she'd brought.

Since caves maintained a constant temperature, she went
back in and settled into the car. She could only hope Rieka
would forgive her once she did return.

"If I ever get out of here," she told the cave, her voice
echoed down the winding tunnel, "I'm going to soak in a
hot bath until my bones melt."

She looked at her wrist chrono. She'd been stuck here
for over two hours. Thirty minutes had passed since the
last time she'd checked outside. She flexed her stiff muscles
and climbed out of the car.

The snow wasn't quite as bad, now. She thought she
could distinguish the building's outside security light in the
eerie darkness. Her feet would be frozen by the time she got
there, but Jeniper knew she had no other choice. The console had to have EarthCom access. She needed to call for
help.

No longer disconcerted by the curtain, Jeniper pushed
through the last layer, then stopped. Something had moved.
A dark, lumpy shape. The light turned it into a man's sil-
houette. It lurched toward her.

Not knowing what else to do, Jeniper clutched Jonik's
bag and retreated to the cave. Though she'd been struck
there for hours, she couldn't decide on a decent hiding
place. Finally, she dropped the bag onto the floor of a car
and hurried farther down the cave, where she could conceal
herself around the first winding turn.

Pressing against the rock, Jeniper heard a noise from
above. The cavern distorted everything, but she distinctly
made out the sound of footsteps. Whoever it was had
come inside.

"Jeniper? It's—" the person's shout had been so loud,
the rest of the sentence became drowned out in the echo.

Her breath caught. They knew her name. She looked
around frantically and found a shadowy niche. Silently, she
eased into it. What else had they said? she wondered.
Could it be Jonik, worried that she hadn't made it back
to Canberra?

The sound of footsteps came closer. The person came
around the corner and she shrank back against the wall,
ignoring a rock as it pressed into her back.

The figure held something and turned it directly toward her. It stepped closer. Clad in a parka that covered most of its face, she couldn't even tell the person's gender, but she guessed it to be a man. "Jeniper?"

Whoever it was knew her, and the voice wasn't Jonik's. The object in his hand didn't look like a maitu, but it could be some other type of weapon. She realized Jonik's influence on her when she wondered if her assailant intended to kill her here, or take her someplace else, then do it.

She willed herself to stay calm. What would Rieka do in such a situation? Jeniper had no idea, but she knew she couldn't give up Jonik's treasure without a fight.

Pushing off the wall, Jeniper plowed into the stranger. They spun together for a brief moment, and she jerked away, hoping to run back up toward the entrance. But a hand reached out and caught her arm.

"Jen?"

Thrown off-balance on the uneven surface, Jeniper teetered before she fell. She thought she might still get away until she realized her attacker hadn't let go. They crashed together onto the tunnel's hard floor, the blow knocking the air from her lungs.

"Jeniper? *Shadana,* are you all right?" Robet tugged the parka's hood away from his face and looked down at her. "Why did you run like that?"

Her wide-eyed expression was incredulous. "Robet?" she asked, gasping for breath, "Captain DeVark? Why didn't you say who you were?"

"I did when I came in the cave. And I meant to again just now—but then you hit me." Suddenly conscious of their intimate position, he rolled off her and sat up. Not that he minded the body contact, but this was neither the time nor place. "Are you all right?" he repeated, pushing himself to his feet.

"I think so," she answered warily, scrambling off the ground. "Did you . . . did you just call me your *shadana*?"

Robet helped her steady herself on the uneven terrain. The word had come out unbidden. "Yes. I did," he admitted wincing at how contrite he sounded. "And I beg your pardon, Jeniper. I have no right to lay claim on you. It was . . . disrespectful. And I apologize."

To his amazement, she lifted a hand and caressed his cheek with cool fingers. "Perhaps it was—wishful thinking?"

Even in the tunnel's dim light, he could see her bibbets darken. He had to stop himself from following up on the urge to kiss them. He focused on her eyes, instead. "Perhaps."

Her expression softened, and she leaned closer. Slowly, he brought his lips to hers, brushing them gently, waiting for Jeniper to respond.

When she did, Robet thought he might never again experience such joy. Since he'd played at loving so many women before, this reality overwhelmed him. Somehow, she had become more valuable to him than his life.

"Jen, Jen," he whispered, nuzzling her bibbets, relishing how they thickened under his cheek. "I thought I'd never find you. Don't ever scare me like that again."

"I won't. I promise." Suddenly, she pulled back from his embrace, and he saw fear replace the passion in her eyes. "We've got to get out of here."

Robet nodded. "I told Rieka I'd bring you back to New SubDenver as soon as I found you." He'd almost switched on his TC when she stopped him.

"I have to get something first."

"What?"

"It's not far," she said, catching his hand and pulling him back up the tunnel. "I dropped it in one of the cars."

He followed and watched as she pulled a small knapsack from beneath a seat.

"What's in there?"

"I'm not exactly sure, but it's very important to my brother." Hugging it to her side, she turned to him and nodded. Less than a minute later, they were standing in the embassy's InterMAT station in New SubDenver.

Robet tugged off his thermal parka as they left the chamber. He turned down the hallway to Rieka's office. Jeniper turned the other way.

"I want to stop at my apartment, first," she explained with a shy smile. "I need a cup of *colan*—and I'm a mess."

Robet hesitated only a second before nodding. "Okay. Take this for me?" He handed her his coat. She took it, silently promising they'd be alone later when he went to retrieve it.

EIGHTEEN

Gundah woke to the sound of her comm console beeping. She lifted her head from the pallet and sniffed disapprovingly at both the noise and the darkness. Cimpa had billeted them in the subterranean city called Johannesburg, and despite the light she'd left on, the sense of being underground disturbed her.

Pulling herself to her feet, Gundah stretched before padding to the console. If Cimpa required her services at this hour, she'd never get any sleep. Sometimes she wondered why she didn't kill him and be done with it. She flipped the toggle. "Adjutant Gundah."

Gellath's face appeared on the small screen. "I am uneasy," she began without preamble. "We left Earth orbit three hours ago. The *Prospectus* arrived yesterday and doesn't look as if it's planning to go anywhere."

"Yes, I know," Gundah told her. "I made some inquiries on Cimpa's behalf this afternoon. The ship has a mechanical problem and is awaiting parts."

Gellath snorted. "You do not think this is suspicious?"

Gundah sighed tiredly. "I hardly think a malfunctioning Fleet ship is going to alter our plans. All you need do is rendezvous with the *Barnel* and *Garner* at the appointed place and time. Gimbish will provide you with my instructions, then."

"You are sure we can put an end to Humanity's association with the Commonwealth?"

"Very sure," Gundah replied, curling her black lips into a toothy smile. She sobered quickly, and added, "Do not try to contact me again unless there is an emergency. Gundah, out."

She shut down the console and the room again plunged into darkness. After thumping her pallet until it felt comfortable, Gundah relaxed against the firm support. Gellath's worries were completely unwarranted. The plan had been moving along with great precision and would continue to do so. Very soon, Tarrik would fulfill his part of their bargain, and she'd have the means to destroy the Human race.

When the Reaffirmation failed to be the entertainment spectacular the ads implied, a shadow would cloud Earth's image. Rieka Degahv would founder helplessly for months trying to recover from her naive notions of a productive homeworld. She would be so busy making amends, she would never suspect the ceremony's sabotage might have been a decoy.

Heaving a contented sigh at her foresight, Gundah slid a paw under her cheek. The only thing she hadn't yet decided on was what to do with that vermin, RadiMo.

"What do you mean you left her in the corridor?" Rieka snapped in disbelief. She gripped the arms of her chair and glared across her desk at Robet. Jeniper had been gone for almost twenty hours, and his behavior was completely nonchalant. Exasperated, she said, "I asked you to bring her directly to me, Robet. What were you thinking?"

"That she needed a few minutes to herself," he said, then settled into one of the chairs in front of her desk.

"Well, I suggest you redefine your priorities. Fast."

"There's no point in getting upset," Robet advised. "She's fine. She'll be here in a minute."

"Good." Rieka paused, hoping to control her frustration. "Thank you. And I am not upset. I am . . . disappointed." She heaved a disgruntled sigh. "I expected you to do something and you—"

"Maybe we should clear up that little gray area, Rieka," he said, suddenly on the offensive. "I have orders given to me by Nason to stay here and maintain peace and security until he tells me otherwise."

Surprised by his comeback, Rieka frowned. She pushed out of her chair and came around the desk to sit next to him. "Robet," she began in the calmest tone she could muster, "I appreciate both Nason's orders and you're being here. But what you're forgetting is a Herald's request takes top priority in an emergency situation. And we both considered Jeniper's disappearance an emergency. If this were any other planet, you'd have coordinated with the established authorities. But we're still hiring our peace officers and the resident population is less than a million people. The hierarchy simply isn't set up yet."

"There's no emergency situation," he told her adamantly. "And unless one does occur, I'm not taking orders from you. Possibly not even then."

Rieka bit her tongue to keep from saying things she'd later regret. She wished Triscoe were here, or Setana. Then she might begin to understand what had made her Aurian friend suddenly belligerent.

"Great. Have it your way. And the next time—" The door opened, and Jeniper appeared, effectively cutting her off. "Jeniper. Come in. Are you all right?"

"I'm fine, thank you, Rieka." Jeniper took a few tentative steps into the office. "I need to apologize for my leaving so suddenly. I would have returned sooner . . . but the weather complicated things."

The look on Jeniper's face told Rieka her problems were more than weather-related. "Accepted," she replied easily. "What don't we make ourselves comfortable." She gestured for everyone, including Wang to adjourn to an alcove in her office she called the "sitting room."

Robet and Jeniper sat together on the sofa. "Okay," Rieka began, after settling in the chair next to Wang, "now that we've established that everybody's fine . . ."

"I need to explain," Jeniper blurted. "I haven't been honest with all of you and it's . . . it's gotten to a point where I can't keep it to myself anymore."

A dozen nightmarish ideas swam in Rieka's head, including one that said she'd allowed herself to be manipulated. Again. She watched Jeniper's bibbets fluctuate. They darkened and lightened, then thickened slightly. She looked at Robet, who placed his hand in hers. "Do you know about this?" she asked him.

Robet swiveled his jaw, and he looked both insulted and angry. Rieka felt Wang tense, but Jeniper held up her free hand, and softly said, "No, he doesn't. Nobody knows anything about this. Please. Just let me tell you and . . ."

"And what?"

"And then accept my resignation."

Rieka sat up straighter. That remark had come out of nowhere. "I'll decide that once I've heard your story."

Jeniper took a deep breath. "It started the same day you hired me," she began, glancing once to meet Rieka's gaze, but mostly focusing on the floor. "My brother Jonik is—basically a good person. But he's made a lot of bad decisions in his life. He came to me for money, and I wouldn't give him any. He warned me that someone might come after *me* if he didn't repay the loan."

"Why didn't you say something?" Wang asked.

"I didn't believe him. And Rieka had just offered me the job. I thought the situation would turn out to be nothing."

"But it didn't," Rieka added softly.

"No. It was just the beginning. When we arrived for the inauguration, Jonik had already sent me a message, here, on Earth. He'd asked me to meet him in an old mining town outside of Canberra that's been renovated for tourists."

"Bywong," Robet supplied.

"Yes. When I went there, the place was deserted. But Jonik had sent another message warning me to be extremely careful. He wouldn't supply the name, but he did say that this person was ready to make good on her threats." She sighed. "Two days later, you told us about your mother—how you thought she meant to hurt, maybe kill you." Jeniper glanced at Rieka then away again.

"I remember," Rieka said, strangely enthralled with Jeniper's story. "And so you thought he was mixed up with her." Knowing Candace, the idea wasn't so far-fetched as Jeniper seemed to think.

She nodded. "Then RadiMo disappeared, and we went to Yona. And that accident happened, and I thought it was my fault. We all would have died if it hadn't been for Captain Marteen. I keep thinking—" Jeniper stopped speaking when her voice cracked. Robet slid an arm around her shoulders.

"It's all right, Jeniper," she said gently, handing her a tissue from the container next to her chair. "Can you tell me the rest?"

"When we came back . . ." She sniffed and blew her nose. "When we came back, Jonik was here. I got another message to meet him. I thought it wouldn't take long, so I went. I needed to see him."

"Of course you did," Rieka agreed. "He's your brother."

"Jonik isn't working for Candace Degahv, or any of the companies she owns. He told me he owes a great deal of money, nearly a hundred thousand credits, to an Oph named Gundah."

Wang perked up at the name. "Gundah? The Oph adjutant?"

"I don't know—he didn't know. But *I* think it must be. Gundah was the one who told me about the *skiff* on Yona. Maybe she somehow—"

"—set us up," Rieka finished. "Dammit." She frowned and raked her fingers through her hair. "I can't believe I could have been so blind. I was so focused on Candace, I didn't even consider another angle."

A wave of confusion and guilt washed over her as it had when she'd been arrested for treason. Then as now, she'd done all the appropriate things, made the correct decisions, but it hadn't been enough. The Procyons' machinations had nearly toppled the Commonwealth. She had no idea whether Candace and Gundah were working together, nor could she guess their ultimate goal. But she did know they were shrewd individuals who thought nothing of using treachery to get what they wanted.

"You couldn't have known," Robet told her. "And this might tie in to the reason the *Prospectus* is still in orbit."

She looked at him and noticed his bibbets darken slightly. "Yes, it could."

Wang cleared his throat. "Would somebody like to explain that?"

Rieka waited for Robet to nod before she answered the question. "The Fleet has intercepted illegal transmissions between Oph, Earth, Yadra, and some of its ships. Until they figure out what's going on, one Fleet ship has been assigned to remain at those planets. The *Prospectus* is not awaiting parts from Dani."

She let Wang digest that information and tried to see the situation from a new perspective. She had always known Humans were considered the dregs of Commonwealth society, no matter who claimed otherwise. She had earned respect as a Fleet captain, but even that rank had not exempted her from the undercurrent of xenophobia that prevailed.

She'd been so busy on her crusade for Human equality, she hadn't realized someone might actually take a stand to defend the status quo. And the time to strike was when Earth presented itself as a productive member world. More than once, she'd wondered if the Reaffirmation was being sabotaged and ignored those thoughts as paranoid. Now, she realized her instincts had been right.

While Wang asked Robet a few more questions, she let her military training kick in. They needed to define the enemy and design a suitable counteroffensive.

"Where's Jonik now?" she asked. "We need to get him here so he can be protected."

Jeniper shook her head. "I don't know. He left just before the snow began falling. He wouldn't say where he was going."

"We need to find him. I'll leave that to you, Wang-Chi." He nodded, and Rieka looked at Jeniper. "Do we know when Cimpa is arriving?"

"I think they're already here," she said. "His entourage planned some tours for tomorrow. They'll be in Damascus before the ceremony. They leave for Oph as soon as it's over. He's reserved eight or ten seats. Gundah is probably attending with him."

"I'd bet on it," Rieka agreed, "but as things stand now, our hands are tied. We can't detain her without proof. And we need to know who's working with her."

"I can access her financial record," Wang said. "It might help determine if she's the right individual."

"Is that legal?" Robet asked.

Wang shrugged. "Not . . . necessarily."

"We need some kind of implicating evidence before we can have her arrested," Rieka told him. Wang simply grinned, so she looked at Robet. "You'll look the other way on this?"

He squeezed Jeniper's shoulder and nodded. "I wasn't even here."

"Good." Rieka felt her anxiety level drop a hair. Despite whatever had bothered Robet before, at least he was willing to cooperate. "Who knows, maybe we'll untangle all of this and the Reaffirmation will be a success."

"Yeah." Wang smiled rakishly. "And RadiMo will show up, too. And Candace will recant her wicked ways. And—"

"—and I can see I'm not the only one who can dole out sarcasm."

Rieka sat behind her desk and massaged her forehead with her fingertips. After a long argument, she'd convinced Jeniper to stay on the job, at least temporarily. But her Aurian adjutant's self-confidence had dropped considerably. Even with Robet's emotional support, she wasn't sure Jeniper could defeat the personal demons that still surrounded her. If she couldn't, Rieka knew she would have to let her go.

The console screen activated, and Jeniper's face appeared. "Are you free, Herald? You have a visitor."

Friend or foe? she wanted to ask, but stopped herself just in time. Jeniper offered the information before she had a chance to reword the question.

"It's Admiral Nason."

She frowned. With Nason, one could never predict the objective. "Send him in, Jeniper. And bring some refreshments, please."

"Yes, ma'am."

Rieka had barely enough time to take a deep breath before the admiral marched in the door. He stopped, looked around, then smiled at her. "The job suits you, Herald. You're looking well."

Rising, Rieka shook her head. "I look as though I've pulled a double shift, sir, and you know it." Jeniper entered, pushing a small cart. "Just leave that by the sofa, Jen. Thank you."

Jeniper nodded and left.

"Come in, Admiral. Sit down. Have a cup of *colan* and tell me what brings you here."

Nason nodded and sat. Rieka retrieved a mug from the cart and filled it with the strong-smelling brew. After handing it to him, she poured herself a cup and eased onto a chair so she could face her old boss.

"So, tell me what's gone wrong, now," she said.

Nason chuckled. "I told you I was coming to make a speech at the Reaffirmation. What makes you think anything is wrong?"

"Admiral, I probably shouldn't admit this, but I will. I can read bibbets pretty well. Even yours. As a captain, I picked up a lot of information by reading bibbets. You're controlling yours the best you can, right now," she said, knowing he respected her frankness. "They haven't fluctuated since you came in this room." She leaned forward, her elbows resting on her knees. "That tells me two things. One—you have news. And two—it's bad."

Rieka leaned back against the cushion. "Am I right?" she asked.

Nason pinched at his well-trimmed beard with his thumb and index finger. "First Setana and now you," he murmured.

"What?"

"Individuals—women—who can somehow manage to read me like a book," he admitted. "It's uncanny. And you aren't even Indran."

Rieka chuckled and set her cup down. "I shall be gracious, Admiral, and take that as a compliment."

"So intended. And now that we've shared a few pleasantries, I'm sure you want me to get to the point of my visit."

Rieka smiled tightly and nodded. "I assume this has something to do with those illegal transmissions."

"Unfortunately, yes." Nason took another sip of *colan* and set his mug on the table. "Robet DeVark did show you my communiqué, did he not?" She nodded. "We're still unable to decode them."

"Nothing's been sent recently from here. If it had, Wang would have pinpointed the source, and we'd have someone in custody."

"Wang?" Nason asked.

"Hong Wang-Chi is his full name. My bodyguard and all-around security man. He's in his office now, working on a project. Otherwise, he'd be sitting here making you nervous."

"He's that intimidating?"

"He's that big," she told him. They shared a smile. "Since Wang's people haven't intercepted any illegally coded messages, incoming or outgoing, do you think someone is getting nervous?"

"I wouldn't begin to speculate," Nason said. "All questionable communications stopped abruptly once the Fleet ships in orbit were given CO-3. As much as I would like to think we've put an end to whatever was going on—I sincerely doubt it."

"You're right," Rieka agreed. She considered telling him about Jeniper's brother and Gundah, but decided against it. There wasn't any evidence to connect them to this odd situation, yet, and it would only serve to complicate matters.

The desk console sounded. "Excuse me." He nodded as she got up and went to the desk. She pressed the appropriate spot and Jeniper's concerned face appeared.

"Sorry to interrupt," the Aurian began. "Herald Marteen and Captain DeVark are here. You have a dinner engagement in ten minutes."

"Damn, I forgot. Thanks, Jeniper. Could you access my apartment and see what I've got to wear that's appropriate. And send the Herald and captain in."

"Of course."

Rieka switched off the console and looked at Nason. "Would you care to join me for dinner, Admiral? I'm hosting an intimate dinner for seventy of the Commonwealth's finest business and social leaders."

He chuckled at her facetious tone. "Thank you, Rieka. I'm sure that would be refreshing. Most of my social engagements are with stodgy old Fleet types."

"I beg your pardon, sir?" Robet said as he followed Setana Marteen into the room.

The admiral stood. "Present company excluded, Captain." They exchanged salutes, then Nason turned toward the Indran Herald. "You're looking lovely as ever, Setana," he said, offering her his palms. "Is Ker here, too? I haven't played a decent hand of Cranbonie in months."

"He's coming on the *Providence*," she replied. Rieka detected more than a trace of amusement in her tone. Apparently Ker was an easy mark when it came to Cranbonie.

As long as I've got the three of you here," the admiral said, "I suppose I should present my news."

Rieka came around the desk to stand near Setana. "I was wondering when you'd get around to it."

Nason smiled gallantly and inclined his head. "Officially, I'm here to represent the Fleet at the Reaffirmation ceremony. I'm in your office this afternoon to tell you something you've very nearly heard before." His eyes blazed with a mixture of excitement and anxiety, and his bibbets flushed slightly from pink to rose. "You may take this information and do with it what you will. But I don't want it made public knowledge."

"Of course," Rieka assured him.

Nason took a deep breath. "Just before I left Headquarters at Yadra, an astounding thing happened. I received confirmation that three Fleet ships are off their routes."

"Missing?" Robet asked, his eyes growing large.

"Perhaps. They have been *listed* as missing."

"This sounds far from coincidental," Rieka said. "Whether they're actually 'missing' or not, three ships disappearing at the same time sounds like—"

"A conspiracy," he finished. "Yes, it does. And with the additional fact that I'm about to divulge, I'm sure it will more than *sound* like one."

"What?"

"The missing ships—*Garner, Barnel,* and *Dividend,* are all captained by Ophs."

NINETEEN

The dining area's antechamber overflowed with Commonwealth personalities. They had booked three rooms at the Continental Hotel: a dining hall, a reception area with an open bar, and a quieter visiting room for private conversations. With dinner still thirty minutes away, most all the guests remained here nibbling finger food as they held their beverages in lead crystal.

Above the friendly chatter, Rieka recognized Candace's strident voice. "Of course the Earth was considered a garden spot before the Collision," her mother said. Rieka couldn't see to whom she was speaking. "But that's what I'm saying, don't you see? That it should remain a garden spot. People don't need to be immigrating to this planet simply because they're Human. Why that's the most ridiculous thing I've ever heard."

"Well I certainly don't want *you* here," Rieka grumbled under her breath.

"Do you want me to say something, dear?" Setana asked. "Shall I speak to Candace?"

"No. It'll probably just instigate a tirade on the fact that I'm so weak I can't defend myself."

She watched Setana's gentle face fold into a frown. "I am not a violent person, but I most assuredly would find pleasure in slapping her face."

Rieka laughed lightly at the image of Setana hauling off to smack her mother. "I know that feeling. And compared to you, I *am* a violent person."

Candace's voice rose again. "Unfortunately, my daughter doesn't particularly listen to my advice."

"I've had it," Rieka muttered. To Setana she said, "Be

back in a minute." Jeniper had planned this evening to show off Rieka's plans, not to have them denounced as inappropriate. She wasn't about to let Candace get away with undermining their work.

She eased through the crowd until she found her quarry and Ekatarina Volshoy, one of Earth's senators. Rieka recognized the man standing next to her as her husband, but couldn't remember his name.

"It's good to see you again, Mrs. Volshoy," Rieka said, offering her hand. "Mr. Volshoy."

The senator grasped and shook it firmly, as did her husband. "The pleasure is mine, Mrs. Degahv," she said. "I've been having a remarkable conversation with your mother."

Rieka glanced at Candace. "So I heard. From across the room. I hope you didn't take her seriously."

Her mother grimaced but Volshoy smiled softly and replied, "I . . . try not to discount anyone's opinion until I have some facts."

"As I said," Candace countered, her tone dripping superiority, "my people have amassed a great deal of evidence. I can forward that report to your office, Madam Senator, if you'd like."

"Mother, this isn't the time for your anti-Earth campaign. Please stop it," Rieka hissed at her as quietly as she could.

Whether she'd heard or not, Volshoy nodded noncommittally. "This isn't a business trip, but you may forward the information to my office on Yadra. My door is always open."

"Why thank you, Senator," Candace trilled. Rieka wanted to strangle her.

When the Volshoys moved on, Candace scanned the crowd, apparently for her next victim. "Don't do anything you and I both will regret," Rieka warned.

Her mother's eyes turned cold. "Don't threaten me. You have no idea what could happen to you."

Rieka nodded and set her jaw. "Ditto," she said. "You've been warned."

Candace went still for a moment, then noticed someone else in the crowd. "There's Senator DeWilt. Charming man. I believe I'll say hello."

As she moved off, Rieka doubted that was all she

planned to say. Glancing around, she saw Setana's concerned expression and went to join her.

"It didn't go well," Setana said.

"No."

"Dinner in twenty-four minutes," Jeniper said as she passed them.

Rieka watched Jeniper disappear through the crowd. "It won't be too soon for me," she muttered. Catching a whiff of *ciffa* dust, Rieka turned to look past Setana. "Cimpa is here? I thought his secretary had sent word he wasn't feeling well enough to come this evening."

"That was what I understood," Setana replied, angling in the direction of a small commotion. "Perhaps we'd better investigate."

Rieka saw Wang moving through the crowd from his post near the wall. "Yes. Let's go."

It took only a few seconds for them to squeeze around several guests before they found Cimpa standing in a small knot of fellow Ophs trying to face down Admiral Nason.

"What are you implying, sir? That my people seek to monopolize the hydroponics industry?"

Nason, to his credit, remained unruffled. "I haven't implied anything, Herald," he said, his smile all innocence. "I've simply asked you a question. A *hypothetical* question regarding transport of goods."

Rieka tried to say something, but Setana put a hand on her arm. Instead of speaking, she watched Cimpa's face. He didn't seem himself. He licked away foam from the corners of his mouth.

"And have you brought your *hypothesis* to all the other Heralds as well?" Cimpa demanded, adding a growl.

"I had planned on it," Nason said smiling. "You just happened to be the first Herald I've spoken to this evening."

"*Vigaran!*" Cimpa growled. "I will not have you defaming my people."

"I've done nothing of the kind, sir."

A female with no gemstones in her ear jewelry put a paw on Cimpa's shoulder. She spoke to him too softly for Rieka to hear, but he calmed almost immediately, so Rieka took the opportunity to jump in.

"Gentlemen, this evening we're celebrating Earth's accomplishments and its entry into the community of productive planets. We're not here to create obstacles or negative feelings. If you have something you'd like to settle, please take it outside and away from my guests."

"Of course, Herald," the female murmured as she edged her way in front of Cimpa. "I am Gundah, adjutant to Oph. The Herald is going through a difficult time. We apologize profusely for any problems we may have caused."

Rieka looked at Gundah's face and could tell the words obviously meant nothing. "Accepted," she said in a tone equally discordant. She then turned to the watery-eyed Cimpa. "Herald, I realize your journey to Earth has been tiring. Perhaps you and some of your staff would care to retire to a more comfortable room. Through those doors is a quiet sitting area. I'll make sure someone notifies you when dinner is ready."

"Very gracious, Herald," Cimpa replied. "Attend me, Grellah . . . Gundah."

Gundah looked pointedly at Rieka before she turned to follow her boss. Rieka inched to trail after them and address the issue of what had happened on Yona. She felt Setana's light touch on her arm and sighed.

"Now isn't the time, dear," the Indran Herald told her softly.

"Now is never the time." She glanced at Wang. "I want them under observation, Wang-Chi," she said quietly. "Subtly."

"I'm on it." He turned and went back to his post.

Rieka welcomed several others as she stood chatting with Nason and Setana. Then, quite suddenly, she heard her name called and turned to see her father-in-law walking toward them.

She waited while he greeted Setana, then said, "Ker, how wonderful that you could come." She purposefully extended her right hand in the characteristic Human greeting. He stared at it for a second, then shook it.

"I wouldn't miss this," he told her. "I rarely get the opportunity to see my family anymore."

"Where is Triscoe?" Setana asked.

"He sends his regards. He'll be a bit late." He studied his wife admiringly. "You are looking lovely this evening, my dear," he offered.

"I thank you for the compliment," she said.

"And you," he returned his attention to Rieka, "look quite elegant, especially wearing a Herald's insignia on your collar."

"I preferred the captain's insignia, myself," Nason interjected.

Rieka felt herself smile. Quite honestly, she thought the same thing. She ignored the admiral, however, and kept her attention on her father-in-law as he watched her carefully. "Ker, you look as if you have a request."

"True," he admitted and a dimple appeared on his cheek that reminded her of Triscoe. "I was wondering, my dear, if you might possibly be able to procure something for me."

"And what is that?" she asked, her curiosity piqued. This was a first for them.

"Well, they're very difficult to find—especially since they're only grown on Earth, you see. And after you sent the first box, I believe I really became addicted."

"The first box?" Rieka searched her memory and frowned. "You mean the macadamia nuts I sent you?"

Ker made a strange face, then sighed. "Do you remember where you got them?"

"The ones I sent were from Australia," Rieka said. "I don't know if they're grown elsewhere, right now. I'll have Jeniper look into it for you. We can probably have some here by tomorrow morning. Or, better yet, I'll see if Jeniper or one of her staff can get you a grove tour. Do you think you'd be interested in that?"

"I would be," Nason interjected. "If you've found something that makes Ker Marteen sit up and ask for more, I'd like to see where it comes from."

"Merik," Ker said, clapping him on the shoulder, "you're welcome to come along. And if you're free later, let's play a few hands of Cranbonie."

"You're on, old man," Nason said.

Candace's voice caught Rieka's attention again. Her mother had attracted a small audience just to their left. Listening to the annoying chatter, Rieka didn't think they could announce dinner one second too soon.

"Candace never gives up," Setana remarked. "I think she's insulted you haven't spent more time with her, Rieka."

"I didn't think it wise," she said.

Ker reached and touched Rieka's jawline. "This obnoxious woman with the white hair is your mother?" Rieka nodded, speechless at this unanticipated sign of affection. "Stay here," he said. "I've heard enough. I'll take care of this right now."

"No, don't—" she began. But he ignored her, and she could do nothing but stare wide-eyed as Ker walked into the fray.

Ker edged his way closer to Candace's voice.

"Of course, she was always a recalcitrant child," she trilled, batting her eyes at a particularly handsome young Aurian male. Ker didn't recognize him, but he instinctively knew the lad would be forgotten the minute he escaped Mrs. Degahv's sight. "She always did whatever she wanted—never did a thing she was told—and of course that trait has continued to this day."

"Why, Mrs. Degahv, how nice to finally meet you," Ker said, shouldering his way forward. "Ker Marteen. Triscoe's father."

For a brief moment, Candace said nothing. Then a smile blossomed on her well-preserved face. "Of course, the resemblance is uncanny." She thrust a hand at him.

Ker shook it, trying not to be offended that she hadn't extended both hands and offered an Indran greeting. His daughter-in-law had earned his respect, but he still held a particular dislike for Humans in general. He wondered if Candace Degahv would soon top the list.

"I have been meaning to speak to you," he told her, purposely keeping his voice light. "Perhaps we can go into the lounge and have a talk before dinner is announced."

He watched her swirl the orange liquid in her glass before nodding. "Certainly, Mr. Marteen. If you'll all excuse us . . ." She gestured to the young man. He stepped closer, and she patted his arm. "I'm sure I'll see you after dinner, Torry."

Watching her performance, Ker began to wonder if he'd have any appetite at all by the time they assembled at the table. Once inside the lounge, Candace walked past several members of Herald Cimpa's party, including the Herald himself, and gestured at a pair of chairs near a small fountain feeding a pool occupied by several large orange-and-white fish.

"Now, Mr. Marteen," she began once they were comfortable, "what did you wish to talk about?"

"Your daughter. Is there any other common subject?"

"I—wouldn't know."

Ker leaned back in his chair. "Perhaps I should begin by explaining that, in general, I cannot tolerate Humans. They are arrogant, selfish, and deceitful. I've known them to lie, cheat, and commit criminal acts to get what they want—with absolutely no regard for anyone who gets in their way."

"I will not sit here and be insulted by you, Mr. Marteen. I don't care whether you consider yourself family, or not." She huffed and began to push out of the chair.

Ker raised both hands innocently. "I meant no offense, madam. But I like to speak plainly. As an astute businesswoman, I assumed you'd appreciate that."

When Candace neither replied, nor departed, he took it as a sign to continue. "I am *sure*," he went on, emphasizing the last word, "you are familiar with the type I'm describing."

"Exactly what is the point of this conversation?" she asked, her voice hard and accusatory.

Ker smiled. Goading her was as much fun as he'd thought it would be. "My point, dear lady, is that nearly all of the Humans with which I've had contact are exactly as I have described, with one rather impressive exception—your daughter, Rieka."

"I don't see—"

"You needn't *see* anything, madam," Ker cut in harshly. "Simply listen and take heed. Your daughter is now the Earth Herald. She represents a planet populated by roughly one million people—hardly an impressive number. She has a great deal to do in order to see this planet gain the respect it deserves."

"But the Earth should not be repopulated to any extent," Candace interjected vehemently. "There are ten subterranean cities completed now and that is enough. Ten million people living here will not have a negative effect on the Commonwealth—or on this planet. But there are plans for over fifty *more* cities to be built. Some of them five times the size of New SubDenver. And who knows what might come after that. The effect on the economy is bound to be dramatic." She tapped her finger on the chair's arm to reinforce her point.

"What you say may be true, Mrs. Degahv. But your attitude toward what Rieka envisions for Earth—your words and actions speak against your daughter. I will not tolerate that."

"How dare you threaten me." This time Candace pushed farther out of her chair, but Ker put a hand on her arm.

"Please," he said in his sternest voice. "Sit. And listen."

Frowning, and obviously furious, Candace slowly sat back. Ker remained on guard, ready to stop her should she decide to make a quick getaway.

"Say what you want then, and have done with it," she told him, her voice steely.

He let go of her arm and nodded. "Thank you, Mrs. Degahv. As I understand it, you've been saying your piece for several days. Now it is my turn."

Ker took a breath and wondered exactly where to begin. "As I have mentioned, I do not like Humans. When I learned of my son's marriage, I was outraged. I thought he must have been insane to consider a Human for a mate. According to the media, she'd also disobeyed a direct order and attacked and destroyed a Procyon ship—thus committing a treasonous act.

"I didn't like her and I didn't trust her. That mistrust nearly cost me my life. I was present at Dani when the Procyons commandeered the *Prodigy*. In the aftermath of the assault, I met your son."

Candace, thus far giving the appearance of boredom, perked up. "Paden? You knew Paden?"

Ker nodded. "I understand you think Rieka killed him. Is that right?"

"She was responsible for his death. Yes."

Candace's steely blue eyes stopped him for a moment. Carefully, he continued the narrative. "Paden didn't trust Rieka, either. Nor did he have any faith in the Fleet's decision to drop the charges against her. I agreed to accompany him aboard the *Prodigy* and stop her before she attempted to do anything that might seem seditious."

He sighed. "I don't know how we were discovered, but

when your daughter arrived and found us held hostage by some Procyons, she traded herself for me." Ker paused, reliving the moment when he realized what Rieka had done. "In the process of negotiating with them, shots were fired and Paden was hit. He died immediately."

He watched as Candace again pursed her lips and made an oddly Human face at him. "And what exactly am I supposed to learn from your little story?" she asked coolly.

"I thought you might learn to trust your daughter, perhaps more than you did your son. She is a very capable Human. I would not say that if I didn't believe it."

"I see." She lifted her chin and looked down her nose at him.

"I don't think you do." Ker sighed and shook his head. Candace's attitude required another tactic. "It is my understanding that you are rather an astute businesswoman."

She shifted in the chair and smoothed her skirt. "That is correct."

"Then you realize that image is very important."

"Rieka's image is not my—"

"I'm not talking about hers, Mrs. Degahv," Ker interjected, leaning forward and looking directly into her eyes. "*Your* image is in jeopardy. One who speaks against a person with high ideals and commendable goals comes off looking the fool. I tell you this from personal experience."

Candace huffed. "Rieka is a child who does not comprehend the complexity of the situation she's in. She thinks that—"

"I beg to differ, madam," Ker said. "She is no child. She has served the Commonwealth nearly all her life—in the Fleet and now as Earth Herald. She knows how to get her job done. All she requires from us is a little faith."

Candace shook her head. "*You* are a fool to believe in her. She thinks that a few million Humans on Earth will cause the Commonwealth to hold *all* Humans in higher esteem."

Ker heard the musical tones signaling the dining room had opened, but Candace continued her lecture. "Trust your instincts, Prefect Marteen. Humans are contemptible creatures. Perhaps my daughter did not murder my son, but she hated him all the same. For that, she will never have my respect." She rose and turned to leave.

Ker stood and hoped he intimidated her with his size. "The same way you hate her, madam?"

Candace had the decency to look shocked before she straightened her shoulders and walked away.

Rieka leaned forward in her chair and tried to listen to everything the Aurian Senator DeWilt said, but a sense of Triscoe kept distracting her. She also felt an unwelcome sense of urgency but couldn't tell if it originated within her or her husband.

"But you do agree," Setana offered, "that the seasonal variety of produce is going to increase consumer interest throughout the Commonwealth."

"Most definitely," DeWilt agreed. "The studies I've seen of Earth's potential grain crops are phenomenal. When the workforce arrives to start achieving that potential—"

"—prices will be driven through the floor," Candace finished.

Rieka itched to kick her mother under the table. But with her target a third of the way around, it would have been too far to reach, anyway. She didn't try to hide her smile, however, when Ker shot Candace a menacing look.

"Not necessarily, Mrs. Degahv," DeWilt said. Rieka couldn't tell whether he'd missed the interchange or simply ignored it. "Our population on Aurie has been growing steadily, and we have several new colonies to support as well. If Earth hadn't been ready to be reinhabited and brought to a productive level, the Senate would now be voting to send several Fleet ships on a mission to search for a similar planet."

"Inhabited or uninhabited?" Robet asked.

"Preferably uninhabited," Senator Ekatarina Volshoy replied. "We terraformed Yadra two hundred years ago— and could terraform another world again, if necessary."

Rieka had only just met Mrs. Volshoy that day and liked her immediately. "Then a productive Earth actually fits into the Commonwealth's future plans," she said, looking pointedly at her mother.

DeWilt nodded. "Very much so. The only things in question are quality and quantity."

"Quality will not be a problem," Rieka said. "Earth, even when all seventy-two self-contained subterranean cities are completed and occupied, won't suffer from the pollution problems associated with several other Commonwealth planets. Water, earth and atmosphere are as pure now as they've ever been. Pests, both animal and vegetable, can be controlled naturally. Processing plants are under construction. As far as agriculture goes, I'd say we're ready to go."

Volshoy nodded, her smile contagious. "And we must credit the Degahv ancestors for their farsighted leadership."

Rieka accepted the compliment with a nod. Everything on Earth today had been built on their shoulders.

"I'm afraid you missed dinner, dear," Setana said.

Rieka turned and found Triscoe standing behind the chair left vacant for him. *Not funny sneaking up on me like that,* she chided.

Thought I'd try behaving like a Human husband, he replied while he smiled at the others, then said, "It's midmorning to me, anyway."

Rieka introduced him to her distinguished tablemates, and added, "If we're through here, shall we retire to the lounge?"

Senator DeWilt deferred to his redheaded wife. Even before she nodded, Volshoy's husband pushed his chair away from the table. He helped her from her chair.

Rieka let Setana and Ker lead the way in order to have a private moment with Triscoe. They followed as far as the reception area before Robet broke off his conversation with Nason and came toward them.

"What's new?" Robet asked.

"I've learned a few things," Triscoe answered. "I take it the situation here is secure."

Rieka glanced over her shoulder to find Wang positioned near the door. He acknowledged her silent inquiry with a nod. "As secure as it's going to get," she said. "But we still don't know what's become of RadiMo. And Jeniper's got a few problems. Hopefully they'll wait until after tomorrow's Reaffirmation ceremony."

Not everyone can wait that long.

Rieka got an instant sense of Triscoe's desire. She took a breath and tried to push it away. "And . . . uh . . . Robet's got some charming news," she managed.

Totally oblivious to the heat that Rieka felt, Robet launched into the Fleet's current problems. He and Triscoe carried on a short conversation that she could barely follow.

Stop it. Almost immediately the sensation abated.

"And Nason's already had words with Cimpa—even though he didn't imply anything much," Robet concluded.

Rieka frowned as a new thought hit her. "Could be Cimpa doesn't know what's going on."

"You may be right," Triscoe agreed.

"If you are, then our prime suspect is Gundah," Robet said. "Have we got anything on her, yet?"

Rieka looked over her shoulder, again. In the relatively empty room, Wang had come close enough to hear their conversation. "Have we, Wang-Chi?"

"She's clean," Wang admitted, stepping closer. "Very clean," he amended. "Too clean. She's got three personal credit accounts and doesn't spend half of her adjutant's salary. No mate, no kids. A perfect Oph enigma."

"So you're saying this Gundah probably has inaccessible accounts?" Triscoe asked.

"I'm saying her lifestyle and documented spending habits are suspicious. She owns property that wasn't paid for by any traceable funds. She's smart enough to conduct her business in a way normal inquiries won't reach."

"That's suspect in itself," Rieka pointed out.

Triscoe frowned as he watched her, and she could tell he'd thought of something she didn't want to air, yet.

Could you say good night to your guests without appearing impolite? he asked.

Probably.

Then please do.

It didn't take as long as he thought. When Rieka finally returned to the apartment, Triscoe was lounging in a chair, scanning the news channels. He'd found nothing much to hold his interest, save a listing of available SubDenver real estate.

She came in with Hong Wang-Chi and flopped on the sofa. "I hate these shoes," she groused, kicking them off. "See you at zero-six-hundred, Wang."

"Bright and early—if that can be applied to living three hundred meters below ground level."

Triscoe said good night and watched Wang turn the corner to his room. He then picked himself up and settled next to Rieka. "How are you, love?" he whispered after kissing her cheek.

"I feel like I need about four clones of myself to get through tomorrow," she said. "I need to play hostess, tour guide, master of ceremonies—and probably five or six other things I can't even think of."

"Has Mother been of any help?"

"She's been wonderful, Triscoe." He watched her smile wistfully. "I can almost imagine what it would have been like to grow up with a real mother, myself. I couldn't have got this far—and remained sane—without her."

"Good." He reached and put a hand on her shoulder. The thin, shimmery blue material felt like nothing under his fingers. "You're tense."

"Big surprise."

"You don't need to snap, love." He turned her around and put both hands against her neck. "I'm here for at least three days. We'll sort through everything before my next tour starts." He kneaded the bands of stiff shoulder muscles. "We'll have lots of time to relax you."

Her eyes closed and she dropped her head forward as far as the muscles allowed. "Just as long as—ouch, ahh—that hurts."

Triscoe worked the spot, then pressed his lips against it. "Better?"

"Infinitely."

"You were saying?"

"I can't remember."

Her skin, her voice, her scent was intoxicating. He nuzzled her nape and kissed the back of her left ear. She turned slightly and pressed her lips against his.

Doo natti karan, Rieka.

Da nattu, Triscoe, she replied. He could tell she'd become so absorbed in emotion she hadn't even known she'd spoken Indran. Her hands slid up his arms and over his shoulders to lock behind his neck.

"Not on the sofa, I know," he whispered, easing off the cushions and bending to lift her as the door chime sounded.

Rieka stiffened and sighed. She waited until he'd set her

on her feet before grumbling, "What now? Your mother said not to expect them till late."

The chime sounded again, and Wang appeared. Triscoe watched Rieka smooth her dress and nod. Wang hit the switch to open the door.

Jeniper rushed in without preamble. "I just got this from Jonik," she told them, holding a communiqué chip in her hand. "He's been kidnapped."

TWENTY

They huddled around the console screen as Jonik Tarrik's frightened face appeared, his bibbets a dark rose. "Jeniper," he began, his voice wavering, "I need you to bring me the . . . the package I gave you for safekeeping. The person who hired me insists she needs it now."

He looked away from the camera for a moment, licked his lips and sighed. "You need to bring it to me on the Oasis. Nothing will happen if you bring it in an hour. We'll both be free to go once it's here."

His bibbets went darker. "Please don't be late, Jen. And please don't tell anyone. Anyone at all. Gundah says I won't survive any—any more reckless behavior."

The image on the screen faded. Rieka switched off the console and sighed. She knew each of the three other people in the room had his or her own ideas about what should be done. But Jonik Tarrik's plea to his sister had been nonnegotiable. No peace or Fleet officers were to be involved or he would be killed.

She dropped the plastic chip into Wang's outstretched hand. "Do you think you can get anything out of it?"

"Place of origin, probably," he said. "Maybe more. You can never tell." He dropped the chip into his pocket, then gestured to her dining table. "Conference time, Boss?"

Rieka nodded and stood. If anything, Jeniper looked even more tense than she did when she'd come in. "Jen, why don't you fix some *colan*? And maybe make yourself some tea."

"Yes. Yes, I can do that," she replied. Her bibbets fluctuated strangely as she turned and headed to the kitchen.

Rieka gestured toward the table. "Gentlemen."

Patting his pocket, Wang said, "I'll be right back."

Rieka waved him off, then sat and looked at Triscoe. "I need your cooperation on this. I think we ought to let Nason know whatever we decide to do—but the Fleet needs to appear oblivious."

"I'm not sure I understand," Triscoe answered, leaning back in his chair.

Rieka sensed him becoming defensive and knew nothing she said would satisfy him. "I'm saying the Herald's office will handle this, and the Fleet needs to be involved as backup only."

"I disagree."

"And what would you rather do, Triscoe? Make an assault on this place where Jonik says he's being held? Risk a lot of people's lives?"

"No. But certainly there is another way."

"Of course there is. I just haven't thought of it, yet." Frustrated because it would take a direct order for him to do as she asked, Rieka dropped her face into her hands and waited for the others to return.

A few moments later Jeniper set a tray of cups and a decanter on the table. "Servebot's bringing some fruit and cheese," she said softly. "I'll just go and get my tea."

By the time she returned, Wang rejoined them and reported. "The message originated on Earth and was routed through EarthCom to Jeniper's address."

"So, Gundah lied—because there's no city with that name on this planet," Jeniper said.

"Earth origin means everything both terrestrial and in orbit," Wang told her. "I verified the name: Oasis. It's one of three hydroponics labs built to support the restoration crews. It's been orbiting Earth for about 175 years. Dimensions are one kilometer by 100 meters by 100 meters. Energy is provided by a small cold-fusion system. Most of the equipment was salvaged a decade ago. It's pretty much just a shell now. The file says an Indran company bid on it last month. I don't know whether they intend to use the structure or scrap it." He shrugged. "That's all I got."

"It's enough—for now," Rieka told him. She looked at Jeniper. "I need you to tell me what's so important about the package Gundah is ransoming your brother for."

Jeniper shrugged and her bibbets paled. "I don't know.

He gave it to me in the mine just before Robet came. He'd hidden it there. I have no idea what's in it, but he said it was worth our lives."

"Apparently he was right," Triscoe offered. "Unfortunately, Gundah now holds the upper hand. Once she's had the ransom paid, do you think she'll just let your brother go?"

Jeniper paled visibly, bibbets included, and Rieka kicked Triscoe under the table. "Kidnappers like to *think* they have control at all times," she said carefully. "Trust me on this, I've had a lot of experience dealing with them."

As Triscoe bent to rub his skin, he said, "What we need is some information that can be used against Gundah. It seems to me she's one who apparently plans things out in advance. If we can get her to act on impulse, we might have an advantage."

Jeniper shook her head. "If? Might? Those aren't very substantial words, Captain. We're talking about my brother's life."

"The Human term for your attitude is 'wet blanket,' Triscoe," Rieka scolded. "We're searching for possibilities, here. We'll worry about the details later."

Jeniper drummed the table with her fingertips. "I'm supposed to be there in forty minutes. There doesn't seem like a lot of time to work out a detailed plan."

"There's plenty of time, Jen. We're going to use the *Providence* and InterMAT there rather than take a shuttle."

"We?" Triscoe inquired.

"A figure of speech," Rieka said, offering what she could only hope didn't look like a phony smile.

"But Jonik said—" Jeniper began.

"The Fleet is involved," Triscoe told her, "despite Gundah's wishes."

"But—"

"That doesn't matter," Wang cut in, stopping Jeniper's complaint with a stern look. "This Oph craves power. And for some unknown reason, she does it without craving attention, too. She had Jonik record the message in order to remain incognito. She doesn't even know we're onto her. So we'll do what she wants—but not the way she wants it.

That cuts into her power and makes her think on her feet. Many wrong decisions are made that way."

Hoping they could capitalize on those faulty decisions, Rieka looked at her wrist chrono. "I've got twenty-three-twenty. Gundah expects you to show up by zero-hundred. Let's get ready by changing out of these party clothes and regrouping on the *Providence*. We'll talk to Nason, there, and let him decide how visible he wants the Fleet to be."

"Sounds good," Wang agreed. He slid the communiqué chip across the table to Jeniper and stood. "Give me five minutes."

Rieka nodded and looked at Jeniper. "Everything will be fine. Once we're aboard ship we'll have your whatever-it-is scanned. Maybe that will tell us something, and we can plan our strategy. Go get changed."

Jeniper nodded nervously. "Should I tell Robet?"

Rieka glanced once at Triscoe. "If you want to—but I'm sure he'll find out soon enough."

"I appreciate you backing me up on this, Admiral," Rieka said as they strode down the corridor toward an InterMAT station on the *Providence*.

"It seems the most logical course of action," he said. "We can't make any kind of assault on the station—at this point, anyway," he added.

Rieka grinned at his phraseology. "I like the way you think. And you agree we substitute a dummy package for the real thing? Twanabok supplied us with a metal cylinder similar to the one Jonik Tarrik gave Jeniper. He said they're used to transport tissue samples."

"Makes you wonder what's so special in the real one."

"Yes," she agreed, "it does. Especially since Twanabok's scan was inconclusive."

They entered the station and found Jeniper and Wang outside the transfer chamber. Jeniper held a small sack containing the stand-in cylinder. Two tech-pros put the finishing touches on Wang's body equipment.

"How's it rigged?" Rieka asked him.

Wang turned toward her. "The TC has been repro-grammed to pick up both my voice and any other noise in the room—so you'll be able to hear exactly what's happening. I've got a regulation maitu here in my pocket and a chemical packet under my shirt."

Rieka nodded and looked at Nason. "We're expecting them to disarm Wang. But they shouldn't be able to detect the smoke bomb. If there's trouble, he can activate it—thus giving us time to InterMAT him out."

"And Miss Tarrik?" Nason asked.

"Jeniper's got a signal tracer injected behind her left ear. The InterMAT is already programmed with her code."

"Then it looks like we've done all we can," Nason commented.

Rieka nodded but remained silent. More and more she felt suffocated by her Heraldship. Not long ago she'd chafed at the idea of being recalled to duty. Now, she realized how badly she wanted to do just that.

Sending two inexperienced individuals into a potentially hazardous situation was not her idea of doing all she could. Her sense of responsibility worked like a double-edged sword. If it weren't for Triscoe's *quantivasta* gift, she'd be preparing to settle the score with Gundah, herself. She could feel her adrenaline pumping at the thought and frowned in frustration.

Nason nudged her, and whispered, "It does get easier in time, Rieka. Right now, though, a smile would help more than a frown."

She forced herself to do as he asked, and said, "When did you learn to read minds?"

"I haven't," he replied. "I've been there—and it was you I sent into the fray."

"But *you* never smiled."

Nason shrugged slightly. "I didn't have the advantage of someone advising me."

Trying not to laugh, Rieka ended up snorting softly. "What's the time, Lieutenant?" she asked.

"Twenty-three-fifty-eight, Herald," he replied.

"Contact the bridge and tell Captain Marteen you're ready to transport."

Rieka left Nason to step closer to Jeniper and Wang. "No fancy heroics, understand? Just trade the bag for Jonik, and we'll get you out of there."

Jeniper nodded. Wang, however, offered a one-sided smile. "Simple plans are the best ones, Boss. See you in a few minutes." He gestured to Jeniper, and they entered the chamber.

Rieka backed away from the door and went to stand with Nason near the console. She listened to Lieutenant Kyliss's conversation with the bridge while he prepared to send his charges to New SubDenver. From there, they'd be rerouted to the Oasis, thus avoiding any suspicion of having involved the Fleet. In a moment, she heard a pop as Wang and Jeniper were sent to the orbiting station via synthetic wormhole.

Jeniper gasped when the two Ophs grabbed her and pulled the bag from her hands. One shoved a maitu against her neck and she closed her eyes, sure he meant to kill her. She realized Wang was receiving similar treatment when she heard him curse. She turned toward him as far as the guards allowed and watched as he was disarmed and pummeled when he fought back.

"Stop fighting," she yelled, her voice echoing eerily in the distance.

Remarkably, all three of them did. Her guard's pushed her forward and they began to walk down a long covered walkway made of strong, metal mesh. Dim overhead lights lit the path and disappeared in the darkness ahead. Hoping they wouldn't be separated, Jeniper listened for Wang behind her. He and his guards stayed a few paces back. She heard them struggling and wished Wang would cooperate.

Finally, they came to a junction with another walkway. When she got close enough to recognize the individual waiting for them, Jeniper took a breath and pushed her shoulders back. Her guards stopped her a short distance away from Gundah.

"Adjutant Tarrik, how nice to see you again. And who have you brought with you?"

"His name is Hong Wang-Chi," Jeniper said. "A Human on the Earth Herald's staff."

Gundah took her time as she looked him over. "Your mate?"

Jeniper decided not to dignify the question with more than a simple answer. "No." She watched as Gundah ambled toward Wang and growled at him in her throat. He looked her in the eye, but didn't move.

"He had this," one of Wang's guards said. He handed Gundah the maitu.

"That's all?" she asked.

The creature nodded and Gundah leaned close to Wang. Jeniper watched him clench his jaw when she sniffed his neck, then jerk violently when she licked him. "Take care, Human," Gundah told him. "Your life is in my paws." She punched him in the chest, sending both Wang and the guards a few steps back. "Mind yourself."

A hiss emanated from the vicinity of the blow and the three men were immediately surrounded with smoke. Jeniper watched as Gundah stepped forward and all but disappeared in the cloud. She heard clothing rip and the sound of the tape being pulled from Wang's chest. When the smoke cleared, Jeniper felt her chin quiver. Wang's shirt was in tatters and his chest raw from the chemical and tape.

Gundah waved off the guards and they stepped back a pace. "He will behave," she said.

Jeniper felt a shiver run down her spine as Gundah casually turned to scrutinize her. "And now Adjutant Tarrik, I believe you and I have some business to attend to." She reached out a paw and a guard handed her the sack.

"Where's Jonik?" she asked, hoping her voice wouldn't betray her terror.

"He is here," Gundah replied casually. Jeniper watched as she hefted the bag.

"On this station?" she persisted.

"Perhaps." Gundah's paws fumbled with the canvas material.

While Jeniper waited nervously for her to open the knapsack, she heard an odd humming sound. Odd, but familiar, she realized. She glanced away from Gundah and felt one of her *ribah* flip. Jonik stood in front of an ornately carved *skiff*.

"I told you she'd come," Jonik said, moving toward her.

"Jonik, are you all right? Is that a *skiff*?" Jeniper asked, knowing that back on the *Providence* they could hear everything being said. She wanted to touch him, but the guards held her arms immobile. Ophs, she knew, were much stronger than any other bipeds. She glanced at the two who stood beside Wang. One had a dark streak near his mouth. Blood? Had Wang actually injured an Oph?

"I'm healthy enough," Jonik said. He looked pointedly at Gundah. "For now."

"Your debt will be paid once I verify the contents of this," Gundah replied, slipping the silvery cylinder from the sack.

Wishing she knew what she hadn't truly delivered, Jeniper thought hard for something to say. "How can such a tiny thing be so important?" she asked.

"That is not your concern, Aurian," Gundah said. "My business with your family is almost complete."

Before Jeniper could respond, the *skiff* slid out into the small area formed by the intersecting walkways. RadiMo popped up from a hole and his digits began to dance over the keys.

"When the Aurians return to Earth, this creature would accompany them," the voice said.

"That wasn't exactly our deal," Gundah replied. A low growl came from her throat. "I told you to wait in the lab."

"This creature no longer trusts Adjutant Gundah of Oph, and will cease to comply with her requests."

As Gundah walked toward RadiMo, Jeniper could tell she had some difficulty with the reduced gravity. "You'll do what I tell you, you little bug, or that bitch of yours won't see her next litter."

"This would be blackmail," RadiMo's *skiff* announced.

"Yes. It would." Gundah turned the cylinder over in her paws and frowned, if that could be said of Ophs. Jeniper felt her breath catch when Gundah walked under a light to examine it more closely.

"We've given you what you wanted," Wang said quickly. "At least let RadiMo and Jeniper go."

"I do not take orders from Humans," Gundah replied, making the term sound vile. She scrutinized the metal and ran her paws over it.

Jeniper looked at Wang and saw him nod at her. He figured Gundah had realized she'd been given a phony whatever-it-was. She wondered if the *Providence* could InterMAT just the four of them back, leaving the Ophs behind, but doubted it. The guards still held her and could probably kill her in an instant.

"You all thought you were very clever, didn't you?"

Gundah said finally, turning to glare at them with yellow-ringed eyes.

Jeniper said nothing. She felt her knees weaken as the Oph approached, but thanks to the guards, remained standing. "I . . . I have no idea what you mean," she managed.

"I am insulted at both your attempt at duplicity and your underestimation of my intelligence," Gundah said easily. "Someone will die for that."

"This is an outrage," RadiMo's *skiff*-voice announced. "You assured this creature no one would be harmed by the plan."

She turned slightly and bared her teeth at him. "I hate to disillusion you, vermin, but I lied." In a movement too smooth for Jeniper to believe it could have been anything other than calculated, Gundah grabbed a maitu from the nearest guard's holster and blasted a hole through the far end of RadiMo's *skiff*.

He shrieked as the device dropped to the floor, then disappeared down a hole. Gundah's barking laugh filled the walkway, but Jeniper distinctly heard Wang say, "Boss? I think we need help."

Rieka couldn't imagine how she'd let the situation slip from bad to worse. Now, as she stood in Triscoe's conference room, staring into his worried face, the beginnings of a plan came to her. She could only hope he'd cooperate. Not daring to form the thoughts into words he'd perceive through their link, she realized she needed to get aboard the Oasis, herself.

She glanced at her companions. Nason and Setana occupied two chairs at the table, and Robet's concerned face lit the console's screen.

Gundah's voice clearly said, "You'll do what I tell you, you little bug, or that bitch of yours won't see her next litter."

"We've got to do something," Rieka insisted. "She doesn't care what's in that cylinder. She'll kill them all."

"InterMAT them here?" Setana suggested softly over Wang's voice asking Gundah to let RadiMo and Jeniper go.

"No," Triscoe said. "The guards are too close to Jeniper and Wang to separate the signals. Plus, there's a brief moment before and after transport in which the guards could discharge their weapons."

"And we need to get RadiMo out of there, too. We just have to find something to distract the guards," Rieka said, raking her fingers through her hair. Unfortunately, she had no idea what that might be.

They eavesdropped on the conversation until Gundah said, "Someone will die for that."

Rieka gasped as they heard the maitu's blast and Radi-Mo's terrified squeal. Then, Wang's quiet plea did something to her. She felt as if he'd drilled through a facade she'd worn and reached her true self. The urge to act overcame the conventions of her office. Lives were at stake, now, because she'd made the decision to send the fake canister.

Striding past the admiral, she sat in the chair at the console and switched on two-way communications. "Tell her I'm listening, Wang-Chi."

"No," Triscoe barked, but it was too late. They heard Wang relay the message.

"All right then," Gundah's disembodied voice replied. "I will accept that the Earth Herald is privy to this conversation. How does she wish to contribute to it?"

"Ask her what she wants," Rieka said.

Wang relayed the message. They heard Gundah's barking laugh, then she said, "I want Earth under my control, again."

"Again?" Rieka frowned and looked at Nason. He shrugged.

Setana offered, "Perhaps she's deluded herself into believing that—and your Heraldship has altered her warped perception."

Rieka shook her head and looked at Triscoe. "Somehow I doubt that. There's some kind of connection here—but I can't see it."

"However," Gundah's disembodied voice continued, "provided you bring along the genuine canister, I am willing to trade one Herald for another."

"Tell her I'll be there in ten minutes, Wang-Chi," she told him over Triscoe's loud objection. "And if she hurts anyone in the meantime, I'll destroy her merchandise."

"What do you think you're doing? You simply can't—"

It took both Nason and Setana's efforts to quiet Triscoe, but he managed to control himself long enough for them to hear Gundah's reply. "That is acceptable."

"You are Earth Herald," Triscoe insisted, pointing a long finger at her. "You cannot simply trade your life for another. The welfare of your planet rests on your shoulders."

Rieka glared at him, and she sensed the flare of his emotions, but it didn't alter her decision. "Don't tell me my responsibilities, Triscoe," she warned, slapping his finger away. "Those aren't your people being held at gunpoint."

"That would make no difference."

"The hell it wouldn't!" She pushed away from the table to put some distance between them. "You haven't lost—anything. Ever. In your whole life." She turned and glared into fierce brown eyes. "You only *think* you know the burden of responsibility."

"And you do?"

"You're damn right I do." She paused and brought herself under control. "How many people have died under your command?"

Triscoe frowned and shook his head. "That isn't fair."

"Really?" Rieka glanced at Nason. "I'm guessing fewer than twenty. on the other hand, I've lost dozens, including my brother. I'm well aware of the consequences my decisions bring, and I don't intend for anyone else to die on my account."

"That isn't fair, Rieka," Triscoe persisted.

"Maybe not. But we don't have time for discussion. Gundah expects me in nine minutes, and I've got a lot of preparing to do." Rieka glanced at Nason for support, but he simply frowned down at the table, presumably in deep thought.

She realized Triscoe and Setana were communicating silently and turned to leave them alone when Robet's voice stopped her. "I'll go instead," he announced.

Embarrassed she'd forgotten him, Rieka moved to the console. "A generous offer, my friend," she said. "But you aren't the Earth Herald."

"Is that so important?" he asked.

"Apparently. I intend to find out exactly why."

"Good luck, then. *Prospectus* out."

Rieka looked at the grim faces of her companions. Nason's bibbets fluctuated wildly. She nodded at him and hurried out the door. Triscoe's mind-voice hit her in the corridor.

Rieka stop.

No. He continued to try to talk to her, but Rieka discovered that humming to herself did a good job of drowning him out. She went to their rooms and collected the canister from the desktop. She'd almost made it back to the corridor when Triscoe arrived.

"You can't ignore me," he insisted.

"And you can't order me."

He grabbed hold of her arm when she attempted to pass him. "Have you forgotten that we are bound? That if something happens to you, I suffer as well?"

"I haven't forgotten, Triscoe. I simply don't intend to die." She pulled free of his grasp and left the room. He caught up quickly, and they took a Chute to Station Four.

"Your arrogance is astounding, Rieka. You cannot control the future," he argued. "You don't know what will happen."

"You don't trust me, do you?" she snapped.

He stood mutely for a moment as if shocked by her question. "That was uncalled for."

"I disagree," Rieka told him, hands on her hips. "I think I just hit ground zero."

The door opened, and she strode the last few meters to Station Four with him in her wake. "Lieutenant Kyliss, I need two InterMat transponders," she told the chief.

"Right away, Herald," he said, then went through a doorway opposite the chamber.

Rieka went to the console and tapped in the command to receive Wang's TC signal. She boosted the sound until she could hear Gundah speaking clearly. "Dorah, keep that rat quiet."

"Yes, Adjutant."

Triscoe stepped close and doused the volume. "We need to talk."

Kyliss returned with two small disks the size of communiqué chips. "Here you are, Herald. I've programmed your ID into this one just like I did for Jeniper's."

"Thank you," Rieka said pleasantly. She took it from

him, thinking of the best place to wear it. "And the second?"

"It's not coded."

"Okay." She clutched the second one in her palm.

"Clear the Station," Triscoe ordered. "I need to speak to Herald Degahv alone."

"Yes, sir." Kyliss nodded and left.

Rieka turned to face her Indran husband. She knew what had to be done and didn't like it any more than he did. But the emergency facing them had to take precedent over their personal needs.

"Rieka," he said, grasping her by the shoulders, "don't do this."

"Because if I die—you die?"

"I did not say that. But Gundah is like a nuclear reactor with an exposed core. We don't know when she'll blow."

Rieka shook her head. "That's a fine argument, Tris, but RadiMo doesn't stand a chance. We've still got what Gundah wants. That has to be enough reason to believe in my decision." She tugged the jumpsuit's zipper and shoved the transponder into her bra.

"Not for me."

"Because your life is at stake, too?" He said nothing, but the look in his face told Rieka all she needed to know. "All right. Then let's fix that. I've got a couple of minutes left before I'm late. Disconnect me."

He reeled back but didn't let go. "Do what?"

"You heard me, Triscoe," she said, her heart pounding. "Get out of my head. Now."

His normally pale face looked ashen. "I . . . I can't do that. I don't want to. The Singlemind is complete. Without that connection—"

"—what, precisely, will happen?" Rieka interjected. "You don't know, do you? That's because you're convinced this is the same type of Singlemind as that of a 'Gifted Pair.' Well, it isn't, Triscoe. I'm Human. I'm not a Gifted Indran. I didn't begin to understand the difference until you made me . . . get into your mind."

She paused and took a shaky breath. "If you refuse to get out of my head, then I want you to *stay* out. Can you do that?"

Staring at her as if she'd grown a third eye, he nodded. "However, that would not . . . be wise."

"I don't give a damn about what you think right now," she said, her heart aching. She'd gone this far and wasn't about to turn back. If Triscoe could actually separate himself, then maybe he'd be safe if anything did happen to her. It might not be the best idea she ever had, but they didn't have time to explore any other options.

She saw the recognition of her strategy in his eyes. "But I must protect you," he protested.

She aimed a finger at him. "That's another Indran thing we need to work on." Glancing at her wrist chrono, she added, "Another time. Take this"—she thrust the silver cylinder into his hands—"scan it again, and don't send it to the Oasis."

"But you told Gundah you'd—"

"I know what I told her. Now please, Triscoe, trust me. As soon as my signal and this one separate, InterMAT this one." She held out her hand, still holding the chip.

Looking completely dumbfounded, he nodded.

Her throat burned, but at least her eyes hadn't teared up. "Thank you," she whispered, then turned and walked smartly to the InterMAT chamber.

TWENTY-ONE

Arriving at the orbiting station with a soft pop, Rieka realized how alone she suddenly felt. With her mind as her only weapon, she thanked whatever gods might be watching that Triscoe had not called her bluff and disconnected them. Even so, she knew it had to be torture for him not to speak to her.

She moved cautiously along an enclosed catwalk structure, glancing out occasionally into the darkness and imagining the station as it once was, growing every sort of edible plant for the planet below. This place was only one of many gifts the Commonwealth had given Humanity. Rieka wondered why Gundah had chosen it.

The dimness grew brighter and the sound of distant voices became stronger. She crept quietly along the mesh flooring, wondering if the Ophs could either hear her approach or feel the vibrations as she moved.

RadiMo's *skiff*-voice sounded, a loud complaint. She heard the unmistakable sound of metal rending. Someone had discharged a maitu.

Knowing she'd run out of time, Rieka hurried on toward what she could now make out to be the junction of at least two catwalks. The gravity created by the station's spin had decreased a bit as she neared the pivot point, but she still managed to maintain contact with the grillwork under her feet.

Ignoring everything but RadiMo and his *skiff,* she took a deep breath, straightened her shoulders, and strode regally past the guards standing beside Jeniper and Wang. Gundah made some kind of growling noise, and Jonik gaped, but Rieka didn't stop until she reached the Bournese Herald.

"Herald Degahv would greet Herald RadiMo and inquire as to his health," she said.

RadiMo pulled himself up from his hole and typed on his console. "This creature is well. But the Oph, Gundah, has lied, and this creature is displeased."

"All will be well, RadiMo," Rieka said, squeezing the TC transponder in her palm.

Gundah bared her teeth. "You are *my* prisoner, Degahv," she snarled. "You will do as I say, or die."

Ignoring her, Rieka bent to examine the *skiff*'s damage. She could see sparks down one of the holes and caught a whiff of something pungent. "You will require major repairs to this unit, Herald," she said, slipping the transponder onto his console. "I am glad that this area remains undamaged."

Gundah growled again and RadiMo blinked strangely when he saw what she'd done. He typed. "It is just a machine."

"Replaceable, yes. Unlike the rest of us."

"Shoot her!" Gundah snapped angrily.

Still kneeling, Rieka looked directly at the Oph guards. All four held their weapons ready, but none of them appeared very anxious to kill a Herald. "Not a good idea, Gundah," Rieka said pleasantly, "even your men know that. If you kill me, then there's absolutely no reason why anyone would consider bargaining with you. With that hurdle crossed, there's also no reason not to move up the schedule and scrap this station early. Say, in the next few minutes. My guess is a couple of spheres ought to do it."

"You could not do this," Gundah hissed.

Rieka smiled. "Try me." She stood and took a step away from the *skiff*.

"I still have RadiMo," the Oph argued. "The Fleet ships would not attack with him aboard."

A second later, the Bournese Herald and his *skiff* were gone.

Rieka released the breath she'd held and crossed her arms over her chest. "You were saying, Gundah?"

Her nemesis growled strangely. "I accepted the trade, Human," Gundah replied, switching tactics. "You are infi-

nitely more valuable to Earth than the Bournese Herald."
Her nostrils flared and hatred was evident in her yellow-
ringed eyes. Rieka took her emotional state as a good sign
and shifted her attention to assess Jeniper, Jonik, and
Wang.

Even in the minimal light, she could see Jeniper's bibbets
had gone dark under her disheveled hair. Her powder blue
eyes were wide and uncertain, but she nodded slightly that
she hadn't been hurt. Jonik's bibbets were pale, as if in
shock. Rieka wondered if he'd been drugged.

Wang, on the other hand, had a conspicuous bruise over
one cheekbone and a swollen lip. His chest, exposed by the
shredded shirt, looked burned. Rieka couldn't tell if he'd
received any other injuries, but he seemed to be leaning
heavily on the mesh wall. Unable to tell if that was a ruse
or not, she looked him in the eye. "Wang-Chi?"

"I'm okay," he whispered hoarsely.

"Good," she replied brightly, then turned her attention
back to Gundah. "Now, Adjutant, I would like an explanation."

"I do not explain myself to Humans."

"Oh really?" Rieka uncrossed her arms. "My curiosity is
piqued. Do you happen to have a reason?"

"An Oph does not answer to a subspecies."

"I see," Rieka replied, still keeping her tone light, though
she wanted to get her hands around the Oph's throat. Gundah's reasoning might be the evidence she needed to convince others the Commonwealth harbored a double
standard. "Now, would that be subspecies as in subordinate
or—"

"As in—inferior," Gundah spat. "Deficient. Insignificant."

"Second-class?" Rieka prompted, knowing Triscoe could
hear this conversation via Wang's altered TC.

"Precisely. Humans are worthless creatures. They were
unworthy of Commonwealth aid two hundred years ago—
and they are unworthy of possessing their own planet
today."

"What an interesting statement, especially coming from
an Oph," Rieka replied. "And how, precisely, did you intend to rectify the situation? You're holding two Humans

and two Aurians hostage and everything we say is being transmitted to the *Providence*."

"I am not obligated to explain myself to you," Gundah stated, twitching her nose. "I want the container Jonik gave to his sister. The *real* container. Now." She growled again.

Refusing to be intimidated, Rieka waited until the eerie echoes died away. "Sorry. I didn't bring it with me—but I do have it," she assured Gundah quickly. "So let's say I get the canister to you. What then?"

Gundah let a moment of silence pass before she said, "Then, I will consider letting you go."

Rieka shook her head. "I'm afraid that isn't good enough."

Gundah snorted then, and Jonik stepped back. Rieka glanced at him and recognized fear in his face, his stance. She was scared, too, but didn't dare show it. Individuals like Gundah thrived on intimidation.

Gundah's black lips drew taut around her teeth, "Do nothing, Aurian," she warned. To Rieka she said, "You are your mother's daughter."

Thrown by the odd turn in the conversation, Rieka frowned. "You know Candace?"

Gundah raised her chin and grinned. "Intimately."

Triscoe had assembled his mother, Admiral Nason, and Commander Aarkmin in the InterMAT lab. They all heard the conversation unfold, each registering shock every time Rieka goaded Gundah to divulge something.

Cursing himself for honoring his wife's request, Triscoe looked at Aarkmin. "Find Candace Degahv. I want her brought here as soon as possible."

"Yes, sir." Aarkmin nodded and strode from the room.

"Do you think that's wise, dear?" Setana asked.

"Candace has been threatening Rieka since before the election. If she has some connection with Adjutant Gundah, then I want her to explain it to me—before I have her arrested."

"Do you have any evidence?" Nason asked.

"Not yet. But a high-ranking Oph with an admittedly xenophobic streak has just implicated Candace. I mean to find out exactly what is going on."

The admiral nodded, and Triscoe felt his anxiety drop a

notch. Rieka had convinced Gundah not to kill her, and Nason agreed to an inquiry. The situation didn't seem quite so out of control. Unfortunately, he wasn't sure how long that would last. Nor was he certain he could last much longer, himself. *Not* communicating with Rieka had to be the most difficult thing he'd ever done.

"And what shall we do with the cylinder?" his mother asked, gesturing beyond the lab to the innocent looking object sitting on the station's InterMAT console.

"I'm not sure. Our scans have only identified an interior chamber containing discordant strands of molecules."

"What kind of molecules?" Nason asked.

"Simple sugars . . . bases . . . Nothing, apparently."

"Gundah thinks it's something," Setana reminded them.

Nason frowned. "Do you think it *could* have been something once—and has since broken down?"

"If that is the case, then we don't lose anything by letting Gundah have it," Setana said, looking first at Triscoe, then at the admiral.

He felt his mother's scrutiny and knew some strategy was in the works as Nason asked, "Do you think that is wise?"

"I'm not sure," she admitted. "But it does present itself as a possibility."

Triscoe's TC clicked on in his ear and he held up a hand. "Marteen."

Aarkmin's voice sounded in his head. "Candace Degahv is in her quarters on Earth, Captain. In New SubDenver."

"If you've found her, then why isn't she here, Commander?"

"It is zero-two-hundred hours local time, sir. Apparently my rank was only sufficient to warrant waking her. She refuses to comply with my request."

Aware now of where Rieka got her stubborn streak, Triscoe asked, "Do you have the InterMAT coordinates to her quarters?"

"Affirmative."

"I'll access them from here. Thank you, Aarkmin. That's all for now." He terminated the link and looked pointedly at his mother. "Would you mind collecting Candace Degahv for me, Mother?" he asked. "She requires . . . motivation."

*   *   *

From his captain's chair, Robet activated communications with the *Providence*, hoping for news.

"Aarkmin here, Captain DeVark," Triscoe's EO replied.

"Any news?" he asked.

"Captain Marteen and Admiral Nason have been in conference in an InterMAT station and have asked not to be disturbed," Aarkmin offered. "Otherwise, I would put you through to them."

"I see." Robet nodded as a *ribah* flipped, silent evidence of his concern for both Rieka and Jeniper. He had infinite confidence that should either Triscoe or the admiral require his services, they would ask. He set down his cup and tried to smile at his DGI. "Thank you, Commander. If the opportunity arises, please inform the admiral that I've put my ship on standby alert."

"I will sir," she said. "*Providence*, out."

"*Prospectus*, out." Robet flipped the toggle and cut the communication. The Reaffirmation ceremony was only hours away. It would take a miracle to work through this crisis and still go forward with the celebration. Rieka, he knew, had managed a few miracles in the past. He decided to help her however he could.

Working along that idea, Robet let his thoughts slip back to the admiral. Nason had ordered him to stay here to protect Earth. Wondering just exactly what that might entail, he leaned toward his navigator.

"I want you to do a sweep of the inner planets, Pita," he said to the Aurian lieutenant. "Everything inside Mars's orbit. Go above and below the solar plane, too."

"What am I looking for, Captain?" Pita asked.

"I'm not exactly sure, Lieutenant," he answered, frowning. "Anything unusual, unexpected, out of the ordinary."

Rieka blew into her cupped hands. "Just for the sake of curiosity," she began, "is there a warmer place on this hunk of junk? I mean, your fine illumination leads me to believe the power is still on," she added, a touch of sarcasm in her tone when she referred to the dim bulbs along the ceiling.

"The manager's office is warm," Jonik volunteered. "It's one level up."

"Silence," Gundah barked. She grabbed a maitu from

the guard near Wang and turned it on Rieka. "I want that cylinder, now."

Rieka saw Wang stiffen as the weapon was leveled. She looked at the maitu in Gundah's paw, then at her eyes. The yellow rings had disappeared. Gundah knew exactly what she was doing.

She shrugged. "I'm not the one with the TC, Gundah," she said. "If you want to talk to the *Providence,* you'll have to use Wang to do it. And, of course, it only works if he's alive."

Gundah glared at her, but turned slightly to address Wang. "*Providence,* I am aiming a maitu at Herald Degahv. Transport the cylinder to me immediately, or I will kill one of my hostages." She waited a moment, then barked, "Well?"

Wang nodded, frowning as if trying to concentrate on what only he could hear. "Okay." He looked at Gundah. "The EO on the ship," he began slowly, "Commander Aarkmin—says that Captain Marteen has given permission to send the cylinder. But he wants to trade it for the hostages."

Rieka gritted her teeth as Gundah growled and turned the weapon on him. He pointed to his ear. "I'm only repeating what she's telling me."

"No hostages," Gundah barked.

A moment passed and Wang shook his head.

"How about two?" Rieka offered. "Send back the Tarriks. They're just excess baggage now, anyway."

Gundah took a moment to consider that option. She looked Rieka in the eye and nodded once. "All right. Tell your captain I will let them go."

"Unharmed," Rieka prodded.

"Unharmed."

Rieka watched Wang as the messages were relayed. "It's in the chamber now," he said.

"Have the guards step away from Jeniper and Jonik," Rieka told Gundah.

The Oph nodded, and they did. Fear and concern in her eyes, Jeniper looked at Rieka while she moved closer to her brother. Rieka nodded once, and Wang said, "Okay, they're ready."

A moment later, the Tarriks disappeared and, to Rieka's

amazement, Candace appeared holding Gundah's ransom. She couldn't imagine Triscoe's reasoning in sending her mother. Did he think, as she'd been wondering herself, that they were working together toward a common goal?

Gundah immediately reached forward and Candace recoiled. "Give me the canister," the Oph barked.

"I will not!" Candace countered, clutching the prize closer to her chest. "I demand an explanation."

"Why do you Humans keep insisting upon explanations when you do not control the situation?" Gundah growled ferociously and lunged.

Rieka watched, amazed, as Candace actually struggled to keep hold on the object. Gundah, of course, had little trouble wrestling it from her, but it seemed almost comical the way her mother wouldn't let go.

As Gundah held up the canister, Rieka watched its polished surface reflect the station's dim lights. "Do you have no curiosity about this, Herald?" the Oph asked.

"Not particularly."

"It contains something of yours."

That caught her attention. "Mine? Is that so?"

"Oh, yes. Your adjutant's brother owed Candace a great sum of money. We struck a deal that when he delivered this to me, I would pay the debt."

Rieka nodded. She glanced at Candace who looked as though she had no idea what Gundah was talking about. "I'm listening," she said. "And I haven't heard anything that remotely involves anything belonging to me."

Gundah grinned, if that could be said of an Oph. "I hold your children." While Rieka frowned trying to figure that out, Gundah went on. "And many more."

Her words registered, and Rieka felt her blood pressure rise. They hadn't scanned the canister to ID anything on the molecular level. "Are you telling me that's what left of—of Sati Labs? That Jonik stole my DNA and then blew up the lab to cover his tracks?"

"Actually," Gundah began, suddenly modest, "it was my plan. And it worked marvelously. No one had any idea your sample survived."

For a brief moment, Rieka found her temper difficult to control. "And what do you intend to do with it?" she managed stiffly.

"Control you. Control Earth. Until you are of no further use, that is."

For some reason, Rieka didn't believe her, but she said, "Blackmail."

"Precisely."

Thankful that Jeniper was safe, but still worried for Rieka, Robet scanned the file he'd retrieved on the Oph Adjutant. He hoped to find some clue as to why she hated Earth so much.

Lieutenant Pita shifted in his chair. "Captain?"

Robet leaned toward him. "What is it, Lieutenant?"

"You said to watch for anything out of the ordinary."

Sensing his bibbets thicken, Robet concentrated on keeping their color light. "That's right, Pita. What's the panoply picking up?"

"Well sir, it isn't exactly out of the ordinary—considering Earth's had a lot of traffic recently. But three Fleet ships have just entered the solar system, about one-point-five AUs from the sun."

Robet sat straighter. "Three ships. Are you sure?"

"Absolutely, Captain."

"Give me a tactical on the DGI. I want them identified." Pita carried out his orders and Robet watched the three-dimensional image form before him. The four inner planets appeared around the sun, their orbits traced by a blue line. Two red spots well above the solar plane blinked, indicating a pair of Fleet ships. A lone red blip appeared below.

"No response on the IDs, Captain. Maybe they're too far to pick up."

He doubted it. "Three . . . ships." He felt his jaw swivel and turned to the ensign manning the communications console. "Contact the *Providence*. I need to speak to Captain Marteen or Admiral Nason immediately."

"As we speak, sir," the woman said.

It took several seconds longer than he hoped, but finally Triscoe's face appeared, slicing the DGI's image into two sections. "Yes, Robet?"

"Tris, I think we have a situation."

"Of what sort, Captain?" Nason's unmistakable voice asked. A moment later, he stepped into the video pickup.

The camera automatically zoomed out, and Robet realized they were in an InterMAT station.

"My navigator has informed me three ships have just entered an area of less than one-point-five AUs from Sol. Their autorecognition beacons have apparently been deactivated. Could these be our missing Ophs?"

He watched Triscoe work the console adjacent to the InterMAT. Nason turned to look at the screen which displayed a two-dimensional image similar to Robet's own DGI. "It is possible, Robet," Nason admitted. "Ready your crew for combat. I'll issue further orders shortly."

"Yes, Admiral."

When the signal had been cut, Robet leaned back in his chair and took a deep breath. After the Procyon War, he never thought he'd need to fire another antimatter sphere. Now, with Earth poised to enter the Commonwealth as an equal partner, he realized Rieka had been right. Humanity and all it represented had not been universally accepted. And he would have to defend this planet and all the individuals on her against once-friendly ships.

The *Barnel.* The *Garner.* The *Dividend.* Pita would ID them soon enough, but Robet instinctively knew it had to be them.

And he knew those captains and respected them. It would not be easy to engage onetime comrades, but he would. He had sworn to protect every Commonwealth planet nearly two decades ago and had lived his life by those words.

Reminding himself to concentrate on what, rather than whom, Robet flipped a toggle on his console. The intercom lit and he spoke into the microphone. "All hands, this is the captain. We are now at red-alert status. Please man your stations and prepare for battle. This is not a drill. Repeat. This is not a drill."

Rieka wasn't precisely sure when Candace's maternal instinct switched on, but once it did, Gundah's earlier reference about their mother-daughter similarities made a whole lot of sense.

"And just who do you think you are, speaking to my daughter like that?" Candace demanded.

The Oph remained unruffled. "I have absolutely no motivation for entering into a debate with you, but since you've served me well in the past, Candace Degahv, I may let you live if you behave yourself."

"Served you well?" Candace echoed. "I have never met you—or done business with you. You must be—"

"Surely you have heard of TechLine Enterprises," Gundah said smoothly.

Rieka watched a number of expressions cross her mother's face. Confusion. Recognition. Disbelief. "Yes," she said, a dubious tone surrounding the word.

"I am TechLine," Gundah announced.

"But there are at least a dozen companies under that umbrella," Candace replied, glancing at Rieka. "No one individual could . . . Why, the combined fortune . . ."

"Is in the quadrillions of credits, yes," Gundah answered easily. "The only entities larger than myself are Extensa Communications and the Commonwealth Fleet."

"Then why risk it all for a few strands of DNA?" Rieka asked.

"Earth has been a growing ulcer for some time. I have managed, in my way, until now. And then the Procyons came along and ruined everything. You," she said, aiming her maitu again at Rieka, "must be controlled. If that is impossible, there are other less-cost-efficient ways to rectify the situation."

Rieka searched Gundah's face and saw more than a hint of evil. She glanced at Candace. Somehow, the Oph had managed to manipulate her mother who, in turn, had control of Paden. Without him as Earth Herald, Gundah had lost her bid for control of Earth. The idea was at once astonishing and absurd. The connection Rieka and Jeniper had been looking for in recent weeks seemed suddenly clear.

"You," she announced, pointing an accusing finger at Gundah. "You murdered him, not Candace."

"You're very clever," Gundah conceded, dipping her head in a small salute.

"Murdered who?" Candace inquired.

Gundah flipped an ear and her jewelry tinkled softly. "Stephen, of course. Your dear, estranged, most uncooperative husband. It was very simple, really."

"Oph ground crew," Rieka supplied. "Accident on entering the atmosphere."

"Could happen to anyone," Gundah said with a faint smile. "I'd be careful if I were you, Herald."

"You had him *killed*?" Candace demanded. "Whatever for?"

Gundah made a small gesture with the paw holding the maitu. "Because unlike you—my small, furless Human chattel—he refused to cooperate. A lesson you should learn soon, Herald."

Rieka refused to dignify that threat with a comment. But Candace huffed and glared at their captor. "I've never cooperated with you," she insisted. "I've never met you until now."

"But you've dealt with TechLine for over two decades. I fed you numbers and you reacted accordingly. Surely you recall your good fortune after the Garacci deal. I believe your investment in Aurian produce netted you enough to buy Paden's administrator's seat."

"I didn't buy his seat," Candace protested.

Gundah gestured with her paw. "For want of a better term."

"I—dear God—can that be true?" Rieka heard the distinctive sound of hysteria in her mother's voice and readied herself to spring. "I can't believe—you have manipulated me. You . . . you killed my husband. You! You . . . animal!"

In her peripheral vision, Rieka saw the maitu come up, but her attention remained on her mother, watching the signs of fear and rage gone out of control. She caught Wang's eye and before her mother could move more than a step toward Gundah, they both lunged.

Rieka saw a guard intercept Wang as she shoved Candace down, but Gundah had already fired. The blast hit Rieka in the shoulder and she heard someone shout her name before everything became shrouded in black.

TWENTY-TWO

"She's unconscious!" Triscoe gasped, raking a hand through his hair. He glanced at Nason long enough to see a concerned frown appear as his bibbets darkened, then began to pace. He tried to list every option in this scenario and their possible results, when his mother entered the InterMAT station.

"What happened?" she asked.

"It isn't good," Nason replied before Triscoe could speak. "How are things on Earth?"

"Organized chaos," she replied. "Damascus and the stadium are awaiting the influx of people—but EarthCom has complied with your request. No shuttles will be launched until you give the word. Jeniper and Ker are personally speaking to as many individuals as they can—asking for their cooperation." She sighed. "What more can we do?"

"Hopefully something," Triscoe grumbled. "Rieka's been stunned."

"Bring her back then, Triscoe. She's wearing a TC signal."

"I can't, Mother. In the moment before the signal takes its full effect, they could kill her."

"I'm not sure leaving her there is a better option," she complained.

Nason pinched at his goatee. "We'll think of something, Setana."

Triscoe's TC clicked on. "Captain to the bridge, please."

"On my way." To his companions, he said, "I'm needed on the bridge." Without waiting for the admiral's permission to leave, Triscoe hurried into the corridor.

As he eased into his chair a few moments later, Aarkmin

gestured at the DGI. "Long-range visual ID shows it's the *Garner*," she said, indicating a ship maneuvering into orbit. "She doesn't respond to our request for communication."

"Of course not." Triscoe swiveled toward the lieutenant at the comm console. It was still the late shift and it took a moment for him to remember her name. "Stolik, ask EarthCom if the *Garner* has made contact."

"As we speak, sir," she replied and a moment later added, "negative, Captain."

"Link to the *Prospectus*."

"On-line now, sir."

The incoming signal reorganized the DGI, splitting it in two. Robet's face looked determined but his bibbets remained pale. "Good morning, Captain DeVark," Triscoe began brightly. "From your expression, I take it the *Garner* refuses to acknowledge you, too."

"Can't believe Gimbish would turn traitor," Robet replied, shaking his head.

Triscoe frowned as a new thought hit him. He'd heard Gundah's blatant prejudice as she'd spoken to both Rieka and RadiMo. While her use of words simply disturbed him, the motivation behind them was shocking. Now, he sensed Gundah had a following larger than any of them had imagined. "Perhaps he doesn't see it that way."

"What do you mean?"

"We've been monitoring the standoff closely. Gundah's reach is far and her financial base is greater than we'd guessed. Though we don't know her reasons, she doesn't want Earth to become an equal partner. It's possible she's convinced these Oph captains they're doing the right thing."

"Against Nason's orders?"

Triscoe shrugged. "Without contact, all we can do is speculate."

Robet looked away for a moment. "My position is about thirty thousand kilometers aft of you. I'm picking up the other two ships. Looks like it's the *Dividend* and the *Barnel*. They're not talking, either."

"Are they close enough for you to tell if they've powered up their weapons systems?"

Robet nodded. "They haven't. Yet."

Triscoe turned toward Aarkmin. "Put us on full alert, Commander. I want Becker to man the weapons station."

While she made the announcement, Triscoe contacted InterMAT Station Four. "Kyliss, I need to speak to the admiral."

"Here, Captain," Nason's voice replied immediately.

"Sir, the *Garner* is now in Earth orbit. The *Barnel* and *Dividend* will arrive shortly. None respond to our hails. Perhaps you should come to the bridge."

"I appreciate the offer, Captain," Nason replied. "But the situation is better served if you remain in command. I'll commandeer a conference room on level one and coordinate things from there."

"Understood. Thank you, Admiral." Triscoe closed the channel and leaned back in his chair. Nason's decision to remain off the bridge was at once a relief and an onus. By choosing to "coordinate things," Nason had implied they would soon engage the renegade ships.

A brief moment passed and Nason reopened the intercom. "Yes, Admiral?"

"Gundah has established contact with the *Garner,*" Nason said. "I think it's time to risk transporting our people out of there."

"About time, Gimbish," Gundah said, adding a small snarl as she hauled Candace out of the *Garner*'s InterMAT station.

Her cousin looked both frightened and excited, his eyes open wide enough for her to see a narrow yellow ring around his dark iris. He gestured for her to move closer.

Gundah shot Candace a lethal look. "Do not move, Human," she warned.

"I wouldn't think of it," the woman replied.

Gimbish snorted in confusion as Gundah moved toward him. "As per your order, Oasis is destroyed," he reported.

"Were the two Humans rescued?"

He nodded once. "Your request was to wait until there were no life signs aboard. They left almost the moment you did."

Gundah bared her teeth and offered him an approving growl. When he did not relax, she flipped an ear. "Something is amiss?"

"The *Barnel* and *Dividend* are approaching Earth. I cannot possibly launch an attack on the planet and defend myself against so many ships."

"Fool," Gundah whispered. "The *Barnel* and *Dividend* will fight with us, not against us."

"You neglected to mention that," Gimbish snapped, pulling himself to his full height. "It now occurs to me that you neglected to mention quite a bit."

"Whatever I choose to mention to you is everything you need to know, Gimbish," she said. "Now enough of your whining. I have much to do in the next several hours."

His lips thinned, but he nodded smartly.

"I shall need a guard for this Human," she said, gesturing toward Candace Degahv. The original plan had not included her, but when she appeared with the canister, Gundah had had to rethink her strategy. Keeping Degahv hostage made more sense than letting her go. "She and her guard will accompany me wherever I am on this ship—unless she becomes uncooperative," she added loud enough for Degahv to hear. "In that case, you may put her in one of your holding cells unless I decide to kill her."

"Understood."

She waited and watched while the captain used his TC to request a guard for Degahv. "Has my control center been outfitted as I requested?"

"Of course," Gimbish replied, looking insulted. "My people have constructed the room to your exact specifications. As soon as the guard arrives, I will take you there, if that is what you desire."

"It is," she said, glancing back at the Human who seemed to be studying both her and the captain intently.

By the time they reached her control room, Gundah realized that her stomachs were demanding food. She followed Gimbish as he toured the small facility, explaining the console functions and the DGI's abilities. The room also contained a table large enough for eight individuals and a comfortable-looking lounge area. Across the hall, Gimbish explained, were sleeping quarters for both herself and Mrs. Degahv.

"Good," Gundah said, glancing again at the console. "And this directly connects me with your station on the bridge?"

"Correct. You can communicate over the audio channel, here," he replied, gesturing to a toggle, "or via screen, here." He indicated another spot on a light-panel board. "This unit uses verbal-initiate software. No keyboard is required."

"The VI is articulate in Commonwealth Standard or Oph?"

"Both," he replied. "But you need to key in what language you're speaking before you start."

"That should be simple enough." Gundah looked around the room once more, her gaze sweeping past Degahv and the guard standing just inside the door. "This will do nicely, Captain. I expect you would like to return to your duties."

"Yes." He nodded and left.

Gundah turned her attention to the console. She sat before the computerized atoll and began familiarizing herself with each function. "Degahv," she said after listening to her stomachs rumble again, "fetch something to eat."

"I am not your lackey," the woman replied. She'd seated herself at the table without permission and looked as indignant as Gundah had ever seen a Human look. "And I imagine there are plenty in the crew just waiting to serve you." She crossed her arms over her chest. "If I have inadvertently helped you in the past, you can be sure I intend to redeem myself at the earliest opportunity."

Amused, Gundah swiveled in her chair and squinted at the creature who might still be of use in her quest for revenge. Candace Degahv appeared disheveled, but her eyes were sharp and her jaw set. "Ah. Human spirit." Gundah smiled. "That intangible thing that has kept your species going for two very long centuries. And what has it got you?" She paused for a brief moment, then said, "Can't answer for your entire race? Then how about yourself, Candace Pirez Degahv? What has your Human spirit done for you?"

The Human didn't answer, but Gundah sensed the silence was belligerent. "I'll tell you, then," Gundah went on. "Your husband died because of his 'spirit.' And your daughter will live out her life as my thrall. As for you—money, even small amounts of it such as you have, will not buy you respect. You're still an inferior species. And I have made it my personal goal to see that you either accept that—or are exterminated."

Rieka heard moaning and wondered who'd been hurt before she realized the noise was coming from her. She lifted a hand to protect her closed eyes from the invading brightness and thought she heard Setana's voice.

"I think she's coming around, Doctor. Mr. Hong, you stay right there. You've been told several times not to move."

Eyes still closed and covered, Rieka recognized Twanabok's approving hiss somewhere close to her right side. She gritted her teeth through the pins-and-needles sensation where the stun had hit her. From experience, she knew it would be gone in an hour or so.

"You're conscious," Twanabok stated as he shifted his position, moving toward her head. She felt his claws contact her still-unusable shoulder before recalibrating the light. When it dimmed, she uncovered her eyes and looked up at him.

"Everyone okay?"

"Mr. Hong has several contusions and a chemical burn on his chest. He is lucky he did not further damage his arm," Twanabok answered.

"And the others?" She watched the doctor's leathery green face meander through several subtle expressions. His pink eyes skimmed over her, then looked away. She'd been a Fleet captain long enough to interpret this indecision as bad news.

Setana stepped to her other shoulder. "Jeniper and Jonik are fine, dear," she said, straightening the blanket across Rieka's shoulders. "They're both back on Earth. Jeniper felt she needed to make arrangements for postponing the ceremony. RadiMo, of course, has been with us for some time."

"Where's Candace?"

Setana gently ran a finger along Rieka's jaw. "I'm so sorry, dear, Gundah took her."

Rieka sighed. "To keep me in line."

Twanabok took her numb hand and wrapped it around his lower arm. "Squeeze, Herald." She did as best she could, and he grumbled something unintelligible. Then he manipulated her shoulder and jabbed it in two places with a claw coated in something.

"Ow!"

"Neural transmitter," he said, attaching a small device to her upper arm. With the heat light off and his pads now registering on her skin, Rieka realized they'd removed her clothes.

Willing her expression to appear as alert as possible, she looked up into Twanabok's pink Vekyan eyes. "Does that mean I'm ambulatory? I can't stay here much longer. Where are my clothes?"

Twanabok flicked his tongue at her. "I'll authorize your release as soon as I return to my office. Your clothes are stowed in the locker. Herald Marteen has offered to help you into them."

"Why are you being so cooperative, Vort?" she asked warily.

He made a strange sound in his chest. "Nason's orders," he replied before turning away.

"Wang-Chi," Rieka called, and waited until he stood beside the bed before she spoke. "I need a TC like yours."

He looked at her skeptically. "Okay, Boss. Can I ask why?"

"Sure you can"—she glanced at Setana as she opened the clothes locker—"but you'll have to wait for your answer."

He, too, glanced at Setana. "I understand. I'll get one ready." Wang nodded once and left.

Setana turned and studied her with a strange look. "Are you planning something with Mr. Hong?"

Rieka sat up, felt the room spin for a minute, then heaved a grateful sigh as it steadied itself. Having no intention of answering Setana's question, since she would go directly to Triscoe with it, Rieka evaded the issue. Twanabok's resistance to her earlier query propelled her to ask, "You going to tell me the bad news?"

"No," Setana answered brightly. "I'll leave that to Merik."

"Then it must really be bad," she said, taking the bra Setana handed her.

"I watched the nurse remove that," her mother-in-law

remarked, deftly changing the subject. "But I'm interested to see how it goes on."

"Nothing to it," she said, slipping it around her. "Even Triscoe—well never mind," she added diplomatically. "The jumpsuit may give me some problems, though."

Working together, they got her into the outfit. Rieka slid her feet into her boots and nodded. "Guess I'm ready. Is the admiral still aboard?"

"Yes," Setana answered. "But before you see him, RadiMo would like an audience."

"Okay," she said, nodding. Taking it slow, they left the ward and found Twanabok waiting at the doctors' med station.

"You have been placed on the board," Twanabok told her without preamble. "If you require pain relief, request it."

"Thank you, Vort." Rieka offered him a smart salute. He returned it, then shook his head and shuffled off toward his office. She turned to Setana. "Where's RadiMo?"

Setana led the way, and a few moments later CariMo greeted them at the guest room's door. "Enter, please," CariMo's *skiff*-voice said. She gestured for them to sit and carefully guided her mobile device to a position near RadiMo's.

The Bournese Herald popped up from a hole and frantically began tapping his board. "This creature would thank Herald Rieka Degahv and wishes her to know he owes her a great debt."

Just seeing his little black eyes blink at her gave Rieka a sense of relief. She sighed and nodded. Wondering if she was about to break some kind of taboo, Rieka left the couch and squatted before RadiMo's floating *skiff*. "You gave us all quite a scare, Herald RadiMo," she told him softly. "I am glad to know you are well."

"You may not be," the *skiff*-voice replied. Before she could ask what he meant, his digits danced over the console and the voice continued. "An explanation is in order."

"Yes."

"Adjutant Gundah has plans for Earth. She communicated with this creature many months ago, seeking cooperation and mutual satisfaction. In return for information about Earth subcities, Bourne received a contractual agreement to mine precious metals and gemstones."

Trying to make sense of what he'd said, she asked, "From Earth?"

"From Earth."

"But Gundah has no authority to offer such a contract." Rieka settled herself into a more comfortable position on the floor and glanced first at Setana, then CariMo. "You must have realized an Oph can't negotiate a contract from Earth."

"Gundah owns controlling shares in TechLine. TechLine owns Kaypak Corp. Kaypak holds mineral rights on three Earth continents," CariMo explained.

"Kaypak is a . . . Human-owned company," Rieka said.

"This is true," CariMo agreed.

"But Gundah owns Kaypak," RadiMo said.

Rieka felt her jaw go slack for a moment, then clamped it shut. Too stunned by Gundah's seemingly endless reach, she switched gears. "What did she want to know about the cities?"

"Their precise positions," RadiMo answered.

"And their proximity to geologic faults or other subterranean structures," added CariMo.

"Such as?"

"Caverns. Aquifers. Deposits of oil and gas. New intrusions of magma."

Rieka immediately saw the impact of such information. If Gundah was out to destroy Earth's ability to be productive, the easiest way to do it would be reducing the workforce. Destroying the underground cities by "accident" would accomplish that without suspicion.

Working hard to keep anger from her voice, she asked, "And you agreed to this in exchange for mineral access?"

"Correct," RadiMo replied.

"Did you confer with the Earth Herald before striking the deal?"

"Affirmative," CariMo said.

RadiMo made an elaborate gesture with his upper body, then attacked his console again. "Herald Alexi Degahv would offer similar access but required monetary compensation."

"I see." Rieka frowned.

"And we . . . that is . . . the Bournese tribal council voted negative to deal with Humans," added CariMo.

"For Earth rights," Rieka said, empathizing with his frustration and trying to understand their thought process. This duplicity had to be a Bournese characteristic. Alexi would have altered the deal if he'd known a second party was involved. He had warned her the Bourne were shrewd, but he hadn't anticipated them selling out Earth in order to get their paws on precious gems.

"Yes."

"So you took the easy way out. You didn't have to pay anything and you didn't have to deal with Humans."

"Precisely," CariMo's *skiff* said.

"This creature now understands that our reasoning may have been in error," RadiMo added. "The bargain did not take into account ill effects toward Humans—who are now perceived as valuable citizens. Though we chose not to do business with you, we would not wish to see you harmed."

"Thank you," Rieka said, unsure whether she believed his excuse. She glanced at Setana, then back to RadiMo. "And the agreement you did make with Alexi? What was that for?"

"This was simply a way for our presence to be uncontested. A Herald sanction is indisputable," RadiMo replied.

"I thank you for your honesty, Herald RadiMo," Rieka told him. "If you should wish to continue your business with Earth, I would request you do it only through my office."

"This would be acceptable."

"Good." She got to her feet and offered both Bournese a crooked smile. "For your protection, please remain aboard the *Providence* until Captain Marteen deems it safe to return to the planet."

"We will do this," CariMo's *skiff* said.

"Thank you. Until I return—be well."

"And you," the synthetic voices echoed.

Back in the hallway, Rieka shook her head. "Who would have guessed that 'funny little guy' would have fooled us like that."

Setana made a strange gesture with her hands. "The Bournese are very straightforward—when one asks precise questions. Apparently Alexi did not ask the right questions."

"And made some incorrect assumptions," Rieka added.

They continued walking for a few more moments, then Setana gestured toward a door. "In here," she said.

Wang stepped from a nearby Chute and joined them. "Your TC is waiting for you in the medical suite, Boss," he said.

"Thank you, Wang." Rieka turned and entered the room to find Nason ensconced at one end of a conference table. Judging by the number of discarded cups, datapads, and the like, he'd been there for some time. "Admiral, you're still here," she said lightly as she moved toward him.

"For the duration," he replied. "Sit down. Everyone." He gestured for Setana and Wang to join them. Not bothering to wait for them to comply, Nason looked at Rieka and asked. "You're better?"

"The arm's a little tingly, still. But Twanabok released me."

"Good."

Rieka read something in that singular word. She stared at him for a long moment, steeling herself to the realization. Dread and anticipation warred within her. When she managed to say the words, they didn't sound quite as unpalatable as she thought they would.

"You're going to recall me."

Nason glanced at his screen before focusing his attention on her again. "That's very possible, yes," he admitted.

"Why?"

"Several significant things have happened since you were stunned, Rieka," he began. When he glanced at Setana, Rieka saw her mother-in-law shake her head.

"What haven't you told me?"

"The abandoned station is now destroyed," Nason answered. "We transported you and Mr. Hong here only moments before it happened."

Frowning with confusion, Rieka asked, "How?"

"Gundah's escape was apparently well-planned. She and your mother are now aboard the *Garner,* captained by an Oph named Gimbish. The *Garner* destroyed the Oasis with a sphere—as I said—just seconds after we InterMATted you here."

Rieka digested that information and decided it wasn't anything she couldn't have guessed for herself. But none of that, as far as she could tell, warranted her returning to active duty. Not wanting to seem too eager, she crossed her arms over her chest and leaned back in her chair. "And?"

Nason nodded once. "And . . . the *Barnel* and *Dividend* have entered Earth orbit. They remain unresponsive to our hails and are considered hostile."

"How many loyal ships are in orbit?"

"Two right now, the *Prospectus* and *Providence*. The *New Venture* should arrive shortly. Captain Tohab has two senators aboard who are scheduled to speak at the Reaffirmation."

"So Midrin doesn't know the situation," Rieka said.

"I've just sent her an update," Nason told her. "Fortunately, we've got battle-experienced people manning all three ships."

"You're expecting shots to be fired?" Setana asked.

"I have to anticipate anything. Adjutant Gundah apparently has a plan. We don't know what it is, but with—"

"Wait." Rieka lifted her hand, indicating he should backtrack. "She only wanted the genetic material in the canister, right? And we gave her what she wanted. So what's keeping her here? The Reaffirmation? Jeniper's announced its postponement. What if I tell her to reschedule it for next year? That ought to throw off Gundah's plans."

"It may not be that simple," Nason countered. "She has a hostage and our attention. I think she wants a great deal more."

Setana sighed tiredly. "If only Cimpa was not so . . . disoriented. We might be able to get some information out of him."

"Or one of the other Heralds," Rieka added. "If Gundah struck a deal with RadiMo, she could have easily done it with anyone." Nason nodded and swiveled slightly to study his console.

"True," Setana agreed. "Perhaps I could—" She stopped and looked wide-eyed at Nason. "Merik?"

Rieka glanced back to him to discover his bibbets had darkened considerably in the moment her attention had been directed at Setana. "Admiral?" she asked, echoing her mother-in-law's concern.

Nason ignored them for a moment. He'd already switched on audio communications with the bridge. "I'm monitoring your tactical screen, Captain," he advised. "What do you make of that maneuver?"

Rieka heard Triscoe's voice reply, "They've dropped to a closer orbit and have gone geosyncranous over the Earth city, Winnipeg. It's an above-ground. Many structures predate the Collision."

Nason looked at Rieka. "What's in Winnipeg?"

Rieka shook her head, frantically trying to think. "Uh, it's above ground, like Triscoe said. Probably about ten thousand residents. Lots of historical landmarks." She continued to rattle off increasingly insignificant details until she couldn't recall anything else. "I . . . I don't know what she wants there."

"The kids," Wang blurted.

"The kids?" It took her a moment to realize what he meant. "The Blue Planet Future?" In a heartbeat, the faces of the children she'd met flashed across her mind. "That's right. Their Camp Future in Winnipeg."

"Are you sure?" Nason asked.

"Yes."

"Intercept that ship, Captain," Nason ordered. "Do whatever you can to get it away from the city."

"As we speak, sir," Triscoe replied. "Two minutes to intercept."

Rieka glanced at Setana. "Yillon said to beware for the children. I thought he meant the genetic material but do you think he could have—"

"Damnation!" Nason shouted, pounding his fist against the table. "We're too late. They've begun transport."

TWENTY-THREE

Triscoe watched, horrified. The *Garner* had InterMATted a number of individuals from the surface. And Gimbish had used a technique Triscoe had adopted when attacked by the *Venture* during the Procyon War. He'd called up a screen fragment during transport, a simple but effective way of moving objects while still protecting your ship. Did that mean he anticipated friendly fire?

His horror at the abduction was augmented by Rieka's frustration and rage. He'd purposely kept out of her mind, but the involuntary connection still bridged their feelings. He let her snap and squabble with Nason. If the admiral really wanted her back in uniform as he's suggested, he'd have to accept both Rieka's talents and her temperament.

"Update positions on the *Barnel* and *Dividend*," he said.

"They're closing on the *Garner,* sir," the lieutenant replied. "Still ignoring our requests for communication."

"If we knew what she wanted, we'd know how to prepare," he mumbled.

"What was that, Captain?" Nason's voice asked at his elbow.

"I was lamenting that we still do not know what Gundah wants. We thought it was the DNA. Now, it's the Human children. There isn't a pattern to follow, sir."

"You may be looking at the problem too closely," Nason advised. "This Oph has something against Earth. What, exactly, we don't know. She's managed to acquire the allegiance of three Fleet captains—and convinced them to accept her commands."

"You're saying she wants to destroy the Earth?" Triscoe

asked, bewildered. Now that he thought about it, three ships could do that job rather efficiently.

"Or something close to it," Nason replied.

"Captain," Stolik interrupted, "they've opened communications with each other."

"Can you tap into it?"

"I have," she replied, turning toward him with a strange expression on her green, Vekyan face. "It's encoded in such a way the translator won't process it. It throws the garbled transmission back at me."

"Keep trying," Triscoe told her, though he knew it probably would do them no good. Judging from the section of his DGI that maintained a muted image of the *Prospectus*'s bridge, he figured Robet's crew had drawn the same conclusion.

"Sir, they're powering up the weapons systems," Aarkmin informed him.

For a split second Triscoe wondered how to respond. "Power up, Becker," he ordered. "Repulsion screens to maximum."

"As we speak, Captain," the Human at the weapons console replied.

Robet looked into his camera, and the audio suddenly came on. "*Dividend*'s closer to me," he said. "I'll keep them busy. You take the *Barnel*."

Triscoe nodded. "Target the *Barnel*, Becker. Minimally charged spheres to start with."

"Aye, Captain." Becker bent to carry out the order, and Triscoe acknowledged the feeling of dread he'd thus far kept at bay. Having to use weapons rankled, and firing on a sister ship went against the fealthy oath he'd taken when he'd become a captain.

"Admiral," he began, "is there anything—"

"They're InterMATting again!" Aarkmin's strident voice interrupted.

Triscoe snapped his attention to his console screen and felt his heart flip. The *Garner* had transferred cargo to her companions. They were now forced to assume the children had been dispersed to all three Oph vessels. An effective shield, Triscoe realized.

"Hold your fire," Nason said. "No Fleet ship is to fire on them without my express order."

Robet's voice echoed Triscoe's as they replied in unison, "Yes, sir."

"Gods, no!" Becker's voice rang out across the bridge.

Triscoe glanced up from his small screen to the image on the DGI. All three rogue ships had just released spheres headed for the Earth's surface.

Rieka watched Nason's DGI as six spheres converged on a single spot in central North America. They disappeared in the atmosphere, but the imager compensated and she felt her heart cringe as Winnipeg ceased to exist.

Wang dropped his face in his hands, and she gripped the table, her body shuddering at the unspeakable act. "Thousands of people," she managed, her voice rough with emotion. "She's just murdered thousands of people."

Setana's face contorted, but she didn't immediately speak. "What can we do, Merik?" she finally asked, turning toward the admiral. "We can't let this continue."

From the look on his face, Rieka realized Nason was in shock. Who could prepare themselves to face such destruction? While he grappled for a reply, her mind clicked into gear. Maria and little Po's face flashed across her mind. They had to get those children back. All of them.

"Earth doesn't have a squad to handle this sort of thing." Rieka glanced at Wang. "And while the Fleet has security personnel on every ship—this situation is probably beyond anything they've ever handled."

Nason couldn't seem to pull his eyes from the screen. "Unfortunately, that's true," he said.

"So what can be done?" Setana asked.

"We can start by recalling me to active duty," Rieka told them, relieved now that the choice had been so easy.

The admiral's head snapped around. He stared at her for a brief moment before nodding decisively. "I'll process your recall immediately."

"Good."

"Is that wise, dear?" Setana asked, both concern and confusion in her voice.

"No. It's not," Wang interjected.

She shrugged. "It's necessary. That's all that matters. The way things are now, Gundah can destroy Earth piece by piece while I stand by and watch her. A Herald can do almost nothing in this situation. But a Fleet officer can, and I'm going to get those kids back, too."

She paused for a moment to think. "As my adjutant, Jeniper will have to take over my Herald's duties." Rieka glanced at her mother-in-law. "She may need some help."

"Don't worry about a thing," Setana replied.

Knowing they would not disappoint her, Rieka smiled wryly, then looked at Nason. "How long before the *New Venture* gets here?"

"Less than twenty minutes," he said. "What are you thinking?"

"I'm thinking . . . somebody needs to get aboard the *Garner* and stop Gundah before she does any more damage."

The admiral nodded. "And what role does the *New Venture* play in that objective?"

"I think there's someone aboard her who can help me do that."

Wang pulled himself straighter. "Us," he said.

"Us?"

Wang's look told her not to argue. "Herald or captain, it makes no difference. You're not going anywhere without me."

From her position at the table, Candace studied her captor. Gundah opened communications with someone via the Digital Graphics Imager. An Oph in a captain's uniform appeared three-dimensionally near the wall.

The captain curled her lip before she spoke. "What now, Gundah? A third Fleet ship is approaching the planet. I do not have time for—"

"You have as much time as I tell you, Gellath," Gundah snapped. Candace heard the ring of irritation in her voice. "We are three ships. They are three ships. But we have Human children aboard and a planet to destroy below. They will not fire on us."

"Don't be so sure."

"Humans have mush for hearts. They will not sacrifice the children," Gundah assured her.

Gellath shook her head. "The other Fleet ships are battle-experienced, too. This concerns me. My people are following orders—but I sense they are wondering about the objective."

"You have few aliens aboard and none on the bridge. Correct?" Gundah asked.

"Of course."

"Then don't worry. I will contact you when we reach the next target. Gundah out."

The screen went dark and Candace watched Gundah frown. Perhaps things weren't running as smoothly as she had led everyone to believe. Fleet captains pledged an oath to serve and protect all Commonwealth citizens. It seemed reasonable that the Oph officers might be having second thoughts. If she handled this situation correctly, Candace realized, she might do far better than simply coming out of it alive.

"That captain knows what she's talking about," Candace said from her seat at the table. "You're running a big risk taking on the likes of Captains Marteen and DeVark."

"I fail to see any point in discussing this with you," Gundah said. She gave a little snort to punctuate her annoyance.

"Have it your way."

"It is always my way," Gundah reminded her.

Sure the Oph would eventually decide to kill her, Candace taxed her mind for some strategy to delay the inevitable. If she could manage to make herself seem useful, Gundah might choose to keep her on retainer. A good plan, she decided—if the Fleet didn't elect to destroy this ship, first.

That thought inspired a roundabout strategy. "I'm sure you have everything . . . under control." She made her voice sound soothing. "I just hope you haven't left out any of the variables."

Gundah's ears pricked up ever so slightly. "Explain," she said.

Candace gestured with her long-fingered hands. "As you've already noted, we Humans know all about survival. We understand that sometimes a few people have to die in order to save many, many more."

"And you expect me to believe that?" Gundah sneered. "All you creatures do is cry about how everything must be

protected from harm. Nothing is to be sacrificed." She
growled deep in her throat. "It's uncivilized."

"You underestimate us. My daughter—"

"—your daughter and her father are the only Humans I
have ever met with a backbone," Gundah finished. She left
the console and went to the table. "Every last one of you
worships money more than integrity."

Candace held herself straight, moving only her eyes to
look at the Oph. "You're mistaken."

Gundah laughed and peered down at her captive. "This
from you, Candace? From the Human so predictable that
you have never once done something without my telling
you?"

"You said that before," she replied. "And I still don't
understand. I've never met you and have done very limited
business with TechLine. The Garacci deal you mentioned
before had nothing to do with you."

"Didn't it?" The Oph settled into the chair nearest the
tray of food and began to move its contents about with an
extended, lethal-looking nail.

While Gundah waited, Candace tried to find the connection. "I dealt exclusively with Auries," she replied, shrug-
ging slightly.

"How do you make your business decisions?"

Candace considered that for a moment. She fingered her
bracelet while Gundah played with her food. "The way
everyone else does," she said, finally. "I watch the trends,
consult the market reports, consider sales projections. . . ."

"And if the decisions prove to be wrong?"

"I either change the marketing strategy, downsize the
project, or cut production entirely."

Gundah pounded the table with her paw. "Typical
Human philosophy," she hissed, jaw clenched.

Surprised, Candace forced herself to sit straighter. She
schooled her face into an indifferent mask. "I don't see
what is wrong with that. I've built quite a large reputation
based upon that philosophy.

"*Everything* is wrong with it," Gundah told her. "You
are looking at the Commonwealth through a microscope.
One does not get ahead by altering oneself to meet the
needs of others. That is passive. That produces nothing."

She pounded the table again, but this time Candace didn't budge. "A philosophy of fools."

"I see." Candace lifted her chin. "And your philosophy?"

"I have changed the Commonwealth to meet *my* requirements," Gundah replied proudly. "You should be honored that I have decided to share this information with you."

"Oh, I am," she said. Her tone betrayed the words, and she wondered if Gundah would catch the sarcasm. "Please, go on."

Gundah studied her a moment and Candace wondered what she might be thinking. Finally the Oph tapped the table and said, "Power, not money, is the key. The two often go together, I will admit," she went on, "but *power* is the key."

Candace nodded. "And that's what you've got."

"Ahh . . . yes." Gundah squinted and sighed, giving Candace the idea this conversation went beyond the words being spoken. It was as if Gundah, despite her hatred for Humans, had chosen to take Candace under wing. "You see me commanding three starships and holding a planet for ransom and think this is the extent of my power." She threw her head back and laughed, the yellow rings visible in her eyes. "This is the beginning!"

Candace shook her head. "From my perspective, it looks rather like the end."

Gundah aimed a paw at her. "That is because your thinking is flawed, Candace Degahv. It always has been. Did I not risk my life for that canister?"

"I wouldn't say that, exactly," Candace replied.

"Fortunately, what you think is immaterial. I have the canister now. And with it I will control Humanity's destiny."

Candace leaned back in her chair. "You'll forgive me for not making that leap."

"That is because you do not know what it contains."

"I heard Rieka say it was a sample of something—from a lab that was destroyed."

"The canister contains your daughter's DNA."

Candace frowned and shook her head again. "Where do you get power from that?" she asked.

Leaning forward, Gundah snatched a bloody tidbit from

the tray and ate it. Candace tried not to watch. "Think of this, Human. The Earth Herald is the advocate of equality for her species. In the past, she has been the one to complain loudest about Human mistreatment. How ironic it would be, don't you think, for her own DNA to destroy her race?"

Realizing the canister was the angle she'd been looking for, Candace knew instinctively how to handle her captor. "Destroy it? How?" she asked, hoping she sounded both curious and interested.

Gundah wrinkled her nose and took another morsel off the tray. "Sati Labs was not the only genetic-research facility in the Commonwealth. I own another—a company I removed from the TechLine umbrella and set out on its own. My people there have assured me they can both alter and replicate a strand of Human DNA. It does not even need to be complete." Gundah smiled to herself at her cleverness.

"Go on," Candace coaxed.

"The Degahv sample will be altered and duplicated and turned over to another little company I own called Pulsar Pharmaceuticals." She stopped when she noticed Candace's confused reaction. "Surely you see where this is leading. Pulsar's main business is providing serum inoculations. It produces almost eighty percent of the vaccinations given to Human infants."

Candace fought to maintain her stoic expression. "What are you doing to do?"

"I won't hurt them," Gundah assured her. "It will take a number of years, though, using this—civilized approach. And the expense will be more than simply controlling your daughter. But I alone will eradicate the Human species and no one will ever know."

"I don't understand how you can do this," Candace persisted. "If you don't plan to harm them—?"

"The vaccine will mutate them slightly," Gundah explained. "Every Human inoculated with serum from Pulsar will be sterile."

Candace forced herself to remain aloof as she absorbed the impact of Gundah's monstrous plan. "I don't understand why you've gone to all this trouble. You could use *any* Human DNA to do that."

Gundah gobbled another morsel of flesh before she answered. "Theoretically, you are correct. But I have my reasons for proceeding with Degahv DNA."

"I'm fascinated," Candace said, leaving forward. "Why?"

"Stephen ruined my life," Gundah replied simply. "When I was still a pup, my father invited him to our home. For some reason that escapes me, he impressed my mother."

Candace nodded, remembering her tall, handsome husband. "In his youth, he was quite—impressive."

Gundah tilted her head back. "I recall he seemed large, for a Human." Her eyes wandered the room and Candace waited patiently for her to continue. "He visited frequently after that first time. Until the day my father caught my mother sniffing him."

"And that was bad?"

Gundah stared straight into her eyes. "A criminal act."

"But . . . Ophs mate for life," Candace said softly, sure Stephen hadn't provoked such an intimacy.

"Precisely." Gundah's voice grew hard. "She was banished from our clan. My father fell into a *vesch*. You would call it—depression. He took up games of chance and lost huge sums of money. Eventually, in my seventeenth season, he took his life."

"And it was Stephen's fault," Candace forced herself to say with conviction.

"Oh, yes."

Cautiously, Candace leaned over the table, and softly said, "I hated him, too. That's why Rieka thought I was behind the shuttle accident. And I can accept why you've taken this stand against Earth. I, too, believe that Humans are base, reprehensible creatures. And while your plan for the inoculations is—nothing short of genius, it will take time."

She waited for Gundah to react, but the Oph simply watched her. "And I'm sure you realize I abhor Rieka's designs for Earth. Perhaps . . ."

"Perhaps what?"

"Well, it just occurred to me . . . it might be amusing if we worked as a team."

At that, Gundah bared her teeth. "I like your choice of words, Human."

* * *

Rieka glanced at Lieutenant Kyliss and offered him a reluctant smile. Pacing across the InterMAT station did little to calm her nervousness, but it was better than talking to Triscoe. True to his promise, he'd kept out of her head, but it didn't stop him from arguing mightily that she should not go through with the plan. While she empathized with his sense of frustration, Rieka could not sympathize with his inherent fear for her safety. They both knew she would do everything possible, including laying down her life for the Humans of Earth. And now that the *Providence* had been placed in battle-ready status, Triscoe faced a similar predicament.

"*New Venture*'s within range, Captain," Kyliss told her.

"Notify the bridge, Lieutenant. We're standing by for transport." Nodding at Wang, who had stood like a statue near the console, she positioned herself in the chamber.

Wang stepped up to her shoulder. He looked good in the Fleet's colors. A black ensign stripe ran up his sleeve. "You love this, don't you?" he asked quietly.

Rieka noticed how comfortable it felt to be in uniform. She wore her captain's rank bar on the blue-and-rust tunic, but had a lieutenant's bar in her pocket that matched the bronze stripe on her sleeve. "Is it that obvious?"

She watched while he tried not to smile. "Only to someone who knows you."

She nodded. "Think of it this way, Wang-Chi, I'm much better at doing something rather than nothing. And while it might seem to you like my DNA is just a strand of molecules, to me—she's got my child. I can't turn my back on that."

Wang sighed. "Gundah's got your mother, too. She seemed genuinely surprised back there—when she found out about Stephen."

Rieka shrugged. "Candace can put on a pretty good act."

"Here we go, Captain," Kyliss said.

Rieka stood straighter. The InterMAT effect began, and in a moment she found herself standing in an identical chamber on the *New Venture*. Midrin Tohab waited for her out in the lab. Rieka smiled and saluted. "Permission to come aboard, Captain."

"Granted, Captain Herald—and Mr. Hong," Midrin replied, returning both the smile and the salute. "We're assembled in the conference room on this level." She shook her head as they moved into the corridor. "Do you really think you can do this?"

"Truthfully I have no idea," Rieka admitted. "But no one can come up with anything better."

Midrin nodded. "You'll do fine I'm sure. They won't know what hit them."

"I hope so."

The door opened to reveal four Ophs seated at the conference table. They stood and saluted her. Rieka returned the greeting and nodded to them in turn. "Good morning, Lieutenant Giffah, Lieutenant Gebrah, Lieutenant Gennath, Lieutenant Gorah."

"Captain Degahv," they replied.

She didn't correct them. Rieka then gestured to Wang. "And this is Mr. Hong."

They eyed him carefully, but said nothing.

"Let's sit down," Midrin said, gesturing toward the table. She took the end seat and Rieka sat opposite her, Wang on her right. "Now, all four of you have volunteered for this duty and the plan has been outlined to each of you. Before we brief Captain Degahv, have you any questions?"

The lieutenants shook their heads, their collective jewelry clinking pleasantly for a short moment. Rieka studied them all and wondered if any had been approached by Gundah in the past. It was possible, she decided, but unlikely. The three ships threatening to redesign the Earth's surface were captained by Ophs and had primarily Oph crews. She knew Nason was kicking himself for not noticing how the transfers and promotions had slowly trickled past him. Gundah, they'd realized belatedly, was both devious and patient.

"Before we start," Rieka said, looking each lieutenant in the eye, "I'd like to know why you volunteered for this mission. It's dangerous, and some of us might not survive."

Lieutenant Gennath, the one with the cream-colored coat, spoke first. "We are mothers," she began, gesturing toward the ornate metal symbol fused to her left ear. In it, two of the four jewel spaces contained stones. "My two sons will respect my decision to save other children. They will be taken care of by my family if I do not return."

Rieka nodded. "I appreciate the help, Lieutenant."

Lieutenant Gorah leaned closer. "You conducted my Advancement, Captain," she said. "I will always assist you whenever possible."

Honored, Rieka simply nodded. "Thank you, Gorah."

"My child grows within my body," she continued, "but our research has found that Gundah went past her prime without seeking a mate or having pups. This phenomenon can make an Oph . . ."

"Insane," Lieutenant Giffah finished. "We believe Adjutant Gundah is suffering from a disorder called Encephalostemic Syndrome. Most Oph females seek chemical therapies if they have no pups. Apparently, Gundah has not. While we are not doctors, it is plain to us that she requires medical help."

Rieka shook her head. "I'm afraid I don't understand. Gundah's behavior doesn't strike me as—insane."

Giffah's fur ruffled slightly across her shoulders. "This is a chemical imbalance," she explained. "It is difficult to explain fully. But a female with ESS appears normal in most respects. Their aberrant behavior is difficult to pinpoint. They become obsessive, deceptive, secretive . . . their desire for intercourse is heightened."

Nodding her understanding, Rieka said, "I can only vouch for the secretive aspect as of right now, but I'm guessing she's probably deceived a lot of people, too."

Lieutenant Gebrah nodded. Her spotted ears reminded Rieka of a stuffed animal she'd once had. "She must not be allowed to achieve her objective, Captain Herald. We intend to help you secure the children and the planet and take Gundah into custody so that she can be examined and treated. She is, after all, a sister Oph."

Rieka accepted their reasons and sighed. She looked down the table at Midrin. "And you're willing to let them do this."

"You're going to need all the help you can get," Midrin replied.

Rieka shot her a cantankerous look. "Thanks a lot, I think." She pulled her attention back to the four Ophs in front of her and looked them all in the eye. "Okay Lieutenants," she began, "this is a covert operation. Admiral Nason wants the hostages off those ships as soon as possible. We've got three targets and six of us. Who is taking the InterMAT detail?"

"I am," Giffah replied.

"And me," added Gebrah.

"Then we'll put you on the *Barnel* and the *Dividend*." They nodded. "You'll just man the InterMAT stations and transport the kids off the ships. Giffah, you'll be on the *Barnel*. Send the children to the *Prospectus*. Lieutenant Gebrah, you've got the *Dividend*. Transport to the *New Venture*."

"Gennath and Gorah—you'll be with us." She gestured at Wang and herself. "We'll start with the *Barnel*. You're going to locate the children and bring them to the InterMAT station."

"And what will you do, Captain?" Gorah asked.

"In addition to helping you, Admiral Nason has empowered me to incapacitate the ships. First, Wang and I will disable their weapons systems, then we're going to confer with their engineers."

"How will we keep in contact?" Midrin asked.

"We both have TCs," Rieka answered. "Twanabok glued one into my ear canal because we didn't have time to install it properly. Just ask for Lieutenant Dee and I should receive you."

Midrin nodded. "The admiral hasn't briefed me on what to do if something goes wrong, but I'm sure he'll—"

"Nason doesn't expect me to fail, Midrin. He'll be monitoring our progress as we go, but Gundah may have a few surprises for us. In the event that something untoward happens, I'm sure he'll issue new orders."

"You don't think he'll choose to destroy the ships, do you?" Midrin asked, visibly concerned.

Rieka blinked, surprised she'd ask such a question. Knowing the possibility existed for Nason to do just that, she diffused the suddenly tense atmosphere. "He'd better not—if he wants to stay on my good side."

TWENTY-FOUR

Rieka removed her insignia and pinned the lieutenant's bar on her tunic. She turned toward Wang. "Is it on straight?"

"I guess so."

Annoyed with his answer, she glanced at Gorah. "Is it?"

"Yes, Captain."

"Lieutenant," she corrected, lifting her arm and pointing to the bronze lieutenant's stripe running down the sleeve.

Gorah nodded once. "It's on straight, Lieutenant Dee."

The others joined them in the InterMAT station. Midrin looked anxious but determined, and the three Ophs' ears were perked up a bit more than before. "Let's get started then," she said.

Midrin turned to her InterMAT chief. "Have you coordinated with Damascus?"

"Yes, Captain," the Aurie said. "They're waiting for our signal."

"We'll be all right, Midrin," Rieka assured her, hoping her bravado wasn't transparent. "The *Barnel* won't have any idea we're from the *New Venture*. They'll think we're from Damascus. The odds are with us that Gundah's got some of her people there, waiting to wreck the ceremony. If we need you, we'll call."

Midrin's eyes met Rieka's for a moment, then she said, "Everyone have their stasis cuffs?" Rieka and the others nodded. "Good. Remember—all of you—no TC transmissions over ten seconds."

The Ophs nodded again. Wang clipped his maitu to his waistband and stepped close enough to Rieka for her to feel his warmth. She smiled. "See you in a couple of hours."

Rieka's anxiety moved up another notch as they stepped from the chamber in Damascus. The Boo ensign stationed at the InterMAT controls, who had already been briefed by Nason, saluted and stepped back out of the DGI range. Gorah signaled the ship while the other two Ophs aimed their maitus at Rieka.

"*Barnel*," an Oph lieutenant answered.

"Lieutenant Gorah, here, *Barnel*. We've got a Human in custody and thought it best to secure her aboard one of our ships. Is that acceptable?"

"I do not have the authority for such a transfer. I'll put you through to the captain," the lieutenant said.

"Stay calm," Rieka whispered.

Gorah's nod was slight as a second Oph's face appeared. "Captain Goverah," she began before he had a chance to speak, "we have taken this Human into custody. She apparently knows something of the plan and we are unsure what to do with her. Is it acceptable that we quarter her in your brig until Adjutant Gundah has a moment to decide her fate?"

"This is an unusual request, Lieutenant," Goverah said.

"True, Captain," Gorah replied. Then she began to speak in what sounded to Rieka like growls and yips. The captain nodded slowly. The name Gundah was used several times before the communication terminated.

"Well?" Rieka asked.

Gorah licked her black lips and shrugged. "An Oph that can be bought responds predictably to threats."

"You threatened him?"

"I wouldn't exactly say that, Cap—Lieutenant," Gorah replied. "I simply implied that Gundah would be displeased if anything went wrong." She turned to the Boo that had shuffled back toward the InterMAT control. "The *Barnel* will accept our transport signal."

"Good," it said. "Go now to the cliffs of Rothiwa and search for Varannah."

Rieka couldn't help but smile at Gorah's confused look. To the Boo, she said, "Let us hope Karina remains on the Rock." To Gorah she added, "Let's go," then led the way back into the chamber.

They arrived on the *Barnel* a moment later. Gorah led the way toward the station's attendant, who barked something incomprehensible. Rieka watched as Gorah nodded and gestured toward Rieka with her maitu. Then, she leisurely aimed her weapon toward the attendant and discharged it. He slumped to the floor.

"So far, so good," Rieka smiled. Gorah and Giffah bound the unconscious attendant in stasis cuffs and hauled him into the station's office.

Giffah took her place behind the controls. "I'll hold the children here until I receive confirmation from you, Dee," she said.

"We shouldn't be too long," Rieka told her while she tapped in commands on the InterMAT's auxiliary console, calling up an infrared inventory for the main hull.

"Okay. There's nothing here that points to where they've got the kids. The cargo holds read dark and cold—so my guess is they're holding them in a relatively public place. A conference room, crew's quarters—something like that. We don't even know how many there are. A dozen, at least, I'd guess. Obviously we need information, and we're not going to get it here." She opened a cabinet attached to the wall and searched through the equipment inside. She found a datapad with the power pack missing and picked it up. "Let's go."

"Where?" Gennath asked when they reached the corridor.

"Security office."

The *Barnel* had been refitted after the Procyon War, but that didn't alter its internal structure. Laid out like every other Fleet ship except the *Prodigy,* Rieka led Wang and the Ophs directly to the security office. "We all go in," she told them quietly, "but I'll do the talking. Gennath, you're with me and remember—we do this fast and loose."

A moment later, the door opened and she strode to the counter. Gesturing at the inoperative datapad, Rieka addressed the lieutenant on duty. "Engineering sends me to install an energy grid where they're holding the kids—but I didn't understand the commander. I heard the captain doesn't want to be bothered—so I figured we'd come in and ask you. Where am I supposed to set up? I can't even order up the right equipment if I don't know where to set up."

"Quad B second level dining hall," the Oph replied.

Rieka smiled. "Thanks, Lieutenant." She pretended to consult the datapad then glanced at Gennath. "Oh, sorry, Gennath. Your turn."

The lieutenant lifted her maitu and fired. While Rieka watched Gorah and Gennath secure the unconscious Oph with stasis cuffs, she asked, "You sure you haven't done this before?"

"This is too easy," Wang whispered as they approached the dining area. One Oph stood outside the door. Rieka figured there were at least two more inside.

"They're not expecting us," she replied softly. "Relax, Wang-Chi. Gorah, this time you do the honors."

Gorah moved forward. "This is the holding room, correct?" she asked.

The ensign guarding the door nodded. "We've got two more Humans to put in with them." Gorah gestured at Rieka and Wang.

The ensign stepped aside. They went through the door and stood near the menu counter. Three Ophs had positioned themselves around the room. The children had been seated at the tables and given food, probably to keep them occupied. Glancing around quickly, Rieka estimated twenty-five children were there, all wearing pajamas. She could imagine them being kidnapped from their beds and wondered what they must have thought when they found themselves aboard a Fleet ship. Judging by the noise level, Rieka wondered if they even knew they'd been kidnapped.

Two Oph guards approached, but Rieka let Gorah and Gennath handle them. Smiling, she wound her way around the table toward the third guard and recognized Maria seated nearby. The teenager seemed nervous and looked up as Rieka and Wang slowly came forward.

Sensing the girl wanted to call out to her, Rieka shook her head slightly. Maria, apparently understanding, deliberately looked down.

A glance in Gorah's direction told her they weren't yet ready to take down the guards. Quietly, she said, "Sit down, Wang."

"What?"

She pulled out a chair. "I said sit. We need to wait until there aren't any children in the cross fire."

Parking himself in the proffered chair, he grumbled, "That could take days."

She smiled at him. "You're such a comedian." Turning to a nearby child who reminded her of Po but looked a bit older, she said, "I'm Dee."

"I'm Joe."

"Guard's watching us," Wang whispered.

"It's nice to meet you, Joe," she replied, ignoring Wang. "I was wondering if you could do me a favor."

Joe looked skeptical. "I guess."

"It's nothing hard," she assured him. "Can you pass a message to the others?"

Joe shrugged. Wang tapped his fingers on the tabletop.

"Okay. Here's what you tell them: when Dee yells 'Down,' hit the deck. Do you think they'll know what that means?"

"I guess," Joe told her. He tapped a child at the next table and whispered to her, then got up and spoke to an older boy at another table.

Rieka watched the message cross the room and saw that Gorah and Gennath had positioned themselves near the other guards.

"No one's said anything to this guy, and he looks suspicious," Wang informed her.

She glanced at the guard. "I'll take care of it, right now." She stood and he reached to stop her, but Rieka was faster. "Just be ready," she told him and moved in the third guard's direction.

When she'd got close enough for a clear shot, a boy at Maria's table called out, "It's Herald Degahv!"

"No, Garret," Maria warned.

Before the Oph guard could make the connection, Rieka shouted, "Get down!"

Having received the message, most of the children complied. She aimed her maitu and fired, but the guard was moving she only hit an arm. Rieka heard the other maitus discharge while the guard scooped up the boy next to Maria.

Wang had already taken a position a few meters away, his maitu aimed steadily at the Oph.

"All clear here, Dee," she heard Gennath call.

"Understood," she replied. Keeping eye contact with the

Oph, she said, "Okay now, kids, I need you to move behind us toward the door. Can you do that?" They began to crawl away from the tables. "Your turn, Wang-Chi," Rieka said conversationally. Then, while he got himself into position, she addressed the guard and his hostage. She needed to keep him occupied so that he didn't have time to use his TC and call for help.

"Let him go."

"Not possible."

"Oh, it's entirely possible, my friend," she replied. "And it would make things so much easier."

"I have sworn not to make anything easy for you."

"You really are Herald Degahv, aren't you?" the boy persisted, apparently thrilled to be the center of attention.

Rieka sighed. She hadn't anticipated this. The Oph shifted his aim between her and Wang. Slowly, she lowered her maitu. "Yes, I am," she admitted. "And you need to do what I tell you—Garret, is it?"

"Uh-huh."

Held as he was by the guard, Garret would suffer from Wang's forthcoming stun. She needed the Oph to remain against the wall and the boy out of his grasp. Fortunately, she realized, the restraining arm was the one she'd stunned. "Good. Now, do you know the tickle game?"

"Sure."

Rieka smiled. "Then let's play and he's it." She nudged her chin forward to indicate the guard.

Instantly, Garret began to wiggle until his pinned arms reached the Oph's sides. Rieka didn't have any idea whether Ophs were ticklish, but she hoped the unexpected attack would be enough.

A second later, the Oph jerked. Then he jerked again, his arm coming up for a better grip on Garret's waist.

"Keep going, Garret," she coached. Hands free now, the boy went at his task enthusiastically. The Oph groaned and lurched, his hold on Garret gradually loosening, his maitu all but forgotten.

Rieka decided to speed up the process and unclipped the dummy datapad from her belt. Knowing Wang would fire at the first opportunity, Rieka lunged, smacking the data-pad's edge against the Oph's elbow. At the same time, she grabbed Garret and pulled as hard as she could.

She heard Wang fire and the sound of a body hitting the floor. Taking a deep breath, she set Garret down. "Are you okay?"

"Sure," he chimed. "That was a-mazing."

"Yes," she agreed, looking over his head at Wang. "It sure was."

Maria appeared at her shoulder. "The Ophs told us we were supposed to stay here until the ceremony. But that's not what Mrs. Giovanni told us. What's going on?"

While Wang dealt with the stunned guard, Rieka turned to see that Gorah and Gennath had secured their guards and gathered the other children near the door.

Rieka knew they'd never make it to the InterMAT station unless each one cooperated. She slid a comforting arm around Maria's shoulder. "I'll tell you, but I need you to promise that you'll do exactly what I ask. It's very important."

Maria and the others nodded. "Something has happened involving Earth and the ceremony today . . . and the Blue Planet Future."

"We were all together at Camp Future and then they transported us here," Maria explained. "Then they brought us to this room. Where are the others?"

"You're on the *Barnel*," Rieka said. "And you can't stay here. It isn't safe. I've come to make sure you're transported to the *New Venture*."

"Why?" another child asked.

"Because . . . some confused people don't like Humans. It would take me too long to explain more—and we haven't got a lot of time. I need you all to go with Lieutenants Gorah and Gennath. Go as quietly as possible. They'll take you to the InterMAT and make sure you get to the *New Venture*. Can you do that for me?"

Most of the children nodded that they could. Maria asked, "Aren't you coming, too?"

"I've . . . got something else to do. I'll see you all again soon."

It took a few minutes, but they finally got the youngsters queued up in two lines at the door. Rieka went out first and stunned the ensign. Wang helped her lug the body inside while Gorah and Gennath led their charges to the nearest Chute door.

"We'll send the children on and wait for you at the station," Gorah said, then hurried to catch up with Gennath.

Rieka led Wang in the opposite direction and took the nearest Chute to the weapons lab. She didn't expect it to be manned or guarded but checked the entire lab before stationing Wang as lookout while she went to work. Although the easiest way to incapacitate the ship would be via the panoply systems, Rieka avoided those panels. The bridge would be alerted the moment she touched them.

"How long is this going to take?" Wang whispered.

"Not long."

Rieka opened the access panels to the IRB and sphere-production circuitry. Setting her maitu on its lowest energy level, she discharged it against the IRB board. The panel matrix went from clear to opaque, and she knew she'd charred the circuitry. She did the same to the sphere-production unit and clipped the panels shut.

"We've been aboard fourteen minutes," Wang told her as she headed for the hardware storage area where the backup panels were kept.

"I'm going as fast as I can."

Suddenly, Rieka felt a wave of anxiety wash over her. Triscoe. She sensed his mind concentrating on the bridge but a worried shade of ocher came through the link. His concern was genuine and, apparently, for more than her. Was he preparing for battle? Without speaking to him directly, she couldn't tell.

Rieka sighed. She couldn't risk finishing the job in the hardware storage area. If the *Barnel* tried to fire its weapons and found them disabled, repair crews would be dispatched immediately. There was no way she could find the backups, corrupt them, and get off the ship without being discovered.

"Dammit." Frustrated, she turned and hurried back toward Wang.

"What's wrong?"

"Nothing." Together, they headed for the InterMAT station.

Wondering how he could break the news to Rieka that New SubBrasilia had been destroyed, Triscoe looked up from his console when the DGI switched on the *Prospectus*'s audio. "What do you make of that?" Robet asked.

He studied the tactical display for a moment. "Looks like they're planning to regroup over the northern section of the Pacific Ocean," Triscoe said. "What's there? Nothing that I can see."

"Only two population sites nearby, Captain," Aarkmin reported, studying her own console screen. "There's a city about 150 kilometers inland on the Asian continent, New SubBeijing. And about fifteen hundred kilometers east of it, there's another one still under construction. It's called New SubKyoto."

"Both are underground," Robet said. "It's going to take them several rounds like it did with New SubBrasilia."

Watching the three ships slowly regroup to form a triangle, Triscoe frowned. "A piece of this puzzle is missing," he murmured. He'd eavesdropped for a moment or two when his mother and Rieka had spoken to RadiMo, but hadn't heard the entire story. He'd realized enough, though, to understand that the Bournese Herald knew something of Gundah's plans.

Mother.

Triscoe?

What did RadiMo tell Rieka about the Earth cities?

She paused for a moment, then replied, *Their deal was to scout the local geology in exchange for mining rights.*

For what purpose?

I'm not sure. He said they were looking for faults, aquifers, oil deposits. That sort of thing.

Thank you. He brought his attention back to the bridge as Midrin Tohab's face split the DGI into a third section.

"Captains," she began, "one-third of the missing property has been recovered. My people are still working on the problem."

Triscoe saw Robet's face brighten at the news. Honoring his promise not to contact Rieka, he'd been following her progress silently. She and the others were already aboard the *Dividend* and had located the second group of children.

"Thank you, Captain Tohab," Triscoe said. "Right now, we're wondering what our . . . friends are planning in the North Pacific."

"I've been monitoring them," Tohab said. "My guess is they're going to target New SubKyoto."

"Why?"

"Earth history records the detonation of two atomic bombs over this island chain, Japan. It's relatively small and located on a line of geologic instability called the Pacific Rim. The bombs may or may not have caused additional stress fractures in the strata. Your other possible target, New SubBeijing, the nearest populated city, is hundreds of kilometers from either an active or dormant volcano."

"That's true," Triscoe agreed.

"The other possible strategy, though I doubt she's going to use it, would be to simply target stress points in the crust to stimulate undersea earthquakes. This is potentially more devastating than destroying a single city—since the resulting tsunamis have a tremendous impact on the coastline."

Triscoe saw Robet frown. "How do you know so much about this?"

"I served as Rieka's EO for several years, Captain DeVark," she said. "It is difficult to be in her company and not learn . . . Earth trivia."

"Why wouldn't Gundah opt for this, do you think?"

"It would take too long. Hours, in fact. She made a decisive move when she annihilated Winnipeg and New SubBrasilia. It seems to me she wants to make an immediate statement."

Triscoe smiled. "And we appreciate the fact that you were paying attention. The question now is: What do we do?"

"Do you think we could stop their spheres with ours?" Tohab asked.

"In space, I would try just about anything," Robet offered. "But we're dealing with a planetary atmosphere. That's risky."

Triscoe nodded. "I agree. Even though we don't know their target for sure, I suggest we begin evacuating New SubKyoto. Until we can engage the ships themselves, I suppose we can't do much more than that."

"Captain," Aarkmin began, "two of the ships are firing."

Triscoe watched the DGI as four dots indicating spheres

descended on Earth. The *Barnel* had not fired, he noted.
Rieka had managed to disarm it. He waited helplessly along
with his companions, to see what damage the Ophs would
do.

When the DGI registered the explosion, Becker turned.
"They didn't hit the city, Captain," he said.

"What?"

"They didn't hit it. Of course it's underground, anyway.
But the detonation point is northeast of Kyoto, midway
between it and Lake Biwako."

It took a moment for the information to register, but
Triscoe understood the implication immediately. He flipped
a toggle and Nason's face replaced the map of Japan on
the DGI. "Did you hear that, Admiral?" he asked.

"Yes. And I want the *Providence* and *New Venture* to
begin immediate evacuation of all life signs in New Sub-
Kyoto. Activate every station aboard until that city is
empty. The *Prospectus* will stand by for the scheduled
transport initiated by Lieutenant Gebrah."

"Understood, Admiral," Tohab said. Her image left the
DGI as she ordered her crew to comply with his orders.

Robet nodded, though he looked somewhat disappointed. "Yes, sir."

Triscoe disconnected the admiral's channel and relayed
the orders to his InterMAT chief. Before Kyliss had the
three other stations working, Triscoe had Lisk move them
closer to the island.

The lieutenant complied, bringing them in from the
north. "Why the hurry, Captain?" he asked.

"It seems that Gundah likes to watch a progression of
disaster," he replied. "If the admiral is correct in his assumption, New SubKyoto will be flooded by that lake in a
matter of moments."

Rieka ground her teeth when she felt Triscoe's shock
and frustration. Some new horror had befallen Earth. She
was sure of it. Staring at the computer decks in the *Dividend*'s weapons lab, she couldn't quite suppress a fountain
of rage, herself. Not bothering to think, she reset her maitu
and destroyed the banks controlling the IRB and sphere
production.

Knowing both repair and security crews were being dispatched, she clicked on her TC and hurried toward Wang, stationed at the door. "Dee to Gebrah. Got those kids off yet, Lieutenant?"

"Last five are leaving now."

"Good. You're going to need to transport us directly from here. We're about to be pinned down."

"What did you do?" Wang whispered as they heard the muffled sounds of voices and footsteps approach.

"Lost my temper," she mumbled. Studying the lock's programming panel, she tapped in her command-code override and hoped no one over the rank of lieutenant would be dispatched to investigate the lab. If a commander accompanied them, the override wouldn't buy much time. "As soon as you're ready, Lieutenant."

"Understood," Gebrah replied.

Rieka felt the InterMAT effect begin and a moment later found herself crouched beside Wang in the *New Venture*'s chamber.

She stood and walked out the door and into what seemed like a sea of children. She looked over the smaller ones' heads to Lieutenant Giffah. "Why aren't they in the Medical suite?"

"They wanted to wait for you," Giffah replied.

Rieka turned as a small popping sound behind her announced the arrival of Lieutenants Gebrah and Gorah. "Everything go okay?"

Gorah shrugged as she stepped around a young boy. She leaned forward and said softly, "I had to fuse the lock to the station's door—but we got out without incident."

She nodded, knowing Gorah tended to underplay problems. "That's fine. I told you it would get progressively harder. They'll be waiting for us on the *Garner*."

"I expect so."

Rieka took a breath and looked out over the ragtag group of young performers. The *Dividend*'s party had responded to the teenagers' leadership and followed their orders to the letter. "Okay, everybody. You've seen me, and I've seen you. And we all made it to the *Prospectus* in one piece. If you could please go with Lieutenant Giffah to the Medical suite, we'll get the rest of your group off the *Garner*."

She watched the kids leave the InterMAT station, then

glanced at Wang, Gorah, and Gebrah. "Ready for round three? It's going to be a little different."

When they nodded, she clicked on her TC again. "Link to main computer."

"Linked," the animated voice said.

"Request name of engineering superintendent on the *Garner*."

"Commander Bashid," the voice replied.

"End main computer link. Link with *Garner*. Lieutenant Dee to Commander Bashid."

"I know no Dee," the Boo's voice gurgled after a moment.

"That is my TC registry, Commander," Rieka said. "In truth you speak to Captain Herald Degahv, newly recalled."

"You have been resting at the parallax too long, Captain," the Boo told her.

Rieka wholeheartedly agreed with that, but answered, "I suppose so. My question, Bashid, is—do you follow Gimbish and Gundah—or Nason?"

A moment of silence passed before Bashid replied, "The Ophs are on a nonlinear path of destruction. They slide far from the quanta. It is the zone Milari took before she fell from the White Cliffs."

Rieka nodded. The reference to Milari made sense. But the commander hadn't answered her question. "But do you follow them?"

"If Nason issues order to me, I will act upon them."

Chastising herself for bringing the admiral's name into this, she asked, "Then would you assist me in following his orders?"

"The Karina of the Rock? You are as a high pass of Morado. Even Herald Dzan would follow Karina."

"He would, eh?" Rieka smiled at both the thought and Wang as he frowned, listening to the one-sided conversation. "Bashid, I need you to cut power to your weapons system. And I need to come aboard."

"These requests show symmetry."

Gorah looked up from the console. "The *Garner*'s repulsion screens have been activated."

Rieka frowned, though she'd expected Captain Gimbish

to have set the screens before now. "Bashid, we cannot transport safely through your screen."

"Then it shall fluctuate for the next twenty-four seconds."

"Clever, Commander. I'm heading for the chamber now."

"I will await your arrival."

"Dee out." She turned toward the InterMAT operator. "Good morning, Lieutenant," she said.

"Morning, Herald . . . Captain . . . ma'am." He replied, saluting.

She responded with a less-than-enthusiastic salute, and said, "For the moment I'm just Lieutenant Dee. I need you to pick up Commander Bashid's TC signal on the *Garner* and transport the four of us to him." She gestured behind her as Wang, Gorah, and Gebrah made their way into the InterMAT chamber.

"Yes, Lieutenant . . . ma'am." With a task to perform, he attended to his console.

By the time Rieka stood next to Gorah, the lieutenant was nodding at his board. "Commander Bashid's signal is coming in clear and the ship's repulsion screen is pulsing regularly. I'm in sync with it, so you're clear to transport."

Rieka nodded. She nudged the maitu strapped to her hip. "We're ready," she said, and hoped that they were.

TWENTY-FIVE

"It may have been unwise to bring only three," Bashid said as he towered over her.

Rieka looked up at the huge blue being. She heard the slow click of his kroi and watched his eyes double-blink. "Possibly, Commander Bashid," she said. "But nature shows us how easily a small stream becomes a raging river. Like the Driel over Kolini Falls."

The flesh above his eye wrinkled. "This is true," he said.

"Will you assist our cause again?"

"Should the factors follow your tangent." He double-blinked at her.

Rieka nodded. She turned to her Oph companions. "This is Lieutenant Gennath and Lieutenant Gorah from the *New Venture*. They will coordinate with you when they require alterations in the power grid."

Bashid's starfish hand made a sweeping gesture toward the rest of the engineering suite. "My control of this ship is extensive," he said. "I will follow the equation and induce it toward a satisfactory outcome."

She nodded. "And this is Hong Wang-Chi," Rieka said. "He is my Watcher—as Karina before the Light."

"Understood," Bashid gurgled. He double-blinked at Wang. "See that your eyes bring Karina to the Light."

Obviously perplexed by the request, Wang nodded once. "That's my job."

Rieka looked at Gorah and Gennath. "Okay. This time we need to split up right away. Don't use any InterMAT stations. Coordinate transport through Commander Bashid."

"What about you?" Gorah asked.

"Don't concern yourself with us, Lieutenant. The two of you go find those kids and get them off this ship."

"The Earthlings have been moved like a flock from a cargo hold to the weapons lab on level three," Bashid rumbled.

Gorah nodded. "Thank you, sir." She and Gennath saluted him and left the suite.

Rieka craned her neck to look up at Bashid, again. "My function here is to neutralize Gundah and secure the ship. May I count on engineering as a factor?"

His kroi clicked again, this time the cadence lighter. "I can float this over the equation, Dee," he said ominously. "Roda!"

"Chief," a paler Boo replied as it came toward them, clicking its kroi with a rhythm Rieka identified as curiosity. Roda wore a lieutenant's bar pinned to the drape that fell across broad, sloping shoulders.

"This Human has need of your datapad. It is hers until she departs the *Garner*. Further, like factors in a double-star system, you will now follow her orders."

Roda handed over the datapad. Rieka took it. "I don't need another companion."

Bashid leaned closer. "Perhaps you will," he rumbled, then waddled off on his three stumpy legs.

"Okay then Roda," she began dismissing the engineer from her mind, "we need to neutralize Adjutant Gundah's control. I've used an attack-and-retreat strategy so far. But now I think it's time for a direct frontal assault."

Gundah cursed and cut communications with Gimbish. "Buffoon," she muttered. She'd seen the readouts on the repulsion screens when they'd fluctuated. It had only happened for a few seconds. But InterMAT transport was nearly instantaneous. Whoever had gotten aboard the *Barnel* and *Dividend* had quite probably made their way onto the *Garner*. At least Gimbish had not argued about stepping up security and ordering a search.

She glanced over her shoulder at Candace Degahv. The woman looked up from her Human food and gestured with a hand. "Is something wrong?"

"Nothing significant. Captain Gimbish is sometimes difficult. He forgets who is in charge."

Degahv nodded. "I have several employees like that."

Gundah squinted and studied her further. The Human's attitude had changed once she assumed she'd become something of a partner in this endeavor. "I see we are more alike than I originally thought," Gundah said smoothly. "Now," she added in a businesslike tone, "I require some information. I want to know where the Heralds and senators are."

Candace shrugged. "There's no way we could possibly get that information. The ceremony has been canceled by now. They could be anywhere."

"Well, I suppose that's true—to a degree," Gundah conceded. She'd seen the short announcement Jeniper Tarrik had made about postponing the event. "I am guessing the Indran, Human, and Bournese Heralds are on the *Providence.* Cimpa is probably still in SubDenver. That leaves Herald Honutik. I know I saw Senators Volshoy and De-Wilt at the banquet," Gundah went on. "Did you happen to notice any others?"

"I'm afraid I didn't," Candace said.

Gingerly reaching for proof of the Human's loyalty, Gundah pressed her. "Had they briefed you on any contingency plans? Where to go in case of an emergency?"

Candace shrugged and shook her head. "All there was—was a brief notice on the back of the guest room's door. To evacuate New SubDenver, you take the stairs to the surface."

Dissatisfied by the Human's generic reply, Gundah inhaled and let the air escape her lungs accompanied by a low growl. "That's hardly helpful."

Candace rubbed her temples. "Maybe we should do a little research."

"Maybe I'll destroy Damascus." Gundah thrilled at the flash of horror that crossed the woman's face. "It won't take a minute," she assured her. "I've already practiced on Winnipeg, SubBrasilia and SubKyoto. And . . . of course, they're only Humans."

Candace leaned toward her, her lips drawn in a tight line. "You're doing this the wrong way, Gundah. I thought the plan wasn't to hurt anyone else. I thought you wanted to control Rieka and sterilize the next generation of Humans.

If you continue to openly attack Earth, the Commonwealth will return fire."

"I'm just having some fun while motivating your daughter to do as I say." To herself, she thought: or I could kill you and anyone else who disagrees with my thinking.

"The Fleet might decide to destroy this ship," Candace countered. She left the table and began pacing the length of the room. "You have everything to gain if we leave, now."

"But I still have unfinished business," Gundah said, hoping to draw the Human out. Surely a mother would know her child well enough to predict her actions. And Humans were such homebound creatures. "Your daughter strikes me as a doer—rather than a spectator. One of my ships has had their weapons circuitry damaged and the other is completely incapacitated. I find that rather odd, don't you?"

Candace frowned. "I'm not following you."

"The Procyon War's venerated hero. Earth Herald. RadiMo's savior. It just doesn't follow that she'd sit back and let others do the work."

Candace made a strange face and puckered her lips. "Captain Marteen is very protective of her."

Gundah glanced back at her console. "So I've heard. But I've also heard he doesn't always get his way."

Candace said nothing.

Abruptly, Gundah snatched up her maitu. She flipped a switch on her console and Gimbish's face appeared on her screen.

"Yes?" he asked.

"We're leaving Earth orbit, Captain. Have your people set a course for Oph. Begin acceleration as soon as the course is set."

He nodded. "Understood."

"Well, it's about time," Candace Degahv said. She heaved a sigh and sat down.

"We're leaving because I have the information I needed, thanks to you."

"But I didn't say anything."

"Of course you did. You told me that Rieka Degahv is aboard the *Garner*. And now we are taking her away from those who could protect her. I could not have planned this better, myself."

*   *   *

Triscoe suppressed a shudder as he watched the *Garner* suddenly depart Earth orbit. The other two ships took off on divergent paths but remained close to the planet. He flipped a toggle. "Admiral . . ."

"I see what's happening, Captain," Nason replied. "Do not pursue the *Garner.*"

"But sir—"

"Trust me, Captain. I had a surprise scheduled for Herald Degahv later today. The surprise will work equally well for Adjutant Gundah."

"I don't understand, sir," Triscoe replied, frustrated and confused by Nason's reply.

"That's because I didn't explain it to you. Let's just say I have a reunion of sorts planned. Right now I have other orders." Triscoe watched him open communications with the other two ships. "Captain DeVark, Captain Tohab, once again we have Fleet ships prepared to do battle with Fleet ships. Since there are no longer children aboard either the *Barnel* or *Dividend,* your orders are to attack and disable them."

Triscoe glanced first at Aarkmin then at Becker. They nodded, indicating their readiness.

"Is there any specific strategy you wish to employ?" Tohab asked.

"Negative," Nason replied. "Use whatever method you see fit. But I want the ships disabled—not destroyed."

"Understood, Admiral," she said.

"Do we coordinate through you, sir, or among ourselves?" Robet asked.

Triscoe didn't know whether to feel worried or relieved when Nason replied, "I'll stay out of it—unless you require my input. Nason out."

"Yes, sir." Triscoe watched Robet cut his channel to the admiral, then address his DGI pickup. "Well, how do you want to do this?"

Triscoe replied automatically though he wasn't sure he liked the ease with which he solved the problem. "The three of us should target each ship in turn. We'll use our spheres and try for simultaneous impact on their screens."

Tohab nodded. "That will remove their only defense."

"And then do what to disable them?" Robet asked.

"A single, low-charged sphere to the panoply ought to do it," he said.

"Take out their ability to see, aim, and navigate," Tohab said with a sigh. "But they will retain the ability to fire on us."

Triscoe agreed with Tohab's reluctance. "If Gellath and Goverah don't surrender once we've incapacitated them, then we'll take the admiral up on his offer—and request his input." A physical assault was the logical next step in such a scenario, but he resisted giving such an order without Nason's counsel.

Tohab's face took on a determined look. "Which one first?" she asked.

He glanced at the tactical display on his console. "The *Dividend* hasn't fired any weapons since Rieka was aboard. Let's start with the *Barnel*."

"Gorah to Dee," the TC said softly in her ear.

Rieka allowed Lieutenant Roda to exit the Chute first as she said, "Dee. What's your status?"

"Unable to extract the cargo," Gorah's gravelly Oph voice said. "Still examining alternative methods."

"Understood. Dee out." She sighed. Gundah knew they'd get aboard and attempt a rescue. She'd probably planned a strategy for that and implemented it as soon as the children turned up missing on one of the other ships. But Rieka hadn't figured on Gundah attacking a second target so soon.

The *Barnel*'s inability to fire would have alerted the Oph long before any of the guards turned up missing. By now both the *Barnel* and *Dividend* must have reported their hostages gone. The *Dividend* wouldn't be using her weapons anytime soon, but the *Barnel*'s tech-pros might have repaired the minimal damage Rieka had done. She would've liked to confirm her assumptions with Triscoe via TC, but didn't want to risk going past the ten-second limit.

Gundah had also correctly guessed a rescue team would board the *Garner*. She needed to buy herself some time, which was why she'd kept her hostages heavily guarded.

Rieka empathized with Gorah's frustration. They both needed to find a way through the obstacles as quickly as possible. At the same time, she knew Lieutenant Gorah wouldn't do anything to risk either herself or the children. Fortunately, the lieutenant was both patient and methodical. Her own team had already taken two Chutes to avoid security personnel in the corridors.

Roda stopped and leaned his great head toward her. "Commander Bashid communicates. We slide from Earth orbit."

Rieka frowned, then realized Bashid had sent the message via Roda so that he wouldn't have to speak to her directly. Even he didn't want to chance the communication being traced. And she credited Gundah with enough paranoia to be tracing every signal.

"All three ships?"

"Negative. Just the *Garner*," Roda replied.

"Not good," Wang whispered.

Rieka nodded. "Tell Bashid my thanks for this information are exponential."

Roda wiggled the fleshy patch over his eyes and double-blinked. His kroi clicked, stopped, and clicked again. "He is pleased to assist like the dew of the morn."

They continued slowly down the empty corridor. Rieka felt like kicking herself for making Triscoe promise to stay out of her head. She needed information now, and the only one she could access was Bashid. On the other hand, avoiding contact made things safer for them. The paradox confounded her, and she began to wonder if they'd ever sort it out.

Roda stopped, and she realized they'd arrived. "Mautu on stun?" she asked softly.

"Ready and waiting, Boss," Wang said.

"The door is a short *vondine* down that intersecting corridor," Roda's translator box said. His starfish-shaped hand indicated a cut in the main hallway about two meters to the right.

She nodded. "Wang and I will deal with the guards. You need to disconnect whatever equipment she's got in there." With an unwelcome sense of foreboding, Rieka realized that if Gundah had decided to make a run for it, she might be pursued. If that happened, shots would be fired. "Ask Commander Bashid to power down the weapons from engineering. I don't think the captain will do anything stupid once Gundah's in custody, but I don't want to chance it."

"Captain Gimbish is predictable as *pi* in most situations," Roda agreed.

"Good. Let's go then." To Wang, she whispered, "If there is more than one guard at the door, take the right."

They crept toward the intersection, turned the corner, aimed and fired. Rieka doubted the Ophs even knew they'd been attacked. Leaving the stunned bodies on the deck, she studied the door. Remarkably, it wasn't locked. Roda entered first and Rieka hid behind his immense bulk until they were inside. Then she stepped out from behind him, aiming her maitu at the first Oph she saw.

Candace stood in front of it, effectively blocking off a clear shot. As a bolt of energy barely missed her head, Rieka realized Gundah, on her far right, had a weapon, too. A gut-wrenching sound emanated from Roda. He'd been hit. But Boos was incredibly sturdy beings. He remained on his three stubby feet and fired off a return blast at Gundah.

While Rieka ducked and rolled behind a chair, Wang scuttled away, obviously trying to find a better angle at the guard. For some unknown reason, Candace stayed in front of the Oph, acting as a shield.

"Mother, for heaven's sake, get down," she ordered.

"You have no idea what you're doing," Candace told her.

Rieka watched as Wang squeezed off another ineffectual shot at the guard. The deck below her feet shuddered. Turning, she saw Roda had fallen. His kroi clicked strangely, and he didn't try to speak.

Peeking out from behind the chair, Rieka once again saw Gundah's yellow-ringed eyes as she ducked behind her console. The Oph was breathing hard, her maitu clenched unsteadily in a paw. Roda had hit her at least once.

Rieka didn't allow herself the luxury of satisfaction. She knew Gundah understood the situation was a standoff and anything might happen. A quick glance at Wang showed him behind a table, still trying for a shot at the guard.

Figuring she'd been right about Candace all long, Rieka toyed with the idea of shooting her, too. But Gundah was the main threat here, and Candace was unarmed, so she focused her attention on the Oph.

"I want the canister, Gundah."

"You'll never find it."

"I'll have it even if I have to kill you to get it."

Gundah snorted. "Your fragile Human sensibilities wouldn't allow you to murder me, Herald."

"I wouldn't assume anything if I were you, Adjutant," Rieka told her.

"You see?" Candace spoke from somewhere across the room. "I tried to warn you about her."

"Stay out of this, Mother. This is between me and Gundah."

She heard the Oph respond with a barking laugh. "So you would like to think. The stakes are much higher than you can conceive, Human. And I alone will save Oph and the Commonwealth from the scourge your planet has inflicted upon us."

Rieka consciously ignored that remark, not wanting to give her opponent the satisfaction of knowing she'd hit a tender spot. Right now, she needed to tip the Oph off-balance, either physically, mentally, or both. "I'm afraid you've got it all wrong, Adjutant. You've already lost," she said in her best captain's voice.

"I? What have I lost?" Gundah demanded.

Rieka could tell that Gundah had moved, her voice had come from a different direction. She wondered how much of Roda's stun had managed to hit her after all. "The Fleet knows your identity. And that you're running back to Ophiuchus."

"And once I get there . . ." Gundah paused and took a deep breath. "Once I get there, I'll be safe. You'll never find me."

Rieka found her patience flagging. The guard and Wang exchanged shots again, but Rieka paid them no mind. She could hear Gundah crawling around behind the console, planning to do—what?

Suddenly, Gundah moved. Rieka raised her weapon to take aim, but the guard fired at her, effectively stopping her shot. She ducked and fired anyway, but Gundah had already slipped out the door.

"Dammit!" Rieka banged the floor with a fist.

"Boss, you okay?" Wang asked.

"Yes," she hissed.

"The guard's down. What do I do with Candace?"

Frowning because she hadn't heard Wang fire, Rieka stood to find him holding his weapon on her mother. "Cuff the guard," she told him. "I'll take care of her."

Wang nodded and pulled the last set of cuffs off his belt. While he tended to the unconscious guard, Rieka glared at Candace.

"Where'd she go?"

"I have no idea."

Glancing at Roda, she saw his chest move in and out and saw him suck from his atmosphere compensator. He'd be fine in a few hours.

Two steps brought her within arm's distance of Candace. "Don't give me that, Mother. You're protecting her. What's the payoff, this time? Controlling shares in one of Tech-Line's companies?"

To her credit, Candace pulled herself straighter and lifted her chin. "Don't be ridiculous. I have nothing to do with her. I never have."

Rieka shook her head. "You are quite a piece of work. I'm actually supposed to believe that?"

"I'm not lying to you."

"Right." Silently, Rieka wished Setana were here to verify that. Unfortunately, the only evidence she had was to the contrary. She nodded solemnly. "So, what am I supposed to believe, instead? That you protected him because you had feelings for him?" She indicated the guard.

"Don't be impertinent," Candace argued. "I almost had her trust. She would have told me what she'd done with your DNA."

Rieka wanted to believe her, but couldn't. Holding her maitu in Candace's general direction, she watched Wang finish dealing with the Oph. "Shut down those consoles Wang-Chi," she said. She clicked on her TC. "Lieutenant Dee to Captain Gimbish."

"This is the captain," his barking voice replied. "I have no officer aboard named Dee."

"How astute," Rieka commented. She looked down at Roda again. He double-blinked at her, but spoke with only slow clicks of his kroi.

She heard Gimbish tap at his console, then he addressed her directly again. "Who is this?"

Rieka debated divulging her identity. She'd met Gimbish once or twice before at Fleet functions and couldn't remember much about him. She glanced at her mother and figured Gundah had probably already contacted Gimbish, herself.

"You're speaking to Captain Herald Rieka Degahv."

"Impossible."

"Nothing is impossible, Gimbish. We learned that in the Procyon War."

"Captain Degahv no longer exists," Gimbish persisted. "She is now the Earth Herald and would be a fool to risk her life to rescue my hostages."

"I've been called lots of names before, Captain, fool included," she said. "But that's not the issue here. Surrender command to me, and we'll see if we can't work something out with the admiralty."

"Never. Humans *are* inferior beings," Gimbish insisted. "You can't win, Captain."

"*We* most certainly can."

The link cut off abruptly and Rieka's anxiety level jumped. The last voice had been Gundah's. She looked into Wang and Candace's expectant faces and knew something awful was about to happen. "We've got to get out of here, right now."

"I don't understand," Candace said.

"We've got to move!" Rieka shoved her mother toward the door. "Out of here, now." She turned as Roda tried to push himself upright. "Can you make it, Lieutenant?" she asked.

His kroi clicked positively, and she nodded. "Wang, help me." She realized that, for the time being, she'd have to trust Candace. "Mother, watch the corridor." Together, they steadied Roda on his three stubby feet. He wobbled a little, but remained upright.

"Someone's coming," Candace reported, excitement threading through her voice. "But I can't see them, yet."

Roda followed them toward the door and Wang sniffed the air. "Do you smell something?"

Rieka nodded. "They're gassing the room." Knowing the effort would be all but futile, she willed Roda to hurry out the door. Seconds later, it closed behind them.

"They're here!" Candace gasped.

Rieka looked down the corridor to see a squad of six

Ophs running around the corner, their weapons drawn. Pinned in the short hallway, she stepped forward beside Wang.

"Shoot. Shoot!" Rieka ordered. She lifted her maitu and discharged it just as they received return fire.

TWENTY-SIX

She looked at the guards where they'd fallen, then at her own unorthodox crew. "Roda, can you make it to the Chute?" she asked. His kroi clicked again, and he blinked at her. She took that as a yes. "Okay. Let's go. Wang, you take the rear and keep an ear out."

"Right."

Rieka took the point and felt oddly secure when her mother stepped in behind her. She still didn't know how much she could trust her, if at all. But feelings, she knew, had little to do with facts. "Chute's just down here," she said. "Won't take a few seconds to reach it."

They moved along as quickly as Roda could manage and Rieka clicked on her TC again. "Dee to Bashid."

"Bashid," the Boo engineer's voice replied.

"Gundah is still in the equation and the captain's plans are reciprocal to ours, Commander. He does not wish to slide to Varannah—and seeks another place—like the vortex of Drazid."

"His is a calculable endeavor, Dee. I shall be vigilant with the factors."

"Then add this to the equation—he gassed the conference room."

"Understood."

The connection switched off as they reached a Chute door. Rieka triggered the motion sensor and stood ready with her maitu when the door opened. Fortunately, the car was empty.

"Roda, inside," she said, looking up into his dark multi-faceted eyes. "You have done well, my friend. Karina hopes you find Varannah."

His kroi clicked in response, and she ordered the Chute to the main engineering deck. "Bashid will see to you," she told him, then saluted quickly as the door closed.

"What about us?" Wang whispered.

The light above the door pulsed as a second car arrived to take the other's place. She replayed the same precautions with the new car, but it, too, was empty. "Everybody in." While she waited for Wang to take a final look around the corridor before he joined them, Rieka contacted Gorah.

"We found a way to get to the kids, Dee," she said softly. "We're in the enviro lab. It's secure."

"We'll meet you there." She clicked off the connection and ordered the Chute's destination. "Environmental lab, level two."

"Why are we going there?" Candace asked, irritation obvious in her voice. "Why don't we just get off this ship?"

Rieka couldn't bring herself to make eye contact. "Because I said so."

Triscoe felt a wave of relief when Rieka's emotional state eased from an alarmed, fiery red to a more controlled gold-orange. But he still hated the thought of her aboard the *Garner* as it increased its speed away from Earth.

He'd managed to move the *Providence* into the path of every sphere the *Barnel* sent their way. Using his own repulsion screens to neutralize the attack, Triscoe's strategy to keep the Earth from suffering any more damage had thus far worked. But he knew Lisk couldn't keep at it indefinitely.

His weapons specialist, Becker, had unfortunately endured nothing but bad luck. Trying to coordinate the counterattack with his counterparts on the *Prospectus* and *New Venture* proved to be nearly impossible. With the ships dodging every which way to intercept spheres, their positions were constantly changing with regard to the target.

They'd already tried half a dozen volleys against the *Barnel* to no avail. Repulsion screens cold be worn down eventually by many contacts in close succession, but that would take minutes they didn't have. What they needed was a simultaneous hit that would disrupt the *Barnel*'s defense screen.

He watched the Human lieutenant pound a fist on the

console and mutter an oath when their latest attempts failed. "What was the margin this time?" Triscoe asked.

"Three-tenths."

"We'll do it, Lieutenant," Triscoe said with assurance. "The *Barnel*'s crew will eventually tire. Be patient."

"Yes sir." Becker shook his head, then bent toward his board once again. Three-tenths of a second seemed like nothing to them, but to the computer in charge of the repulsion screen, it was more than enough time to recover from a strike.

The *Dividend* had apparently been rendered defenseless. It had moved south, far away from the battle, and had fired no spheres at all since Rieka had been in their weapons lab. The only viable strategy was to keep after the *Barnel* until Captain Goverah either surrendered on his own, or was forced to.

"V'don," Triscoe said, switching his attention to the lieutenant in charge of communications, "can you link to the *Barnel*?"

V'don's fingers attacked his console. He nodded. "Go ahead and activate your position, Captain," he said.

Triscoe flipped a toggle. "*Providence* to *Barnel*. This is Captain Marteen," he began briskly. "I wish to speak to Captain Goverah."

He let five seconds of silence pass before he said, "As you may or may not have guessed, Admiral Nason has issued a warrant for Adjutant Gundah's arrest. She is wanted for treason. Any efforts on your part to support her will be considered additional acts of treason committed of your own volition. Please feel free to both verify this fact with EarthCom and pass on my message to Captains Gellath and Gimbish."

Not expecting a response, Triscoe nodded at the DGI pickup. "*Providence,* out."

A few seconds later, Lisk sat straighter in his chair. "They're firing again, Captain."

Rieka cautiously peered out of the Chute into the empty corridor. No Fleet personnel lurked in either direction. She found that odd for a ship with known intruders on the loose. Then, considering Gundah was in charge, Rieka accepted their good fortune. It seemed as though Gennath's assumption had been accurate. Gundah appeared to be lucid, but several of her decisions had been far from logical. Why had she murdered Stephen? Why did she need to control Earth? None of it made any sense.

"Okay, let's go," she said. "The environmental lab is just on the right."

While they headed for the lab, she clicked on her TC. "Dee to Gorah. We're here. Is the door locked?"

"I'll have Gennath open it," Gorah's voice said before the connection went dead.

Wang reached the door first and turned to look at her. Rieka nodded for him to go in, but he hesitated, glaring suspiciously at Candace. "Watch yourself, Candace," he warned. "I'm not above using this on you." He pointed the maitu at her.

"Watch yourself," Candace replied, stepping past the threshold.

Shoving him into the lab, Rieka whispered harshly into his ear, "You just watch my back, Wang-Chi. I said I'd take care of her." As Gennath secured the door, she added, "Stay here, you two. Guard the exit. No one else is expected."

"Yes, Captain," Gennath said.

Rieka turned and found Gorah surrounded by a sea of equipment and young people. The Oph lieutenant had somehow managed to keep them seated and quiet, no simple feat when dealing with Humans.

"Status, Lieutenant?" she asked, stepping forward.

"Everyone's out of the weapons lab, Dee," Gorah told her. "We cut our way through from this side and neutralized the guards. Then we brought the children in here and resealed the opening. What happened with Gundah?"

"She . . . got away," Rieka replied, trying not to sound fatalistic. As far as she could see, it would take a miracle to bring Gundah in alive.

Gorah sighed and licked her black lips. "I understand, Captain," she said softly. Her eyes seemed sad. "She may be beyond help. But I am glad you are unhurt. And most importantly, the children are safe."

She nodded for Gorah to follow her and moved away from their young audience. "Just between us, that . . . that may be premature," Rieka replied softly. She shrugged

apologetically at Gorah's questioning look. "We're not in
Earth orbit anymore. There's nowhere to InterMAT them
to. Gimbish is preparing for a slide to Oph. Commander
Bashid is still powering down nonessential systems, but it
might take a while."

"Understood," Gorah said, her ears pinning back slightly.

Rieka was still smiling her keep-the-faith captain's smile
when the ship shuddered hard enough to knock anyone
standing to the deck. Her natural instinct when she went
down was to fall to absorb the impact. Unfortunately, a
chair slid into her path and caught her in the midsection.
She rode it for a moment before it slammed into a console.

Gorah clambered to her side and pulled her around to
sit in the chair. "Are you injured, Captain," she asked.

Rieka nodded both no and yes. Her diaphragm had momentarily ceased to function, and she couldn't get her lungs
to move. Finally she managed to reply, "Fine. Go. See to
them." Gorah nodded and went to calm the terrified
children.

It was then that she realized two of the group had come
to stand by her. She looked up and into Samantha's frightened blue eyes.

"Are you okay, Herald?" she asked. "What happened?"

Someone touched her shoulder, and she turned to find
Po. "Can't you talk?"

Rieka nodded. She tried to inhale and managed a short
breath. Po rubbed her back, and she took in a little more
air. "Thanks, Po," she said, finally. "Is everyone all right?"

"We're okay," he told her. "The Ophs gave us ice
cream."

Rieka found enough breath to laugh, but it came out
sounding like a cough. "They did?"

"Yes, but we didn't like the way they dragged us
around," complained Samantha. "I mean one second we
were all sleeping in our beds and suddenly we were here."

"I know." Rieka drew another painful breath. "The
Ophs on this ship are—confused. We're doing our best to
get you all back to Earth safe." She couldn't tell them the
painful news of what had happened to Winnipeg and the
other cities. That would have to wait for later.

While she squeezed Samantha's hand, her mother appeared out of the crowd of children. "What happened just then?" she demanded.

Rieka shook her head, and whispered, "I'm not sure." She pushed out of the chair. "Samantha, Po, I need you to do something for me."

"What?" Po asked, excitement crossing his cherubic face.

"You need to keep the others calm. Things might get worse before they get better." She looked at Samantha. "Can you all stay together and out of the way?"

"Sure," Samantha assured her. "Come on, Po."

Rieka smiled encouragingly. "It might help if you told them I want everyone to sit down against the back wall."

"Okay," he said.

While Samantha dragged Po away by his arm, Rieka touched the nearest console's comm board. "Environmental to Engineering."

"Engineering." Watching the small screen, Rieka was glad the gravelly voice belonged to a Vekyan rather than an Oph. The lieutenant flicked out his tongue and looked off screen as if distracted.

"We don't have a DGI here," she explained. "What's happening?"

"Could be bad, Lieutenant," the Vekyan replied. "Captain Gimbish is not standing down."

"Standing down? To what?"

"The *Prodigy*." Abruptly, he terminated the link.

Rieka's mind reeled. The *Prodigy* was here? An image of the huge ship designed for both defense and deep-space research flashed across her thoughts. She'd captained that ship and knew the damage it could do. What in the world was Gimbish thinking?

She considered cutting back through to the weapons lab to disable the equipment, then figured that would both take too long and expose the children to greater danger. It seemed they'd run out of alternatives. No longer caring whether or not the signal was traced, Rieka clicked on her TC.

"Degahv to Gimbish." She heard the link connect but Gimbish didn't reply. "Are you insane? Captain Saxen has more than double your firepower. Stand down, Gimbish."

"Never," the Oph growled in her ear. "Never will I surrender to a Human or a Human-lover!"

The connection went dead before she could say anything more. She decided another strategy was in order. "Link to the *Prodigy*."

A tinny automated voice replied, "Intership links are unavailable at this time."

"Dammit. Dee to Bashid."

"Commander Bashid."

"What's our power situation, Commander?"

"Sixteen minutes left—if the captain continues sphere production."

That wasn't a question, in her mind. "Can we get through to the *Prodigy* somehow?"

"Negative, Dee," he replied. "Another equality remains beyond the horizon."

"Okay. I'll try to think of something. Dee out." She clicked off the TC and looked around. Beyond her mother's disapproving scowl, the seated children had gone amazingly quiet. It was then that she heard the singing. Peering over the console, she saw Samantha and Po leading several of the younger ones is a soft, slow, repetitive children's song. As she watched, Gorah nodded approvingly, adding her voice. Rieka smiled at them.

"Well, what are you going to do?" Candace rasped instantly in her ear.

She turned and glared. "I'm thinking, Mother." She eased back in the chair and set her elbows on the console before her. If the *Prodigy* hadn't arrived, she'd have had a whole lot more than sixteen minutes to figure a solution.

There wasn't much she could do from the environmental lab. Other than a comm board, the console controlled nothing of great import. In front of her, she recognized pressure gauges, a set of indicators for mixing elemental gasses, filtration and temperature controls. The board behind her controlled oxygen and nitrogen production, and the air scrubbers. Nothing useful, there. She hadn't felt this helpless since she'd been arrested.

A thought hit her. "Gorah," she called.

The lieutenant came immediately. "Yes, Captain?"

"Have a look at this console." She leaned back so the Oph had an unobstructed view while she moved around Candace who stood steadfastly in the way. "Can we mix the right elements in the right proportions to generate a

knockout gas? And can we pump it directly to the bridge—
like Gimbish did to Gundah's conference room?"

Gorah studied the indicators for a moment. "I don't
know this equipment very well, Captain. But ammonium
nitrate is available. If we heat it, we'll get nitrous oxide.
That should do it."

Rieka looked up at her skeptically. "Laughing gas?"

Gorah shrugged and sniffed. "Maybe it makes Humans
laugh."

"What does it do to Ophs?"

"In high concentrations, it's deadly. Otherwise, it will do
just what you asked."

Rieka nodded. "And how can we route it to the bridge?"

Gorah pointed to a light board on her far right. "That
panel down there controls individual vent sections."

"Okay." Rieka nodded approvingly. "You heat the ammonium nitrate. I'll figure a way to pump it."

Rieka found the computer easier to use than she'd imagined. She'd very nearly worked out the route, closing some
vents and opening others, when Wang's strident voice filled
the room.

"They're cutting their way in!"

Rieka glanced up to see sparks in the vicinity of the
doorway. "Damn." Not bothering to look up from her task,
she knew Candace was still nearby. "Can you handle a
maitu, Mother?"

"I think so. Yes."

"Do I have your word you won't use it on me?" After
a moment of silence, Rieka looked up at her mother's indignant expression. "Answer the question, please."

"Of course I won't shoot you."

"Then take mine and find something to hide behind—
but don't let anyone in that door." Rieka reached and
pulled her maitu from her waistband.

Candace took it. "They'll regret if it they try," she muttered, striding away.

"I've got positive ID for nitrous oxide, Captain," Gorah
said.

"What's the pressure?"

"Minimal now. Less than point-five pascals. We're going
to need to triple that to one-point-five if we want any speed
built up."

Rieka nodded and worked another calculation on her board. "It's going to have to travel thirty-eight meters through the vents to reach the bridge. Can you tell the ratio of the mix in that volume of air?"

"It should be enough to knock them out—but not be fatal."

"Good." A squeal from beyond the console pulled at Rieka's attention. Samantha and her companions stared wide-eyed at the door. More sparks were flying as the Ophs cut through the metal. Rieka clicked on her TC. "Dee to Bashid. We're in the environmental lab on level two. The door is locked and an unknown number of security personnel are cutting their way in. Can you assist?"

"Hold steady, Karina. Help comes."

"Point-seven," Gorah said.

"Not enough." Rieka's finger hovered over the release switch. "I'm not so sure we can wait, Lieutenant."

Gorah looked up at the door, now nearly breached. Her eyes had gone wide and yellow-ringed, but her voice remained steady. "I think you might be right, Captain." She glanced down at her board. "One-point-one."

Rieka counted to three and punched the button. The board began to flash with indicators announcing the gas's progress. Together, they watched it flow toward the bridge.

Addressing the twenty or so children Samantha and Po had moved to the back wall, Rieka said, "Some Boos are going to help us. When I know you're safe, Lieutenant Gorah, Mr. Hong, and I are going to go to the bridge. Everyone is to stay here and do exactly what Lieutenant Gennath says. Is that understood?"

The young people nodded. "Good." She smiled, hoping to boost their confidence, then turned and went back to the console.

"They should be feeling some effect by now, Captain," Gorah told her. "I'm reading ten percent N_2O on the bridge, and I've terminated production."

"Good. Grab your maitu. We'll be heading there once we handle this mess."

Gorah tapped at the console and followed her toward the door. Almost immediately it was kicked from the outside. Wang instinctively stepped back and braced for the onslaught, his maitu aimed at the door. Rieka grabbed her weapon from her mother's hand as she joined her behind some equipment. "Everybody get ready."

The door shuddered twice before it fell in. More Ophs than she thought possible stormed through the opening. Fortunately, it was narrow enough for them to be cut down by maitu fire before they could get very far.

Unfortunately, the Ophs returned fire.

Some of the smaller children began to scream. Rieka doubled her firing speed, hoping to draw the Ophs' attention away from her young charges. The noise grew to an unbearable level before the room grew eerily quiet. She heard thumping sounds from outside and a large blue head peered over the pile of bodies in the doorway. A single little girl shrieked again, and was silenced by Samantha. The Boo's dark eyes double-blinked for a moment, and she heard the distinctly solemn click of kroi. "Karina of the Rock?"

"Here," she said, stepping away from the scorched console.

"You are steady," it told her. "The equation seeks its conclusion."

She nodded and looked back at the terrified faces of the Blue Planet Future. "You did great," she told them. "Now, remember to do what Lieutenant Gennath tells you. Samantha, Po, thanks for your help."

For once, Po had nothing to say.

Rieka winked at him, then gestured for Gorah to follow. They climbed over the stunned Ophs on their way to the corridor. "How long until we're out of power?" she asked the lieutenant. Before he could answer, she saw Wang and her mother come out the lab door.

"Another nine is the estimate," the Boo reported. "We have attained the Symmetry of Six. Sphere production is discontinued."

She nodded to him and looked at Candace. "I want you to stay here, Mother."

"You're not going anywhere without me," Candace said, her tone defiant.

Deciding it would be worse to stand there arguing, Rieka shrugged. "Fine. It's your funeral."

Wang sighed. "I wish you wouldn't say things like that."

*   *   *

"Finally!" Becker shouted. In his excitement, he jumped up from his chair.

Triscoe smiled. "Congratulations, Lieutenant." He turned toward the DGI. "Robet, you and Midrin can see to things now that the *Barnel* is disabled. I'm going after the *Garner*."

Robet nodded. He flashed a triumphant smile as his bibbets returned to their normal pale pink tint. "We won't start the party until you get back."

Triscoe didn't bother to give that comment more than a nod. "Lisk. Let's go. Maximum speed."

"Course has been plotted and updated, Captain," Lisk replied. "We're looking at an ETA of about twenty minutes."

Triscoe groaned inwardly at the time, but said nothing. He could tell Rieka wasn't in immediate physical danger, but that situation could change. Knowing her, he predicted it would. Frustrated and fearful, he silently wished the InterMAT could traverse great distances.

Nason's face appeared on his screen. "Status, Captain?" he asked.

"You've been monitoring, sir, I'm sure," Triscoe replied, snapping back to attention. "Earth is secure, and we're on an intercept course with the *Garner*."

Nason nodded. "Do you confirm there have been shots fired between the *Garner* and *Prodigy*?"

Triscoe consulted his tactical board. "Yes, Admiral."

He watched as Nason sighed, then tapped at his own console. Triscoe realized he'd set up a comm link with the big ship. "Admiral Nason to Captain Saxen on the *Prodigy*," he began. "Cease fire. Repeat. Cease firing on the *Garner*."

Maitu at the ready, Rieka held her tongue as Wang eased his way onto the bridge ahead of her. The six Ophs within were either slumped in their chairs or on the floor. Gorah held back, and she couldn't blame her. The sweet taste of nitrous oxide remained in the tainted air.

"We'll handle this, Lieutenant. Mother, stay with Gorah." While Wang checked the bodies, she stepped to the weapons board and shut it down before hurrying on to the comm console. Shoving the unconscious Oph onto the floor, Rieka tapped out an order for an intership link.

"*Garner* to *Prodigy*," she said. The DGI melted quickly from a view of the stars to an austere-looking Indran face. "Saxen, cease fire. I've shut everything down."

"Who is speaking?" the Indran captain inquired.

"It's Rieka Degahv. Nason put me here to get control of the ship."

She saw him study his own DGI before saying, "The admiral has just informed me of the situation. I see that you've managed to get the job done, Herald. Or is it Captain?"

"Either will do," she commented dryly. "Can you possibly lend me a hand, though? I need a safe haven for the children. They're in the environmental lab."

"We'll bring them aboard right away."

"Thank you, sir," she said with an approving nod. "With regard to the crew, the bridge and engineering are secure—but I don't know what else. Don't know how many I can trust."

"I believe we can manage that," Saxen began, "in one of two ways. We can either contain them on the *Garner*, or sequester them aboard the *Prodigy*."

"I hadn't thought of that," Rieka admitted. "They'd be easier to manage in a couple of your cargo holds—if you have any available."

"Several," Saxen said. "How many squads do you think it will take?"

Rieka shrugged. "As many as you've got, Captain, so long as none of them are Ophs. I know that's a strange request—you'll just have to trust me. I'll explain it as soon as I've got a minute."

Saxen inclined his blond head. "I'll be waiting."

She watched while he began issuing orders to his crew and noticed Gorah slip into the room.

Wang had assembled a small pile of bodies. "Looks like Gundah's still on the loose, Boss," he announced.

"Put your maitu on the lowest setting and stun them, Mr. Hong," Gorah said. "I doubt the nitrous oxide effect will last much longer."

"Be glad to." Rieka watched as he set the weapon and, with Gorah's assistance, stunned the prone bodies.

Rieka tapped in another request on the communications board. "*Garner* to *Providence*."

"*Providence,*" V'don's voice answered. A split second later, the DGI image reconfigured to show their bridge. All positions were manned, the officers tending to their specific jobs. At the center back sat a worried looking Triscoe.

"Your status, Rieka?" he asked.

"Fairly secure," she replied, glancing over her shoulder to watch Gorah and Wang lift Gimbish out of his chair. Candace had edged into the room and stood watching them. "We've been in contact with the *Prodigy,* and Captain Saxen is collecting the last group of hostages and sending a few squads to secure the entire ship."

"Will that be enough?"

"Don't know. He's going to transfer the prisoners to a cargo hold."

Triscoe nodded, agreeing with that strategy. "Our ETA is about ten minutes. How is everyone?"

"We're okay," she said, studying the navigation console to verify his statement. "Gundah's still at large, and we need to find the canister."

"Don't go after her on your own," he warned.

Rieka shook her head. "She's getting desperate, Triscoe. And we've pushed her hard. She might do anything. We can't wait."

TWENTY-SEVEN

As Rieka finished telling Bashid he could put the reactor back on line, Gorah called her name. "What?"

The lieutenant sat at a console, a schematic on her screen. "I'm reading activity in the quad B perimeter hold. Section Three."

"A team from the *Prodigy*?"

Gorah shook her head. "One individual."

"What's in the hold?" She caught Wang's inquiring glance and shrugged a shoulder.

Gorah consulted the computer. "Manifest lists for the section include two ground transport vehicles, four cases of industrial recyclers, a shipment of textiles, and an interplanetary shuttle."

"Gundah's going to try to make a run for it. Reset the hatch overrides. Command level only."

"As we speak," Gorah replied, her paws flitting over her board.

"And secure that door." Rieka saw her mother move toward the exit. "Where are you going?"

Candace turned, a determined look on her face. "The same place you are. That cargo area."

Rieka sighed. Another lie? Impossible to say. Her better judgment told her to wait. With Gundah effectively locked in the hold, they could afford to proceed slowly. On the other hand, Gundah probably had the canister with her. When she found out she'd been trapped, she might decide to destroy it. The shuttle had an onboard cold-fusion reactor. If she get desperate enough, Gundah could even blow the reactor and scuttle the *Garner*.

She'd rescued the other children. Now it was time to tend to her own.

Something on her face must have given away her decision. Wang smiled and gestured toward the door. "After you, Boss—until we get to that cargo hold."

Triscoe paced the floor in the conference room as Nason and his mother watched. "She's anxious," he growled. "She's gone to apprehend Gundah. I just know it. What's wrong with that bodyguard of hers? Why doesn't he stop her?"

"Do you actually think he'd accomplish that any better than you?" Nason asked quietly.

"Merik, please," Setana chided. She caught Triscoe's eyes. "Why don't you just speak to her?"

"I promised I wouldn't," he said, trying to keep from sounding ridiculous.

His mother frowned. "Why?"

"It's Rieka's attempt to keep me from harm in the event she's . . . she doesn't survive."

Setana put a hand to her throat. "This is unprecedented."

"*Rieka* is unprecedented," he said, swiping a hand through his hair. "Sometimes I think Father was right. Marrying her was insane."

"Don't be ridiculous, Triscoe," Setana chided. "Now, we'll be there in a few minutes. Surely she can keep out of danger until then."

He sighed at her and looked at Nason. "Admiral, with your permission, I intend to leave Aarkmin in command of the *Providence* and board the *Garner* as soon as we reach InterMAT range."

Almost smiling, Nason said, "Granted, Captain."

"Thank you, sir." Leaving his elders to think whatever they wished of him, he saluted, then turned smartly and strode out the door. On the way to Station Two, Triscoe promised himself he and Rieka would settle this risk-taking business before the day was out.

Rieka checked that her maitu still had a reasonable charge, then glanced at Wang, Candace, and Gorah. "Unlock it, Lieutenant," she said.

While Gorah tapped in her code, Wang sidled in front of her. "No heroics, Boss," he whispered.

She made a face at him. "You wound me, Wang-Chi. There's only one Oph in there—and three of us."

"Four," corrected Candace.

"It's impolite to eavesdrop, Mother," Rieka said. "And I want you to stay out here."

"It's unlocked, Captain," Gorah said.

"Open it."

The door slid aside and they peered into the hold. The interior lights were on, enabling them to see everything clearly. Boxes were stacked in neat rows, vehicles parked end to end. Gorah stepped inside and moved quickly to crouch behind some crates.

Wang nudged Rieka. "Go. I'll cover you."

With a warning glance at Candace to do as she'd been told, Rieka moved to join Gorah. By the time Wang slipped next to her, Rieka was frowning. "We need to check the vehicles," she whispered, silently kicking herself for not collecting some sensory equipment first. A general infrared sweep would have been able to pinpoint Gundah's position. "My best guess is she's hiding in one of them."

"Okay."

Rieka led the way to the first vehicle, a ground transport. Looking through the clear windows, they found no evidence of either Gundah or the canister.

The shuttle was next. Designed to travel relatively short distances through space, it stood just over four meters high. Rieka estimated its length at about fifteen meters. It had been floated in through the cargo doors and sat on an immense platform. The air lock wasn't open, but the gangplank had been extended to the floor.

"Check the perimeter, first," Rieka told them. Cautiously, they moved down the ship's port side. Wang stayed a short distance in front of her. She saw him tense when he turned a corner, but he continued around and headed back toward the entry port. She'd almost caught up to him when they heard a small sound.

Rieka pivoted instantly. She retraced her steps around the little ship's aft area. Gorah was gone. Cursing herself for underestimating Gundah, she hurried back to Wang.

"Gundah's out here, somewhere," she whispered. "She surprised Gorah."

Wang's jaw tightened as he looked down at her. "This is your show, Boss."

She nodded, and called out, "Lieutenant?"

"Your misguided friend can't answer you, Herald," Gundah's unmistakable voice replied.

Wang pointed to the right. Rieka nodded. The sound had come from that direction. "Keep her talking," he whispered, then crept off behind a stack of crates.

Trying for a conversational tone, Rieka said, "Actually, I'm not particularly surprised. Is she dead?"

"Not yet," Gundah's disembodied voice replied. "I'm waiting for just the right time."

"I see," Rieka answered. "Why kill Gorah now—when you might use her to control me?"

"Precisely, Herald. I do like the way you think."

Knowing she needed to keep speaking in order to cover whatever noise Wang might make, Rieka grasped for something else to say. "So . . . what kind of a deal did you make with Candace?"

"I'm not about to discuss that with you."

The direction of her voice had moved. Rieka was sure of it. "But surely you came to some . . . mutual understanding." They hadn't come too far into the hold. She wondered if Candace could hear this, too. "I mean, you've used her in the past."

"Without her knowledge," Gundah added.

The voice had moved again. Rieka took a few tentative steps around the shuttle. Three rows of crates were stacked on the right. Both Wang and Gundah were back there. "Oh, of course not. But she knows what you're doing, now. Your objectives. Your strategy," Rieka coaxed.

"Possibly," Gundah hedged. "I never tell anyone all my secrets. On the other side of the coin, I still require the assistance of certain Humans. And your mother is . . . well beyond the reproductive years. Her price is worth the cooperation."

Rieka frowned. Beyond the reproductive years? What in the world did that mean? "I'm sure it is. So . . . is that what we're doing now, Gundah. Working out a deal to

secure *my* cooperation, too?" Rieka left the shuttle and
crept toward the first row of crates.

"Possibly."

Gundah's voice had come from behind the third row. If
she would just stay in one place for another few seconds,
Wang could grab the opportunity to stun her.

"What's the deal, then?" she asked.

"I've been thinking about that," Gundah replied conversationally. "I've decided to help you with your greatest desire—in exchange for your cooperation."

"My greatest desire?" Rieka couldn't imagine what that
might be.

"You want a child," Gundah's voice answered. "I can
give you one. I own a research lab similar to the one I
destroyed on Indra."

"A child in exchange for . . ."

"Your life."

Gundah leapt around the far side of the shuttle's gangplank, surprising Rieka. She crouched instinctively, bringing
her weapon to bear on Gundah's chest. She'd been sure
the Oph had been behind the crates.

"What good is a baby if I'm not alive?" she asked. Her
maitu was aimed, but then so was Gundah's.

Gundah bared her teeth and issued a barking laugh.
"Even with you dead, I can produce your children. As
many as I want. Hundreds of them."

Gundah lifted her maitu higher. Rieka had waited for
some small distraction, and realized something must have
happened to Wang. She watched the Oph's eyes, gauging
the moment when she would fire.

A second later, Rieka dropped to the floor and rolled to
the left, hoping to squeeze off a shot since Gundah now
had to come past the gangplank to correct her aim. Wang
appeared then, hurtling himself toward Gundah as he came
around the shuttle's far corner.

"No!" Rieka shouted, but it was too late to stop him.

Wang leapt on the Oph, fouling her aim and knocking
them both to the floor. The blast hit a crate above her.
Rieka scurried away and got to her feet as it tumbled to
the floor.

"Wang, get loose of her," she shouted. She didn't dare

shoot and hit Wang by mistake, though she did consider the possibility of stunning them both.

She watched helplessly while he tried, but Gundah wouldn't let go. They rolled, crashing into the shuttle's platform. Wang grunted, and she knew he couldn't last much longer. Taking a chance she'd rather not, Rieka ran up the gangplank to get a better angle. She aimed her weapon and fired.

Gundah's howl echoed across the hold, but Rieka realized instantly she'd only been hit in the leg. Then, in a maneuver that looked almost unreal, the Oph lifted Wang like a shield in front of her and got to her knees. He struggled mightily, clouting her with vicious kicks, but she ignored his blows.

"Humans," Gundah managed, "are so tedious."

Rieka barely saw Gundah move. But she heard a loud snap and saw Wang's body go limp. In the second it took for her to realize his neck had been broken, the Oph flung his body at her. His foot knocked the weapon from Rieka's hand. Before she could recover it, Gundah had snatched up her own maitu from the floor, aiming it with unwavering precision.

"You said you'd let me handle her," Candace's voice rang out, breaking the eerie silence. "We had a deal."

She kept her eyes locked on Gundah, but in her peripheral vision, Rieka saw her mother come forward. Her heart breaking over Wang's senseless death, she realized it had been foolhardy to trust Candace even a little bit. Not knowing how much time had passed since they'd been on the bridge, Rieka held her breath.

Triscoe?

Silence.

Gundah glanced momentarily at Candace when she came a step closer. "I gave you your chance. Apparently you have no more control over her now than you did when she was a child."

Triscoe, answer me! Silently berating herself for ever suggesting they disconnect, Rieka realized the irony of that demand. In a few seconds she would probably die. Without their intimate mental connection, at least she knew he'd survive.

"I have my own way of doing things," Candace snapped.
"She would have done exactly as you asked."

Gundah shrugged. "Too bad we won't have the opportunity to test your theory."

The look appeared in her eye, again. Rieka recognized it for what it was. Gundah experienced a strange type of ecstasy when she held someone's life in her hands. The Oph savored it for a moment, then smiled.

Rieka dropped to the floor as the maitu went off. Her hand slid under Wang, and she groped for her weapon.

"You can get up now," her mother said.

Looking past Wang's body, Rieka saw that Candace was still standing and Gundah had collapsed onto the floor. While she took a second to figure out what had happened, Candace stepped up to the ramp and extended her arm. In her open palm, she held what had to be Gorah's maitu.

Gingerly, Rieka lifted the weapon and saw it had been calibrated for the highest stun setting. Hoping her voice still worked, she asked, "Do you know where the canister is?"

"Inside the shuttle."

Triscoe looked around as soon as the InterMAT deposited him in the *Garner*'s cargo hold and saw a strange tableau. Two women stood over a pair of bodies. Not knowing what had happened, he gestured for the security team to wait while he walked toward Rieka and her mother.

"Rieka?" he asked cautiously. Closer now, he recognized Wang and knew from the stillness of his body that he was dead. "Rieka?"

Her attention shifted from Candace to him. He saw her nostrils flare and could sense she was on the verge of an emotional collapse. He knew that feeling well, himself. The last few minutes as the *Providence* approached the *Garner* had been torture.

She held two maitus in her hand and offered them to him as he approached. "Just let me . . ." She stopped, pressed her lips together, and took a deep breath. "Candace is under arrest. Have your men look for Lieutenant Gorah. I'll be right back."

She strode up the ramp and went through the shuttle's air lock before he had time to formulate a question. Trusting her word, Triscoe turned to his people, and said, "Place

Mrs. Degahv in custody and secure the area. Report if you find Lieutenant Gorah."

Triscoe desperately wanted to be with her, but knew Rieka would not accept his comfort until she'd done what she'd set out to do. He didn't know what had happened here, but was glad when one of his people led Candace away.

Rieka returned holding the silvery cylinder. She stopped and knelt near Wang's body. He watched as her trembling fingers gently touched him. "His hair is the most interesting color," she whispered, smoothing a wayward lock. "It's so black it looks blue."

A moment of silence passed, and she stood. Triscoe saw the tears pooling in her eyes and felt the chaotic swirl of her anguish. Carefully stepping around Wang, he took her in his arms.

She shuddered, and he squeezed her tighter. He wanted to tell her it would be all right. That she was safe, and that's all that mattered. But he couldn't lie to her. Rieka had known the stakes. And she'd paid the price.

She took a deep breath and leaned back to look at him. "I'm sorry, Triscoe," she said, her voice gravelly. With her free hand, she wiped her cheeks. "I should never have suggested we . . . disconnect."

"Don't apologize, love. I should have trusted you."

Oddly, she frowned and gave a little shake of her head. "Sometimes . . . sometimes doubt is a good thing."

Triscoe nodded. He wiped another tear as it slid down her cheek. "Wang didn't doubt you. He was a good man."

He watched her clutch the cylinder tighter. "The best."

Rieka sat on the sofa with a pillow in her arms, finding it odd to see both Nason and Setana here, in the rooms she shared with Triscoe aboard the *Providence*.

"Perhaps you should rest now, dear," Setana suggested.

"I'm fine," she said, her voice steady again. She'd cry for Wang later. There were still too many unanswered questions. "I simply want to interrogate Candace. Is there something odd about that request?"

"No," Nason said as Triscoe came in the door. "I just want to make sure you're up to it."

She glared at him for a long moment. Not even a Fleet

admiral could dent her determination in this. Finally, Nason looked at Triscoe and nodded. He went back to the door and led Candace in.

Eyeing her mother carefully, Rieka said, "If you don't mind, I'd like to speak to my mother privately."

"Of course," Triscoe said. He gestured for Nason and his mother to leave. Before he followed them out, he added, "We'll be outside."

"You murdered her," Rieka began without preamble, watching Candace. She stood regally near the console as if nothing could touch her. "I want to know why."

"She was going to kill you," Candace countered.

Rieka shook her head. "I chose my words carefully. I said you *murdered* her. You could have stopped Gundah without seeing her dead." She looked sharply into Candace's eyes. "You reset the maitu."

"I—may have."

Rieka set the pillow aside and stood. "You know something, Mother. I can see it in your face. You felt justified, didn't you? She'd already been shot twice. There wasn't a chance she could have survived three hits in a row like that."

"I'm not a weapons expert. I had no idea—"

"—and you waited until after she'd killed Wang to act."

Candace faltered briefly. Rieka saw her frown. "I . . . I wasn't able to help him. I would have—but it took time to find Gorah's maitu."

Frustrated by the answers she got, Rieka balled a fist. "Too much time," she said, the words infused with accusation.

Candace lifted her chin. "Do you intend to have me charged with murder?"

Rieka recognized that defiant look. She'd seen it in the mirror. Shaking her head, she muttered, "No. I doubt any court would even hear the case." Feeling oddly detached, she walked the room's length. "But I still don't have the answer I'm looking for. There is more to this than some kind of retribution for her having Dad killed. What else did she tell you?"

Candace looked at her a long moment before heaving a tired sigh. "Two things."

"And they are?"

Candace sank down in one of the chairs. Rieka realized the day had been grueling for her, too. "Gundah's business acumen was incredible. Her holdings were easily a hundred times greater than mine. She owned TechLine, for heaven's sake. I do business with them on a daily basis. Almost everyone does." She stopped speaking and shot Rieka a defiant look.

"Go on, Mother," she prodded.

"You uncovered part of it." Candace glanced at her once, then studied the floor as she spoke. "Gundah admitted to manipulating me. For years. She thought she owned me and did these things to protect her investment. She studied me well enough to be able to predict my reactions to certain situations—and then she made them happen."

Gundah's strategy came as less a surprise than her mother's admission of it. Rieka nodded sympathetically. "Do you believe me now?"

"About what?"

"That we've been deliberately degraded. That individuals like Gundah have worked hard to keep us in the Commonwealth's debt."

"At this moment," Candace admitted, "I'd believe just about anything."

Rieka nodded and returned to her chair. "So. She manipulated you and had Stephen killed. You said there was another thing."

Her mother frowned and pressed her lips together. "I'd rather not say."

Rieka huffed. Did Candace really expect to be excused with that lame answer? She aimed an accusatory finger. "I don't care what you'd rather do, Candace," she said, her jaw tight. "Adjutant Gundah is dead now by your hand. And Wang by hers. I want my questions answered."

Another moment passed before Candace said, "She intended to destroy Humanity."

"What?"

"She could have used any Human's DNA to do what she planned. But it was very important to use yours."

Frowning, Rieka shook her head. "That's sheer fantasy. How could she possibly pull something like that off?"

"She intended to sterilize an entire generation."

For a moment, Rieka could think of nothing intelligent

to say. The statement was unbelievable. Perhaps the Oph lieutenants had been right after all. Finally, she stammered, "That—that's insane."

Candace shook her head. "Her influence was incredible, Rieka," she said quietly. "I believe she could have done exactly what she planned to do."

Pushing past acceptance of the plan, Rieka wondered, "Why my DNA, then?"

Candace looked away to study her lap. "I don't think you want to hear this." She paused, but went on before Rieka had a chance to prompt her. "There was some sort of connection between Stephen and her parents. She blamed him for her father's death. Her family's fortune was all but wiped out. Everything she did—she did for revenge."

Rieka nodded. "So she hated him and decided to take it out on all Humanity. Earth's restoration must have felt like a personal insult," Rieka went on. "When Stephen's plans actually started to come about, she created the accident to stop him. Uncle Alexi continued the plan, but at a much slower pace. I wonder if it's coincidental that he's been suffering from a variety of illnesses since he took the office."

Rieka paused and studied her mother. "She influenced you, and probably planned for Paden to become Herald." She shook her head. "This is . . . I'm at a loss for words. If the Procyons hadn't killed Paden, he'd be Earth Herald now and Gundah . . ."

"Gundah would be using *his* DNA to commit genocide."

Rieka took several deep breaths, trying to overcome her shock, indignation, and rage. Purposefully, she tried to think of what to do next. How to proceed. How to behave. Unfortunately, nothing seemed clear. Finally, she said, "And how about you? When you found out what she had planned—"

"—I wanted my own revenge," Candace told her. "I convinced her the two of us could keep on as we were. That all I wanted was the money."

Rieka nodded. Candace's revenge had had nothing to do with insanity. As usual, it had been cold and calculated. And now Gundah was dead. She sighed. "This remains between the two of us, Mother, I don't want anyone else to know." Of course Triscoe had access to her thoughts, but he'd honor her request, and her mother didn't need to know about that part of her relationship with him.

"And," she added, "since you're obviously going to profit from your bargain with her, you're going to stop your petty verbal attacks of me and my office—or I will prosecute you. Is that clear?"

Candace nodded. "I know how to keep a secret."

Rieka studied her for a moment. "I'm sure you do."

Triscoe held Rieka firmly in his lap even after Jeniper and Robet entered the apartment. He'd considered staying aboard the *Providence* for a day or two, but realized Rieka needed to be on Earth. Or in it, he thought wryly, considering they were several hundred meters below the surface.

"How are you feeling this morning?" Jeniper asked.

"I'm fine. I wish people would quit treating me as though I were made of porcelain." She squirmed again, and Triscoe released her to sit beside him.

"Good. Then you're ready to hear my news."

"You've not going to believe this," Robet added, beaming.

Rieka raised both her hands. "Okay. The two of you sit down and tell us your news."

Jeniper and Robet sat. "We're betrothed," he announced.

Triscoe leaned forward and smiled. "Congratulations."

Rieka poked him with her elbow. "I'm glad I didn't listen to you," she murmured, snapping a glance at him.

Jeniper cocked her head. "What is that supposed to mean?"

Before he could respond, Rieka said, "He didn't think you were right for each other. I did." She smiled, her first for the day, and Triscoe breathed a relieved sigh. "I'm really happy for you."

"I am, too," he said.

"But there's more," Jeniper said, moving to the edge of her seat. "I know how disappointed you were, Rieka, when we had to announce the Reaffirmation Ceremony needed to be postponed indefinitely."

Triscoe felt her stiffen. "We decided it was for the best," she said softly.

"Yes. Well, apparently no one else did." Jeniper gestured

with her fingers splayed. "Our office has been inundated
with calls. Heralds, business people, the general public—
everyone thinks Earth needs to be rededicated as soon as
possible." Her voice had the ring of excitement. "They
want us to announce the new date today."

Rieka shook her head. "We can't possibly put it back
together anytime soon. There are hundreds of details . . ."

Triscoe watched Robet's bibbets darken slightly before
he spoke. "You don't seem to understand. These folks want
to cooperate."

Jeniper nodded. "They want to help. Participate. They've
been telling me they want to welcome Earth—not the other
way around."

The room stayed quiet for a moment. Rieka seemed to
be studying the floor, but Triscoe knew better. She was
overwhelmed by the impact of what Jeniper had said. Finally, she nodded. "When, then?"

Jeniper's eyes glowed, excitedly. "Next week?"

"Do you think so?"

"You're the miracle worker."

Rieka chuckled softly. "Okay. Set up a broadcast time
for this afternoon, Jen. If we're going to give them what
they want, we might as well get started."

"I'm on it." Jeniper stood, and Robet followed as she
fairly danced toward the door. "This is the most wonderful
thing that's ever happened in the Commonwealth, Rieka,"
she said, turning and flashing them a huge smile. "And it's
all because of you."

When they were alone again, Triscoe squeezed her shoulder. "I should have trusted you from the start," he said
softly. "Things might have ended differently if I had."

Rieka turned toward him and he saw confusion in her
blue eyes. "Are you saying Wang's death is your fault?
You're no more to blame than I am for not stunning both
of them when I had the chance."

Triscoe felt as if someone had reached into his chest and
squeezed his heart. He had failed her on a most basic level
and still she forgave him. He glanced across the room to
the dining table where the canister set. "We cannot undo
what has been done—no matter how hard we wish it. But
I want you to understand you are more precious to me
than anything else I could possibly imagine."

She put her hand over his. "I know. I feel the same way about you."

"No matter what the future brings, I never want to lose contact again."

"No matter what?" Rieka asked skeptically.

Triscoe rolled his eyes and squeezed his Human wife's shoulder. "Yes, love. I trust you."

At that, Rieka smiled her quirky, one-sided smile.

Five hours later, Rieka sat amazed at what Jeniper had managed to pull together. Not only had she organized a Herald's News Conference, she'd coordinated entertainment to go along with Rieka's speech.

Seated beside Triscoe in New SubDenver's media room, she went over the hastily prepared speech one more time. A variety of entertainers had already performed, including the Blue Planet Future.

Senator Volshoy began Rieka's introduction. She took a deep breath to quell a sudden wave of anxiety.

"Are you all right?" Triscoe whispered, squeezing her hand.

"I think so." She tried to smile. Rieka felt him close in her mind and knew he meant her mental state rather than her physical one. She looked beyond him and saw her mother, seated next to Setana and Ker. They nodded their support.

Volshoy said her name and she went to the podium. In addition to the now-recognizable faces of the Blue Planet Future, she noticed Admiral Nason, Midrin Tohab, and the *Prodigy*'s Captain Saxen. Rieka smiled at them, then grinned when she noticed Jeniper seated next to Robet.

Glancing once more at her speech, she began. "Welcome, Commonwealth citizens, to my planet. As Earth Herald, I am privileged to invite you to experience the wonders my home has to offer. From Damascus, to the restored equatorial rain forests, to undersea laboratories, to the incredible World Zoo—I know you will find yourselves fascinated, educated, accommodated, and entertained."

Glancing away from the camera, she saw Jeniper give her an encouraging nod. Perhaps this speech wasn't as sappy as she thought. She took a breath and went on.

"Additionally, I am proud to announce that the Reaffirmation will take place one week from today. On that day, the Earth will begin to repay the Commonwealth for the investment it made two centuries ago. Our ancestors understood value and potential—and saw both in the Earth and its peoples." There was a smattering of applause from the audience. Smiling, she waited until it died down, then continued.

"Our civilization works on the principle of business, and it has been brought to my attention that some individuals are concerned with the idea of a productive Earth. To them, I say simply—wait and see. There are winners and losers in every business transaction, but I assure you we will work very hard to see that everyone profits. And we will work just as hard to ensure the Earth both achieves its potential and maintains the high standard of ethics so important to the Commonwealth today."

Rieka raised her left hand in a cautious gesture. "But success is never without obstacles," she added. "I can promise the future holds many hurdles for all of us. And I can likewise predict we will gain an amazing return for that effort.

"It is my wish that all of you within the sound of my voice remember this moment and pass on to your children and to their children the sense of excitement and challenge you feel right now. For this is what it is like to be Human and to have your feet on the soil of your homeworld. To remember where you've come from, to hold a vision of the future, and to be proud of who you are."

She paused and looked out onto the sea of faces before her, then returned her attention to the camera. "Welcome to Earth, my friends. I hope you have brought with you an appetite for adventure. I guarantee you won't be disappointed."

TERRIFYING TALES